VENGEFUL

VENGEFUL

V. E. SCHWAB

TOR

A TOM DOHERTY ASSOCIATES BOOK

NEW YORK

VENGEFUL

Copyright © 2018 by Victoria Schwab

Edited by Miriam Weinberg

A Tor Book
Published by Tom Doherty Associates
175 Fifth Avenue
New York, NY 10010

www.tor-forge.com

Tor® is a registered trademark of Macmillan Publishing Group, LLC.

The Library of Congress Cataloging-in-Publication Data
is available upon request.

ISBN 978-0-7653-8752-3 (hardcover)
ISBN 978-1-250-31247-1 (signed edition)
ISBN 978-0-7653-8754-7 (ebook)

Our books may be purchased in bulk for promotional, educational, or business use.
Please contact your local bookseller or the Macmillan Corporate and Premium Sales
Department at 1-800-221-7945, extension 5442, or by email at
MacmillanSpecialMarkets@macmillan.com.

First Edition: September 2018

Printed in the United States of America

0 9 8 7 6 5 4 3 2 1

To Mum, and Holly, and Miriam,
the most powerful women I know

While seeking revenge, dig two graves—one for yourself.

—*Douglas Horton*

GENESIS

SIX WEEKS AGO

THE night Marcella died, she made her husband's favorite dinner.

Not because it was a special occasion, but because it *wasn't*—spontaneity, people insisted, was the secret to love. Marcella didn't know if she believed all that, but she was willing to try her hand at a home-cooked meal. Nothing too fancy—a good steak, edges seared with black pepper, slow-baked sweet potatoes, a bottle of merlot.

But six o'clock came and went, and Marcus wasn't home.

Marcella put the food in the oven to keep it warm, then checked her lipstick in the hall mirror. She freed her long black hair from its loose bun, then put it up again, teasing a few strands out before smoothing her A-line dress. People called her a natural beauty, but nature only went so far. The truth was, Marcella spent two hours in the gym six days a week, trimming and toning and stretching every lean muscle on her willowy five-foot-ten frame, and she never left her bedroom without her makeup expertly applied. It wasn't easy, but neither was being married to Marcus Andover Riggins—better known as Marc the Shark, Tony Hutch's right-hand man.

It wasn't easy—but it was worth it.

Her mother liked to say she'd gone fishing and somehow bagged a great white. But what her *mother* didn't understand was that Marcella had baited her hook with her prize in mind. And she'd caught *exactly* what she'd wanted.

Her cherry red heels clicked across the wood floor before being swallowed by the silk rug as she finished setting the table and lit each of the twenty-four tapers in the pair of iron candelabras that framed the door.

Marcus hated them, but for once Marcella didn't care. She loved the candelabras, with their long stems and branching limbs—they looked like the kind of thing you'd find in a French chateau. They made the home feel luxurious. Made new money feel old.

She checked the time—seven, now—but resisted the urge to call. The fastest way to kill a flame was to smother it. Besides, if Marcus had business, then business always came first.

Marcella poured herself a glass of wine and leaned back against the counter, imagining his strong hands closing around someone's throat. A head forced underwater, a jaw cracking sideways. Once he'd come home with blood on his hands and she'd fucked him right there on the marble island, the metal shaft of his gun still in its holster, the steel hard against her ribs.

People thought Marcella loved her husband in spite of his work. The truth was, she loved him because of it.

But as seven became eight, and eight neared nine, Marcella's arousal slowly turned to annoyance, and when the front door finally swung open, that annoyance hardened to anger.

"Sorry, darling."

His voice always shifted when he'd been drinking, slowing to a lazy drawl. It was his only tell. He never stumbled or swayed, his hands never shook. No, Marcus Riggins was made of stronger stuff—but he wasn't without his flaws.

"It's fine," said Marcella, hating the edge in her own voice. She turned toward the kitchen, but Marcus caught her wrist, pulling her hard enough that she lost her balance. His arms folded around her, and she looked up into his face.

Sure, her husband's waist had widened a little, while hers had narrowed, that beautiful swimmer's body bloating a fraction with each passing year, but his summer brown hair hadn't thinned, and his eyes were still the rugged blue of slate or dark water. Marcus had always been good-looking, though she wasn't sure how much of that was his tailored suits or the way he moved through the world, as if expecting it get out of his way. It usually did.

"You're gorgeous," he whispered, and Marcella could feel the press of him, hungry against her hip. But Marcella wasn't in the mood.

She reached up, nails dragging down his stubbled cheek. "You hungry, sweetheart?"

"Always," he growled against her neck.

"Good," said Marcella, stepping away and smoothing her skirt. "Dinner's ready."

A bead of red wine slid like sweat down the side of the raised glass, tracing its way toward the white tablecloth. Marcella had filled it too full, her hand made clumsy by her worsening mood. Marcus didn't seem to notice the stain. He didn't seem to notice anything.

"To my beautiful wife."

Marcus never prayed before meals, but he always made a toast, had since the night they met. It didn't matter if he had an audience of twenty or if they ate alone. She'd found it endearing on their first date, but these days the gesture felt hollow, rehearsed. Designed to charm instead of being genuinely charming. But he never failed to say the words, and perhaps that was a kind of love. Or perhaps Marcus was simply a creature of habit.

Marcella lifted her own glass.

"To my elegant husband," she answered automatically.

The rim was halfway to her lips when she noticed the smudge on Marcus's cuff. At first she thought it was only blood, but it was too bright, too pink.

It was lipstick.

Every conversation she'd had with the other wives came rushing back.

His eyes start to wander yet?
Keeping his stick wet?
All men are rotten.

Marcus was busy cutting into his steak, and rambling on about insurance, but Marcella had stopped listening. Behind her eyes, her husband traced his thumb across a pair of stained lips, parting them around his knuckle.

Her fingers tightened on the wineglass. Heat was flushing her skin even as a cold weight settled in her stomach. "What a fucking cliché," she said.

He didn't stop chewing. "Excuse me?"

"Your sleeve."

His gaze drifted languidly down toward the bloom of pink. He didn't even have the decency to look surprised. "Must be yours," he said, as if she'd ever worn that shade, ever owned anything so tacky and *twee*—

"Who is she?"

"Honestly, Marce—"

"Who *is* she?" demanded Marcella, gritting her perfect teeth.

Marcus finally stopped eating, and leaned back in his chair, blue eyes hanging on her. "Nobody."

"Oh, so you're fucking a ghost?"

He rolled his eyes, clearly tired of the subject, which was ironic, considering he usually relished any topic that revolved around *him*. "Marcella, envy really doesn't suit you."

"Twelve years, Marcus. Twelve. And *now* you can't keep it in your pants?"

Surprise flickered across his face, and the truth hit her like a blow—of course this wasn't his first time cheating. This was only the first time he'd been *caught*.

"How long?" she asked icily.

"Let it go, Marce."

Let it go—as if his cheating were like the wineglass in her hand, something she'd just happened to pick up, could just as easily set down.

It wasn't the betrayal itself—she could forgive a lot, in the interest of this life she'd made—but it was the look in the other women's eyes that Marcella had always taken for envy, it was the stoic warnings of the first wives, the twitch at the corner of a smile, the realization that they all *knew,* had known, for god knows how long, and she—hadn't.

Let it go.

Marcella set the wineglass down. And picked up the steak knife. And as she did, her husband had the nerve to scoff. As if she wouldn't know what to do with it. As if she hadn't listened to all his stories, hadn't begged for details. As if he didn't go on and on about his job when he was drunk. As if she hadn't practiced with a pillow. A bag of flour. A steak.

Marcus raised a single brow. "What do you plan to do now?" he asked, voice dripping with condescension.

How silly she must look to him, with her perfectly manicured nails gripping the monogrammed hilt of the blade.

"Dollface," he crooned, and the word made Marcella seethe.

Dollface. Baby. Darling. Was that how he really thought of her, after all this time? As helpless, brittle, weak, something *ornamental,* a glass figurine designed to shimmer and shine and look pretty on a shelf?

When she didn't let go, his gaze darkened.

"Don't you turn that knife on me unless you plan to use it . . ."

Perhaps she *was* glass.

But glass is only brittle until it breaks.

Then it's sharp.

"Marcella—"

She lunged, and had the thrill of seeing her husband's eyes widen a fraction in surprise, the bourbon spilling as he jerked backward. But Marcella's knife had barely skimmed his silk tie before Marcus's hand cracked across her mouth. Blood poured across her tongue, and Marcella's eyes blurred with tears as she tumbled back into the oak table, rattling the china plates.

She still had the knife, but Marcus had his hand wrapped around her wrist, pinning it to the table so hard the bones began to grind together.

He'd been rough with her before, but that had always been in the heat of the moment, signaled by some unspoken pact, and she'd always been the one to signal it.

This was different.

Marcus was two hundred pounds of brute strength, a man who'd made his living breaking things. And people. He clucked his tongue now, as if she were being ridiculous. Blowing things out of proportion. As if she'd made him do this. Made him fuck another woman. Made him ruin all that she'd worked so hard to build.

"Ah, Marce, you've always known how to rile me up."

"Let me *go*," she hissed.

Marcus brought his face close to hers, ran a hand through her hair, cupped her cheek. "Only if you play nice."

He was smiling. *Smiling.* As if this were just another game.

Marcella spit her blood into his face.

Her husband let out a long-suffering sigh. And then he slammed her head against the table.

Marcella's world went suddenly white. She didn't remember falling, but when her vision flickered back she was on the silk carpet beside her chair, her head throbbing. She tried to get up, but the room swayed viciously. Bile rose in her throat, and she rolled over, vomited.

"You should have let it go," said Marcus.

Blood ran into one of her eyes, staining the dining room red as her husband reached out and wrapped his hand around the nearest candelabra. "I always hated these," he said, tipping the pole until it fell.

The flame caught the silk curtains on the way down, before the candelabra hit the floor.

Marcella struggled to her hands and knees. She felt like she was underwater. Slow, too slow.

Marcus stood in the doorway, watching. Just watching.

A steak knife gleamed on the hardwood floor. Marcella forced herself up through the heavy air. She was almost there when the blow hit her from behind. Marcus had knocked over the second candelabra. It came crashing down, iron arms pinning her to the floor.

It was disconcerting how fast the fire had spread. It leapt from the curtain to a puddle of spilled bourbon, to the tablecloth and the rug. It was already everywhere.

Marcus's voice, through the haze. "We had a good run, Marce."

That fucking prick. As if *any of it* had been his idea, his doing. "You're nothing without me," she said, her words unsteady. "I made you, Marcus." She heaved against the candelabra. It didn't move. "I will unmake you."

"People say a lot of things before they die, sweetheart. I've heard them all."

Heat filled the room, her lungs, her head. Marcella coughed, but couldn't catch her breath. "I will *ruin* you."

There was no answer.

"Do you hear me, Marcus?"

Nothing, only silence.

"I will ruin you!"

She screamed the words until her throat burned, until the smoke stole her vision, and her voice, and even then it echoed in her head, her last thoughts following her down, down, down into the dark.

I will ruin you.

I will ruin.

I will.

I—

OFFICER Perry Carson had been stuck on the twenty-seventh level of Radical Raid for the better part of an hour when he heard an engine rev to life. He looked up in time to see Marcus Riggins's sleek black sedan peel out of the slate half circle that formed the mansion's drive. It tore down the road, a good thirty over the suburb-mandated speed limit, but Perry wasn't in a patrol car, and even if he had been, he hadn't spent the last three weeks in this shit-heap eating greasy takeout just to bust Riggins for such a minor infraction.

No, the Merit PD needed something that would *stick*—and not just to Marc the Shark. They needed the whole crooked sea.

Perry settled back against the worn leather and returned to his game, cracking the twenty-seventh level just as he smelled smoke.

No doubt some asshole setting a poolside bonfire without a permit. He squinted out the window—it was late, half past ten, the sky an inky black this far from Merit, and the smoke didn't stand out against the dark.

But the fire did.

The officer was out of the car and across the street by the time the flames lit the front windows of the Riggins mansion. Calling it in by the time he reached the front door. It was unlocked—thank god it was unlocked—and he threw it open, already composing his report. He'd say it was ajar, say he heard a call for help, even though the truth was he didn't hear *anything* but the crack of burning wood, the whoosh of flame sliding up the hall.

"Police!" he called through the smoke. "Is anyone here?"

He'd seen Marcella Riggins arrive home. But he hadn't seen her leave. The sedan had gone by fast, but not fast enough to leave any doubt—there was no one in the passenger seat.

Perry coughed into his sleeve. Sirens were already sounding in the distance. He knew he should go back outside and wait, outside, where the air was clean and cool and safe.

But then he rounded the corner and saw the body trapped beneath a coil of iron the size of a coatrack. The tapers had all melted, but Perry realized it was a candelabra. Who even *owned* a candelabra?

Perry reached for its stem and then recoiled—it was searing to the touch. He cursed himself. The metal arms had already burned through Marcella's dress wherever they touched her, the skin raw and red, but the woman didn't cry out, didn't scream.

She wasn't moving. Her eyes were closed and blood slicked the side of her head, matting the dark hair against her scalp.

He felt for a pulse, and found one that fluttered, then seemed to fall away beneath his touch. The fire was getting hotter. The smoke was getting thicker.

"Shit shit shit," muttered Perry, scanning the room as sirens wailed outside. A pitcher of water had spilled across a napkin, leaving it unburnt. He wrapped the cloth around his hand and then took hold of the candelabra. The damp fabric hissed and heat shot toward his fingers as he heaved the iron bar up with all his strength. It lifted, and rolled off Marcella's body just as voices filled the hall. Firefighters came storming into the house.

"In here!" he wheezed, choking on the smoke.

A pair of firemen cut through the haze right before the ceiling groaned and a chandelier came toppling down. It shattered against the dining room table, which split and threw up flames, and the next thing Perry knew, he was being hauled backward out of the room and the burning mansion, and into the cool night.

Another firefighter followed close behind, Marcella's body slung over one shoulder.

Outside, the trucks were splayed across the manicured lawn, and ambulance lights strobed across the slate drive.

The house was going up in flames, and his hand was throbbing, his lungs burned, and Perry didn't give a damn about any of it. The only thing he cared about right then and there was saving the life of Marcella Riggins. Marcella, who had always flashed a wan smile and a pert wave to the cops whenever she was followed. Marcella, who would never, ever snitch on her crooked husband.

But judging by the gash in her head, and the house on fire, and the husband's swift departure, there was a chance her position had changed. And Perry wasn't about to waste it.

Hoses sent jets of water into the flames, and Perry hacked and spat, but pulled away from an oxygen mask as two medics loaded Marcella onto a stretcher.

"She's not breathing," said a medic, cutting open her dress.

Perry jogged after the medics.

"No pulse," said the other, beginning compressions.

"Then bring it back!" shouted Perry, hauling himself up into the ambulance. He couldn't put a corpse on the stand.

"Ox-sat levels tanking," said the first, strapping an oxygen mask over Marcella's nose and mouth. Her temperature was too high, and the medic pulled out a stack of cold packs and began to break the seals, applying them to her temples, neck, wrists. He handed the last one to Perry, who grudgingly accepted.

Marcella's heartbeat appeared on a small screen, a solid line, even and unmoving.

The van pulled away, the burning mansion quickly shrinking in the window. Three weeks Perry had spent outside that place. Three *years* he'd been trying to nail Tony Hutch's crew. Fate had handed him the perfect witness, and he'd be damned if he was giving her back without a fight.

A third medic tried to tend to Perry's burned hand, but he pulled away. "Focus on her," he ordered.

The sirens cut through the night as the medics worked, trying to force her lungs to breathe, her heart to beat. Trying to coax life out of the ashes.

But it wasn't working.

Marcella lay there, limp and lifeless, and Perry's hope began to gutter, die.

And then, between one compression and the next, the horrible static line of her pulse gave a lurch, and a stutter, and finally began to beep.

1
RESURRECTION

I

FOUR WEEKS AGO

HALLOWAY

"I won't ask you again," said Victor Vale as the mechanic scrambled backward across the garage floor. Retreating—as if a few feet would make a difference. Victor followed slowly, steadily, watched as the man backed himself into a corner.

Jack Linden was forty-three, with a five-o'clock shadow, grease under his nails, and the ability to fix things.

"I already told you," said Linden, jumping nervously as his back came up against a half-built engine. "I can't do it—"

"Don't lie to me," warned Victor.

He flexed his fingers around the gun, and the air crackled with energy.

Linden shuddered, biting back a scream.

"I'm not!" yelped the mechanic. "I fix *cars*. I put *engines* back together. Not people. Cars are easy. Nuts and bolts and fuel lines. People are too much *more*."

Victor didn't believe that. Had never believed that. People were more intricate perhaps, more nuanced, but fundamentally machines. Things that worked, or didn't, that broke down, and were repaired. *Could be* repaired.

He closed his eyes, measuring the current inside him. It was already in his muscles, already threading his bones, already filling his chest cavity. The sensation was unpleasant, but not nearly as unpleasant as what would happen when the current peaked.

"I swear," said Linden, "I'd help you if I could." But Victor heard him shift. Heard a hand knocking against the tools strewn across the floor. "You have to believe me . . ." he said, fingers closing around something metal.

"I do," said Victor, eyes flicking open right as Linden lunged at him, wrench in hand. But halfway there, the mechanic's body slowed, as if caught in a sudden drag, and Victor swung the gun up and shot Linden in the head.

The sound echoed through the garage, ricocheting off concrete and steel as the mechanic fell.

How disappointing, thought Victor, as blood began to seep across the floor.

He holstered the gun and turned to go, but only made it three steps before the first wave of pain hit, sudden and sharp. He staggered, bracing himself against the shell of a car as it tore through his chest.

Five years ago, it would have been a simple matter of flipping that internal switch, killing power to the nerves, escaping any sensation.

But now—there was no escape.

His nerves crackled, the pain ratcheting up like a dial. The air hummed with the energy, and the lights flickered overhead as Victor forced himself away from the body and back across the garage toward the wide metal doors. He tried to focus on the symptoms, reduce them to facts, statistics, measurable quantities, and—

The current arced through him, and he shuddered, pulling a black mouth guard from his coat and forcing it between his teeth just before one knee gave way, his body buckling under the strain.

Victor fought—he always fought—but seconds later he was on his back, his muscles seizing as the current peaked, and his heart lurched, lost rhythm—

And he died.

II

FIVE YEARS AGO

MERIT CEMETERY

VICTOR had opened his eyes to cold air, grave dirt, and Sydney's blond hair, haloed by the moon.

His first death was violent, his world reduced to a cold metal table, his life a current and a dial turning up and up, electricity burning through every nerve until he finally cracked, shattered, crashed down into heavy, liquid nothing. The dying had taken ages, but death itself was fleeting, the length of a single held breath, all the air and energy forced from his lungs the moment before he surged up again through dark water, every part of him screaming.

Victor's second death was stranger. There had been no electric surge, no excruciating pain—he'd thrown that switch long before the end. Only the widening pool of blood beneath Victor's knees, and the pressure between his ribs as Eli slid the knife in, and the world giving way to darkness as he lost his hold, slipped into a death so gentle it felt like sleep.

Followed by—*nothing*. Time drawn out into a single, unbroken second. A chord of perfect silence. Infinite. And then, interrupted. The way a pebble interrupts a pond.

And there he was. Breathing. Living.

Victor sat up, and Sydney flung her small arms around him, and they sat there for a long moment, a reanimated corpse and a girl kneeling on a coffin.

"Did it work?" she whispered, and he knew she wasn't talking about the resurrection itself. Sydney had never revived an EO without consequences. They came back, but they came back wrong, their powers skewed, fractured. Victor felt gingerly along the lines of his power, searching for frayed threads, interruptions in the current, but felt—unchanged. Unbroken. Whole.

It was a rather overwhelming sensation.

"Yes," he said. "It worked."

Mitch appeared at the side of the grave, his shaved head glistening with sweat, his tattooed forearms filthy from the dig. "Hey." He drove a spade into the grass and helped Sydney and then Victor up out of the hole.

Dol greeted him by leaning heavily against his side, the dog's massive black head nestling under his palm in silent welcome.

The last member of their party slumped against a tombstone. Dominic had the shaken look of an addict, pupils dilated from whatever he'd taken to numb his chronic pain. Victor could feel the man's nerves, frayed and sparking like a shorted line.

They'd made a deal—the ex-soldier's assistance in exchange for taking away his suffering. In Victor's absence, Dominic clearly hadn't been able to keep his end of the bargain. Now Victor reached out and switched the man's pain off like a light. Instantly, the man sagged backward, tension sliding like sweat from his face.

Victor retrieved the shovel and held it out to the soldier. "Get up."

Dominic complied, rolling his neck and rising to his feet, and together the four of them began filling Victor's grave.

TWO days.

That's how long Victor had been dead.

It was an unsettling length of time. Long enough for the initial stages of decay. The others had been holed up at Dominic's place, two men, a girl, and a dog, waiting for his corpse to be buried.

"It's not much," said Dom now, opening the front door. And it wasn't—a small and cluttered single bedroom with a beat-up sofa, a concrete balcony, and a kitchen covered in a thin layer of dirty dishes—but it was a temporary solution to a longer dilemma, and Victor was in no condition to face the future, not with grave dirt still on his slacks and death lingering in his mouth.

He needed a shower.

Dom led him through the bedroom—narrow and dark, a single shelf of books, medals lying flat and photographs facedown, too many empty bottles on the windowsill.

The soldier scrounged up a clean long-sleeve shirt, embossed with a band logo. Victor raised a brow. "It's all I have in black," he explained.

He switched on the bathroom light and retreated, leaving Victor alone.

Victor undressed, shrugging out of the clothes he'd been buried in—clothes he didn't recognize, hadn't purchased—and stood before the bathroom mirror, surveying his bare chest and arms.

He wasn't free of scars—far from it—but none of them belonged to that night at the Falcon Price. Gunshots echoed through his mind, ricocheting off unfinished walls, the concrete floor slick with blood. Some of it his. Most of it Eli's. He remembered each and every wound made that night—the shallow cuts across his stomach, the razor-sharp wire cinching over his wrists, Eli's knife sliding between his ribs—but they left no mark.

Sydney's gift really was remarkable.

Victor turned the shower on and stepped beneath the scalding water, rinsing death from his skin. He felt along the lines of his power, turned his focus inward, the way he'd done years before, when he'd first gone to prison. During that isolation, unable to test his new power on anyone else, Victor had used his own body as a subject, learned everything he could about the limits of pain, the intricate network of nerves. Now, bracing himself, he turned the dial in his mind, first down, until he felt nothing, and then up, until every

drop of water on bare skin felt like knives. He clenched his teeth
against the pain and turned the dial back to its original position.

He closed his eyes, brought his head to rest against the tile wall,
and smiled, Eli's voice echoing through his head.

You can't win.

But he *had*.

THE apartment was quiet. Dominic stood out on the narrow balcony, puffing on a cigarette. Sydney was curled on the sofa, folded
up carefully like a piece of paper, with the dog, Dol, on the floor beside her, chin resting by her hand. Mitch sat at the table, shuffling and
reshuffling a deck of cards.

Victor took them all in.

Still collecting strays.

"What now?" asked Mitch.

Two small words.

Single syllables had never weighed so much. For the last ten years,
Victor had focused on revenge. He'd never truly intended to see the
other side of it, but now, he'd fulfilled his objective—Eli was rotting in a cell—and Victor was still here. Still alive. Revenge had been
an all-consuming pursuit. Its absence left Victor uneasy, unsatisfied.

What now?

He could leave them. Disappear. It was the smartest course—a
group, especially one as strange as this, would draw attention in ways
that solitary figures rarely did. But Victor's talent allowed him to
bend the attention of those around him, to lean on their nerves in
ways that registered as aversion, subtle, abstract, but efficient. And
as far as Stell knew, Victor Vale was dead and buried.

Six years he'd known Mitch.

Six days he'd known Sydney.

Six hours he'd known Dominic.

Each of them was a weight around Victor's ankles. Better to un-shackle himself, abandon them.

So leave, he thought. His feet made no progress toward the door.

Dominic wasn't an issue. They'd only just met—an alliance forged by need and circumstance.

Sydney was another matter. She was his responsibility. Victor had *made* her so when he killed Serena. That wasn't sentiment—it was simply a transitive equation. A factor passed from one quotient to another.

And Mitch? Mitch was cursed, he'd said so himself. Without Victor, it was only a matter of time before the hulking man ended up back in prison. Likely the one he'd broken out of with Victor. For Victor. And, despite knowing her less than a week, Victor was certain Mitch wouldn't abandon Sydney. Sydney, for her part, seemed rather attached to him, too.

And then, of course, there was the issue of Eli.

Eli was in custody, but he was still alive. There was nothing Victor could do about *that,* given the man's ability to regenerate. But if he ever got out—

"Victor?" prompted Mitch, as if he could see the turn of his thoughts, the direction they were veering.

"We're leaving."

Mitch nodded, trying and failing to hide his clear relief. He'd always been an open book, even in prison. Sydney uncurled from the sofa. She rolled over, her ice blue eyes finding Victor's in the dark. She hadn't been sleeping, he could tell.

"Where are we going?" she asked.

"I don't know," answered Victor. "But we can't stay here."

Dominic had slipped back inside, bringing a draft of cold air and smoke. "You're leaving?" he asked, panic flickering across his face. "What about our deal?"

"Distance isn't a problem," said Victor. It wasn't strictly true—once Dominic was out of range, Victor wouldn't be able to *alter* the threshold he'd set. But his influence *should* hold. "Our deal stays in effect," he said, "as long as you still work for me."

Dom nodded quickly. "Whatever you need."

Victor turned to Mitch. "Find us a new car," he said. "I want to be out of Merit by dawn."

And they were.

Two hours later, as the first light cracked the sky, Mitch pulled up in a black sedan. Dom stood in his doorway, arms crossed, watching as Sydney climbed into the back, followed by Dol. Victor slid into the passenger's seat.

"You sure you're good?" asked Mitch.

Victor looked down at his hands, flexed his fingers, felt the prickle of energy under his skin. If anything, he felt stronger. His power crisp, clear, focused.

"Better than ever."

III

FOUR WEEKS AGO

VICTOR shuddered back to life on the cold concrete floor.

For a few agonizing seconds, his mind was blank, his thoughts scattered. It was like coming off a strong drug. He was left grasping for logic, for order, sorting through his fractured senses—the taste of copper, the smell of gasoline, the dim glow of streetlights beyond cracked windows—until the scene finally resolved around him.

The mechanic's garage.

Jack Linden's body, a dark mass framed by fallen tools.

Victor pulled the mouth guard from between his teeth and sat up, limbs sluggish as he dragged the cell phone from his coat pocket. Mitch had rigged it with a makeshift surge protector. The small component was blown, but the device itself was safe. He powered it back on.

A single text had come in from Dominic.

3 minutes, 49 seconds.

The length of time he'd been dead.

Victor swore softly.

Too long. Far too long.

Death was dangerous. Every second without oxygen, without blood flow, was exponentially damaging. Organs could remain stable for several hours, but the brain was fragile. Depending on the individual, the nature of the trauma, most doctors put the threshold for brain degradation at four minutes, others five, a scant few six. Victor wasn't keen on testing the upper limits.

But there was no use ignoring the grim curve.

Victor was dying more often. The deaths were lasting longer. And the damage . . . He looked down, saw electrical scorch marks on the concrete, broken glass from the shattered lights overhead.

Victor rose to his feet, bracing himself against the nearest car until the room steadied. At least, for now, the buzzing was gone, replaced by a merciful quiet—broken almost immediately by the short, clipped sound of a ringtone.

Mitch.

Victor swallowed, tasting blood. "I'm on my way."

"Did you find Linden?"

"I did." Victor glanced back at the body. "But it didn't work. Start looking for the next lead."

IV

FIVE YEARS AGO

PERSHING

TWO weeks after his resurrection, the buzzing started.

At first, it was negligible—a faint humming in his ears, a tinnitus so subtle Victor first took it for a straining light bulb, a car engine, the murmur of a television rooms away. But it didn't go away.

Almost a month later, Victor found himself looking around the hotel lobby, straining to find a possible source for the sound.

"What is it?" asked Sydney.

"You hear it too?"

Sydney's brow furrowed in confusion. "Hear what?"

Victor realized she hadn't been asking about the noise, only his distraction. He shook his head. "Nothing," he said, turning back to the desk.

"Mr. Stockbridge," said the woman, addressing Victor, "I see you're with us for the next three nights. Welcome to the Plaza Hotel."

They never did stay long, bounced instead from city to city, sometimes choosing hotels, and other times rentals. They never traveled in a straight line, didn't stay at places with any regularity, or in any particular order.

"How would you like to pay?"

Victor drew a billfold from his pocket. "Cash."

Money wasn't a problem—according to Mitch it was nothing but a sequence of ones and zeroes, digital coinage in a fictional bank.

His favorite new hobby was skimming minute quantities of cash, pennies on the dollar, consolidating the gain into hundreds of accounts. Instead of leaving no footprint, he created too many to follow. The result was large rooms, plush beds, and space, the kind Victor had longed for and lacked in prison.

The sound inched higher.

"Are you okay?" asked Syd, studying him. She'd been studying him since the graveyard, scrutinizing his every gesture, every step, as if he might suddenly crumble, turn to ash.

"I'm fine," lied Victor.

But the noise followed him to the elevators. It followed him up to the room, an elegant suite with two bedrooms and a sofa. It followed him to bed and up again, shifting subtly, escalating from sound alone to sound and sensation. A slight prickle in his limbs. Not pain, exactly, but something more unpleasant. Persistent. It dogged him, growing louder, stronger, until, in a fit of annoyance, Victor switched his circuits off, turned the dial down to nothing, numbness. The prickling vanished, but the buzzing only softened to a faint and far-off static. Something he could almost ignore.

Almost.

He sat on the edge of his bed, feeling feverish, ill. When was the last time he'd been sick? He couldn't even remember. But with every passing minute, the feeling worsened, until Victor finally rose, crossing the suite and taking up his coat.

"Where are you going?" asked Sydney, curled on the sofa with a book.

"To get some air," he said, already slipping through the door.

He was halfway to the elevator when it hit him.

Pain.

It came out of nowhere, sharp as a knife through his chest. He gasped and caught himself on the wall, fought to stay upright as another wave tore through him, sudden and violent and impossible. The dials were still down, his nerves still muted, but it didn't seem to matter. Something was *overriding* his circuits, his power, his will.

The lights glared down, haloing as his vision blurred. The hallway swayed. Victor forced himself past the elevator to the stairwell. He barely made it through the door before his body lit again with pain, and his knee buckled, cracking hard against the concrete. He tried to rise, but his muscles spasmed, and his heart lurched, and he went down on the landing.

His jaw locked as pain arced through him, unlike anything he'd felt in years. Ten years. The lab, the strap between his teeth, the cold of the metal table, the excruciating pain of the current as it fried his nerves, tore his muscles, stopped his heart.

Victor had to move.

But he couldn't get up. Couldn't speak. Couldn't breathe. An invisible hand turned the dial up, and up, and up, until finally, mercifully, everything went black.

VICTOR came to on the stairwell floor.

The first thing he felt was relief—relief that the world was finally quiet, the infernal buzzing gone. The second thing he felt was Mitch's hand shaking his shoulder. Victor rolled onto his side and vomited bile and blood and bad memories onto the landing.

It was dark, the light overhead shorted out, and he could just make out the relief on Mitch's face.

"Jesus," he said, slumping backward. "You weren't breathing. You didn't have a pulse. I thought you were dead."

"I think I was," said Victor, wiping his mouth.

"What do you mean?" demanded Mitch. "What happened?"

Victor shook his head slowly. "I don't know." It wasn't a comfortable thing for Victor, not knowing, certainly wasn't something he cared to admit to. He rose to his feet, bracing himself against the stairwell wall. He'd been a fool to kill his sensitivity. He should have been studying the progression of symptoms. Should have measured the escalation. Should have known what Sydney seemed to sense: that he was cracked, if not broken.

"Victor," started Mitch.

"How did you find me?"

Mitch held up his cell. "Dominic. He called me, freaking out, said you took it back, that it was like before, when you were dead. I tried to call you but you didn't answer. I was heading for the elevator when I saw the light burned out in the stairs." He shook his head. "Had a bad feeling—"

The cell started ringing again. Victor took it from Mitch's hand and answered. "Dominic."

"You can't just *do that* to me," snapped the ex-soldier. "We had a *deal.*"

"It wasn't intentional," said Victor slowly, but Dominic was still going.

"One minute I'm fine and the next I'm on my hands and knees, trying not to pass out. No warning, nothing in my system to dull the pain, you don't know what it was like—"

"I promise you, I do," said Victor, tipping his head back against the concrete wall. "But you're fine now?"

A shuddering breath. "Yeah, I'm back online."

"How long did it last?"

"What? I don't know. I was kind of distracted."

Victor sighed, eyes sliding shut. "Next time, pay attention."

"*Next* time?"

Victor hung up. He opened his eyes to find Mitch staring at him. "Did this happen before?"

Before. Victor knew what he meant. Once his life had been bisected by the night in the laboratory. Before, a human. After, an EO. Now, it was split down the line of his resurrection. Before, an EO. After—this. Which meant that it was Sydney's doing. *This* was the inevitable flaw in her power, the fissure in his. Victor hadn't avoided it after all. He'd simply ignored it.

Mitch swore, running his hands over his head. "We have to tell her."

"No."

"She's going to find out."

"No," said Victor again. "Not yet."

"Then when?"

When Victor understood what was happening, and how to fix it. When he had a plan, a solution as well as a problem. "When it will make a difference," he said.

Mitch's shoulders slumped, defeated.

"Maybe it won't happen again," said Victor.

"Maybe," said Mitch.

Neither one of them believed it.

V

FOUR AND A HALF YEARS AGO

FULTON

IT happened again.

And again.

Three episodes in less than six months, the time between each a fraction shorter, the duration of death a fraction longer. It was Mitch who insisted he see a specialist. Mitch who found Dr. Adam Porter, a compact man with a hawkish face and a reputation as one of the best neurologists in the country.

Victor had never been fond of doctors.

Even back when he wanted to *become* one, it had never been in the interest of saving patients. He'd been drawn to the field of medicine for the knowledge, the authority, the control. He'd wanted to be the hand holding the scalpel, not the flesh parting beneath it.

Now Victor sat in Porter's office, after hours, the buzzing in his skull just beginning to filter into his limbs. It was a risk, he knew, waiting until the episode was in its metastasis, but an accurate diagnosis required the presentation of symptoms.

Victor looked down at the patient questionnaire. Symptoms he could give, but details were more dangerous. He slid the paper back across the table without picking up the pen.

The doctor sighed. "Mr. Martin, you paid quite a premium for my services. I suggest you take advantage of them."

"I paid that premium for privacy."

Porter shook his head. "Very well," he said, lacing his fingers. "What seems to be the problem?"

"I'm not entirely certain," said Victor. "I've been having these *episodes*."

"What kind of episodes?"

"Neurological," he answered, toeing the line between omission and lie. "It starts as a sound, a buzzing in my head. It grows, until I can feel the humming, down to my bones. Like a charge."

"And then?"

I die, thought Victor.

"I black out," he said.

The doctor frowned. "How long has this been happening?"

"Five months."

"Did you suffer any trauma?"

Yes.

"Not that I know of."

"Changes in lifestyle?"

"No."

"Any weakness in your limbs?"

"No."

"Allergies?"

"No."

"Have you noticed any specific triggers? Migraines can be triggered by caffeine, seizures by light, stress, lack of—"

"I don't care what caused it," said Victor, losing patience. "I just need to know what's happening, and how to fix it."

The doctor sat forward. "Well, then," he said. "Let's run some tests."

VICTOR watched the lines chart across the screen, spiking like the tremors before an earthquake. Porter had attached a dozen electrodes to his scalp, and was now studying the EEG alongside him, a crease forming between his brows.

"What is it?" asked Victor.

The doctor shook his head. "This level of activity is abnormal, but the pattern doesn't suggest epilepsy. See how closely the lines are gathered?" He tapped the screen. "That degree of neural excitation, it's almost like there's too much nerve conduction . . . an excess of electrical impulse."

Victor studied the lines. It could be a trick of the mind, but the lines on the screen seemed to rise and fall with the tone in his skull, the peaks in rhythm growing with the hum under his skin.

Porter cut the program. "I need a more complete picture," he said, removing the electrodes from Victor's scalp. "Let's get you into an MRI."

The room was bare save for the scanner in the center—a floating table that slid into a tunnel of machinery. Slowly, Victor lay back on the table, his head coming to rest in a shallow brace. A framework slid across his eyes, and Porter fastened it closed, locking Victor in. His heart rate ticked up as, with a mechanical whir, the table moved and the room disappeared, replaced by the too-close ceiling of the machine in front of Victor's face.

He heard the doctor leave, the click of the door shutting, and then his voice returned, stretched thin by the intercom. *"Hold very still."*

For a full minute, nothing happened. And then a deep knocking sound resonated through the device, a low bass that drowned out the noise in his head. Drowned out everything.

The machine thudded and whirred, and Victor tried to count the seconds, to hold on to some measure of time, but he kept losing his grip. Minutes fell away, taking with them more and more of his control. The buzzing was in his bones now, the first pricks of pain—a pain he couldn't stifle—crackling across his skin.

"Stop the test," he said, the words swallowed by the machine.

Porter's voice came over the intercom. *"I'm almost done."*

Victor fought to steady his breathing, but it was no use. His heart thudded. His vision doubled. The horrible electric hum grew louder.

"Stop the—"

The current tore through Victor, bright and blinding. His fingers clutched at the sides of the table, muscles screaming as the first wave crashed over him. Behind his eyes, he saw Angie, standing beside the electric panel.

"I want you to know," she said as she began to *fix sensors to his chest,* *"that I will never, ever forgive you for this."*

Alarms wailed.

The scanner whined, shuddered, stopped.

Porter was somewhere on the other side of the machine, speaking in a low, urgent voice. The table began to withdraw. Victor clawed at the straps holding his head. Felt them come free. He had to get up. He had to—

The current crashed into him again, so hard the room shattered into fragments—blood in his mouth, his heart losing rhythm, Porter, a pen light turning the world white, a stifled scream—then the pain erased everything.

VICTOR woke on the exam table.

The lights on the MRI were dark, the opening threaded with scorch marks. He sat up, head spinning, as the world came back into focus. Porter lay several feet away, his body contorted, as if trapped in a spasm. Victor didn't need to feel for a pulse, or sense the man's empty nerves, to know that he was dead.

A memory, of another time, another lab, Angie's body, twisted in the same unnatural way.

Shit.

Victor got to his feet, surveying the room. The corpse. The damage.

Now that his senses had settled, he felt calm, clear-headed again. It was like the break after a storm. A stretch of peace before bad weather built again. It was only a matter of time—which was why every silent second mattered.

There was a syringe on the floor next to Porter's hand, still capped.

Victor slipped it into his pocket and went into the hall, where he'd left his coat. He drew out his cell as the text came in from Dominic.

1 minute, 32 seconds.

Victor took a steadying breath and looked around the empty offices.

He retraced his steps to the exam room, gathered up every scan and printout from Porter's tests. In the doctor's office, he cleared the appointment, the digital data, tore off the sheet on which the doctor had made his notes, and the one beneath it for safe measure, systematically erased every sign that he'd ever been inside the building.

Every sign aside from the dead body.

There was nothing to be done about that, short of setting fire to the place—an option he considered, and then set aside. Fires were temperamental things, unpredictable. Better to leave this looking as it did—a heart attack, a freak accident.

Victor slipped on his coat and left.

Back at the hotel suite, Sydney and Mitch were sprawled on the sofa, watching an old movie, Dol stretched at their feet. Mitch met Victor's gaze when he walked in, eyebrows raised in question, and Victor gave a small, almost imperceptible head shake.

Sydney rolled upright. "Where were you?"

"Stretching my legs," said Victor.

Syd frowned. Over the last few weeks, the look in her eyes had shifted from pure worry to something more skeptical. "You've been gone for hours."

"And I was trapped for years," countered Victor, pouring himself a drink. "It makes a body restless."

"I get restless too," said Sydney. "That's why Mitch came up with the card game." She turned to Mitch. "Why doesn't Victor have to play?"

Victor raised a brow and sipped his drink. "How does it work?"

Sydney took the deck up from the table. "If you draw a number card, you have to stay in and learn something, but if you draw a face card, you get to go out. Mostly just to parks or movies, but it's still better than being cooped up."

Victor cut a glance at Mitch, but the man only shrugged and rose, heading to the bathroom.

"You try it," said Syd, holding out the deck. Victor considered her a moment, then lifted his hand. But instead of drawing a card, he brushed the deck from Syd's palm, spilling cards across the floor.

"Hey," said Syd as Victor knelt and considered his options. "That's cheating."

"You never said I had to play fair." He plucked the king of spades from where it lay, upturned. "Here," he said, offering her the card. "Keep it up your sleeve."

Sydney considered the card for a long moment, and then palmed it right before Mitch returned. His eyes flicked between them. "What's going on here?"

"Nothing," said Syd without a second's hesitation. "Victor's just teasing me."

It was disconcerting how easily she lied.

Syd returned to the couch, Dol climbing up beside her, and Victor stepped out onto the balcony.

A few minutes later, the door slid open at his back, and Mitch joined him.

"Well?" asked Mitch. "What did Porter say?"

"He didn't have answers," said Victor.

"Then we find someone else," said Mitch.

Victor nodded. "Tell Syd we're leaving in the morning." Mitch slipped back inside, and Victor set his drink on the railing. He drew the syringe from his pocket, reading the label. Lorazepam. An anti-seizure drug. He had been hoping for a diagnosis, a cure, but until then, he would find a way to treat the symptoms.

"I don't normally meet with patients after hours."

Victor sat across the table from the young doctor. She was slim, and dark, eyes keen behind her glasses. But no matter her interest, or suspicion, her practice was located in Capstone, a city with strong government ties, the kind of place where privacy was paramount, discretion mandatory. Where loose lips could end careers, even lives.

Victor slid the cash across the table. "Thank you for making an exception."

She took the money and considered the few lines he'd filled out on his intake. "How can I help you, Mr. . . . Lassiter?"

Victor was trying to focus through the rising sound in his skull, as she asked all the same questions, and he gave all the same answers. He laid out the symptoms—the noise, the pain, the convulsions, the blackouts—omitting what he could, lying where he had to. The doctor listened, pen scratching across her notepad as she thought. "It could be epilepsy, myasthenia gravis, dystonia—neurological disorders are hard to diagnose sometimes, when they present overlapping symptoms. I'll order some tests—"

"No," said Victor.

She looked up from her notes. "Without knowing what exactly—"

"I've had tests," he said. "They were . . . inconclusive. I'm here because I want to know what you would prescribe."

Dr. Clayton straightened in her chair. "I don't prescribe medications without a diagnosis, and I don't diagnose without compelling evidence. No offense, Mr. Lassiter, but your word is not sufficient."

Victor exhaled. He leaned forward. And as he did, he leaned on her, too. Not with his hands, but with his senses, a pressure just below pain. A subtle discomfort, the same kind that made strangers bend away, allowed Victor to pass unnoticed through a crowd. But Clayton couldn't escape so easily, and so the discomfort registered for what it was—a threat. A fight-or-flight trigger, simple and animalistic, predator to prey.

"There are plenty of dirty doctors in this city," said Victor. "But their willingness to prescribe is often inversely proportional to their skill as a physician. Which is why I'm here. With you."

Clayton swallowed. "The wrong diagnosis," she said steadily, "and the medication could do more harm than good."

"That is a risk," said Victor, "I'm willing to take."

The doctor let out a short, shaky breath. She shook her head, as if clearing her mind. "I'll prescribe you an anti-seizure medication and a beta blocker." Her pen scratched across the page. "For anything stronger," she said, tearing off the sheet, "you will have to admit yourself for observation."

Victor took the slip and rose. "Thank you, Doctor."

Two hours later, he tipped the pills into his palm and swallowed them dry.

Soon, he felt his heart slow, the buzzing quiet, and thought, perhaps, that he had found an answer. For two weeks, he felt better.

And then he died again.

VI

VICTOR was late, and he knew it.

Linden had taken longer than expected—he'd had to wait for the garage to clear, wait for them to be alone. And then, of course, wait for the death he knew was coming, see it through so it didn't follow him back to the house where they'd been for the last nine days. It was a rental, another one of those short-stay places you could book for a day or a week or a month.

Sydney had chosen it, she said, because it looked like a *home*.

When Victor walked in, he was met by the smell of melted cheese and the crack of an explosion on the large TV. Sydney was perched on the arm of the couch, tossing Dol pieces of popcorn while Mitch stood at the kitchen counter, arranging candles on top of a chocolate cake.

The scene was so extraordinarily . . . normal.

The dog spotted him first, tail sliding back and forth across the hardwood floor.

Mitch met his gaze, forehead knotted in concern, but Victor waved him away.

Syd glanced over her shoulder. "Hey."

Five years, and in most ways Sydney Clarke looked the same. She was still short and slight, as round-faced and wide-eyed as she'd been the day they'd met on the side of the road. Most of the differences were superficial—she'd traded the rainbow leggings for black ones with little white stars, and her usual blond bob was constantly hidden by a collection of wigs, her hair changing as often as her mood. Tonight, it was a pale blue, the same color as her eyes.

But in other ways, Sydney had changed as much as any of them. The tone of her voice, her unflinching gaze, the way she rolled her eyes—an affectation she'd clearly taken on in an effort to stress her age, since it wasn't readily apparent. In body, she was still a child. In attitude, she was all teenager.

Now she took one look at Victor's empty hands and he could see the question in her eyes, the suspicion that he'd forgotten.

"Happy birthday, Sydney," he said.

It was a strange thing, the alignment of Syd's birthday with her arrival in Victor's life. Every year marked not only her age, but the time she'd been with him. With them.

"Ready for me to light the candles?" asked Mitch.

Victor shook his head. "Give me a few minutes to change," he said, slipping down the hall.

He closed the door behind him, left the lights off as he crossed the bedroom. The furnishings really didn't suit him—the blue and white cushions, the pastoral painting on one wall, the books on the shelf picked out for decoration instead of substance. The last, at least, he'd found a use for. An attractive history text sat open, a black felt-tip pen resting in the center. At this point, the left page had been entirely blacked out, the right down to the final line, as if Victor were searching for a word and hadn't found it yet.

He shrugged out of his coat and went into the bathroom, rolling up his sleeves. He turned the faucet on and splashed water on his face, the white noise of the tap matching the static already starting again inside his skull. These days the quiet was measured in minutes instead of days.

Victor ran a hand through his short blond hair and considered his reflection, blue eyes wolfish in his gaunt face.

He'd lost weight.

He had always been slim, but now when he lifted his chin, the light glanced off his brow and cheekbone, made shadows along his jaw, in the hollow of his throat.

A short row of pill bottles sat lined up along the back of the sink. He reached for the nearest one, and tipped a Valium into his palm.

Victor had never been keen on drugs.

Sure, the prospective escape held some appeal, but he could never get over the loss of *control*. The first time he'd purchased narcotics, back at Lockland, he wasn't even trying to get high. He was just trying to end his life, so he could come back *better*.

Irony of ironies, thought Victor, swallowing the pill dry.

VII

VICTOR hadn't spent a lot of time in strip clubs.

He'd never understood their appeal—never been aroused by the half-naked bodies, their writhing oiled forms—but he hadn't come to the Glass Tower for the show.

He was looking for someone special.

As he scanned the hazy club, trying not to inhale the cloud of perfume and smoke and sweat, a manicured hand danced along his shoulder blade.

"Hello, honey," said a syrupy voice. Victor glanced sideways and saw dark eyes, bright red lips. "I bet we could put a smile on that face."

Victor doubted it. He had craved a lot of things—power, revenge, control—but sex was never one of them. Even with Angie . . . he'd *wanted* her, of course, wanted her attention, her devotion, even her love. He'd cared about her, would have found ways to please her— and perhaps found his own pleasure in that—but for him, it had never been about sex.

The dancer looked Victor up and down, misreading his disinterest for discretion, or perhaps assuming his proclivities went to less feminine places.

He brushed her fingers away. "I'm looking for Malcolm Jones." Self-styled entrepreneur, specializing in all things illicit. Weapons. Sex. Drugs.

The dancer sighed and pointed toward a red door at the back of the club. "Downstairs."

He made his way toward it, was nearly there when a small blonde crashed into him, releasing a flutter of apology in a high sweet lilt as he reached to steady her. Their eyes met, and something crossed her face, the briefest flutter of interest—he would have said recognition, but he was sure they'd never met. Victor pulled away, and so did she, slipping into the crowd as he reached the red door.

It swung shut behind him, swallowing the club from view. He flexed his hands as he followed a set of concrete steps down into the bowels of the building. The hall at the bottom was narrow, the walls painted black and the air thick with stale cigar smoke. Laughter spilled out of a room at the end, but Victor's way forward was blocked by a heavyset guy in a snug black shirt.

"Going somewhere?"

"Yes," said Victor.

The man surveyed him. "You look like a narc."

"So I've been told," said Victor, spreading his arms, inviting a search.

The man patted him down, then led him through.

Malcolm Jones was sitting behind a large desk in an expensive suit, a gleaming silver gun resting atop a stack of bills at his elbow. Three more men perched on various pieces of furniture; one watched the flat-screen mounted on the wall, another played on his phone, the third eyed the line of coke Jones was cutting on his desk.

None of them seemed overly concerned by Victor's arrival.

Only Jones bothered to look up. He wasn't young, but he had that hungry, almost wolfish look that came with people on the rise. "Who're you?"

"New customer," said Victor simply.

"How'd you hear of me?"

"Word spreads."

Jones preened at that, clearly flattered by the idea of his budding notoriety. He gestured at the empty chair across the desk. "What are you looking for?"

Victor lowered himself into the chair. "Drugs."

Jones gave him a once-over. "Huh, would have taken you for a weapons guy. Are we talking heroin? Coke?"

Victor shook his head. "Prescription."

"Ah, in that case . . ." Jones waved a hand, and one of his men rose and opened a locker, displaying an array of plastic pill bottles.

"We've got oxy, fentanyl, benzos, addy . . ." recited Jones as the other guy lined the bottles on the desk.

Victor considered his options, wondering where to start.

The episodes were multiplying, and nothing he did seemed to make a difference. He'd tried avoiding his power, on the theory that it was a kind of battery, one that charged with use. When that didn't work, Victor changed tactics, and tried using his power *more,* on the theory that perhaps it was a charge he had to *diffuse.* But that approach yielded the same results—again the buzz grew louder, again it became physical, again Victor died.

Victor surveyed the array of pills.

He could chart the electrical current's progress, but he couldn't seem to change it.

From a scientific perspective, it was damning.

From a psychological one, it was worse.

The pain itself he could hijack, to a point, but pain was only one facet of the nervous system. And only one aspect of most opiates. They were suppressants, designed not only to smother pain, but also sensation, heart rate, consciousness—if one kind didn't suffice, then he'd need a cocktail.

"I'll take them," he said.

"Which ones?"

"All of them."

Jones smiled coolly. "Slow down, stranger. There's a house limit of one bottle—I can't go giving you my whole supply. Next thing I know, it shows up on a corner at triple the price—"

"I'm not selling," said Victor.

"Then you don't need much," said Jones, his smile tightening. "Now, as for payment—"

"I said I'd *take* them." Victor leaned forward. "I never said anything about payment."

Jones laughed, a humorless, feral sound, taken up in a chorus by his men. "If you were planning to rob me, you could have at least brought a gun."

"Oh, I did," said Victor, holding out his hand. Slowly, as if performing a trick, he curled three of his fingers in, leaving his thumb up and his index extended.

"See?" he said, pointing the finger at Jones.

Jones no longer seemed amused. "You some kind of—?"

"Bang."

There was no gunshot—no earsplitting echo or spent cartridge or smoke—but Jones let out a guttural scream and fell to the floor as if hit.

The other three men went for their own guns, but their actions were slowed by shock, and before they could fire Victor leveled them all. No dial. No nuance. Just blunt force. That place beyond pain where nerves snapped, fuses blew.

The men crumpled to the floor like puppets with their strings cut, but Jones was still conscious. Still clutching his chest, searching frantically for a bullet wound, the wetness of blood, some physical damage to match what his nerves were telling him.

"The fuck . . . the fuck . . ." he muttered, eyes darting wildly.

Pain, Victor had learned, turned people into animals.

He gathered the pills, dumping bags and bottles into a black leather briefcase he found leaning against the desk. Jones shuddered on the floor before rallying, his attention latching on to the glint of metal on his desk. He started to lunge for it, but Victor's fingers twitched, and Jones sagged, unconscious, against the far wall.

Victor took up the gun Jones had been going for, weighed the

weapon in his palm. He didn't have any special fondness for guns—
they'd been rendered largely unnecessary, given his power. But in
his current condition, it might be useful to have something . . .
extraneous. Plus, it never hurt to have a visible deterrent.

Victor slipped the gun into his coat pocket and snapped the briefcase shut.

"A pleasure doing business with you," he said to the silent room
as he turned and walked out.

AT THE SAME TIME . . .

June adjusted her ponytail and slipped through the velvet curtain
into the private dance room. Harold Shelton was already inside, waiting, rubbing his pink hands on his thighs in anticipation.

"I've missed you, Jeannie."

Jeannie was home sick with food poisoning.

June was just borrowing her body.

"How *much* have you missed me?" she asked, trying to sound soft,
breathy. The voice wasn't perfect, it never was. After all, a voice was
nature *and* nurture, biology and culture. June could nail the pitch—
that came with the body—but her real accent, with its light musical
lilt, always snuck through. Not that Harold seemed to notice. He
was too busy ogling Jeannie's tits through the blue-and-white cheer-
leading outfit.

It wasn't really June's preferred type, but it didn't have to be.

It just had to be his.

She did a slow circle around him, let her pink nails trail along his
shoulder. When her fingers grazed his skin, she saw flashes of his
life—not all of it, just the pieces that left a mark. She let them slide
through her mind without sticking. She knew she'd never borrow
his body, so she'd never need to know more.

Harold caught her wrist, pulling her into his lap.

"You know the rules, Harold," June said, easing herself free.

The rules of the club were simple: Look, but don't touch. Hands in your lap. On your knees. Under your ass. It didn't matter, so long as they weren't on the girl.

"You're such a fucking tease," he growled, annoyed, aroused. He tipped his head back, eyes glassy, breath sour. "What am I even paying for?"

June passed behind him, draped her arms around his shoulders. "You can't touch *me,*" she cooed, leaning in until her lips brushed his ear. "But I can touch *you.*"

He didn't see the wire in her hands, didn't notice until it wrapped around his throat.

Harold started fighting then, but the curtains were thick, and the music was loud, and the more people fought, the faster they ran out of air.

June had always liked the garrote. It was quick, efficient, tactile.

Harold wasted too much energy clawing at the wire instead of her face. Not that it would have made a difference.

"Nothing personal, Harold," June said as he stomped his feet and tried to twist free.

It was the truth—he wasn't on her list. This was just business.

He slumped forward, lifeless, a thin line of spittle hanging from his open lips.

June straightened, blew out a short breath, put away the wire. She studied her palms, which weren't *her* palms. They were marked with thin, deep lines where the wire had bit in. June couldn't feel it, but she knew that the real Jeannie would wake up with these welts, and the pain to go with them.

Sorry, Jeannie, she thought, stepping through the curtain, flicking it shut behind her. Harold was a big spender. He'd shelled out for a full hour of Jeannie's teen queen, which gave June a good fifty minutes to get as far from the body as possible.

She rubbed the welts from her hands as she started down the hall.

At least Jeannie's roommates were home—she'd alibi out. No one had seen June go into Harold's room, and no one had seen her leave, so all she had to do—

"Jeannie," called a voice, too close, behind her. "Aren't you on the clock?"

June swore under her breath, and turned around. And as she did, she *changed*—four years of collecting everyone she touched had given her an extensive wardrobe, and in a blink she shed Jeannie and picked out someone else, another blonde, one with the same shade, same build, but smaller tits and a round face, clad in a short blue dress.

It was a bloody work of art, that shift, and the bouncer blinked, confused, but June knew from experience—when people saw something they didn't understand, they couldn't hold on. *I saw* became *I think I saw* became *I couldn't have seen* became *I didn't see*. Eyes were fickle. Minds were weak.

"Only dancers and clients back here, ma'am."

"Not gunning for a peek," said June, letting her accent trip rich and full over her tongue. "Just looking for the ladies' room."

Max nodded at a door on the right. "Back out the way you came, and across the club."

"Cheers," she added with a wink.

June kept her pace even, casual, as she crossed the club. All she wanted now was a shower. Strip clubs were like that. The smell of lust and sweat, cheap drinks and dirty bills, so thick it coated your skin, followed you home. It was a trick of the mind—after all, June couldn't feel, couldn't smell, couldn't taste. A borrowed body was just that—borrowed.

She was halfway there when she knocked into a man, thin, blond, and dressed in all black. Not unusual, in a place like this, where businessmen leered alongside bachelors, but June reeled at the contact—when she'd brushed his arm, she'd seen . . . *nothing*. No details, no memories.

The man had barely registered her, was already moving away. He disappeared through a red door at the back of the club, and June forced herself to keep walking too, despite feeling like her world had shuddered to a stop.

What were the odds?

Slim, she knew—but not none. There'd been another, a few years ago, a young guy she'd passed on the street one summer night; knocked into, really—she'd had her head tipped back, he'd had his down. When they touched, she'd felt that same flush of cold, the same stretch of black where the memories should be. After months of taking on looks and forms with every touch, the absence of information had been startling, disconcerting. June hadn't known, then, what it meant—if the other person was broken, or if she was, if it was a feature or a glitch—not until she followed the guy and saw him run his hand along the hood of a car. Heard the sudden rumble of an engine starting under his touch, and realized he was *different*.

Not in the way *she* was different, but still, miles from *ordinary*.

She'd started looking for them, after that.

June, who'd never before been a fan of casual contact, unwanted touches, now found every excuse to brush fingers, kiss cheeks, searching for those elusive patches of darkness. She hadn't found another.

Until now.

June slipped behind a column, shedding the blond girl in favor of a man with a forgettable face. Up at the bar, she ordered herself a drink and waited for the stranger to resurface.

Ten minutes later, he did, carrying a black briefcase. He slipped out into the dark.

And June followed behind.

THE streets weren't empty, but they also weren't crowded enough to hide a tail. Every time she dipped out of streetlight, she shifted form.

What would June do if the man in black noticed her?

What would she do if he didn't?

June didn't know *why* she was following the man, or what she planned to do when he stopped walking. Was it a gut feeling pulling her along, or just curiosity? She hadn't always been able to tell them apart. Before . . .

But June didn't like to think about before. Didn't want to, didn't need to. Dying might not have stuck, but her death itself had been real enough. No point in prying open that coffin.

June—that wasn't her real name either, of course. She'd buried that with the rest.

The only thing she'd kept was the accent. *Kept* was a strong word—the stubborn thing didn't want to go. A wisp of home in a foreign world. A memory, of green, and gray, of cliffs and ocean . . . She probably could have shed it, scrubbed it out along with everything else that made her *her*. But it was all she had left. The last thread.

Sentimental, she chided, quickening her step.

Eventually June stopped shifting, and simply followed in the stranger's wake.

It was strange, the subtle way other people veered around him, leaned out of his path.

They *saw* him, she could tell by the way they shifted, sidestepped. But they didn't really *notice*.

Like magnets, thought June. Everyone thought of magnets as having pull, attraction, but turn them around and they repelled. You could spend ages trying to force them together, and you'd get there, almost, but in the end they'd slide off.

She wondered if the man had that effect on the world around him, if it was part of his power.

Whatever it was, she didn't feel it.

But then again, she didn't feel anything.

Who are you? she wondered, annoyed by the man's opacity. She had been spoiled rotten by her power, by the easy knowing that came with it. Not that she saw everything—that would be a short road to long madness—but she saw enough. Names. Ages. Memories, too, but only the ones that really left a mark.

A person, distilled into so many bites.

It was disconcerting, now, to be deprived.

Ahead, the man stopped outside an apartment building. He stepped through the revolving door into the lobby, and June stood in the shadow of the building's eaves and watched him get into the elevator, watched the dial ascend to the ninth floor and then stop.

She chewed her lip, thinking.

It was late.

But it wasn't *that* late.

June turned through the wardrobe in her mind. Too late for a delivery, perhaps, but not a courier. She selected a young woman—more disarming, especially at night—in navy cycling gear, scooped up an undelivered envelope from the lobby, and pushed the call button on the elevator.

There were four doors on the ninth floor.

Four chances.

She put her ear to the first door and heard the dead silence of an empty apartment.

The same with the second.

At the third, she heard footsteps, and knocked, but when the door swung open she was greeted not by the man in black, but by a girl, a large dog at her side.

The girl was on the small side, with white-blond hair and ice blue eyes. The sight of her caught June off guard. She was twelve, maybe thirteen. Madeline's age. Madeline belonged to the Before—*before*, when June had had a family, parents, siblings, one older, three younger, the youngest, with those same strawberry curls—

"Can I help you?" asked the girl.

June realized she must have the wrong place. She shook her head and started to back away.

"Who is it?" asked a warm voice, a big guy with tattooed sleeves and a friendly smile.

"Delivery," said the girl. She was reaching for the package, her fingers nearly brushing June's, when *he* appeared.

"Sydney," said the man in black. "I told you not to answer the door."

The girl retreated into the room, the large dog trailing behind her, and the man stepped forward, his eyes, a colder, darker blue, flicking down to the package in June's hands.

"Wrong address," he said, closing the door in her face.

June stood in the hall, mind spinning.

She'd expected him to be alone.

People like them, they were supposed to be alone.

Were the others human, the big guy and the young girl? Or did they have powers too?

June came back the next day. Pressed her ear against the door and heard—nothing. She knelt before the lock, and a few seconds later the door swung open. The apartment was empty. No signs of the girl, or the dog, the big guy, or the stranger.

They were just—gone.

VIII

IT was happening again. Again. Again.

Victor braced himself against the dresser, the pills from Malcolm Jones's supply arrayed before him, that ever-present hum turning to a high whine in his skull. He searched the labels again for something he hadn't tried—oxycodone, morphine, fentanyl—but he'd tried all of them. Every permutation, every combination, and they weren't working. None of them were working.

He stifled a frustrated growl and swept the open bottles from the counter. Pills rained down onto the floor as Victor surged out into the apartment. He had to get away before the charge reached its peak.

"Where are you going?" asked Sydney as Victor crossed the room.

"Out," he said tightly.

"But you just got back. And it's movie night. You said you'd watch with us."

Mitch put a hand on her arm. "I'm sure he won't be long."

Sydney looked between them, as if she could see the omissions, the lies, the space where truth had been carved out. "What's going on?"

Victor pulled his coat from the hook. "I just need some air." The charge was spilling out now, into the air around him, energy crackling through his limbs. Dol whimpered. Mitch winced. But Sydney didn't back down.

"It's raining," she protested.

"I won't melt."

But Sydney was already reaching for her own coat. "Fine," she said, "then I'll go with you."

"Sydney—"

But she made it to the door before him.

"Get out of my way," he said through clenched teeth.

"No," she shot back, stretching her small body across the wooden frame.

"*Move,*" said Victor, a strange desperation creeping into his voice.

But Sydney held her ground. "Not until you tell me what's going on. I know you're hiding something. I know you're lying, and it's not fair, I deserve to—"

"*Move,*" ordered Victor. And then, without thinking—there was no room for anything beyond the rising charge, the slipping seconds, the need to escape—Victor took hold of Sydney, and *pushed,* not against her nerves, but against her whole body. She stumbled sideways, as if hit, and Victor surged past her for the door.

He was almost there when the spasm hit.

Victor staggered, braced himself against the wall, a low groan escaping between clenched teeth.

Sydney was on her hands and knees nearby, but when he stumbled, all the anger drained out of her face, replaced by fear. "What is it? What's wrong?"

Victor bowed his head, struggling for breath. "Get her—out—"

Mitch was finally there, dragging Sydney back, away from Victor.

"*What's happening to him?*" she sobbed, fighting Mitch's grip.

Victor got the door open, and managed a single step before pain closed over him like a tide, and he fell.

The last thing he saw was Sydney, tearing free of Mitch's arms, Sydney, rushing toward him.

And then death erased it all.

"SYDNEY?"

Victor dragged in a shallow breath.

"Sydney, can you hear me?"

It was Mitch's voice, the words low and pleading.

Victor sat up and saw the man kneeling on the floor, crouched over a small shape. Sydney. She was stretched on her back, her pale hair pooling around her head, her skin porcelain and her body still. Mitch shook her by the shoulder, put his ear to her chest.

And then Victor was up, the room tilting under his feet. His head felt heavy, his thoughts slow, the way they always did in the wake of an episode, and he turned his own dials up, sharpened his nerves to the point of pain. He needed it, to clear his mind.

"Move," he said, dropping to a knee beside her.

"Do something," demanded Mitch.

Sydney's skin was cold—but then, it was always cold. He searched for a pulse, and after several agonizing seconds of nothing, felt the faint flutter of her heart. Barely a beat. Her breath, when he checked, was just as slow.

Victor pressed a hand flat against her chest. He reached for her nerves and tried, as gently as possible, to turn the dial. Not far, just enough to stimulate a reaction.

"Wake up," he said.

Nothing happened.

He turned the dial up a fraction more.

Wake up.

Nothing. She was so cold, so still.

Victor gripped her shoulder.

"Sydney, *wake up*," he ordered, sending a current through her small form.

She gasped, eyes flying open, then rolled onto her side, coughing. Mitch rushed forward to soothe her, and Victor sagged backward, slumping against the door, his heart pounding in his chest.

But when Sydney managed to sit up, she looked past Mitch to Victor, her eyes wide, not with anger but sadness. He could read the question in her face. It was the same one crashing through his own head.

What have I done?

VICTOR sat on the balcony and watched the snow fall, flecks of white against the dark.

He was freezing. He could have put on a coat, could have turned his nerves down, muted the cold, could have erased all sensation. Instead, he savored the frost, watched his breath plume against the night, clung to the brief period of silence.

The lights had come back on, but Victor couldn't bring himself to go inside, couldn't bear the look on Sydney's face. Or Mitch's.

He could leave.

Should leave.

Distance wouldn't save him, but it might protect them.

The door slid open at his back, and he heard Sydney's light steps as she padded out onto the balcony. She sank into the chair beside him, drawing her knees up to her chest. For a few minutes, neither spoke.

Once upon a time, Victor had promised Sydney that he wouldn't let anyone hurt her—that he would always hurt them first.

He'd broken that promise.

He studied his hands, recalling the moment *before*—when he'd forced Syd out of his way. He hadn't touched her nerves then, or at least he hadn't turned the dials. But he'd still *moved* her. Victor rose from his seat, thinking through the implications. He was halfway to the door when Sydney finally broke the silence.

"Does it hurt?" she asked.

"Not right now," he said, sidestepping the question.

"But when it happens," she persisted. "Does it hurt then?"

Victor exhaled, clouding the air. "Yes."

"How long does it hurt?" she asked. "How bad does it get? What does it feel like when you—"

"Sydney."

"I want to know," she said, voice catching. "I *need* to know."

"Why?"

"Because it's my fault. Because I did this to you." Victor started to shake his head, but she cut him off. "Tell me. Tell me the truth. You've been lying for all this time, the least you can do is tell me how it feels."

"It feels like dying."

Sydney's breath caught, as if hit. Victor sighed and stepped to the balcony's edge, the railing slick with ice. He ran his hand over the surface, cold pricking his fingers. "Did I ever tell you how I got my power?"

Syd shook her head, the blond bob swaying side to side. He knew he hadn't. He'd told her his last thoughts once, but nothing more. It wasn't a matter of trust or distrust so much as the simple fact that they'd both left their pasts behind, ones filled with a few things they wanted to remember, and many more things they didn't.

"Most EOs are the result of accidents," he said, studying the snow. "But Eli and I were different. We set out to find a way to effect the change. Incidentally, it's remarkably difficult to do. Dying with intent, reviving with control. Finding a way to end a life but keep it in arm's reach, and all without rendering the body unusable. On top of that, you need a method that strips enough control from the subject to make them afraid, because you need the chemical properties induced by fear and adrenaline to trigger a somatic change."

Victor craned his head and considered the sky.

"It wasn't my first try," he said quietly. "The night I died. I'd already tried once, and failed. An overdose, which, it turned out, provided too much control, and not enough fear. So I set out to try again. Eli had already succeeded, and I was determined to match him. I created a situation in which I couldn't take back control. One in which there was nothing *but* fear. And pain."

"How?" whispered Sydney.

Victor closed his eyes and saw Angie, one hand resting on the control panel.

"I convinced someone to torture me."

Syd drew a short breath behind him. Victor kept talking.

"I was strapped to a steel table, and hooked up to an electrical current. There was a dial, and someone to turn it, and the pain went up when the dial was turned, and I told them not to stop until my heart did." Victor pressed his palms against the icy rail. "People have an idea of pain," he said. "They think they know what it is, how it feels, but that's just an idea. It's a very different thing when it becomes concrete." He turned back toward her. "So when you ask me what the episodes feel like—they feel like dying all over again. Like someone turning up the dial inside me until I break."

Sydney's face was white. "I did this," she said under her breath, fingers gripping her knees. "I did this to you."

Victor went to Sydney's chair and knelt before it.

"Sydney, I am alive because of you," he said firmly. Tears spilled down Syd's cheeks. Victor reached out and touched her shoulder. "You saved me."

She met his eyes then, ice blue laced with red. "But I broke you."

"No," he started, then stopped. An idea flickered through his mind. The first spark of a thought, bright but brittle. He shielded its fragile heat, trying to coax it into something stronger, and as it kindled, he realized—

He'd been looking in the wrong place. Searching for ordinary solutions.

But Victor wasn't ordinary. What had happened to him wasn't ordinary.

An EO had broken his power.

He needed an EO to fix it.

IX

SOUTH BROUGHTON

IT was amazing what passed for music.

Victor leaned against the bar as sound blared out from the stage, where a group of men slammed their hands against their instruments. The upside, he supposed, was the way they drowned out the rising sound in his own head. The downside was the ache forming in its place.

"Hey!" shouted the bartender. "Get you a drink?"

Victor twisted back toward the bar. Toward the man behind the counter.

Will Connelly was six-foot-three, with a square jaw, a shock of black hair, and all the markers of a potential EO.

Victor had done his homework, had instructed Mitch to rebuild a search matrix, the same one Eli, and then the police, had used to find EOs, the same one that had led Victor to Dominic.

It had taken two months to track down the first lead—a woman down south who could reverse age, but not injury—another three to find the second—a man who could take things apart and put them back together, sadly a skill which didn't really apply to living things.

Finding other EOs was hard enough.

Finding specific ones, with restorative abilities, was even harder.

Their latest lead was Will Connelly, who'd bailed from a hospital bed, sans discharge, a mere two days after his accident. The doctors had been stunned.

That suggested a healing ability.

The question was whether he could heal Victor.

So far, no one could.

"Well?" called Connelly over the music.

"Glen Ardoch," Victor called back, nodding at a bottle on the back wall. It was empty.

"Gotta grab some more," said Connelly, flagging another bartender before ducking out from under the bar. Victor waited a moment, then followed, trailing the other man down the hall. Connelly's hand was on the open storeroom door when Victor caught up.

"I've changed my order."

The bartender swung around, and Victor gave him a single forceful shove, tipping Connelly down the flight of stairs.

It wasn't a long flight, but there was a wall of metal kegs at the bottom and the bartender crashed against them with a noise that would have called attention, if not for the wailing of the band overhead.

Victor followed, taking the steps at a more leisurely pace as the man straightened, clutching his elbow. "You broke my fucking arm!"

"Well, then," said Victor, "I suggest you fix it."

Connelly's expression changed. "What? What are you ta—"

Victor flicked his fingers and the bartender staggered, biting back a scream.

There was no need to quiet him. The bass from the club overhead would have been loud enough to drown out a murder.

"Okay!" gasped Connelly. "Okay."

Victor's hold dropped away, and the bartender straightened. He took a few steadying breaths, and then his whole body shuddered, the motion so small and fast it seemed more a vibration than a shiver. As if he were *rewinding*. A fraction of a second, and his arm hung easily at his side, the pain gone from his face.

"Good," said Victor. "Now, fix *me*."

Connelly's face crumpled in confusion. "I can't."

Victor flexed, and the man staggered back into the crates and kegs. "I—*can't*—" he gasped. "Don't you think—if I could help other people—I would? Hell—I'd be a—fucking messiah. Not working—in this shithole bar."

It was a valid point.

"It only works—on me."

Fuck, thought Victor right before his phone rang. He dragged the cell out of his pocket and saw Dominic's name on the screen.

Dom, who only called Victor when there was trouble.

He answered. "What is it?"

"Bad news," said the ex-soldier.

In the storeroom, Connelly had grabbed a bottle off the shelf behind him and now lunged toward Victor. Or started to. But Victor raised a hand, and Connelly's whole body slammed to a stop as he caught the man's nerves, pinned them in place. He'd been practicing, since the night he moved Sydney. He'd learned that pain and motion were both facets of control. Hurting a body was simple; halting it was harder—but Victor was getting the hang of it.

"Go on," he said to Dom.

"Okay, so you know a lot of the guys who come out of the military, they go into private sector. Security. Task force. Muscle-for-hire kind of jobs. Some of it's aboveboard. Some of it's not. But there's always work for people in a certain field, if you're willing and able."

Connelly was still fighting Victor's hold, throwing all his weight against it as if they were arm-wrestling. As if this were a battle of muscle, not will.

"So I'm having drinks with an old army buddy," continued Dom, "well, he's drinking bourbon, I'm on club soda—"

"Summarize," urged Victor, forcing the bartender to his knees.

"Right, sorry. So he tells me about this new job posting. It's under the radar—no public listings, no paper ads or online posts, just word of mouth. No details. Nothing but a name. Letters, really. EON."

Victor frowned. "EON?"

Connelly tried to shout, but Victor clamped his jaws shut.

"Yeah. EON," said Dom. "As in ExtraOrdinary Observation and Neutralization."

Victor stilled. "It's a prison."

"Or something like it. They're looking for guards, but they're also training officers to hunt down people like us."

Victor turned the information over in his mind. "What else did your friend tell you?"

"Not much. But he gave me a card. Some cloak-and-dagger shit. Just those three letters on one side, a name and number on the back. Nothing else."

"Whose name?" asked Victor, even though he had a feeling he already knew the answer.

"Director Joseph Stell."

Stell. The name scraped against Victor's skin. The cop who'd first come for him at Lockland, on the heels of Angie's death; the reason he'd spent four years in a solitary cell, and another six in standard; the same man who'd tracked Eli to Merit a decade later, only to fall under Serena Clarke's spell. Stell was a dog with a bone—once he got his teeth in, he didn't let go. And now—this. An organization designed to hunt EOs.

"I thought you'd want to know," said Dominic.

"You were right." Victor hung up.

What a mess, he thought, shaking his head. Victor Vale was dead and buried in Merit Cemetery, but all it would take was a hunch—hell, bodies were dug up for a dozen reasons. And he'd left behind an empty coffin. The beginning of a trail. Not an obvious one, but enough to cause trouble. From there, how long would it take EON to catch on? To catch up?

"Let me *go*," growled Connelly through locked teeth.

"All right," said Victor, releasing his hold. The bartender staggered, unbalanced by the sudden freedom, and was halfway to his feet when Victor drew his gun and shot him in the head.

The music continued to rage overhead, unbroken, undisturbed.

"**FIVE** marshmallows," said Sydney, perched on the kitchen counter. Tonight her hair was a shock of purple.

"That's too many," said Mitch at the stove.

"Fine, three," said Syd.

"What about four?"

"I don't like even numbers—hey, Victor." Syd swung her legs absently. "Mitch is making hot chocolate."

"How domestic," he said, shrugging out of his coat. They didn't ask about his evening, or Connolly, but Victor could feel the tension in the air like a taut string. His silence on the subject was answer enough.

He caught Mitch's eye. "I need you to find out everything you can about EON."

"What's that?" asked Mitch.

"A problem." Victor relayed Dominic's intel, watching Sydney pale and Mitch's face shift from surprise to concern. When he was done, he turned toward his room. "Start packing."

"Where are we going?" asked Syd.

"Fulton. Capstone. Dresden. Capital City . . ."

Mitch frowned. "Those are all places we've already been."

"I know," said Victor. "We're going back. We need to clean up."

A shadow crossed Sydney's face. "You're going to kill them," she said. "All the people you've met with . . ."

"I don't have a choice," he said simply.

"Yes, you do," said Sydney, crossing her arms. "Why do you have to—"

"Some know my condition. Some know my power. But *all* of

them have seen my face. From here on out, we leave absolutely no trace, and that means before we go forward, we have to go back."

A trail of bodies, or a trail of witnesses—that was the choice they were faced with. Neither option was ideal, but at least corpses couldn't give statements. Victor's solution was logical, but Sydney wasn't having it.

"If you kill all the EOs you meet," she said, "how are you better than Eli?"

Victor's teeth clenched. "I take no pleasure in this, Sydney, but if EON finds them, they'll be one step closer to finding *us*. Do you want that to happen?"

"No, but—"

"Do you know what they'll do? First they'll kill Dol, and then they will take you, and me, and Mitch, and we will never see the light of day, let alone each other, *ever* again." Sydney's eyes widened, but Victor went on. "If you're lucky, they'll lock you in a cage. Alone. If you're not, they'll turn you into a science experiment—"

"Victor," warned Mitch, but he only stepped closer. Sydney stared up at him, fists clenched. He knelt so they were eye to eye.

"You think I'm acting like Eli? You think I'm playing God? Fine, you play, Sydney. You decide, right now, who should live. Us, or them."

Tears hovered on her lashes. She didn't look at him, kept her gaze focused on his shirtfront as her lips moved, short and soundless.

"What was that?" he asked.

This time, he heard it.

"Us."

X

FOUR WEEKS AGO

VICTOR braced himself against the sink, waiting for the drug to hit his system, wondered if the effects were, at this point, placebic. Less medicine and more a misplaced hope. For calm. For time. For control.

He pushed off the counter and returned to the bedroom, to the dresser, to the shallow stack of paper there, Jack Linden's face staring up from the top. Black streaks cut across the profile, erasing line after line after line until only two words remained. Five letters scattered inelegantly across the page.

F I X   M E

Victor stared at the words for a long moment, then crumpled the paper and flung it away.

They were running out of leads.

And he was running out of time.

3 minutes, 49 seconds.

"Victor!" called Syd impatiently.

He straightened.

"Coming," he called, drawing a shallow blue box from the top drawer.

The living room was dark.

Sydney knelt in front of the coffee table, where a small altar of presents waited beside the cake. Eighteen candles burned on top, their tips sending up colorful sparks. Mitch crossed his arms, looking pleased.

"Make a wish," he said.

Syd's eyes shifted from the cake to Mitch before landing on Victor. A shadow crossed her face, just before she blew the candles out.

EIGHTEEN candles—Sydney marveled at the number as she nudged them into even lines beside the half-eaten cake. Eighteen. Dol tried to lick a fleck of chocolate icing from the table, and Victor nudged the dog's face away as Mitch handed Syd her first present. She took the box, shook it with a mischievous grin, then tore the paper off and pulled out a red bomber jacket.

She had seen it in a shop window a few cities back, and stopped to admire it, admire how cool the lanky mannequin looked, the S curve of its body, hands on hips through the deep side pockets.

What Syd didn't say then was that she'd wanted the mannequin's shape as much as the clothes resting on it. On her, the jacket was too big—the sleeves a good six inches longer than her arms.

"I'm sorry," said Mitch. "It was the smallest size they had."

She managed a smile. "That's okay," she said. "I'll grow into it."

And she supposed she might. Eventually.

Mitch handed her the second box, a package with Merit on the return label. Dominic. She missed him—Victor was always on the phone with the ex-soldier, but none of them had actually *seen* him since they left Merit. It was the one city they never went back to.

Too many skeletons, she supposed.

Now, Sydney staggered at the weight of Dominic's present. Inside was a pair of steel-toed combat boots, each with a sole three inches thick. Syd dropped to the floor and laced them up. When she got to her feet, she made Mitch stand eye to eye with her so she could see how tall she was. She came to his sternum instead of his stomach, and he ruffled her wig playfully.

At last, Victor held out the shallow blue box.

"Don't shake it," he warned.

Syd knelt at the table and held her breath as she lifted the lid.

Inside, nested in velvet, lay the skeleton of a small, dead bird. No feathers, no skin, or muscle—only three dozen attenuated bones perfectly arranged in the narrow blue folds.

Mitch cringed at the sight of it, but Sydney rose, clutching the box to her like a secret.

"Thank you," she said with a smile. "It's perfect."

XI

FIVE YEARS AGO

MERIT

THE night Victor died, Sydney couldn't sleep.

Dominic had taken a handful of pills, washing them down with whiskey before collapsing on the couch, and it was only a matter of minutes before Mitch, bruised and bloody and a thousand miles away, sank into his own fitful doze.

But Syd sat up, with Dol at her feet, thinking of Victor's body in the morgue, of Serena's charred corpse in the Falcon Price lot, until finally she gave up on sleep entirely, tugged on her boots, and snuck outside.

It was just before dawn when Sydney reached the Falcon Price project. The darkest part of the night, Serena used to say. The time when monsters and ghosts came out.

The construction project was marked off with crime scene tape.

Sydney folded herself small and slipped behind the plywood fence, into the gravel lot. The police were gone, the noise and lights were gone, the chaos of the night reduced to numbered markers, and drying blood, and a white plastic tent.

Inside that tent, Serena's body. What was left of it. The fire had been hot—hot enough to reduce most of her sister to blackened skin and brittle bones. Syd knew the fire was out, but as she reached a hand into the charred remains, she still half expected the bones to burn her. But there was no heat, no warmth, no promise of life. Half of the bones had already crumbled, others threatened to fold under the barest touch, but here and there a few pieces retained their strength.

Sydney started digging.

She just wanted a token, something to remember her sister, a piece to hold on to. It wasn't until she was elbows-deep in the scorched heap that she realized what she was really doing.

Looking for a way to bring Serena back.

SYDNEY started dying, but only in her dreams.

The nightmares began when they left Merit. Night after night, she'd close her eyes and find herself back on the frozen lake, the one that had cracked and broken and swallowed her and her sister up three years before.

In her dreams, Serena was a shadow on the far shore, arms crossed and waiting, watching, but Syd was never alone on the ice. Not at first. Dol stayed close, licking at the frozen ground, while Dom and Mitch and Victor formed a loose circle around her.

And in the distance, walking toward them across the lake, a man with broad shoulders and warm brown hair, an easy stride and a friendly smile.

Eli, who never aged, never changed, never died.

Eli, who made every hair on her neck stand on end in a way the cold never did.

"It's okay, kid," said Dom.

"We're here," said Mitch.

"I won't let him hurt you," said Victor.

They were all lying in the end.

Not because they meant to, but because they couldn't make it true.

The lake made a sound like branches breaking in the woods. The ice began to splinter beneath their feet.

"Get back!" she called, and she didn't know if she was talking to them or to Eli, but it didn't matter. Nobody listened.

Eli made his way across the lake, coming for them, for *her*. The ice stayed smooth and solid beneath him, but every time he took a step, someone else disappeared.

Step.

The lake shattered beneath Dominic.

Step.

Mitch sank like a stone.

Step.

Dol crashed and went under.

Step.

Victor plunged down.

Step.

One by one they drowned.

Step.

And then she was alone.

With *Eli*.

"Hello, Sydney," he said.

Sometimes he had a knife.

Sometimes he had a gun.

Sometimes he had a length of rope.

But Sydney's hands were always empty.

She wanted to fight back, wanted to hold her ground, wanted to face the monster, but her body always betrayed her. Her boots always turned toward the shore, slipping and skidding as she ran.

Sometimes she almost made it.

Sometimes she wasn't even close.

But no matter what she did, the dream always ended the same.

XII

FOUR YEARS AGO

DRESDEN

SYD sat up with a gasp.

She'd woken to the sound of cracking ice, the hiss and snap of a lake giving way. It took her a moment to realize the sounds hadn't followed her out of her dreams; they were coming from the kitchen.

The sound of cracking eggs.

The hiss and snap of bacon in a pan.

Sydney's parents had never made breakfast. There was always food—or at least, there was always money for food, in a jar by the sink—but there were no family meals—that would have required them to all be in the house at the same time—and unlike in the movies, no one was ever woken by the smell of breakfast, not on Christmas morning, not on birthdays, and certainly not on a random Tuesday.

Whenever Sydney woke to the sizzle of bacon or the pop of a toaster, she knew that Serena was home. Serena always made breakfast, a veritable banquet of food, way too much for them to eat.

"Hungry, sleepyhead?" Serena would always ask, pouring her a glass of juice.

And for a groggy moment, before the details of the room came into focus, Sydney almost leapt from the bed to ambush her sister in the kitchen.

Sydney's heart quickened. But then she saw the strange apartment walls, and the red metal tin on the unfamiliar nightstand, containing all that remained of Serena Clarke, and the reality came rushing back.

Dol whined softly from the edge of the bed, obviously torn between his loyalty to Syd and his canine love of food.

"Hungry, sleepyhead?" she asked softly, rubbing him between the ears. He gave a relieved huff and turned, nosing open the door. Sydney followed him out into the apartment. It was a rental, the eleventh one they'd stayed in, the fifth city. It was a nice place—they were always nice places. They'd been on the road—on the run—for nearly six months, and she still walked around holding her breath, half expecting Victor to send her away. After all, he never said Sydney could stay with them, after. He had simply never told her to leave, and she had never asked to go.

Mitch was in the kitchen, cooking breakfast.

"Hey, kid," he said. Mitch was the only one who got to call her that. "You want food?"

He was already dividing the eggs onto two plates, three for him and one for her (but she always got half the bacon).

She plucked a strip from her plate, split it with Dol, and looked around the rented apartment.

She wasn't homesick, exactly.

Sydney didn't miss her parents. She knew she should feel bad about that, but the fact of the matter was, she felt like she'd lost them way before she disappeared—her first memories were of packed suitcases and long-term sitters, her last were of two parent-shaped shadows leaving her behind in the hospital after the accident.

What she had now felt more like a family than her mother and father ever had.

"Where's Victor?"

"Oh . . ." Mitch had that look on his face, that carefully blank look that adults got when they were trying to convince you everything was fine. They always assumed that if they didn't *tell* you a thing, you wouldn't know it. But that wasn't true.

Serena used to say that she could tell when someone was lying, because all those unsaid things hung in the air, making it heavy, like the pressure before a storm.

Sydney might not know the full scope of Victor's lie, but the wrongness was still there, taking up space.

"He just stepped out for a walk," said Mitch. "I'm sure he'll be back soon."

Sydney knew Mitch was lying too.

He pushed his empty plate aside.

"Okay," he said, producing his deck of cards. "Draw."

It was a game they'd been playing since the first few days after Merit, when the need to keep a low profile clashed with the urge to go out, and Victor's absences meant Syd and Mitch spent a lot of time together (and the good-natured ex-con obviously had no idea what to do with a thirteen-year-old who could resurrect the dead).

"What would you be doing," he'd asked, "if you were . . ." He let the question trail off.

Sydney knew he was thinking *home* but she said, "Back in Brighton? I'd probably be in school."

"Did you like school?"

Sydney shrugged. "I liked learning."

Mitch brightened at that. "Me too. But I never got to stay in one place long. Foster care and all. So I didn't care much about *school* . . . but you don't need that to learn. I could teach you . . ."

"Really?"

Mitch colored a little. "Well, there's lots I don't know. But maybe we could learn together." That's when he drew the deck from his pocket. "How about this—hearts will be literature. Clubs is science. Diamonds is history. Spades is math. That should give us a good start."

"And face cards?" asked Syd.

Mitch flashed a conspiratorial smile. "Face cards, we go outside."

Now Sydney held her breath and pulled a card from the center, hoping for a king or queen.

She got a six of clubs.

"Better luck next time," said Mitch, pulling his laptop over. "Okay, let's see what kind of experiments we can do in this kitchen . . ."

They were halfway through creating a homemade lava lamp when the door swung open, and Victor walked in. He looked *tired,* his face tight, as if he were in pain. She felt the air go heavy on her shoulders.

"You hungry?" asked Mitch, but Victor waved him away and sank into a chair at the kitchen table. He took up his tablet and began absently swiping through. Mitch set a cup of black coffee at his elbow.

Sydney perched on the counter and studied Victor.

Whenever she'd resurrected an animal, or a person, she'd done it by visualizing a thread, something floating in the darkness. She pictured grabbing that thread and pulling it toward her, drawing them back into the light. But when it was done, she never really let go of the thread. Didn't know how, really. So she could feel it now when Victor was home, and when he was out pacing the city, could feel it still, no matter how far he went, as if his energy, his stress, vibrated up the invisible rope until the tremor reached her.

And so, even without the heavy air, the way Mitch looked at Victor, the way Victor didn't look at her, she *knew* that something was not right.

"What is it, Sydney?" he asked without looking up.

Tell me the truth, she thought. *Just tell me the truth.*

"Are you sure you're okay?" she asked.

Victor's cold blue eyes drifted up, meeting hers.

His mouth twitched into a smile, the way it did when he was lying. "Never better."

XIII

SYDNEY wove around the base of the tree, sunlight dappling her skin.

She'd drawn a face card—the queen of diamonds—but the weather was so nice she would have played the spade Victor had slipped her just to get out of the apartment.

Victor.

Behind her eyes, Sydney saw him buckling against the door, saw him fighting back a scream as his body curled on the floor. There had been pain, too, a jolt of something straight through her chest, and then darkness, but that part didn't haunt her.

Victor haunted her. His pain haunted her. His dying haunted her.

Because it was Sydney's fault.

He had been counting on her, and she'd let him down.

She'd brought him back wrong.

Broken.

That was the secret. The lie.

"It feels like dying."

Sydney kept her eyes on the mossy ground as she paced. If anyone looked her way, they would probably assume she was searching for flowers, but it was late spring, the time when baby birds flung themselves out of the nest and hoped to fly. Not all of them made it. And Sydney was always searching for things to revive. Subjects to practice on.

Sydney already knew how to reach inside a body and pull it back to life. But what if the thing had been dead for a long time? What if the body wasn't all there? How much did there have to be, for her to find the thread? How little?

Dol snuffled in the grass nearby, and across the field Mitch leaned back against a slope, a battered paperback open on one knee, a pair of sunglasses perched on his nose.

They were in Capital City, as hilly as Fulton had been flat, a place with as many parks as skyscrapers.

She liked it here. Wished they could stay. Knew they wouldn't.

They were only here because Victor was searching for someone. Another EO. Someone who could fix what she'd broken.

Something cracked under Syd's foot.

She looked down and saw the crumpled body of a young finch. The bird had been there awhile, long enough for its small body to sink into the moss. Long enough for the feathers to fall away and a wing to come detached, the brittle bones shattering like an eggshell under her shoe.

Syd sank to her knees, crouching over the tiny corpse.

It was one thing, she'd learned, to breathe life back into a body. Another thing entirely to rebuild the body itself. You only got one chance—Sydney had learned that the hard way, threads unraveling, bones crumbling to ash under her touch—but the only way to get stronger was to practice. And Sydney wanted to get stronger—she *needed* to get stronger—so she curled her fingers gently over the bird's remains, and closed her eyes, and reached.

Cold rippled through her as she searched the darkness for a thread, a filament, a wisp of light. It was there somewhere, so faint she couldn't see it, not yet. She had to go by feel instead. Her lungs ached, but she kept reaching, knew she was almost, almost—

Sydney felt the bird twitch under her palm.

Flutter, like a pulse.

And then—

Sydney's eyes flew open, a faint plume of cold brushing her lips as the bird was rising on unsteady wings. Buffeting itself up into the branches of the tree.

Syd rocked back on her heels and let out a shaky breath.

"Well, *that* was quite a trick."

Her head snapped up, and for a second—just a second—she found herself staring at a ghost. White-blond hair, and ice blue eyes, a dazzling smile set into a heart-shaped face.

But it wasn't Serena.

Up close, the girl had higher cheeks than her sister, a broader chin, eyes that danced with a mischievous light. Dol's lip curled a little, flashing teeth, but when the stranger held out her hand, the dog sniffed it cautiously, and then calmed.

"Good boy," said the girl who wasn't Serena. There was a lilt in her voice, a kind of music. Her eyes flicked up to Sydney. "Did I scare you?"

"No," she managed, her throat constricting. "You just looked— like someone else."

The stranger flashed her a wistful grin. "Someone nice, I hope." She pointed up to the branches. "I saw what you did there, with the bird."

Sydney's heart quickened. "I didn't do anything."

The girl laughed, a light, airy sound. And then she crossed behind the trunk of the tree. When she reappeared on the other side, she was *someone else*. Only a second had passed, a step, but the blond girl was gone, and Sydney found herself staring into Mitch's familiar face.

"It's a big world, kiddo," he said. "You're not the only one with talents."

She knew it wasn't really him. Not just because the real Mitch was still reading across the field, but because of the accent that ran beneath his voice, even now.

The stranger took a step toward Sydney, and as she did, her body changed again. Mitch disappeared, replaced by a lanky young woman in a peasant skirt, her loose blond curls pulled up in a messy bun.

The girl looked down at herself. "This one's my favorite," she said, half to herself.

"How did you do that?" asked Syd.

The stranger raised a brow. "I didn't do anything," she said, echoing Syd's words. And then she broke into a smile. "See? Isn't it silly to lie when we both know the truth?"

Sydney swallowed. "You're an EO."

"EO?"

"ExtraOrdinary. That's what they call—us."

The girl mused. "ExtraOrdinary. I like that." She looked down, and chirped in delight. "Here," she said, retrieving a tiny bird's skull from the grass. "You've seen my trick. Show me yours again."

Sydney took the skull, which was no bigger than a ring. It was unbroken, unblemished—but not enough.

"I can't," she said, handing it back. "There's too much missing."

"Syd?" called Mitch.

The stranger drew a folded bookmark from her back pocket, and a pen from her curls. She scribbled something down the side, and held it out.

"In case you ever need a friend." She leaned in close. "Girls like us got to stick together," she added with a wink.

Mitch called Sydney's name again.

"Better go," said the stranger. "Wouldn't want the big guy to worry." She ran her fingers over Dol's muzzle. "You look after our girl," she told the dog.

"See ya," said Syd.

"You bet."

Mitch was waiting for her across the field. "Who were you talking to?" he asked.

Sydney shrugged. "Just some girl," she said, realizing she hadn't asked for a name. She glanced over her shoulder, and saw the stranger still leaning back against the tree, holding the little white skull up to the light.

That night, Sydney put the number in her phone.

The next, she sent the girl a text.

I forgot to tell you. My name is Sydney.

She held her breath and waited.

The reply came a few seconds later.

Nice to meet you, Sydney, it said.

I'm June.

XIV

FOUR WEEKS AGO

SYD was helping Mitch clear the cake when she felt the phone buzz in her back pocket.

She excused herself, slipped into her room and shut the door behind her before reading the text.

> **June**: Happy birthday, Syd xoxo

She felt herself smile.

> **June**: Get anything good?

Syd sent her a photo of the bomber jacket.

> **Syd**: Doesn't fit.
> **June**: Good thing vintage never goes out of style ;)

Sydney turned toward the closet mirror, studying her reflection. Eighteen.

Officially an adult, even if she didn't look it.

She considered the boots. The blue hair. The bomber jacket—it really was too big for her. How long before it fit? Ten years? Twenty?

Victor thought Sydney's aging—the lack of it—had something

to do with the way she'd died, the icy water that froze her limbs and stopped her pulse. All this time, and her vitals were still slow, her skin still cold to the touch. Everyone else was changing—Victor getting leaner and harder by the year, the lines around Mitch's eyes, Dol's muzzle edging white.

Only Sydney seemed to stay the same.

And Eli, she thought, a chill running through her. But he was gone. And she had to stop summoning him, stop inviting him into her head.

Syd sank onto the edge of the bed.

Syd: Where are you?
June: Just got to Merit.

Sydney's pulse quickened.

Syd: Really? How long are you staying?
June: On a job. Just passing through.
Syd: I wish I could be there with you.
June: You could be ;)

But they both knew it wasn't that simple.

Sydney wouldn't leave Victor, and as far as Victor was concerned Merit—and all of its skeletons—belonged in the past.

XV

THE dead mouse lay on Sydney's desk, curled atop a floral dish towel.

A cat had obviously gotten to it—there were bits and pieces missing, leaving the rodent more than half, but less than whole. It was late summer, and Syd had the window propped up to keep the smell from gathering.

Dol had his chin resting on the window frame, sniffing the air on the fire escape while she worked. More than once, she'd resurrected a small animal, only to have it race away from her fingers and out into the apartment, burying itself under a sofa or behind a cupboard. More than once, Mitch had been summoned to help extricate it. Victor had noticed her practicing, even encouraged it, but he had one rule: she couldn't keep any of the animals she brought back. They were to be set free. Or disposed of. (Dol, of course, was the sole exception.)

Down the hall, a door opened, closed, and the dog's ears perked. Victor was back.

Sydney held her breath and listened, hoping to glean good news from the tone of his voice, or Mitch's reaction. But within seconds she could tell—another dead end.

Her chest tightened, and she turned her attention back to the dead mouse, cupping her palms over the tiny furred corpse. Her backpack sat on the bed beside the desk, the small red tin resting on top.

Sydney's gaze flicked toward it, the action almost superstitious—like throwing salt over your shoulder, or knocking on wood—and then she closed her eyes, and reached. Past the body, to the darkness, searching for the thread. With every passing second, the cold climbed her fingers, spread past her wrists and up toward her elbows.

And then, at last, the thread brushing her fingers, a twitch against her palm.

Syd gasped, and blinked, and the mouse was whole, was alive, was scurrying out of her hands and across the desk.

She lunged and caught the small rodent, setting it on the fire escape and closing the window before it could follow her back in. She turned toward the hall, excited to tell Victor and Mitch about the feat, small as it was.

But halfway there, Syd slowed, stopped, held back by something in Mitch's voice.

". . . is it really necessary?"

"It's a calculation," answered Victor coldly. There was a pause. The sound of ice shifting in a glass. "You think I *enjoy* killing people?"

"No . . . I don't know . . . I think sometimes you make the easiest choice instead of the right one."

A low, derisive snort. "If you're still hung up on what happened with Serena . . ."

Sydney's breath caught on the name. A name no one had uttered in almost three years.

"There could have been another way," said Mitch.

"There wasn't," growled Victor, "and you know it, even if you want to pretend you don't."

Sydney pressed her hand over her mouth.

"Make me the villain of that night, Mitch. Wash your hands of any blame. But don't act like Serena Clarke was merely a victim or even a casualty of circumstance. She was an enemy, a weapon, and killing her wasn't just smart, or easy—it was right."

Victor's steps sounded on the hardwood as he came down the hall.

Syd scrambled back into her room. She went to the window and threw it open, stepping out onto the fire escape. She leaned her elbows on the metal rail, tried to pretend she was looking dreamily out at the city instead of making fists so tight her fingers ached.

But Victor didn't even slow down as he passed Sydney's door.

She sank to her knees when he was gone, bowing her head against the bars.

A memory washed over her, of that night. Of Serena's voice in her ear, telling her not to run, of the way Sydney's mind had gone smooth, her limbs soft under the order. Of the cold parking garage, and the gun against her head. Of the long pause, and then her sister's order—to go. To find somewhere safe. Some*where*, which had once been some*one*. Victor.

But Victor—

Some part of her had known.

Had to have known.

Sydney felt like she was going to scream. Instead, she left. Took the fire escape two stairs at a time, didn't even care about the way her steps rattled as she crashed down floor after floor.

She hit the street and kept going.

One block, three blocks, five—Sydney didn't know where she was going, only that she couldn't turn around. Couldn't look Victor in the eyes.

She drew her cell from her back pocket and dialed June. They'd been texting for almost a year, exchanging small notes, anecdotes about where they were, what they were doing, but Syd had never *called*.

The phone rang, and rang, and rang.

But no one answered.

Sydney's steps slowed, the initial wave of shock settling into something heavier. She looked around. She was on a narrow street, not an alley exactly, but not a main road, either. People said cities didn't sleep, but they did get quiet. And dark.

Turn around, said a voice in her head, but it sounded like Victor, so Sydney kept going.

Which was a mistake.

The thing about mistakes was that they weren't always big, or obvious. Sometimes they were simple. Small. The decision to keep walking. The turn left instead of right. Those few extra steps in the wrong direction.

Sydney was trying to call June again when she saw them—two men. One wearing a black leather jacket, the other with a kerchief slung around his throat.

She stopped walking, caught between turning around, which would mean putting her back to the men up ahead, or continuing forward, which would mean passing within arm's reach. They hadn't noticed her, at first, or at least they'd pretended not to, but now they looked at her and smiled.

The men didn't look dangerous, not like in the movies Syd watched with Mitch, but she knew that meant nothing—everyone who'd ever hurt her had *looked* safe. And the longer she stayed put, the more she felt the badness wafting off them like cheap cologne. Something she could smell and taste.

"Hey, little girl," said one, moving toward her. "You lost?"

"No," said Sydney. "And I'm not a little girl."

"Different time we're living in," said the second. "They grow up so fast."

Syd didn't know how they'd gotten so close to her, so quickly, but as she shuffled backward, turned to go, a hand caught her collar. The guy in the leather jacket wrenched her back against him, one arm wrapped around her shoulders. "Aw, now, don't be rude."

"Get off me," she snarled, but he was squeezing too hard, and she couldn't breathe, couldn't think. She felt something hard dig into her ribs, realized it was a gun. She twisted in his grip, trying to grab it.

"Careful," said the other one, closing in. "She's got spirit."

Syd tried to kick out at the other guy but he jumped back, wagging his finger. Her fingers skimmed the gun, but she couldn't quite get it.

The first man's breath was hot and sour on her cheek. "Come on, now, let's have some fun."

Syd slammed her head back into his nose—or tried, but her head only came to his chin. Still, she hit bone, heard the crack of a tooth, and she was free, stumbling to her hands and knees as the man reeled, the gun tumbling from his waistband. Syd lunged for it, fingers closing around the grip right before one of the men grabbed her ankle and *pulled*.

The street bit into her elbows and scraped her shin as she twisted around and raised the gun, barrel leveled at the man's heart. "Let *go*," she snarled.

"Oh shit," said the man in the kerchief, but the other one sneered at her, blood spilling from his mouth.

"That's an awfully big gun for such a little girl."

"Let *go*."

"You even know how to use it?"

"Yes." Sydney squeezed the trigger as she said it, bracing for the recoil, the bang.

But nothing happened.

The man laughed, a short barking sound, and knocked the gun from her hands. It went skidding away.

"Little bitch," he said, raising his boot as if she were a bug, something to crush. He brought it down hard. Or at least, he started to, but his leg seemed to lock up halfway, and then he toppled, a single horrifying sound leaking from his clenched teeth. An instant later, the second guy fell, limbs seizing, as Victor walked toward them, his collar up against the cold.

Relief washed over her, tangled with shock. "What are you doing here?"

The men on the ground writhed in muted agony, blood leaking from their noses and vessels breaking in their eyes.

Victor knelt to retrieve the discarded gun. "A little gratitude would be nice."

She rose on shaky legs, the anger catching up. "You *followed* me."

"Don't try for the moral high ground, Sydney. You snuck out."

"I chose to go. I'm not a captive."

"You're a *child,* and I promised to protect—"

"A promise you can't keep is just another *lie,*" she snapped. She was sick of everyone lying.

Mitch had lied when he told her Victor was fine. Eli had lied when he said he wouldn't hurt her. Serena had lied when she said she'd never leave. And Victor had been lying every day since his return.

"I don't want you to save me," said Sydney. "I want to save myself."

Victor weighed the weapon in his hand. "All right," he said, offering her the gun. "The first step is to turn the safety off."

Sydney took the weapon, marveled at the weight in her hands. It was heavier than she expected. Lighter than she expected. Her thumb slid over the catch on the side.

"If you want," said Victor, turning back toward the mouth of the alley, "I'll teach you how to shoot."

Sydney wasn't ready for him to walk away.

"Victor," she called, gripping the gun. "Did you do it?"

Victor slowed to a stop. Turned. "Did I do what?"

Sydney held his gaze. "Did you kill Serena?"

Victor only sighed. The question didn't seem to take him by surprise, but he didn't answer it either. Sydney raised the gun, training it on his chest. "Did you *do* it?"

"What do you think?"

Sydney's grip tightened. "I need you to say it."

Victor moved toward her slowly, steadily. "I warned you when we met, I wasn't a good person."

"*Say it,*" demanded Syd.

Victor came to a stop an arm's length away, halted only by the gun against his ribs. He looked down at her. "Yes. I killed Serena."

The words hurt, but the pain was dull. Not a knife wound, or a plunge into ice water, but the deep ache of a fear realized, a suspicion turned to truth.

"Why? Why did you do it?"

"She was unstable and unquantifiable, a danger to everyone in her path."

The way he talked about her, about everything, as if they were just factors in an equation.

But Serena wasn't a factor. A problem to be solved.

"She was my sister."

"She would have killed you."

"No," whispered Syd.

"If I hadn't killed her, the cops would still be under her control. Eli would never have been caught. He'd still be free."

Sydney shivered, the gun trembling in her grip. "Why did you burn her body?"

"I couldn't risk you bringing her back." Victor's hand drifted up to the gun. He wrapped his fingers loosely around the barrel, not tight enough to stop the action if she pulled the trigger, just enough to keep the weapon steady. "Is this what you want? Killing me won't bring her back either. Will you feel safer if I'm dead? Think hard, Sydney. We all have to live with our choices."

Sydney shuddered.

And then she let go of the gun.

Victor caught the weapon before it hit the ground. He ejected the clip, and then knelt so they were eye to eye.

"Look at me," he said coldly, catching Sydney's chin in his hand. "The next time you point a gun at someone, make sure you're ready to pull the trigger."

He straightened, set the weapon on a nearby crate, and walked away.

Sydney wrapped her arms around her ribs and sank to her knees on the pavement.

She didn't know how long she sat there before her phone finally rang. She drew the cell from her pocket with shaking hands and answered.

"Hey, kiddo," said June, sounding breathless. "Sorry, I was finishing a job. What's up?"

TEN minutes later, Sydney was sitting in a diner—the kind that stayed open all night—clutching a cup of black tea.

It had been June's idea.

The seat across from Syd was empty, but if she kept her eyes on her tea, and her ear to the cell phone, she could imagine the other girl sitting in the booth across from her. The sounds of another diner in another city—the bell of an order ready for pickup, a spoon stirring sugar in a cup—made a soft curtain of noise on the line.

"You said you were working," said Syd, making small talk. "What do you do?"

A pause on the line. "Do you really want to know?"

"Yeah."

"I kill people."

Sydney swallowed. "Bad people?"

"Sure, most of the time."

"Do you like your job?"

A soft sound, somewhere between an exhale and a laugh. "What would you think of me if I said yes?"

Syd looked up at the empty booth. "I'd think at least you were being honest."

"What happened tonight?" asked June. "Talk to me."

And Sydney did. The words just spilled out. She couldn't believe how easy it was to talk to June, how good it felt, amid so many secrets, to share some truth. She hadn't felt that ease with someone, not since Serena died. It was like taking a deep breath after being underwater.

Talking to June made her feel *normal*.

She told her about Victor, and Mitch. About her sister, about the day they drowned, the way they came back, her slowly, and Serena all at once. She told her about Serena's powers, and about Eli.

"Is he like us?" asked June.

"No," growled Sydney. She took a deep breath. "I mean, he's an EO. But he's not like us. He thinks we're wrong. That we shouldn't exist. So he started killing us. He killed dozens of people before Victor stopped him." Sydney's voice sank until it was barely a whisper. "My sister . . . she and Eli . . ."

But it wasn't all Serena's fault.

Her sister had been lost for a really long time when Eli found her.

Sydney had been lost too, but Victor had been the one to find *her*.

It wasn't Serena's fault that Sydney got the hunter and she got the wolf.

"I know what happened to Serena," said June.

Sydney stiffened in her seat. "What?"

A sigh. "In order to take someone's face," said June, "I have to touch them. And when I do, I see things. Not everything—no room in my head for that much useless memory—just the bits that make them who they are, the ones that matter most. Loves, hates, important moments. Mitch—I touched his arm that day in the park, right before you and I met—and I saw him standing before a fire. There was a girl's body in the flames. But all I felt was his regret."

Sydney closed her eyes, swallowed hard. "Mitch didn't kill Serena," she said. "Victor did."

"Why would he do that?" asked June.

Sydney let out a shuddering breath. "My sister could control people. She had this hold on them. Could make them do anything she wanted, just by saying the words. She was strong, powerful. But . . . she was like Eli. She thought people like *us* were lost. Broken."

"Maybe she was right," said June.

"How can you—" started Sydney.

"Hear me out," pressed June. "Maybe we are broken. But we put

ourselves back together. We *survived*. That's what makes us so powerful. And as for family—well, blood is always family, but family
doesn't always have to be blood."

Sydney felt hollow, worn out. "What about you?" she asked. "Do
you have a family?"

There was a long pause. "No," said June softly. "Not anymore."

"What happened to them? Did they die?"

"No," said June. "But I did." A long pause. "You see, they wouldn't
recognize me."

"But you were *you* first. Can't you just . . . change back?"

"It's complicated. What I can do," she said slowly, "makes me invincible. But only as long as I'm someone else." June hesitated. "I
buried someone. So did my family. There wasn't a grave, but I'm
still gone. And it needs to stay that way. When I came back, I decided that no one would ever hurt me again. I gave up everything—
everyone—in exchange for that."

Sydney frowned. "Was it worth it?"

A long silence.

And then June said, "Yes." The sound of a coffee mug shifting on
a table. "But hey, like I said, not all family is blood, right? Sometimes we have to find a new one. Sometimes we get lucky, and they
find *us*."

Sydney looked down into her tea. "I'm really glad we met."

"Me too."

Neither spoke for a few minutes, the ambient noise of their re-
spective diners collapsing the distance. June hummed softly, and Syd
wished she were really there, sitting across the table.

Sydney closed her eyes. "Hey, June?"

"Yeah, Syd?"

Her voice cracked. "I don't know what to do."

"You could leave."

She'd thought about it. She was so tired of moving, of living out
of a backpack, of chasing down lead after lead, only to find dead
ends. Sick of watching Victor suffer, of knowing it was her fault. But

that was exactly why she couldn't go. Victor had killed Serena, yes, but Sydney was killing him. Over and over. She couldn't abandon him. She *wouldn't* abandon Mitch. They were her family. They were all that was left—they'd taken her in, given her hope.

"Syd?"

"I can't."

"Well, then," said June. Sydney heard coins drop on the table, June pushing back her seat. "I suggest you go home."

XVI

ONE YEAR AGO

EDGEFIELD

IT was too hot for Halloween.

They were in a college town somewhere down south, the air still sticky, the streets crowded with groups of teenagers heading to parties, and Sydney had decided to go out.

She stood at the bedroom mirror, adjusted the dark brown bob, put on the darkest lipstick she could find, traced black lines around both eyes. But the older she tried to look, the more ridiculous she felt. Syd tore the wig off and slumped back onto the bed.

She took up her phone, read the last few texts from June.

> **June**: So go out.
> **Syd**: I can't.
> **June**: Says who?
> **June**: You're 17.
> **June**: You can make your own decisions.
> **June**: They can't stop you.

Syd rolled to her feet, and began again.

She'd gone into a costume shop the day before with Mitch, found a generic anime schoolgirl getup. If looking older wouldn't work, maybe she could pass for someone *trying* to look young.

Syd combed her blond hair, pulled on the pleated skirt, and adjusted the bow at her throat. She slipped the gun—these days, she never went anywhere without it—into a tiny backpack, then marched out into the apartment.

Victor sat at the kitchen table, poring over profiles, Dol asleep at his feet. Mitch was on the couch, watching a college football game. He sat up when he saw her. "You dressed up."

"Yeah," she said, starting toward the door. "I'm going out."

Mitch crossed his arms. "Not alone, you're not." He was already pulling the deck of cards from his back pocket. Anger whipped through Sydney at the sight of them.

"This isn't a stupid game," she said. "It's my life."

"Sydney," said Mitch, a new firmness in his voice.

"Stop treating me like a child."

"Then stop acting like one," said Victor without looking up.

Mitch shook his head. "What's gotten into you?"

"Nothing," she snapped. "I'm just sick of being cooped up."

"Let her go," said Victor. "She's giving me a headache."

Mitch rounded on him. "You're not helping."

"She can take care of herself." His eyes met hers. "Isn't that right, Syd?" She bristled at the challenge in his voice. "Well," he sneered. "What are you waiting for?"

Sydney stormed out, slamming the door behind her. She made it down to the street before she stopped, folding onto the steps.

What's gotten into you?

She didn't know—but she knew that she couldn't stand another minute in that apartment. That cell. That imitation of a life. It wasn't just the heat, or the constant moving, or even having to watch Victor's life force wane like a candle. Sydney just wanted one night of feeling *normal*. Human.

A car flew past, a teen hanging out the window, smiling a rictus skeleton grin. Girls laughed as they stumbled by in too-short skirts and too-tall heels. Across the street, a group of guys in wolf masks threw their heads back and howled.

Sydney got to her feet and made her way to the corner, where a dozen flyers had been tacked to a telephone pole, advertising parties at clubs and frat houses. *Monsters Ball!* said one. *Scream Fest,* promised another, the letters dripping blood. *Heroes and Villains,* announced a third. Underneath, in parentheses, the disclaimer: *No Sidekicks.*

Sydney pulled the last flyer from the post and started walking.

SHE could hear the music from the street.

The heavy bass poured through the open front door, where a guy in a cape was making out with a girl in a horned mask. The house beyond was filled with strobe lights, the staccato flashes paired to the music so the whole place looked like it was moving.

It was the kind of party her sister would have been at. The kind of crowd she would have had wrapped around her finger. That was the thing about Serena. By the time she got her powers, she was already used to being in control. Serena didn't bend to the world. She made the world bend to her.

But as Sydney climbed the steps, her resolve wavered. She hadn't been around this many people at once, not since she went to visit Serena at college. Right before everything went wrong.

Syd closed her eyes, could see her sister leaning in the doorway.

You're growing up.

Could feel the weight of Serena's arms around her.

I want you to meet Eli.

The cold of the soda in her hand.

You can trust him.

The crack of the gun sounding in the woods.

"Kawai'i."

Syd looked around and saw a dark-skinned girl in gladiator sandals perched on the front porch rail, long legs swinging as she smoked.

"Or is it chibi?" she went on, nodding at Syd's costume. "I can never remember . . ."

The girl offered up the cigarette, and Sydney reached to take it. She'd never smoked, but she'd seen Serena do it.

The trick is to hold the smoke in your mouth, like this.

The tip of the cigarette had glowed red, Serena had counted on her fingers one, two, three, and then exhaled a perfect plume of white. Now, Sydney did the same thing.

The smoke filled her mouth, hot and acrid. It tickled her nose, crept into her throat, and she quickly blew it out before she could start coughing.

Her head felt cloudy, but her nerves were settling.

She handed the cigarette back and stepped into the party.

The house was teeming with students. Dancing, shouting, moving, sprawling. Too many. Too much. She felt jostled by elbows, shoulders, capes, wings, caught up in the sea of bodies, motion.

Sydney stepped back, trying to get out of the waves, and collided with a man in a black domino mask. Her heart lurched. Eli. Her fingers flew toward her backpack—but it wasn't him. Of course it wasn't him. This boy was too short, too wide, his voice too high as he shuffled past her, calling out to a friend across the crowded room.

Sydney was just starting to relax when someone caught her wrist.

She spun around to see a tall guy in a metal helmet and skin-tight spandex. "How did you get in here?" He raised her arm, and his voice, at the same time. "Who brought their kid sister?"

Sydney felt her face flush hot as heads turned.

"I'm not a *kid*," she snarled, pulling free.

"Yeah, sure, come on," he said, pushing her toward the front door.

What Sydney would have given, in that moment, for Victor's power instead of hers.

The college boy shoved her across the threshold. "Go trick-or-treat somewhere else."

Sydney stood on the front porch, face burning, as the party raged behind her and more guys and girls started up the path to the house.

Tears threatened to spill down her face. She fought them back.

"Hey, are you okay?" asked a guy in a cape, kneeling beside her. "You want to call someone—"

"Fuck off," said Sydney, marching down the steps, her face on fire.

She couldn't go home—not yet. And she couldn't bring herself to text June, either, so Sydney wandered the town alone for another hour, as the sticky heat finally cooled and the crowds in costumes thinned. She kept the backpack in her hand, the zipper parted and the gun in reach in case anyone tried anything.

No one did.

When she finally returned to the apartment, the lights were all off.

She slipped off her shoes, heard the soft sound of a body shifting on the couch, and turned, expecting to see Mitch.

But it was Victor, stretched out on the sofa, one arm across his eyes, his chest rising and falling in the slow, steady rhythm of sleep.

Dol lay on the floor beside him, awake, eyes shining in the dark, tail swishing softly at her arrival.

As Sydney padded across the apartment, the dog rose and followed in her wake, padding down the hall to her room and climbing up onto her bed without invitation. Syd eased the door shut and slumped back against it.

A few moments later she heard the soft scrape of furniture, the sound of Victor rising, the soft tread of his own steps as he passed her door, and closed his own.

He hadn't been asleep, she realized.

Victor had simply been waiting for Syd to come home.

XVII

IT was late, but Sydney wasn't tired yet—too much sugar in her blood, too many thoughts in her head—and besides, she needed to see the birthday out as well as in.

It was tradition.

A memory, like a splinter—of Syd trying to stay awake as the minutes ticked toward midnight. Serena poking her in the ribs every time she started to doze.

Come on, Syd. You're almost there. It's bad luck to fall asleep. Get up and dance with me.

Sydney shook her head, trying to dislodge her sister's voice. She turned in a slow circle before the mirror, letting her blue hair fan around her face, and then tugged off the wig and undid the clips beneath. Her natural hair—a curtain of straight white-blond—came free, falling almost to her shoulders.

Syd caught her reflection again, but this time out of the corner of her eye.

Sometimes, if she squinted a little, she could almost, almost see someone else in the mirror.

Someone with sharper cheekbones, fuller lips, a mouth tugged into a sly grin. The ghost of her sister. An echo. But then the illusion would falter, and Sydney's eyes would come back into focus, and all she would see was a girl playing dress-up.

SYDNEY shed the red bomber jacket and unlaced the steel-toed boots, turning her attention to Victor's gift. She took up the blue box and carried it to the room's small desk. Dol watched from the floor as she carefully lifted the box's lid, examining the contents. The bird's small skeleton was immaculate, intact. It looked like something out of a natural history museum—knowing Victor, it probably was.

Syd sat down, ran her fingers thoughtfully over the bird's wing, and wondered how old it was. The longer a thing had been dead, she'd learned, the harder it was to bring back. And the less of it remained, the more brittle its life was. So likely to crumble, or break, and when it did, it was gone forever. No second chances.

Nothing to grab hold of.

Sydney glanced at the red metal tin beside her bed. And then she took up a pair of tweezers and began removing bones, erasing the bird one piece at a time, until only a few fragments remained. The long bone at the top of one wing. A section of the spine. The heel of one foot.

She took a deep breath and closed her eyes, resting her hand on the partial skeleton.

And then, she reached.

At first she felt nothing beyond the bones under her palm. But she imagined herself reaching further, deeper, past the bird and the case and the desk, plunging her hand down into cold, empty space.

Her lungs began to ache. The chill spread through her fingers and up her arms, sharp and biting, and when she breathed out she could feel the plume of cold, like fog, on her lips. Light danced—far off and faint—behind her eyes, and her fingers brushed something, the barest hint of a thread. Syd pulled gently, gingerly. She kept her eyes closed, but she could feel the small skeleton beginning to rebuild, the ripple of muscle, of skin, the blush of feathers.

Almost—

But then she pulled just a *little* too hard.

The thread vanished.

The fragile light behind her eyes went out.

Sydney blinked, withdrew her hand, and saw the remains of the bird, its fragile skeleton now beyond repair. The bones—so carefully arranged in their velvet—were split and broken, the pile she'd set aside caving in, crumbling under their own weight.

She still wasn't strong enough.

Still wasn't ready.

When she moved to touch the bones, they fell apart, leaving only an ashy streak on the blue velvet lining, a pile of dust on her desk.

Ruined, thought Sydney, sweeping the remains into the trash.

I will ruin you.
I will ruin.
I will.
I—

Marcella opened her eyes.

She was greeted by sterile fluorescent lights, the antiseptic smell of scrubbed surfaces, and the papery thread count of hospital sheets. Marcella knew she shouldn't be here, shouldn't even be *alive*. But her pulse registered, a wavering green line on the machine beside her head, inexorable proof that she was. She drew a deep breath, and then cringed. Her lungs and throat felt raw, her skull pounding even through the high-grade painkillers being piped into her veins.

Marcella tested her fingers and toes, rolled her head gingerly side to side with calm precision and—she commended herself—startling composure. She had long ago learned to compartmentalize her feelings, shove the inconvenient and the unbecoming into the back of her mind like an old dress in a dark closet.

Her fingers crept along the sheets, and she tried to pull herself up, but at the slightest movement she was assaulted by her own body—her bruised and broken ribs, her burned and blistered skin. Marcella had also learned to embrace the various stings and aches and sears that went hand in hand with maintaining her appearance.

But this pain put those nips and tucks, those elected inconveniences, to shame.

This pain made a home in her skin, in her bones, moved like molten fire through her blood, her limbs. But instead of cringing away, Marcella focused in.

She once had a yoga instructor who compared the mind to a house. Marcella had rolled her eyes at the time, but now she imagined going room to room, switching off the lights. Here was fear, switch. Here was panic, switch. Here was confusion, switch.

Here was pain.

Here was anger.

Here was her husband, that cheating fuck.

Here was him slamming her head into the table.

Here was his arm sweeping the candles.

Here was her voice breaking, her lungs filling with smoke.

Here was his back as he walked away, and left her to die.

That light, she left on. She marveled at the way it grew brighter inside her head, at the warmth that came with it, rippling through her skin. Her fingers tightened on the bedrail. It went soft under her palm, the smooth metal rusting away, a red stain spreading along the steel. By the time she noticed, pulled away, a section the length of her forearm was already ruined, flaking onto the bed.

Marcella stared, uncomprehending.

She looked from her hand to the metal, and back, felt the heat still wicking off her skin. She clutched the thin hospital sheets instead, but they crumbled too, the fabric rotting away in the span of a breath, leaving only a patina of ash behind.

Marcella raised both hands now, not in surrender, but in fascination, the palms turned up toward her face, searching for an explanation, a fundamental change, and finding only her own ruined manicure, a familiar hand-shaped bruise going green around her wrist, a white hospital band with the wrong name printed on it: *Melinda Pierce.*

Marcella frowned. The other details were all correct—she

recognized her age, her date of birth—but it seemed someone had entered her into the system under a false name. Which meant they didn't want Marcus to know she was here. Or to know she was alive. A reasonable choice, she thought, considering the events of earlier that night. Or was it tomorrow? Time felt muddy.

The wounds felt fresh enough.

Without the sheets, she could see the bandages tracing their way up her legs, winding across her stomach, around her shoulder, the mirror image of a candelabra burned into her—

A police radio went off, the sharp static setting it apart from the dozens of other hospital sounds. Marcella's attention flicked to the door. It was closed, but through the glass insert she spotted a cop's uniform.

Slowly, Marcella managed to draw herself up from the bed, despite the various cables and cords connecting her to the medical bay. Her hand reached for the IV stand before she remembered the stretch of rusted steel, the crumbling sheet. She hesitated, but her palm felt cool again, and as her fingers closed around the plastic cord nothing terrible happened. Gingerly, Marcella disconnected the line and then, careful not to dislodge the heart monitor, she reached around and pulled the power cord instead.

The machines went quiet, their screens black.

Marcella's hospital gown hung loose, a mercy given the contact with her tender skin, but also a hindrance: she couldn't slip out wearing nothing but a sheet.

A sterile white wardrobe stood in the corner, and she went to it, irrationally hoping to find her clothes, her purse, her keys, but of course it was empty.

Beyond the door, she heard a gruff voice.

". . . still hasn't woken up . . . no, we've kept it off the news . . . I've already called WITSEC . . ."

Marcella sneered. WITSEC. She hadn't designed this life, built a future from nothing, just to spend it *hiding*. And she'd be damned if she disappeared before her husband. Marcella turned, surveying the room, but there was nothing but the one door, and a window looking out over Merit from at least six stories up.

One room, one door. One window.

And two walls.

Marcella picked the one opposite her bed, pressed her ear to the wall, and heard nothing—just the steady beep of more hospital equipment.

She brought her fingers to the plaster, barely touching.

Nothing happened.

Slowly, Marcella pressed her palm flat against the wall. Nothing. She glared at her hand, the nails cracked where her desperate fingers had dug into the silk-threaded carpet, clawed at the wood floor—

Her hand began to glow. Marcella watched the wall beneath her fingers warping, rotting, drywall slouching as if with damp, or gravity, or time, until a broad hole formed between the rooms, large enough to step through.

Marcella marveled, then, at her hand, at the damage it had done. So it wasn't a matter of force, but feeling.

That was fine.

Marcella had quite a lot of feelings.

She drew the power back into her chest, as if it were a breath. There it burned, less like a fuse than a pilot light. Steady and waiting.

Marcella stepped through the ruined wall, and into the next room.

The door to the room was ajar, and the woman in the bed—Alice Tolensky, according to the clipboard—was three inches shorter than Marcella and a good thirty pounds heavier.

Her clothes hung in the small, hospital-issued wardrobe.

Marcella wrinkled her nose as she considered the slip-on flats, the frills on the collar of the flower-printed blouse, the jeans with their elastic waist.

But beggars couldn't be choosers. Marcella was grateful for the room in the jeans when she had to pull them on. She stifled a breath as the denim grazed her bandages, then turned her attention back to the closet.

A knockoff leather purse slumped on the shelf. Marcella rifled through the contents and came up with a hundred dollars in cash and a pair of glasses.

She finished getting dressed, tugged her hair into a bun at the nape of her neck, slipped on the glasses, and stepped into the hall. The cop in front of her door was picking at a bandage on his hand. He didn't look up as Marcella turned and left.

A queue of taxis waited outside the hospital.

She climbed into the nearest one.

"Address?" rumbled the driver.

"The Heights." It was the first time she'd spoken, and her voice was raw from smoke, a fraction lower and edged with the luscious rasp that so many starlets craved. "On Grand."

The car pulled away, and Marcella leaned back against the leather seat.

She had always been good under pressure.

Other women could afford to panic, but being a mob wife required a certain level of poise. It meant staying calm. Or at least *feigning* calm.

At the moment, Marcella didn't feel like she was feigning anything. There was no fear, no doubt. Her head wasn't spinning. She didn't feel lost. If anything, this road she was on felt paved and straight, the end lit by a single, blinding light.

And beneath that light stood Marcus Andover Riggins.

2

REVELATION

I

FOURTEEN YEARS AGO

EVERYONE was shitfaced.

Marcella sat on the kitchen counter, her heels knocking absently against the cabinets as she watched them stumble past, sloshing drinks and shouting to be heard. The house was filled with music, bodies, stale booze and cheap cologne, and all the other inane trappings of a college frat party. Her friends had convinced her to come, with the weak argument that it was just what students *did*, that there would be free beer and hot guys and it would be *fun*.

Those same girls were lost somewhere in the mass of bodies. Every now and then she thought she caught a glimpse of a familiar blond bob, a high brown ponytail. Then again, there were a dozen of them. Cookie-cutter college kids. More concerned with blending in than standing out.

Marcella Renee Morgan was *not* having fun.

She was nursing a beer in a glass bottle, and she was bored—bored by the music, and the boys who swaggered over every now and then to flirt, and then stormed away, sulking, when she turned them down. She was bored by being called beautiful, and then a bitch. Stunning, and then stuck up. A ten, and then a tease.

Marcella had always been pretty. The kind of pretty people couldn't ignore. Bright blue eyes and pitch-black hair, a heart-shaped face atop the lean, clean lines of a model. Her father told her she'd never have to work. Her mother said she'd have to work twice as hard. In a way, both of them were right.

Her body was the first thing people saw.

For most, it seemed to be the last thing, too.

"You're think you're better than me?" a drunken senior had slurred at her earlier.

Marcella had looked at him straight on, his eyes bleary, hers sharp, and said simply, "Yes."

"Bitch," he'd muttered, storming away. Predictable.

Marcella had promised her friends she'd stay for a drink. She tipped the bottle back, eager to finish the beer.

"I see you found the good stuff," said a deep voice, rich, with a faint southern lilt.

She glanced up and saw a guy leaning back against the kitchen island. Marcella didn't know what he was talking about, not until he nodded at the glass bottle in her hand with the plastic cup in his own. She gestured at the fridge. He crossed to it, retrieving two more bottles. He cracked them open against the counter's edge and offered one to her.

Marcella took it, considering him over the rim.

His eyes were dark blue, his hair sun-kissed, that warm shade between blond and brown. Most of the guys at the party hadn't shed their baby fat, high school still clinging to them like wet clothes, but his black shirt stretched tight over strong shoulders, and his jaw was sharp, a small cleft denting his chin.

"Marcus," he said by way of introduction. She knew who he was. She'd seen him on campus, but it was Alice who'd told her—Marcus Riggins was trouble. Not because he was gorgeous. Not because he was rich. Nothing so bland as all that. No, Marcus was trouble for one simple, delicious reason: his family was in the mob. Alice had said it like it was a bad thing, a deal breaker, but if anything, it only piqued her interest.

"Marcella," she said, uncrossing and recrossing her legs.

He smiled. "Marcus and Marcella," he said, lifting his drink. "We sound like a matching set."

Someone turned the music up, and his next words were lost under the bass.

"What did you say?" she called over the song, and he took the opportunity to close the gap between them. She shifted her legs to the side, and he stepped closer, smelling like apples and linen, clean and crisp, such a welcome change from the sticky, tacky grime of lazy, drunken bodies.

He rested his beer on the counter just beside her arm, the cold glass brushing her elbow and sending a small shiver through her. A slow smile crossed his face.

He leaned in close, as if telling her a secret. *"Follow me."*

He stepped back, taking the scent of linen and the blush of heat with him.

He didn't pull her off the counter, but she felt pulled, drawn in his wake as he turned away, slipped through the crowd. She followed him, through the party, up the stairs, down the hall to a bedroom door.

"Still with me?" he asked, glancing back.

The door swung open onto a room at odds with the rest of the frat house. The laundry was hampered, the desk clean, the bed made, the only clutter a neat stack of books on the comforter.

Marcella hovered in the doorway, waiting to see what he'd do next. If he would come to her, or make her come to him.

Instead, Marcus went to the window, slid up the glass, and stepped out onto a widow's walk. A fall breeze whispered through the room as Marcella followed, slipping off her heels.

Marcus offered his hand and helped her up and through. The city spiraled away beneath them, the darkened buildings a sky, the lights like stars. Merit always looked larger at night.

Marcus sipped his beer. "Better?"

Marcella smiled. "Better."

The music, obnoxiously loud downstairs, was now a muted pulse against her back.

Marcus leaned against the wooden rail. "You from here?"

"Not far," she said. "You?"

"Born and raised," he said. "What are you studying?"

"Business," she said shortly. Marcella hated small talk, but that was because so often it felt like a chore. Just noise, empty words meant to fill empty space. "Why did you bring me up here?"

"I didn't," he said, all mock innocence. "You followed me."

"You asked," she said, realizing he hadn't. There'd been no question in his voice, only a simple command.

"You were about to leave," said Marcus. "And I didn't want you to."

Marcella considered him. "Are you used to getting what you want?"

The edge of a smile. "I have a feeling we both are." He returned her long look. "Marcella the Business Major. What do you want to be?"

Marcella twirled her beer. "In charge."

Marcus laughed. A soft, breathy sound.

"You think I'm joking?"

"No," he said. "I don't."

"How do you know?"

"Because," he said, closing the narrow space between them, "we *are* a matching set." A breeze cut through, just crisp enough to make her shiver.

"We better go inside," said Marcus, pulling away.

He stepped back through the window, offering his hand. But this time he didn't lead.

"After you," he said, gesturing toward the bedroom door. It was still cracked open, music and laughter pouring up from the party below. But when Marcella reached the door, she hesitated, fingers coming to rest against the wood. She could picture Marcus standing a few feet behind her, hands in his pockets, waiting to see what she would do.

She pushed the door shut.

The lock caught with a soft click, and Marcus was there as if summoned, lips brushing the back of her neck. His hands slid, feather light, over her shoulders, against her waist. Heat flooded through her at the almost-touch.

"I won't break," she said, turning in time to catch Marcus's mouth with hers. He pressed into her, pushed her back against the wood. Her nails dug into his arms as he unbuttoned his shirt. His teeth scraped her shoulder as her own came off. They laid waste to the order of his room, shedding clothes, knocking over a chair, a lamp, sweeping the books from the bed as Marcus pressed her down into the sheets.

They fit together perfectly.

A matching set.

II

FOUR WEEKS AGO

DOWNTOWN MERIT

THE cab stopped in front of the Heights, a pale stone spire seated in the heart of the city. Marcella paid the driver in cash and climbed out, her limbs a dull roar of pain with every step.

When she had first discovered the secret apartment—on a goddamn bank statement—she'd assumed the worst, but Marcus had claimed the place was purely practical. A safe house. He'd even insisted on bringing her there, showing off his thorough work—her favorite designer labels in the closet, her brand of coffee in the cupboard, her shampoo in the shower.

And Marcella had actually believed him.

Found a way to make it *their* secret instead of his. Now and then she'd phone him up, insisting there was some emergency, and he'd somberly order her to meet him at the safe house, and he'd arrive to find her waiting, wearing nothing but a gold ribbon carefully wrapped and finished with a bow.

Now the image of the tawdry pink lipstick flared like pain behind Marcella's eyes.

What a fool.

The concierge rose from the front desk to greet her.

"Mrs. Riggins," said Ainsley, surprise lighting his face. He glanced quickly at her ill-fitting clothes, the bandages peeking out from collar and cuff, but the residents at the Heights paid for discretion as much as floor-to-ceiling windows (now Marcella wondered how many times Ainsley had employed that same discretion with her husband).

"Is . . . everything all right?" he ventured.

She flicked a wrist dismissively. "It's a long story." And then, after a moment, "Marcus isn't here, is he?"

"No, ma'am," he said solemnly.

"Good," said Marcella. "I'm afraid I've forgotten my keys."

Ainsley nodded briskly and rounded the desk to summon the elevator. When the doors opened, he followed her inside. As it rose, she rubbed her forehead, as if simply tired, and asked the date.

The concierge told her, and Marcella stiffened.

She'd been in the hospital for almost *two weeks*.

But that didn't matter, not now. What mattered was that it was a Friday night.

She knew exactly where Marcus would be.

The elevator stopped. Ainsley followed her out onto the fourteenth floor, unlocked the cream-colored door, and wished her a pleasant night.

Marcella waited until he was gone, then stepped inside and flicked on the lights.

"Honey, I'm home," she cooed to the empty apartment. She should have felt something—a pang of sorrow, or regret—but there was only the ache in her skin and the rising tide of anger beneath, and when she reached for one of the wineglasses on the counter, it warped under her touch and turned to sand. A thousand grains rained down between Marcella's glowing fingers, spilled onto the floor.

She stared down at her hand, the remains of the glass dusting her palm. The strange light was already sinking back beneath her skin, and when she reached for a fresh glass, it held under her touch.

A bottle of chardonnay sat chilling in the fridge, and Marcella poured herself a drink and flicked on the news—now eager to know what she'd missed—as she clicked the volume up and headed for the bedroom.

One of Marcus's shirts lay thrown across the bed . . . along with one of her own. The glass in her hand threatened to give, so Marcella set it aside. The doors to the walk-in closet were thrown wide, Marcus's dark suits lining one wall, while the rest was given over to a medley of couture dresses, blouses, heels.

Marcella glanced back at the clothes still twined in a lover's embrace atop the bed and felt her anger rising like steam. Fingers glowing, she ran her hand along her husband's side of the closet, and watched the garments fade and rot under her touch. Cotton, silk, and wool all withered and dropped from the hangers, crumbling by the time they hit the floor.

Hell hath no fury, she thought, dusting her palms.

Satisfied—no, not satisfied, nowhere *near* satisfied, but momentarily appeased—Marcella took up her drink and went into the luxury bathroom, where she set the glass on the rim of the marble sink and began to peel away the frumpy stolen clothes. She stripped until she was dressed in nothing but bandages. The sterile white wrappings weren't nearly as seductive as the gold ribbons, but they seemed to trace the same path across her leg, her stomach, her arms.

Marking her. *Mocking* her.

Marcella's hands twitched with the sudden urge to reach out and ruin something, anything. Instead she stood there and took in her reflection, every angle, every flaw, memorized it while she waited for the rage to pass—not vanish, no, simply retract, like a cat's claws. If this new power was temporary, a thing with limits, she didn't want to pass them. She needed her nails sharp.

The painkillers from the hospital were wearing off, and her head was ringing, so Marcella dug two Vicodin out of her emergency supply beneath the sink, washed them down with the last of the chardonnay, and went to get ready.

III

THE phone rang, and rang, and rang.

"Don't answer it," said Marcus, pacing. A dark tie hung loose, unknotted, around his neck.

"Darling," said Marcella, sitting on the edge of the bed. "You knew they'd call."

He'd been on edge for days, weeks, waiting for the phone to ring. They both knew who it would be: Antony Edward Hutch, one of the four heads of the Merit crime syndicate, and *Jack* Riggins's long-term benefactor.

Marcus had finally told her, of course, what his father did. How, for them, the word *family* wasn't just about blood—it was a profession. He'd told her in their senior year of college, looked like death when he said it, and Marcella had realized, halfway through the meal, that he was trying to break up with her.

"Is it like joining the clergy?" she'd asked, sipping her wine. "Did you take a vow of celibacy?"

"What? No . . ." he said, confused.

"Then why can't we face it together?"

Marcus shook his head. "I'm trying to protect you."

"Hasn't it occurred to you that I can protect myself?"

"This isn't like in the movies, Marcella. What my family does, it's brutal, and bloody. In this world, in *my* world, people get hurt. They die."

Marcella blinked. Set down her glass. Leaned in. "People die in *every* world, Marcus. I'm not going anywhere."

Two weeks later, he'd proposed.

Marcella adjusted the diamond on her finger as the phone stopped ringing.

A few seconds later, it started again.

"I'm not answering it."

"So don't."

"I don't have a choice," he snapped, running a hand through his sun-streaked hair.

Marcella rose to her feet and took his hand. "Huh," she said, holding it up between them. "I don't see any strings."

Marcus pulled free. "You don't know what it's like, having other people decide who you are, what you're going to be."

Marcella resisted the urge to roll her eyes. Of course she knew. People looked at her and assumed a whole lot. That a pretty face meant an empty head, that a girl like her was only after an easy life, that she would be satisfied with luxury, instead of power—as if you couldn't want both.

Her own mother had told her to aim high, that she should never sell herself cheap. (The correct saying, of course, was *short*. As in, don't sell yourself *short*.) But Marcella hadn't sold herself cheap *or* short. She'd chosen Marcus Riggins. And he was going to choose *this*.

The phone rang on, and on.

"Take the call."

"If I take the call," he said, "I take the job. If I take the job, I'm in. There's no getting back out."

Marcella caught him by the shoulder, interrupting the pendulum of his movement. He faltered, drew up short as she wrapped her fingers around his silk tie, and pulled him toward her. Something flashed in Marcus's eyes, anger, and fear, and violence, and Marcella knew that he could do this job, and do it well. Marcus wasn't weak, wasn't soft. He was simply stubborn. Which was why he needed her. Because where he saw a trap, she saw an opportunity.

"What do you want to be?" asked Marcella. The same question he'd asked her the night they met. One Marcus himself had never answered.

Now he looked at her, his eyes dark. "I want to be more."

"Then *be* more. That," she said, turning his face toward the phone, "is just a door. A way in." Her nails scraped against his cheek. "You want to be more, Marcus? Prove it. Pick up the phone and walk through the goddamn door."

The ringing stopped, and in the silence she could hear her quickening pulse, and his unsteady breath. The moment stretched taut, and then collapsed. They collided, Marcus kissing her, hard, and deep, one hand already sliding between her legs, the other dragging the nails from his cheek. He spun her around, bent her over the bed.

He was already hard.

She was already wet.

Marcella stifled a gasp of pleasure, *triumph,* as he pressed himself against her—into her—her fingers knotting in the sheets, her gaze drifting to the cell phone beside her on the bed.

And when it rang again, Marcus answered.

IV

FOUR WEEKS AGO

THE HEIGHTS

MARCELLA longed for a hot shower, but the first touch of water sent a searing pain over her tender skin, so instead she settled for a damp cloth, drawing lukewarm water from the bathroom sink.

The edges of her hair were singed beyond repair, so she took up the sharpest scissors she could find and started to cut. When she was done, her black waves ended just above her shoulders. A thick coil swept across her brow, hiding the fresh scar above her left temple and framing her face.

Her face, which had miraculously escaped the worst of the fight and the fire. She brushed mascara along her lashes and painted a fresh coat of red on her lips. Pain followed every gesture—each stretch and bend of tender skin a reminder in the shape of her husband's name—but through it all, Marcella's mind felt . . . quiet. Smooth. Silk ribbons, instead of knotted rope.

She returned to the closet, running her fingers lightly along the symphony of clothes that made up her wardrobe. A small, vindictive part of her wanted to choose something revealing, to put her injuries on display, but she knew better. Weakness was a thing best concealed. In the end she chose a pair of elegant black slacks, a silk blouse that wrapped around her sleek frame, and a pair of black stilettos, the heels as thin and chrome as switchblades.

She was just fastening the buckles on her second shoe when a newscaster's voice rose from the television in the other room.

"New developments in the case of the house fire that raged through the upscale Brighton development last week . . ."

She stepped out into the hall in time to see her own face on the screen.

". . . resulting in the death of Marcella Renee Riggins . . ."

She'd been right, then. The police obviously wanted Marcus to believe she was dead. Which was probably the only reason she wasn't. Marcella took up the remote, turning up the volume as the camera cut to a shot of their house, the exterior charred and smoldering.

"Officials have yet to determine the cause of the fire, but it's believed to be an accident."

Marcella's grip tightened on the remote as the camera cut to a shot of Marcus running his hands through his hair, the picture of grief.

"Husband Marcus Riggins admitted to police that the two had quarreled earlier that night, and that his wife was prone to outbursts, but adamantly denied the suggestion that she'd set the fire herself, saying that she had never been violent or destructive—"

The remote crumbled in her hand, batteries liquefying as the plastic warped and melted.

Marcella let the mess fall from her fingers, and went to find her husband.

V

MARCELLA had always liked the National building. It was a feat of glass and steel, a thirty-story prism at the heart of the city. She'd coveted it, the way one might a diamond, and Tony Hutch owned the whole thing, from the marble lobby all the way to the rooftop gardens where he threw his parties.

They stepped through the front doors arm in arm, Marcus in a trim black suit, Marcella in a gold dress. She caught sight of a plain-clothes cop lounging in the lobby, and shot him a toying wink. Half the Merit PD was in Hutch's pocket. The other half couldn't get close enough to do a damn thing.

The inside of the elevator was polished to a high shine, and as it rose, Marcella leaned against Marcus and considered their reflection. She loved the way they looked together. She loved his strong jaw and his rough hands, loved his steely blue eyes and the way he moaned her name. They were partners in crime. A perfect pair.

"Hello, handsome," she said, catching his eye.

He smiled. "Hello, gorgeous."

Yes, she loved her husband.

Probably more than she should.

The elevator doors opened onto a rooftop covered in lights, and music, and laughter. Hutch always knew how to throw a party.

Gauzy canopies and sofas piled with cushions, low gold-and-glass tables, servers slipping through the crowd with champagne flutes and canapés, but what drew Marcella's eye more than any of it was the city beyond. The view was incredible, the National high enough up that it seemed to look down on all of Merit.

Marcus led her through the bustling crowd.

As they moved, she felt the eyes of every man, and half the women, slide over her. Marcella's dress—made of a thousand pale gold scales—hugged her every curve and shimmered with each step. Her heels and nails were the same pale gold, as was the matching net of wire woven through her black hair, lacing tiny white-gold beads through the glossy updo. The only spots of color were her eyes, a vivid blue framed by black lashes, and her lips, which she'd painted crimson.

Marcus had told her to dress up.

"What's the point of having beautiful things," he'd said, "if you don't put them on display?"

Now he led her to the very center of the roof, to the marble star inlaid in the floor where the boss himself was holding court.

Antony Hutch.

He wasn't unattractive—lean and strong, with warm brown hair and a constant summer tan—but there was something about him that made Marcella's skin crawl.

"Tony, you've met my wife, Marcella."

Hutch's attention, when it landed on her, felt like a damp hand on bare flesh.

"Jesus, Marc," he said, "does she come with a warning label?"

"She does not," quipped Marcella.

But Hutch only smiled. "Seriously, though, how could I forget such a beauty?"

He stepped closer. "Is Marc here treating you well? You need anything, you just let me know."

"Why?" asked Marcella with a smirk. "Are you in the market for a wife?"

Hutch chuckled, and spread his arms. "Unfortunately, I like catching girls more than keeping them."

"That simply means," said Marcella, "you haven't found the right one."

Hutch laughed, and turned toward Marcus. "You got yourself a keeper."

Marcus looped his arms around her waist and kissed her temple. "Don't I know it?"

But his body was already twisting away from her, and soon Marcella found herself pushed to the outside of the circle as the group of men began to talk business.

"We're looking to expand our hold on the south side."

"Territory moves are always dangerous."

"Caprese's eyes are bigger than his stomach."

"You could squeeze him out more subtly," offered Marcella. "Pick up the blocks around him. It wouldn't be a direct attack—no grounds for retaliation—but the message is clear."

The conversation crumbled. The men went quiet.

After a pained moment, Marcus simply smiled. "My wife, the business major," he said blandly.

Marcella felt herself flush as the other men shared a knowing chuckle. Hutch looked at her, his own laugh slack, hollow. "Marcella, we must be boring you. I'm sure you'd be happier with the other wives."

Marcella's answer was already poised on her lips, but Marcus cut in first. "Go on, Marce," he said, kissing her cheek. "Let the men talk."

She wanted to grab his jaw, dig her nails in until they drew blood. Instead, she smiled. Arranged her face into a mask of serenity. Appearance was everything.

"Of course," she said. "I'll leave you boys to it."

She turned away, plucked a champagne flute from a passing server, held the glass so tight her fingers hurt. She felt their eyes follow her across the roof.

What's the point of having beautiful things, if you don't put them on display?

She hadn't realized, at the time, that Marcus had referred to her as a *thing*. The comment had slid off like a silk gown, pretty and weightless, but—

"Marcella!" called a woman in a familiar singsong voice. Her heels were pushing six inches, which was probably why she was sitting down, holding court in a dark red gown. It was the perfect color—Grace was blond, and fair, and the dress stood out like blood on skin.

"Have you been evicted?" asked Theresa, seated as well and sipping a large drink.

"God no," said Marcella, "they were boring me to tears."

"Too much shop talk," said Bethany, bangles clanging as she flicked her wrist. More beauty than brains in that one, thought Marcella, not for the first time.

"They may think they're kings," said Grace, "but we're the power behind the throne."

A tinkle of laughter sounded nearby.

There was a second group of women, clustered in another corner of the roof, in higher heels and shorter dresses. The girlfriends. The second and third wives. The side pieces. Newer models, Grace would say.

"How's Marcus?" asked Bethany. "I hope you're keeping him on a leash."

"Oh," she said, sipping her champagne, "he'd *never* cheat."

"What makes you so sure?" asked Theresa.

Marcella met Marcus's eyes across the roof.

"Because," she said, raising her glass, "he knows I'd kill him first."

"**DID** you have a nice night?" Marcella asked later as the car pulled away from the party.

Marcus was all energy. "It went off without a hitch. Or a hutch."

He chuckled at his own joke. Marcella didn't. "He's taken a liking to me, I can tell. Said he'd call me in the morning. Something new. Something big." He pulled her close. "You were right."

"I'm always right," she said absently, looking out the window. "Let's stay in the city tonight."

"Good idea," said Marcus. He knocked on the partition, gave the driver the address of their place at the Heights, told him to hurry. And then he sat back, pressing against her. "They couldn't take their eyes off you. I don't blame them. Neither could I."

"Not here," she said, trying to force a little humor in her voice. "You'll ruin my dress."

"Fuck your dress," he breathed in her ear. "I want *you*."

But Marcella pushed him away.

"What's wrong?" he asked.

Marcella's gaze flicked toward him. "My wife, *the business major*?"

He rolled his eyes. "Marce."

"Let the men *talk*?"

"Oh, come on."

"You made a fool of me."

He made a sound too close to a laugh. "Don't you think you're overreacting?"

Marcella gritted her teeth. "You're very lucky I didn't *react* at the time."

Marcus soured. "This isn't a good look on you, Marce."

The car pulled up in front of the Heights, and Marcella resisted the urge to storm out. She flicked open the door and rose, smoothing the gold scales on her dress as she waited for Marcus to round the car.

"Good evening," said the concierge. "Nice night?"

"Flawless," said Marcella, stepping briskly into the elevator, Marcus in her wake. He waited until the doors were closed, then sighed, shook his head.

"You know what those guys are like," he muttered. "Old guard. Old money. Old values. You wanted this. You wanted me to do this."

"With *me*," she snapped. "I wanted us to do this, together." He tried to cut in, but she didn't let him. "I'm not a fucking coat, Marcus. You don't get to check me at the door."

The elevator stopped, and she strode out into the hall, heels clicking on the marble floor. She reached their door, but Marcus caught her hand and pinned her back against the wood. On a normal night, she would have thrilled at the swift display of strength, would have arched against him. But she wasn't in the mood.

Let the men talk.

"Marcella."

The laugh. The patronizing smiles.

"*Marcella*," said Marcus, drawing her face toward his. Her gaze toward his. And then she saw it—or maybe she just *wanted* to see it—there, beyond the flat, dark blue. A glimpse of the Marcus she'd met, young and hungry and utterly in love with her. The Marcus who wanted her, *needed* her.

His mouth hovered a breath from hers as he spoke. "Where I go, you go," he said. "We're in this together. Step for step."

Marcella wanted to believe him, needed to believe him, because she wasn't willing to let go, wasn't going to lose him, everything she'd built.

They never seem to realize.

We're the power behind the throne.

Marcella leaned forward and kissed him long, and slow, and deep. "Show me," she said, leading him inside.

VI

FOUR WEEKS AGO

MERIT SUBURBS

MARCUS Andover Riggins had always been a man of routines.

An espresso in the morning, a bourbon before bed. Every Monday after breakfast, he got a massage, and every Wednesday at lunch, he swam laps, and every Friday night, rain or shine, from dusk until dawn, he played poker. Four or five members of Tony Hutch's crew all got together weekly at Sam McGuire's place, since Sam was single—or at least, he wasn't married. He had a rotation of sorts, a new girl every week, but none of them stuck.

Sam's was a nice place—they were *all* nice places—but he had a bad habit of leaving the back door unlocked instead of giving any of his short-term girls a key. Marcella had warned him a dozen times—someone could walk right in. But Sam would just smile, and say that no man would walk in on one of Tony Hutch's crew.

Perhaps, but Marcella Riggins was no man.

She let herself inside.

The back door gave onto the kitchen, where Marcella found a girl doubled over, ass in the air and head in the freezer, as she rummaged for ice. She wobbled in too-high heels, bangles clanging against the freezer, but the first thing Marcella noticed was the girl's dress. Dark blue silk, with a short rippling skirt—the same one that had hung for more than a year in Marcella's own closet at the Heights.

The girl straightened, and turned, her mouth forming a perfect pink circle.

Bethany.

Bethany, who had twice as many tits as thoughts.

Bethany, who asked about Marcus every time they met.

Bethany, who looked like a cheap knockoff of Marcella in those diamond earrings, that stolen dress, which wasn't stolen, of course, because the apartment in town had also been kept for *her.*

Bethany's eyes went wide. "Marcella?"

"Did you always know," she'd asked Marcus once, undoing the buttons on a blood-stained shirt, "that you had what it took to end a life?"

"Not until the gun was in my hand," he'd said. "I thought it would be hard, but in that moment, nothing was easier."

He was right.

But there was, it turned out, a crucial difference between destroying *things* and destroying *people.*

People *screamed.*

Or at least they tried. Bethany certainly would have, if Marcella hadn't already grabbed her by the throat, hadn't eroded through her vocal cords before anything more than a short, futile gasp could escape.

And even then, the men in the other room might have heard, if they hadn't been laughing so loudly.

It didn't take long.

One second Bethany's mouth was open in a perfect *O* of surprise and the next her plump skin had shriveled, her face twisting into a rictus grin that quickly pulled away to reveal the skull beneath, and then even that turned to ash, as all that was left of Bethany crumbled to the kitchen floor.

It was over so fast—there was hardly any time for Marcella to savor what she'd done, and no time to think about all the things she *should* be feeling, given the circumstances, or even to wonder at their peculiar absence.

It was just so *easy*.

As if everything had *wanted* to come apart.

There was probably some law about that.

Order giving way to chaos.

Marcella took up a dishcloth and wiped the dust from her fingers as another raucous laugh cut through the house. Then a familiar voice called out.

"Doll, where's that drink?"

Marcella followed the voice down the short hall that ran between the kitchen and the den where the men were playing.

"Where the fuck is my drink?" bellowed Marcus, chair scraping back. He was on his feet when she walked in.

"Hello, boys."

Marcus didn't have to feign surprise, since he'd expected her to be dead. His face drained of all color—what was the phrase, oh yes: as if he'd just seen a ghost. The other four men squinted through the haze of liquor and cigar smoke.

"Marce?" said her husband, voice laced with shock.

Oh, how she *longed* to kill him, but she wanted to use her bare hands, and there was a table between them, and Marcus was holding his ground, looking at her with a mixture of suspicion and worry, and Marcella knew what she had to do. She began to cry. It was easy—all she had to do was think of her life, the one she'd worked so hard for, going up in flames.

"I've been so worried," she said, breath hitching. "I woke up in a hospital, and you weren't there. The cops said there'd been a fire and I thought—I was afraid—they wouldn't tell me if you'd been hurt in it. They wouldn't tell me *anything*."

His expression flickered, suddenly uncertain. He took a step toward her. "I thought you were dead." A forced stammer, a mockery of emotion. "The cops wouldn't let me see your . . . I thought maybe you . . . what do you remember, baby?"

Still the pet names.

Marcella shook her head. "I remember making dinner. Everything after that is a blur."

She caught a glimpse of hope in his eyes—amazement, that he would get away with it, that he could have the best of both worlds: killing his wife *and* getting her back.

But instead of coming to her, he sank down into his chair. "By the time I got home," he said, "the fire trucks were there, the house was up in flames. They wouldn't let me in." Marcus slumped back, as if reliving the trauma. The grief. As if ten minutes earlier he hadn't been playing poker and waiting for his mistress—her one-time friend—to bring him his drink.

Marcella went to her husband, circled behind his chair, and wrapped her arms around his shoulders. "I'm just so glad . . ."

He took up her hand, pressed his lips against her wrist. "I'm all right, doll."

She nestled her face into his collar. Felt Marcus actually relax, muscles unwinding as he realized he was in the clear.

"Guys," said Marcus, "game's over."

The other men shuffled, about to rise.

"No," she whispered in her sweetest voice. "Stay. This won't take long."

Marcus tipped his head back, a furrow between his brows.

Marcella smiled. "You never were one to dwell on the past, Marcus. I loved that about you, the way things always just rolled off."

She lifted an empty glass from the table.

"To my husband," she said, right before the ruin rushed to her fingers in a blossom of red light. The glass dissolved, sand raining onto the felt poker table. A ripple of shock went through the table, and Marcus jerked forward, as if to rise, but Marcella had no intentions of letting go.

"We've had a good run," she whispered in his ear as the anger and hurt and hatred rose like heat.

She let it all out.

Her husband had told her a hundred stories about the way men died. No one ever held their tongue, not in the end. In the end, they begged and pleaded, sobbed and screamed.

Marcus was no exception.

It didn't last long—not out of some sudden mercy, Marcella simply lacked the control to draw it out. She *really* would have liked to savor it. Would have liked the chance to memorize his horrified face, but alas—that was the first thing to go.

She had to settle instead for the shock and terror on the faces of the other men.

Of course, that didn't last very long either.

Two of them—Sam, of course, and another man she didn't recognize—were scrambling to their feet.

Marcella sighed, her husband's remains collapsing as she knocked them aside and caught Sam's sleeve.

"Going so soon?" she asked, ruin surging to her fingers. He staggered, fell, his body breaking by the time it hit the floor. The other man drew a knife from a hidden fold of his coat, but when he lunged toward Marcella, she wrapped one glowing hand around the blade. It decayed and crumbled, ruin spreading in an instant from metal to hilt and then up the man's arm. He began to scream and pulled away, but the rot was already going through him like a wildfire, his body falling apart even as he tried to escape.

The last two men stayed seated at the card table, their hands up and their faces frozen. All Marcella's life, men had looked at her with lust, desire. But this was different.

This was *fear.*

And it felt good.

She took her husband's seat, settling in among his still-warm ashes. She used a kerchief to clear a streak of him from the poker table.

"Well?" said Marcella after a long moment. "Deal me in."

VII

GROWING up, Dominic Rusher had never been a morning person.

But the army made him a get-the-fuck-up-when-you-hear-the-sound person, and anyway, sleep hadn't come easy since his accident, so Dom was on his feet by the third wail of the 4:30 a.m. alarm. He showered, wiped away the fog on the bathroom mirror, and found his reflection.

Five years had done a lot of good. Gone was the harrowed look of someone in constant pain, the gaunt features of a man trying and failing to self-medicate. In his place was a soldier, lean muscles winding over broad shoulders, tan arms strong and back straight, his hair cropped short on the sides, slicked back on top.

He'd gotten his shit together, too.

His medals were mounted on the wall, no longer thrown carelessly around the necks of empty liquor bottles. Next to them hung the X-rays. Each metal plate and bar, pin and screw, every way they'd put Dominic back together, glowing white against the backdrop of muscles and skin.

The place was clean.

And *Dom* was clean.

He hadn't had a drink or a dose since the night they dug up Victor—he wished he could say *since the night they met*, when Victor erased his pain, but the bastard had gone and *died,* left Dom high and dry and in a world of hurt. Those had been two dark nights, ones he didn't want to remember, but Dominic's control hadn't faltered since.

Even when Victor shorted out, and the pain came rushing back. Dom white-knuckled it, tried to treat the episodes as a reminder, the reprieves as a gift.

After all, it could be worse.

It *had* been worse.

Dom wolfed down a cup of too-hot coffee and a plate of too-runny eggs, slung on his jacket, grabbed his helmet from the door, and stepped out into the gray predawn.

His ride sat waiting in its usual spot—a simple black motorcycle, nothing fancy but the kind of thing he'd always wanted growing up and never been able to afford. Dom wiped the dew from the seat before swinging his leg over, kicked it into gear, and savored the low purr for a moment before setting off.

He rode through the empty streets as Merit began to wake around him. This early, most of the streetlights were in his favor, and Dom was out of the city in ten minutes. Merit tapered off to either side before giving way to empty fields. The sun rose at his back as the engine screamed beneath him and the wind buffeted his helmet, and for fifteen minutes he felt totally free.

He hit the turnoff and slowed, easing his bike down an unmarked road. Another five minutes, and Dom passed through an open gate, slowing as the building came into sight.

From the outside, it looked like nothing at all. A hospital, perhaps. Or a processing plant. A set of white blocks stacked together in a nondescript formation. The kind of place you'd drive by without a second glance, unless you knew what it was.

If you knew what it was, it became something far more ominous.

Dominic parked and dismounted, climbing the front steps. The doors parted onto a pristine white hall, sterile to the point of purity. An officer stood on either side, one manning an X-ray, the other a scanner.

"I've got parts," Dom reminded them, gesturing down his side.

The guy nodded, tapping away at the screen while Dominic set his phone, keys, jacket, and helmet in the tray. He stepped into the machine, waiting for the band of white light to scan up and then back down before reclaiming his possessions on the other side. He performed each task with an ease borne from habit. Amazing how things became normal, actions pressed into memory.

The locker room was the first door on the right. Dom set his jacket and helmet on a shelf and changed into a black uniform shirt, high-collared and long-sleeved. He washed his face, smoothed his hair, and patted his front pocket to make sure he had his access key.

Down the hall, and two floors up, he swiped himself into the control room and showed the senior officer the front of his key, where his face hung in holographic detail, right below the word *EON*.

"Dominic Rusher," he said with an easy smile, "reporting for duty."

VIII

STELL ducked under the yellow crime scene tape.

He didn't flash a badge—didn't need to. Everyone on the scene worked for EON. For him.

Agent Holtz was standing by the back door. "Sir," he said eagerly, his tone too bright for the early hour.

"Who called it in?" asked Stell.

"Good Samaritan called the cops. Cops called us."

"That obvious?"

"Oh yeah," said Holtz, holding open the door.

Agent Rios was already in the kitchen. Tall, tan, and keen-eyed, she'd been Stell's second-in-command for nearly four years. She was leaning against the counter, arms crossed, watching a tech photograph a pile of . . . something . . . on the tile floor. A large diamond glinted amid the mess.

"Same profile as the hospital?" asked Stell.

"Looks like it," said Rios. "Marcella Riggins. Age thirty-two. Spent the last thirteen days in a coma after her husband tried to burn down their house—with her inside. Can't really blame her for being mad."

"Mad is conceivable," said Stell. "Murder is a problem." He looked around. "How many dead?"

Rios straightened. "Four, we think. It's kind of hard to tell." She pointed at the kitchen floor. "One," she counted, then turned and led him down the hall to a room with a poker table, and a fairly grisly tableau. "Two," she said, nodding down at a ruined body on the floor. "Three," she pointed at a withered form only vaguely human. "And four," she said, gesturing to a pile of dust that coated the back of a chair and spilled onto the felt table. "Hell hath no fury . . ."

Stell counted the chairs. "Survivors?"

"If there were, they didn't go to the cops. The house belongs to Sam McGuire," said Rios. "Safe to assume he's here . . . somewhere."

Holtz whistled from the doorway. "You ever seen anything like this before?"

Stell considered. He had seen a lot since his first introduction to EOs a decade and a half before. Vale, with his ability to modulate pain; Cardale, with his ability to regenerate; Clarke, with her ability to control—and those were just the start. The tip of the iceberg. He'd since seen EOs who could bend time, move through walls, light themselves on fire, turn themselves to stone.

But this, Stell had to admit, was something new.

He ran his hand through the mess on the felt. "What is this? Ash?"

"As far as we can tell," said Rios, "it's Marcus Riggins. What's left of him. Or maybe this is. Or this."

"All right," said Stell, brushing the dust from his palms. "Compile the record. I want records of *everything*. Everything from the hospital. Everything from here. Shots and specs of every body, every room, every detail, even if you don't think it matters. It goes in the file."

Holtz raised his hand like a schoolboy. It was impossible to forget that he was new. "Who's the file for?"

"Our analyst," said Stell. But he knew how the agents and techs liked to talk. "You might have heard him called 'the hunting dog.'"

"Well," said Holtz, looking around. "Wouldn't it be easier to bring your dog to the scene, instead of trying to take the whole scene to the dog?"

"Perhaps," said Stell. "But his leash doesn't reach this far."

THE lights in the EON cellblocks came on all at once.

Eli Ever opened his eyes, looking up at the cell's mirrored ceiling, and saw—himself. As always. Clear skin, brown hair, strong jaw; a copy of the boy he'd been at Lockland. A pre-med student at the top of his class, the peak of promise. As if the ice bath hadn't only stopped his heart, but had frozen time itself.

Fifteen years, and though his face and body remained unchanged, Eli had aged in other ways. His mind had sharpened, hardened. He'd shed some of his more youthful ideals. About himself. About God. But those were the kinds of changes that didn't show in the reflected glass.

Eli rose from the cot, stretched, and padded barefoot across the private cell that, for nearly five years, had marked the boundaries of his world. He went to the sink and splashed cold water on his face, then crossed to the low shelf that ran against one wall, folders stacked along its length. All of them were beige, ordinary, except for one—a thick black file at the end with a name printed on the front. *His* name. Eli never reached for that one—didn't need to—he'd memorized the contents. Instead, his fingers danced along the spines before coming to rest on one considerably thicker than the rest, unmarked, save for a simple black *X*.

One of his few open cases. A pet project of sorts.

The Hunter.

Eli sat at the table in the center of his cell and flipped back the cover, turned through the pages of the file, skimming past the reports of older killings to the most recent one.

The EO's name was Jack Linden. A mechanic three hundred miles west of Merit. He'd slipped through EON's algorithm, but not, apparently, the Hunter's notice. A crime scene photo showed the EO on his back, amid a sea of tools. He'd been gunned down at point-blank range. Eli ran a finger absently over the entry wound.

A pressure seal sounded nearby, and a few seconds later the far wall of Eli's cell turned clear, dissolving from solid white to fiberglass. A thickset man with salt-and-pepper hair stood on the other side, carrying another file, and, as always, a mug of coffee. The last fifteen years might not have touched Eli, but every single one had left its mark on Stell.

The man nodded at the beige folder in Eli's hands. "Any new theories?"

Eli let the file fall shut. "No," he said, setting it aside and rising from his chair. "What can I do for you, Director?"

"There's a new case," said Stell, setting the file and mug in the fiberglass cubby. "I want your thoughts."

Eli approached the barrier and collected both offerings.

"Marcella Riggins," he read aloud, returning to his seat and taking a long, slow sip of his drink.

Eli didn't *need* coffee, just as he didn't need to eat or sleep, but some habits were psychological. The steaming mug was a small piece of change in a static world. A concession, a prop, but one that allowed him to pretend, if only for a moment, that he was still human.

Eli set the coffee aside and began to turn through the file. It wasn't enough—it was never enough—but it was all they would give him. A stack of paper and Stell's power of observation. And so he flicked through page after page, skimming the evidence, the aftermath, before finally pausing on a photo of human remains, a diamond glinting in the ash. He set the file aside and met Stell's waiting gaze.

"All right," said Eli. "Shall we begin?"

IX

FIVE YEARS AGO

LOCATION UNCERTAIN

AFTER Eli killed Victor, it was all a blur.

First, the chaos. The red and blue lights, the sirens, the officers storming through the Falcon Price, and the horrible realization they weren't on *his* side.

Then came the cuffs, so tight they cut into Eli's wrists, and the black hood, swallowing the sight of Victor's corpse and the blood-slicked concrete, muffling the voices and the orders and the slammed doors, erasing *everything* but Eli's own breath, his pounding heart, his desperate words.

Burn the body. Burn the body. Burn the body.

Then came the cell—more like a concrete box than a room—and Eli slamming his fists against the door over and over until his fingers broke, and healed, broke, and healed, the only evidence the blood left smeared across the steel.

And then, in the end, there was the lab.

Hands forcing Eli down, cold steel on his back and straps cinched so tight they cut into skin, pale sterile walls and too-bright lights and the chemical smell of disinfectant.

In the center of it all, a man in white, his face swimming above Eli's. Dark eyes set deep behind black glasses. Hands drawing on plastic gloves.

"My name," said the man, "is Dr. Haverty."

He selected a scalpel as he spoke.

"Welcome to my lab."

Leaned in close.

"We are going to understand each other."

And then he began to cut. *Dissect*—that was the word for it when the subject was dead. *Vivisect*—that was the word when they were still alive. But when they couldn't die?

What was the word for that?

Eli's faith had faltered in that room.

He had found Hell in that room.

And the only sign of God was that, no matter what Haverty did, Eli continued to survive.

Whether he wanted to or not.

TIME unraveled in Haverty's lab.

Eli thought he knew pain, but pain for him had become a bright and fleeting thing, an instant's discomfort. In the doctor's hands, it became a solid state.

"Your regeneration truly is remarkable," said the doctor, retrieving the scalpel with bloodstained gloves. "Shall we find its limit?"

You're not blessed, Victor had said. *You're a science experiment.*

Those words came back to Eli now.

And so did Victor.

Eli saw him in the lab, watched him circle the table at Haverty's back, slip in and out of Eli's line of sight as he studied the doctor's incisions.

"Maybe you're in Hell."

You don't believe in Hell, thought Eli.

The corner of Victor's mouth twitched. "But you do."

Every night, Eli would collapse onto his cot, shivering and sick from the hours pinned to the steel table.

And every morning, it would start again.

Eli's power had a single flaw—and ten years after Victor first discovered it, so did Haverty. Eli's body, for all its regeneration, couldn't reject foreign objects; if they were small enough, he healed around them. If they were large enough—a knife, a saw, a clamp, his body wouldn't heal at all.

The first time Dr. Haverty cut out Eli's heart, he thought he might *finally* die. The doctor held it up for him to see before cutting it free, and for a fraction of a second Eli's pulse faltered, failed, the equipment screamed. But by the time Haverty set the heart in its sterile tray, there was a new one already beating in Eli's open chest.

The doctor breathed a single word.

"Extraordinary."

THE worst part, thought Eli, was that Dr. Haverty liked to *talk*.

He kept up a casual stream of conversation as he sawed and sliced, drilled and broke. In particular, he was fascinated by Eli's scars, the brutal crosshatching on Eli's back. The only marks that would never fade.

"Tell me about them," he'd say, plunging a needle into Eli's spine.

"There are thirty-two," he'd say, drilling into Eli's bones.

"I counted," he'd say, cracking open Eli's chest.

"You can talk to me, Eli. I'm happy to listen."

But Eli couldn't talk, even if he wanted to.

It took all his effort not to scream.

X

TWENTY-FIVE YEARS AGO

THE FIRST HOME

ONCE upon a time, when the marks on his back were still fresh, Eli told himself that he was growing wings.

After all, his mother thought Eli was an angel, even if his father said he had the devil in him. Eli had never done anything to make the pastor think that, but the man claimed he could see the shadow in the boy's eyes. And whenever he caught a glimpse of it, he'd take Eli by the arm and lead him out to the private chapel that sat beside their clapboard house.

Eli used to love the little chapel—it had the prettiest picture window, all red and blue and green stained glass, facing east so it caught the morning light. The floor was made of stone—it was cold beneath Eli's bare feet, even in summer—and there in the center of the room was a metal cross, driven straight down into the foundation. Eli remembered thinking it seemed violent, the way the cross broke and split the floor, as if thrown from a horrible height.

The first time his father saw the shadow, he kept one hand on Eli's shoulder as they walked, the other clutching a coiled leather strap. Eli's mother watched them go, twisting a towel in her hands.

"John," she said, just once, but Eli's father didn't look back, didn't stop until they'd crossed the narrow lawn and the chapel door had fallen shut behind them.

Pastor Cardale told Eli to go to the cross and hold on to the horizontal bar, and at first Eli refused, sobbing, pleading, trying to apologize for whatever he'd done. But it didn't help. His father tied Eli's hands in place, and beat him worse for his defiance.

Eli had been nine years old.

Later that night, his mother treated the angry lash-marks on his back, and told him that he had to be strong. That God tested them, and so did Eli's father. Her sleeves inched up as she draped cool strips of cloth over her son's wounded shoulders, and Eli could just see the edges of old scars on the backs of her arms as she told him it would be okay, told him it would get better.

And for a little while, it always did.

Eli would do everything he could to be good, to be worthy. To avoid his angry father's gaze.

But the calm never lasted. Sooner or later, the pastor would glimpse the devil in his son again, and lead Eli back to the chapel. Sometimes the beatings were months apart. Sometimes days. Sometimes Eli thought he deserved it. Needed it, even. He would step up to the cross, and curl his fingers around the cold metal cross, and pray—not to God, not at first, but to his father. He prayed that the pastor would stop seeing whatever he saw, while he carved new feathers into the torn wings of Eli's back.

Eli learned not to scream, but his eyes would still blur with tears, the colors in the stained glass running together until all he saw was light. He held on to that, as much as to the steel cross beneath his fingers.

Eli didn't know how he was broken, but he wanted to be healed.

He wanted to be saved.

XI

STELL knocked his knuckles on the counter.

"I'm here to speak with one of your subjects," he said. "Eli Cardale."

"I'm sorry, sir, he's in testing."

Stell frowned. "Again?"

This was the third time he had come to see Eli, and the third time he'd been fed a line.

The first time, the excuse had been believable. The second, inconvenient. Now, it was obviously a lie. He hadn't pulled rank up until this point, but only because he didn't want the headache, or the reputation. EON was still a new venture, *his* venture—so new that the building around them wasn't even finished—but it was also his *responsibility,* and Stell knew in his gut that something was wrong. The unease pinched, like an ulcer.

"That's the same answer I was given last time."

The woman—Stell didn't know if she was a doctor, a scientist, or a secretary—pursed her lips. "This *is* a research lab, sir. Testing is a frequent component—"

"Then you won't mind interrupting the current session."

The woman's frown deepened. "With a patient such as Mr. Ever—"

"Cardale," corrected Stell. *Ever* had been a self-appointed moniker, aggrandizing and arrogant (if slightly prophetic). His real name was Eliot—Eli—Cardale.

"With a patient such as Mr. *Cardale*," she amended, "testing requires immense preparation. Ending an exam early would be a waste of EON resources."

"And this," said Stell, "is a waste of my time." He pinched the bridge of his nose. "I'll observe the session until it's finished."

A shadow crossed her face. "Perhaps if you'd rather wait here—"

With that, Stell's unease turned to dread.

"Take me to him. *Now.*"

XII

THE FIRST HOME

ELI sat on the porch steps and looked up at the sky.

It was a beautiful night, the strobe of red and blue lights painting the house, the lawn, the chapel. The ambulance and the coroner's van parked in the grass. One unnecessary, the other waiting.

He pressed a worn old Bible to his chest while the cops and medics moved around him as if in orbit, close but never touching.

"Kid's in shock," said an officer.

Eli didn't think that was true. He didn't feel shaken. Didn't feel anything but calm. Maybe that *was* shock. He kept waiting for it to wear off, for the steady hum in his head to give way to terror, to sadness. But it didn't.

"Can you blame him? Lost his mother a month ago. Now this."

Lost. That was a strange word. *Lost* suggested something misplaced, something that might be recovered. He hadn't lost his mother. After all, he'd been the one to find her. Lying in the tub. Floating in a white dress stained pink by the water, palms up as if in supplication, her forearms open from elbow to wrist. No, he hadn't lost her.

She'd left him.

Left Eli alone, trapped in a house with Pastor John Cardale.

A female medic brought a hand to Eli's shoulder, and he flinched, half from the surprise of contact, and half from the fact the latest welts were still fresh under his shirt. She said something. He wasn't listening. A few moments later, they wheeled out the body. The medic tried to block Eli's view, but there was nothing to see, only a black body bag. Death made clean. Neat. Sterile.

Eli closed his eyes and drew up the image of his father lying broken at the bottom of the stairs. A shallow red pool spreading around the pastor's head, like a halo, only in the dim basement the blood had looked black. His eyes wet, his mouth hinging open and closed.

What had his father been going down there to do?

Eli would never know. He opened his eyes and began to absently thumb the pages of the book.

"How old are you?" asked the medic.

Eli swallowed. "Twelve."

"Do you know your next of kin?"

He shook his head. There was an aunt somewhere. A cousin, maybe. But Eli had never met them. His world had been here. His father's church. Their congregation. There was a phone tree, he thought, a communication network used to spread the word when there was a celebration, a birth—or a death.

The woman slipped away from his side and spoke to two of the officers. Her voice was low, but Eli caught some of the words: "The boy has nothing."

But again, she was wrong.

Eli didn't have a mother, or a father, or a home, but he still had faith.

Not because of the scars on his back, or any of Pastor Cardale's less physical sermons. No, Eli had faith because of how it felt when he pushed his father down the basement stairs. When the pastor's head struck the basement floor at the bottom. When he finally stopped moving.

In that moment, Eli had felt *peace*. Like a small sliver of the world made right.

Something—someone—had guided Eli's hand. Given him the courage to place his palm flat against his father's back and push.

The pastor had fallen so fast, bounced like a ball down the old wooden steps before landing in a heap at the bottom.

Eli had followed slowly, taking each step with care as he drew his phone from his pocket. But he didn't dial, didn't push Call.

Instead, Eli sat down on the bottom step, safely away from the blood, and held the phone in his hands, and waited.

Waited until his father's chest stilled, until the pool of blood stopped spreading, and the pastor's eyes went empty, flat.

Eli remembered one of his father's sermons, then.

Those who don't believe in the soul have never seen one leave.

He was right, thought Eli, finally dialing 911.

There really was a difference.

"Don't worry," said the medic, returning to the front porch. "We're going to find somewhere for you to go." She knelt down in front of him, a gesture clearly meant to make him feel like they were equals. "I know it's scary," she said, even though it wasn't. "But I'm going to tell you something that helps me when I'm feeling overwhelmed. Every end is a new beginning." She straightened. "Come on, let's go."

Eli rose to his feet and followed her down the porch steps.

He was still waiting for the sense of calm to fade, but it didn't.

Not when they led him away from the house. Not when they perched him on the edge of the unused ambulance. Not when they drove him away. Eli looked back once, and only once, at the house, the chapel, and then he turned, facing forward.

Every end is a new beginning.

XIII

STELL entered the observation room just in time to see a man in a white lab coat crack open Cardale's chest. The patient was strapped to a steel table, and the surgeon was using some kind of saw, and a collection of clamps and metal pins, and Eli was not only still alive—he was *awake*.

A mask ran across the EO's nose and mouth, with a hose connected to a machine behind his head, but whatever it was feeding Eli, it didn't seem to be helping. The pain showed in every muscle, his whole body tensed against the restraints, the skin around his wrists and ankles white from pressure. A strap held Eli's head back against the steel table, denying him a view of his own dissection, though Stell doubted he needed to look to know what was happening. Beads of sweat ran down Eli's face and into his hair as the surgeon widened the cut in his chest.

Stell didn't know what he'd expected to find, but he hadn't expected *this*.

As the surgeon finished sawing through his patient's sternum and pinned the flesh back, Cardale groaned, the sound low and muffled by the mask. Blood poured out of his open chest, slicking the metal table, the lip of which was too shallow to contain the ceaseless flow. Ribbons of red spilled over the sides, dripping to the floor.

Stell felt sick.

"Remarkable, isn't he?"

He turned to find an average-looking man tugging off a pair of blood-slicked gloves. Behind round glasses, the doctor's deep-set eyes were bright, pupils dilated with the pleasure of discovery.

"What the hell do you think you're doing?" demanded Stell.

"Learning," said the doctor.

"You're torturing him."

"We're studying him."

"While he's *conscious.*"

"Necessarily," said the doctor with a patient smile. "Mr. Cardale's regenerative abilities render any anesthesia useless."

"Then what's with the mask?"

"Ah," said the doctor, "one of my more genius moments, that. You see, we cannot *anesthetize* him, but that doesn't mean we can't dampen his functions a little. The mask is part of an oxygen deprivation system. It reduces the breathable air to twenty-five percent. It's taking all of his regenerative ability to stave off the damage done by starving the cells, which buys us a bit more time on the rest of the body before it heals."

Stell stared at Eli's chest as it struggled to rise and fall. From this angle, Stell could almost see his heart.

"We've never come across an EO like Mr. Cardale," continued the doctor. "His ability—if we find a way to harness it—could revolutionize medicine."

"EO abilities can't be harnessed," said Stell. "They aren't transferable."

"Yet," said the doctor. "But if we could understand—"

"Enough," said Stell, transfixed by the sight of Eli's ruined body. "Tell them to stop."

The doctor frowned. "If they take out the clamps, he'll heal, and we'll have to start all over again. I really must insist—"

"What's your name?"

"Haverty."

"Well, Dr. Haverty. I'm *Director* Stell. And I'm officially discontinuing this experiment. Make them stop, or lose your job."

The sick smile slid from Haverty's face. He pulled a microphone from the viewing room wall and clicked it on.

"Terminate the session," he ordered the surgeons still in the room.

The men and women hesitated.

"I said—terminate it," repeated Haverty curtly.

The surgeons began to methodically remove the various pins and clamps from Eli's open chest cavity. The moment they were gone, the tension in the EO's body began to recede. His back sank to the metal table, and his hands unclenched, the color returning to his limbs as his body put itself back together. Ribs cracked into place. Skin settled and fused. The lines of his face smoothed. And his breathing, while still labored (they left the mask on), began to even.

The only sign that something horrific had happened was the sheer quantity of blood left pooling on the table and floor.

"Are you happy now?" grumbled Dr. Haverty.

"I'm a long way from happy," said Stell, storming out of the observation room. "And you, Dr. Haverty—you're fired."

"PUT your forehead against the wall and your hands through the gap."

Eli did as he was told, feeling for the break in the fiberglass. He couldn't see anything—his world had been a mottled black wall since the soldiers had thrown the hood over his head and dragged him from the concrete cell that morning. He knew, before they came, that something was wrong—no, not wrong, but certainly *different*. Haverty was a man of habit, and even though Eli didn't have a perfect sense of time, he had a tenuous enough hold to know their last session had ended too abruptly.

He found the gap in the fiberglass, a kind of narrow shelf, and rested his wrists on the lip. A hand jerked his hands farther into the gap, but a few moments later the cuffs came free.

"Take three steps back."

Eli retreated, expecting to meet another wall, but finding only space.

"Reach up and remove the hood."

Eli did, assaulted by the sudden brightness of the space. But unlike the sterile overheads of the operating theater, the light here was crisp, and clean, without being glaring. He was facing a floor-to-ceiling fiberglass wall, perforated by holes and interrupted only by the narrow cubby through which he'd placed his hands. On the other side stood three soldiers in head-to-toe riot gear, their faces hidden behind helmets. Two gripped batons—cattle prods, judging by the faint hum, the slight current of blue light. The third was coiling the discarded cuffs.

"What am I doing here?" asked Eli, but the soldiers didn't answer. They simply turned and left, steps echoing as they retreated. Somewhere a door opened, closed, pressurized, and as it did, the world beyond the fiberglass disappeared, the wall, transparent seconds before, becoming opaque.

Eli turned, taking in his new surroundings.

The cell was little more than a large cube, but after the months he'd spent strapped to various surfaces, sealed in a cell no bigger than a tomb, Eli was still grateful for the chance to *move*. He traced the perimeter of the cell, counted off the steps, took note of the features and their absences.

He noted four cameras set flush into the ceiling. There were no windows, no obvious door (he'd heard the fiberglass barrier retract into the floor, rise again behind him), only a cot, a table with one chair, one corner fitted with a toilet, sink, and shower. A wardrobe consisting solely of gray cotton lay folded on a floating shelf.

Victor's ghost ran a hand over the folded clothes.

"And so the angel trades Hell for Purgatory," mused the phantom. Eli didn't know what this place was—only knew that he wasn't being strapped down, wasn't being cut open, and that was an improvement. He peeled off his clothes and stepped into the shower, luxuriated in the freedom of turning the water on and off, washed away the scents of rubbing alcohol and blood and disinfectant, expecting to see the water at his feet run thick with the grime of a year's torture. But Haverty had always been meticulous. They'd hosed Eli down every morning, and every night, so the only traces left behind were the scars that didn't show.

Eli lowered himself onto the cot, pressed his back into the wall, and waited.

XIV

THE SECOND HOME

THE phone tree worked.

Eli arrived at the Russos' house that night with a backpack full of clothes, and the knowledge that his stay was temporary. A place for him to wait while the authorities tracked down a living relative, one willing to collect him.

Mrs. Russo met him at the door in a robe. It was late, and the Russo kids—there were five of them, ranging in age from six to fifteen—were already asleep. She took Eli's bag and led him inside. The house was warm and soft in a lived-in way, the surfaces scuffed, the edges worn smooth.

"Poor thing," she clucked under her breath as she led Eli into the kitchen. She gestured at the table for him to sit, and continued to murmur, more to herself than to him. The sound she made was so different from his own mother, whose whispered words had always been tinged with a hint of desperation. *My angel, my angel, you must be good, you must be light.*

Eli lowered himself into a rickety kitchen chair and stared down at his hands, still waiting for the shock to come, or go, whichever it was meant to. Mrs. Russo placed a steaming mug in front of him, and he curled his fingers around it. It was hot—uncomfortably so— but he didn't pull away. The pain was familiar, almost welcome.

What now? thought Eli.

Every end is a new beginning.

Mrs. Russo sat down across from him. She reached her hands out and wrapped them over his. Eli flinched back at the touch, tried to pull away, but her grip was firm.

"You must be hurting," she said, and he was—his hands were burning from the mug, but he knew she meant a deeper, heavier pain, and *that* he didn't feel. If anything, Eli felt lighter than he had in years.

"God never gives us more than we can bear," she continued.

Eli focused on the small gold cross that hung around her neck.

"But it's up to us to find the purpose in the pain."

The purpose in the pain.

"Come on," she said, patting his hand. "I'll make up the couch."

ELI had never been a good sleeper.

He'd spent half of every night listening to his father move just beyond the door, like a wolf in the woods behind the house. A predator, circling too near. But the Russos' place was quiet, calm, and Eli lay awake, marveling at the way eight bodies under one roof could take up less space than two.

The quiet didn't last.

At some point Eli must have drifted off, because he started awake to raucous laughter and morning light and a pair of wide green eyes watching him from the edge of the couch. The youngest Russo girl perched there, staring at him with a mixture of interest and suspicion.

Four loud bodies came crashing suddenly into the room, a cacophony of limbs and noise. It was Saturday, and already the Russo children were running wild. Eli spent most of the time trying to stay out of their path, but it was hard in such a crowded house.

"Weirdo," said one of the boys, knocking into him on the stairs.

"How long is he staying?" asked another.

"Don't be un-Christian," warned Mr. Russo.

"Gives me the creeps," said the oldest boy.

"What's wrong with you?" demanded the youngest girl.

"Nothing," answered Eli, though he wasn't sure if that was true.

"Then act normal," she ordered, as if that were such a simple thing.

"What does normal look like?" he asked, at which point the girl made a small, exasperated sound and stormed away.

Eli waited for someone to come and get him, take him away—though he didn't know where they would take him—but the day passed, and darkness fell, and he was still there. That first night was the only one he spent alone. They put him in the boys' room after that, a spare mattress tucked in one corner. He lay there, listening to the other boys sleep with a mixture of annoyance and envy, his nerves too fine-tuned to let him rest among the various sounds of movement.

Eventually he got up and went downstairs, hoping to steal a few precious hours of stillness on the sofa.

Mr. and Mrs. Russo were in the kitchen, and Eli heard them talking.

"Something's not right with that boy."

Eli hovered in the hall, holding his breath.

"He's too quiet."

Mrs. Russo sighed. "He's been through a lot, Alan. He'll find his way."

Eli returned to the boys' room, climbed back into his bed. There, in the dark, the words repeated.

Quiet. Weirdo. Creep.

He'll find his way.

Act normal.

Eli didn't know what normal was, or even what it looked like. But he'd spent a lifetime studying his father's moods and his mother's silences, the way the air in the house changed like the sky before a storm. Now he watched the way the Russo boys roughhoused, noted the fine line between humor and aggression.

He studied the confidence with which the oldest—a boy of sixteen—moved among his younger siblings. He studied the guileless innocence the youngest played up, to get what he wanted. He studied the way their faces twisted into a pantomime of emotions like annoyance and disgust and anger. Most of all, he studied their joy. The way their eyes lit up when they were gleeful, the varying tones of their laughter, the dozen ways their smiles shone or softened depending on the exact nature of their delight.

Eli had never known there were so many kinds of happiness, let alone so many ways to express it.

But his study was cut short when, just two weeks into his stay with the Russos, Eli found himself uprooted again, deposited with another family in another house.

Act normal, the Russo girl had said.

And so Eli tried again. Started fresh. It wasn't a perfect imitation, not by far. But it was an improvement. The children at this new house still called him names, but the names had changed.

Timid, quiet, weirdo had been replaced by *strange, curious, intense.*

Soon came another family, and another chance.

Another opportunity to reinvent, to modify, to adjust aspects of that act.

Eli tested his theater on the families as if they were an audience, and used their feedback, the immediate, constant feedback, to tweak his performance.

Slowly *strange, curious, intense* had been refined, honed into *charming, focused, clever.*

Then something else changed.

Another car pulled up, and took him away, but this time it didn't drop him off with another of his father's flock.

This time, it took him to *family.*

THE FIFTH HOME

Patrick Cardale did not believe in God.

He was John's estranged nephew, the son of a dead aunt that Eli had never met. Patrick was a professor at a local college, married to a painter named Lisa. They didn't have children. No one for Eli to mimic. No curtain of normalcy or noise for him to slip behind.

Eli sat on the sofa across from them. A captured audience. A solo act.

"How old are you?" asked Patrick. "Twelve?"

"Almost thirteen," said Eli. It had been more than six months since Pastor Cardale's accident.

"I'm sorry it took us so long," said Patrick, hands between his knees.

Lisa put a hand on his shoulder. "We'll be honest, it wasn't an easy decision."

Patrick shifted. "I knew you'd been raised a certain way. And I knew I couldn't give you that. John and I, we didn't see eye to eye."

"Neither did we," said Eli.

He realized he was making them uncomfortable, so he smiled. Not too wide, just enough to let Patrick know that he was okay.

"Come on," said Lisa, rising. "I'll show you to your room."

Eli rose to follow her.

"We can find you a church," she added, leading him down the hall. "If it's important to you."

But he didn't need a church. Not because he'd given up on God—but because church itself was the one place Eli had never felt Him. No, God had stood with Eli at the top of the cellar stairs. Given him each of those families to learn from. Led him here, to this house, and this couple, this new chance.

His room, when they got there, was comfortable and clean. A double bed, a closet, a desk. A pair of framed pictures hung on the wall over the desk, anatomical drawings, one of a hand, the other a diagram of a human heart. Eli stopped before them, studying the lines, startled by the intricacy, the elegance.

"You can take those down, if you don't like them," said Lisa. "Make the space yours. Put up posters or whatever boys your age do."

Eli glanced toward her. "How long am I staying?"

Lisa's eyes widened in surprise. Her face was an open book—that was the phrase people used. Eli had never really understood it until he looked at Lisa.

"As long as you want," she said. "This is your home now."

Eli didn't know what to say to that. He'd been living in increments of days, weeks, which wasn't really living, of course. Now, his future stretched before him, measured in months, years.

Eli smiled, and this time, it almost felt natural.

XV

FOUR YEARS AGO

EON

STELL sank into his office chair, and waited for the call.

His office, like the rest of EON, was composed of clean lines, spare and minimalist. Three thin screens drew a semicircle over his desk, and a vast grid on the wall live-streamed footage of each hall, access point, cell.

EON's cells were state-of-the-art fiberglass cubes, each floating in the middle of its own concrete hangar. The majority of the screens on the wall were still dark, positioned as they were in half-completed wings, or looking onto empty cells, but on the central screen, Eli paced the confines of his unit like a lion tracing the edges of its cage.

To think, none of this would have happened without Eliot Cardale.

Eli Ever.

Stell took up a black business card, turned it absently between his fingers. The word *EON,* ghosted in spot gloss, showed up only when it caught the light.

EON had been Stell's idea, yes, but it was at first a vague proposal, one motivated by his history with Vale and Cardale, by what he'd stopped, but also what he'd failed to. By the fact that ten years ago, Stell had put Victor in jail, and let Eli go free, and because of that choice—that failing to look beyond the obvious, to see through a single deceptive guise—thirty-nine people had died. It haunted him. Plagued him.

There had to be a way—to find EOs, to contain them. Maybe, one day, to use them. EOs were dangerous, yes, some catastrophically so, but what if, among the lost and the deranged, there were those who could be fixed, given purpose, made whole? What if death didn't change a person's nature, only amplified it?

By that logic, a wounded soldier might still want to serve.

That was the focus, the sharp point at the center of Stell's idea. A world where skilled EOs could help stop crimes instead of start them. And where the rest could be contained, kept from committing more atrocities.

A short, bright ring signaled the incoming call.

The curve of screens on Stell's desk lit up.

Stell brushed his fingers through the air, accepting the call, and seconds later a conference room appeared in front of him, five stern figures seated around a long wood desk.

The board of directors.

Three men and two women, all in dark suits—the standard uniform of government agencies and private ones alike. They looked like vague copies of each other. The same dark hair, the same narrow eyes, the same flat expressions.

"Director," said a man in charcoal, "do you care to explain why you removed a valuable test subject from the lab and fired one of our most prominent—not to mention valuable—scientists?"

"He was *dissecting* an EO."

The silence that followed wasn't loaded; on the contrary, it was empty. The members of the board stared at him as if he hadn't answered the question. As if they didn't see the problem.

"Last time I checked," said Stell, knitting his fingers, "I was the director of this institution. Are personnel changes above my pay grade?"

"Of course not, *Director*," said a woman in navy. "You have an intimate understanding of the needs and challenges on the ground. However—"

"EON may be your operation," cut in a man in black, "but we are its bank."

"And as its bank," said the man in charcoal, "we need to know our money is being well spent. In the interest of national security."

That last sentence, like an afterthought. As if the five wolves in dark suits weren't circling in search of profit.

"Haverty's methods may have been questionable," said the woman in navy, "but his research was promising. As for your EO, his ability made him uniquely qualified to undergo that research. Now you have deprived us of both scientist *and* subject."

"Let's discuss the EO," chimed in a new voice, a woman in black. "Eliot Cardale, alias Eli Ever. What have you done with him?"

"He's been relocated to a cell in the containment unit."

"To what end?"

"To *contain* him," said Stell. "Eli Cardale killed nearly forty people."

A man in gray sat forward. "They were almost all EOs, though, weren't they?"

"Is that supposed to make it better?"

The man waved the concern away. "I simply mean, your subject already has a proven skill."

"Killing EOs."

"Tracking them down."

"Isn't that the point of *your* organization?" asked the woman in navy. "To find and *contain* EOs before they can cause harm?"

"It is," said Stell through gritted teeth.

"Then," said the man in black, "I suggest you put him to use."

THE lights went down, and came back up, and Eli was still alone.

A night passed, and no one came to collect him. No one dragged him from the cell. He wondered if this was what Victor's time in prison had felt like, after his arrest. The endless waiting. Entirely alone.

Eli leaned forward, elbows on his knees. He interlaced his fingers, but instead of praying, he stared over the tops of his knuckles at the farthest wall and listened, straining his senses for any clues. He was met only by the dampened silence of nested space.

"Just going to sit around and wait?" chided Victor, there again, haunting Eli. "How complacent."

Eli rose and went to the fiberglass divide, rapped his knuckles on the surface, then pressed his hands flat against it, testing the material.

"I assure you," said a familiar voice, "the cell is stronger than it looks."

The wall cleared, like a curtain dropping all at once from a window, and there, on the other side of the glass, stood Joseph Stell. The last time Eli had seen the cop was at the Falcon Price project, standing over Victor's dead body while a SWAT team dragged Eli away.

"Officer," he said.

"Actually, it's *Director* now."

"Congratulations," said Eli coolly. "Director of what?"

Stell held out his hands. "This place. Your new home. The department of ExtraOrdinary Observation and Neutralization." He stepped up to the glass. "I think you'll admit it's quite an upgrade from your previous circumstances."

"And as *director,* I assume you were responsible for those, too?"

Stell's expression darkened. "I wasn't adequately informed of the lab's methods. Had I been, it wouldn't have been allowed. As soon as I found out, you were extracted, and that branch of testing terminated. If it's any consolation, so was Haverty."

"Consolation . . ." echoed Eli, splaying his fingers across the fiberglass.

"I should warn you," said Stell, "if you try to strike any of these walls, a warning will go off, and the surface will electrify. Try a second time and, well, we both know it won't kill you, but it will hurt."

Eli's hand fell away. "How thorough."

"I underestimated you once, Mr. Cardale. I don't intend to do so again."

"I was never a danger to you, Director Stell. Wouldn't your energy and resources be better spent on EOs who represent a threat to the general public?"

Stell's mouth twitched into a grim smile. "You killed thirty-nine people. That we know of. You are a mass murderer."

The true number was closer to fifty, but Eli didn't say so. Instead, he turned, surveying his cell. "And what did I do to deserve such accommodation?"

Stell produced a simple manila folder and slid it through the slot in the fiberglass. Eli turned back and took it up, flicking through the pages. It was a profile, much like the ones the Merit PD had developed under Eli's instruction.

"You possess a unique and proven skill set," said Stell. "You are here to assist in the tracking and capture of other—"

Eli laughed, short and humorless. "If you wanted me to help you hunt EOs," he sneered, tossing the file onto the table, "you shouldn't have put me in a cell."

"Unlike you, we treat execution as a last resort."

"Half measures, then."

"*Humane* ones."

"Hypocrisy in action." Eli shook his head. "What you're doing, what *EON* is doing, is nothing but a pale version of my own work. So why am I the one in the cell?" Eli stepped as close as the fiberglass would allow. "Disagree with my methods, Stell. Doubt my motives. But you're a fool if you think what you're doing is different. The *only* difference between us is that you naively insist on preserving what I know should be destroyed. You want to pretend that capturing EOs is a mercy. To what end? So you can sleep easier without their blood on your hands? Or so that you can grow your collection of specimens and play God with their bodies? Because I played God once, Stell, and it did not end well." Eli rocked back on his heels. "I spent ten years trying to make amends for that, to undo the damage I wrought. Yes, I killed a great many EOs, but it wasn't out of cruelty or violence, or spite. I did it to protect people—living, innocent humans—from the monsters I'd found in the dark."

"Are you so sure they're *all* monsters?" challenged Stell.

"Yes," he said forcefully. There had been a time when Eli thought himself exempt from that label. Now he knew better. "EOs may look like humans, Stell, but they don't think or act like them."

Victor would have enumerated any number of symptoms— diminished sense of consequence, lack of remorse, self-absorption, amplification of demeanor and aspect—but Eli said only, "They have no soul." He shook his head. "You want to save EOs? Save them from themselves. Put them in the ground, where they belong. Unless that's your plan, I have no intention of helping."

In answer, Stell set another folder in the fiberglass slot between, this one black.

Eli cut a glance at the file. "Didn't you hear me?"

"This isn't another dossier," said Stell. "It's your other option."

Eli glimpsed his own name printed on the front of the file. He didn't reach for it, didn't need to—he knew what it was. What it meant.

"Take a day to think it over," said Stell. "I'll be back tomorrow for your answer."

He retreated, and the wall went solid again in his wake, turning the cell back into a tomb. Eli gritted his teeth. And then he swiped the black folder from the tray and carried it to the table where the thin manila file already waited.

Eli sank into a chair and flicked back the cover. On top was an X-ray, black and white, seemingly innocuous. He flipped past, and saw an MRI, the body lit up in red and blue and green. And then he turned the page again, and his throat constricted at the sight of the first photograph. A man's chest—*Eli's* chest—pried open by metal clamps to reveal ribs, lungs, a beating heart.

Every pre-med student did dissections. Eli had done a dozen his freshman year, peeled and pinned the skin of small animals out of the way to examine the organs beneath. The photos in the black folder reminded him of that. The only difference, of course, was that *Eli* had been alive.

The pain itself was gone, but the memory of it etched along his nerves, echoed through his bones.

Eli wanted to sweep the file from the table, tear it to shreds, but he knew he was being watched—he'd noted the cameras set into the ceiling, imagined Stell standing in some control room, a smug expression on his face. So Eli stayed seated, and turned through every page of the gruesome, graphic record, studying every photograph, every diagram, every scrawled note, every aspect of torture laid out in sterile detail, memorizing the black folder so that he would never have to look at it again.

You're not blessed, or divine, or burdened. You're a science experiment.

Maybe Victor was right.

Maybe Eli was just as broken, just as damned, as every other EO. It was true, he hadn't felt that presence the night he killed Victor. Hadn't felt anything like peace.

But that didn't absolve him of his task.

He still had a purpose. An obligation. To save others, even if he couldn't save himself.

XVI

TWENTY YEARS AGO

THE FIFTH HOME

ELI ran his fingers over the cover of the book.

It was massive, and heavy, and every single page detailed the marvels and miracles of the human body.

"I thought we should get you tickets to a game," said Patrick, "but Lisa insisted—"

"It's perfect," said Eli.

"See?" said Lisa, shouldering Patrick. "He wants to be a doctor. You've got to start young."

"From ministry to medicine," mused Patrick. "John must be rolling in his grave."

Eli laughed, an easy sound, practiced to perfection. The truth was, he didn't see the two avenues as separate. Eli had seen God the day he arrived, in the drawings on his wall; saw Him again now in the pages of this book, in the perfect fit of bones, the vast intricacies of the nervous system, the brain—the spark, like faith, that turned a body into a man.

Patrick shook his head. "What fifteen-year-old boy would rather have a book—"

"Would you rather I asked for a car?" asked Eli, flashing a crooked smile.

Patrick clapped him on the shoulder. These days, Eli didn't flinch. His attention fell back to the anatomy textbook. Perhaps his interest wasn't strictly normal, but he could afford this small divergence.

At fifteen, the personality he'd crafted was nearly perfect. The day after he arrived, Patrick and Lisa had enrolled him in school, and Eli had realized the hard way that a six-month crash course in normalcy was a pale foundation of what he'd need to survive. But it was a big school, and Eli was a quick study, and soon *charming, focused, clever* had not only been cemented, they'd been joined by *handsome, friendly, athletic.* He ran track and field. He aced his classes. He had a winning smile and an easy laugh, and nobody knew about the scars on his back or the shadows in his past. Nobody knew that it was all an act, that none of it came naturally.

LISA'S laughter rang through the house like bells.

Eli could hear it over the classical music in his earbuds as he did his chemistry homework. A few moments later, Patrick knocked on the doorframe, and Eli hit Pause.

"You guys off?"

"Yeah," said Patrick. "Show starts at seven, so we shouldn't be back late. Don't work too hard."

"Says the professor to the student."

"Hey, studies show that variation is good for retention."

"Come on!" called Lisa.

"I put money on the counter," said Patrick. "At least order a pizza. Steal a beer from the fridge."

"Will do," said Eli absently, already hitting Play.

Patrick said something else, but Eli didn't catch the words over the concerto. At nine, he finished his homework and ate leftovers at the kitchen counter. At ten, he went for a jog. At eleven, he went to bed.

And fifteen minutes later, his cell phone rang, a number he didn't recognize, a voice he didn't know.

"Is this Eliot Cardale?" said a man.

A stillness formed in Eli's chest. Not the kind he'd felt when he pushed his father down the stairs. No, this was colder, heavier. The weight of finding his mother floating in the tub. The exhaustion as he sank like a stone to the chapel floor.

"I'm afraid," continued the man, "there's been an accident."

ELI wondered if *this* was shock. He sat on a flimsy plastic chair, a social worker at his side, the doctor straight ahead, an officer looming like a shadow. The cops had come to the house. Driven him to the hospital, even though there was nothing to see, or do. Dead on arrival. On *impact,* according to the doctor.

"I'm sorry, son," said the cop.

God never gives us more than we can bear.

Eli laced his fingers, bowed his head.

It's up to us to find the purpose in the pain.

"The driver didn't survive," continued the cop. "Toxicology's still out but we think he was drunk."

"How did they die?"

Eli realized, too late, that he'd asked the wrong question. A shadow crossed the doctor's face.

"I'm sorry," he said quickly. "I didn't—it's just—I'm going to be a surgeon, one day. I want to *save* lives. I just—I need to understand." He balled his hands into fists. "If you don't tell me, I'll lie awake, wondering. I think I would rather know."

The doctor sighed. "Patrick suffered a cervical fracture of C2 and C3," he said, touching the bones at the top of his own neck. "Lisa sustained a massive concussion, which resulted in an intracranial hemorrhage. In both cases, it would have been nearly instantaneous."

Eli was glad they hadn't suffered. "All right," he said. "Thank you."

"They didn't name a guardian," said the social worker. "Do you know if there's someone you can stay with? Until we get things sorted out?"

"Yes," he lied, digging out his phone. "I'll call a friend."

Eli rose and walked a little ways down the hall, but didn't bother dialing. There was no phone tree this time. And no point in pretending. Eli was popular, well liked, but he had always been careful to keep a measure of distance. Too close, and someone might see the seams in his facade, the subtle but constant effort of pretending. Better to be friendly, without being friends.

Eli returned to the social worker and the cop. The doctor had left. "I need to get some things from my place," he said. "Could you drop me off there?"

He let himself into the house, listened to the sound of the patrol car pulling away before he closed the door. He stood for several long seconds in the darkened hall.

And then turned and slammed his fist into the wall.

Pain flashed through Eli's hand, up his arm, and he hit the wall again and again until his knuckles split open, and blood dripped down his wrist, and he could breathe.

His legs folded under him, and Eli sank to the floor.

After everything, he was alone again.

God never gives us more than we can bear.

Eli told himself there was a plan, even if he couldn't see it. There was a purpose to the pain. He stared down at his bloody hand.

Stupid, he thought.

It would be hard to hide from the inevitable social workers, the school, the hundred eyes bound to latch on to every misstep, every crack in his persona.

Eli got up and went to the bathroom, rinsed the split knuckles under the sink and bandaged his hand with calm precision and steady fingers. He met his gaze in the mirror and forced the lines of his face back into their proper order.

And then Eli went to his room and began to pack.

"Here we go."

Eli stood in the doorway, holding a box of books. The room was simple, empty save for a window, a narrow bed, and a desk.

"Bit sparse, I know," said the landlord, who insisted he call her Maggie. "But the windows are double glazed and the shower down the hall is hot." She gave him a measuring look. "Awfully young to be living on your own, aren't you?"

"I'm emancipated," explained Eli.

It had been the easiest route. He was nearly sixteen. Not many people wanted to take in a teenage boy, and Eli had no interest in becoming a ward of the state. His parents were dead. Patrick and Lisa were dead. The former had left him only scars, but the latter had left him some money—not much, but enough to cover living expenses so he could focus on finishing high school. Get into a good college.

"Thanks, Maggie," he said, crossing the threshold.

"All right, Eliot. You let me know if you need anything."

The wood floor creaked under her feet as she ambled off, creaked under his as he set the box on the desk and unpacked, arranging his schoolbooks in a neat stack.

"We are so sorry, Eliot," the principal had said.

"We have counselors," added the dean of students.

"Let us know how we can help," echoed his teachers.

"Please," Eli had begged them each in turn, "don't tell anyone."

Normal was such a fragile thing, so easily upset by even good intentions.

And so, under the guise of him wanting to grieve in peace, they kept his secret.

Eli unpacked the last two books—the battered Bible and the anatomy text. He set King James aside and sank into the chair, drawing the textbook closer.

It's up to us, he thought, *to find the purpose in the pain . . .*

Eli opened the heavy tome and paged through until he found the drawings of the head, and neck, the tracery of the brain, the delicate column of the spine.

Find the purpose.

He began to take notes.

XVII

FOUR YEARS AGO

WHEN Stell returned the next day, Eli didn't look up.

He kept his head bowed over the file he was studying, had been studying for the better part of the night.

"I see you've decided to cooperate."

Eli gathered the papers back into a shallow stack. "I need a computer," he said.

"Absolutely not," said Stell.

Eli rose from the chair and carried the file to the fiberglass divide. "I spent *months* researching my targets. Confirming their abilities. Tracking their movements." He let the file fall from his fingers, paper sloughing to the floor. "You want me to do the same work from inside a concrete box, with nothing but basic information. This," he said, gesturing to the pages at his feet, "is not enough."

"It's what we have."

"Then you're not looking hard enough," snapped Eli. He turned his attention to a photo on the floor. "Tabitha Dahl," he said, scanning the paper. "Nineteen. College athlete, young, social, active, adventurer. Suffers a massive cardiac event due to an allergic reaction while hiking. Friend is able to resuscitate her. She makes it to a hospital. And then—she disappears. Parents file a missing persons report two weeks ago." Eli looked up. "Where would she go? How would she get there? Why is there nothing here about the friend she was with? How did she think and feel in the direct aftermath of her accident?"

"How are we supposed to obtain that kind of information?" asked Stell.

Eli threw up his hands. "She's nineteen. Start with social media. Hack the texts she sent to friends. Get into her life. Get into her head. An EO isn't just the product of their catalyst. They are the product of the person they were before. The circumstances, but also the psyche. I can help you find Tabitha Dahl. With the right insight, I can probably make a decent guess as to her power, but I can't do any of that with five pieces of paper."

A long silence followed. Eli waited patiently for Stell to break it. He did.

"I'll get you a computer," he said. "But access will be restricted, and the system will be twinned. I will see everything you search, as you search it. And the moment you go off-book, you will lose more than just your tech privileges. Are we clear?"

"I could do more than postulate," said Eli, kneeling to retrieve the papers. "If you let me out . . ."

"Mr. Cardale," said Stell. "I want to make something very clear. You can help us from inside this cell, or from inside a lab, but you will never, *ever* see the outside of this facility again."

Eli rose to his feet, but the director was already walking away.

XVIII

ELI made his way across campus, his collar up against the fall chill.

Haverford was a good school—not the best, but certainly the best he could afford, and close enough to commute from the boarding-house. It was also massive, sporting a population that could rival most towns', and a campus so large that two months in, he was still discovering buildings.

Maybe that was why he hadn't seen the chapel sooner.

Or maybe, until now, the trees had simply hidden it, red and gold leaves obscuring the classic lines, the simple spire, the sloping white roof.

Eli's steps slowed at the sight of it. But he didn't turn around. The pull was subtle, but persistent, and he let himself be drawn to the steps.

He hadn't set foot inside a church in years, not since God became more . . . personal.

Now, as he stepped through the doors, the first thing he saw was the stained glass. Red and blue and green light dancing on the floor. And there, before the window, a stone cross. His palms began to tingle. Eli closed his eyes, willing back the memory of a deep voice, the whistle of the leather belt.

"Amazing, isn't it?" said an airy voice.

Eli blinked, and glanced sideways, and saw a girl. Slim and pretty, with wide brown eyes and honey blond hair.

"I've never been religious," continued the girl, "but I love the look of the buildings. You?"

"I'm not big on the buildings," he said with a wry smile, "but I've always been religious."

She pouted, shook her head. "Oh no, it will never work between us." The false sadness broke back into a smile. "Sorry, didn't mean to interrupt, you just looked sad."

"Did I?" Eli must have slipped, let the truth show through. But in an instant, he'd recovered, and turned the full force of his attention, and his practiced charm, on the girl. "Were you studying me instead of the building?"

Light danced in the girl's eyes. "I'm more than capable of admiring both." She held out her hand. "I'm Charlotte."

He smiled. "Eli." The bells rang once around them, and Eli held out his hand. "Have you had lunch?"

MAGGIE had appeared in the doorway of Eli's room the week before, a basket of laundry on her hip. "It's Friday night, Eliot."

"And?"

"And you're sitting in here doing calculus."

"Biology," he'd corrected.

Maggie had shaken her head. "All this work and no fun, for a boy your age, it's not normal."

That word. *Normal.* The center line of his calibration.

Eli had looked up from his homework. "What *should* I be doing?" he asked, one eyebrow raised to hide the earnestness of the question.

"Go to parties!" said Maggie. "Drink cheap beer! Make bad choices! Date pretty girls!"

He leaned back in his chair. "Do pretty girls count as bad choices, or are those two separate things?"

Maggie rolled her eyes and walked away, and Eli turned back to his paper, but he'd taken the words to heart. He'd gone to one or two frat parties, plastered on a lazy smile and sipped awful beer (which honestly felt like a bad choice).

But now, he had Charlotte.

A relationship, Eli had learned, was a universal shorthand for *normal*. A societal stamp of approval. Dating Charlotte Shelton in particular was more like a gold seal. She was old money, the breeding so deep she didn't even notice it lining her every seam.

She was cheerful, and pretty, and spoiled—she lived in the school dormitories, but only because she wanted an *authentic* college experience. Not that that desire for authenticity extended much beyond a single twin bed and a communal hall.

Charlotte came to Eli's boardinghouse once, and only once, and on her insistence. She knew he was an orphan (a word that seemed to generate in her an intense protective instinct), but the threadbare truth wasn't as romantic. He'd seen the pity masquerading as sympathy.

"I don't love you for your *stuff*," she'd insisted. "I have enough stuff for the both of us."

But after that, they didn't *share* a life—Charlotte just pulled Eli into hers.

And he let her.

It was easy.

It was simple.

She adored him.

And he enjoyed the attention.

Charlotte liked to say they were a perfect fit. Eli knew they weren't, but only he could see the jagged sides, the empty spaces.

"How do I look?" she asked as they climbed the steps to her parents' house—mansion—for Thanksgiving, sophomore year.

"Stunning," said Eli automatically, pairing the word with a wink.

Charlotte fixed his tie. She ran her fingers through his dark hair, and he let her, his own hand grazing the bottom of her chin, tipping her face up for a kiss.

"Don't be nervous," she whispered.

Eli wasn't.

The door swung open, and he turned, half expecting to see a butler, a grim old man in coattails, but instead he found an elegant, older version of Charlotte.

"You must be Eli!" said the woman brightly as a slim, stern man in a well-tailored suit appeared at her back.

"Thank you for having me," said Eli, holding out a pie.

"Of course," said Mrs. Shelton warmly. "When Charlotte said you didn't have plans, we insisted."

"Plus," said Mr. Shelton, shooting Charlotte a look, "it's about time we meet the boy our girl's been so taken with." They started down the hall, Charlotte and her mother arm in arm.

"Eli," said Mr. Shelton, putting a hand on his shoulder, "why don't I give you a tour while the ladies catch up."

It wasn't a question.

"Of course," said Eli, falling in step behind the man, who led him through a pair of doors into a private study. "This," he said, "is really the only room that matters."

He opened a cabinet and poured himself a drink.

"I can see why Charlotte likes you," he said, leaning back against his desk. "She's always had a weakness for charity cases. Especially handsome ones."

Eli stilled, his easy manner stiffening a fraction. "Sir, if you think I'm with Charlotte for her money or her station—"

"The truth doesn't matter, Mr. Cardale, only the optics. And they don't look good. I've done my homework on you. So much tragedy— you handle it with poise. While I admire how far you've come, the fact is, you're tracking mud into my home."

Eli's teeth clicked together. "We can't shape our past," he said. "Only our future."

Charlotte's father smiled. "Well put. And that's what I'm offering you. A bright future. Just not with my daughter. I've seen your grades. You're a smart young man, Eliot. Ambitious, too, Charlotte tells me. You want to be a doctor. Haverford is a decent college, but it's not the best. I know you got into other schools. Better schools. I assume you couldn't afford them."

Eli stared, amazed. He was being *bribed*.

Mr. Shelton pushed off the desk. "I know you care about my daughter. Hell, you might even think you love her . . ."

But Eli didn't.

If Mr. Shelton was better at reading people—or if Eli hadn't made himself so hard to read—he might have seen the simple truth. That Eli didn't need persuading. That Charlotte Shelton had always been, for him, a vehicle. A way to move through the world on an upward trajectory. What her father was now offering, *if* he was truly offering it, was a true chance for meaningful change, a great gain for a minor loss.

But what came next was a delicate maneuver.

"Mr. Shelton," started Eli, contorting his face with an aspect of tightly controlled defiance. "Your daughter and I—"

The man held up a hand. "Before you play the noble card, and insist you can't be bought, remember that you are both very young, and love is fickle, and whatever you have with Charlotte might feel real, but it won't last."

Eli exhaled, and looked down, as if ashamed. Let his features settle into a semblance of resignation. "What would you have me do, sir?"

"Tonight? Nothing. Enjoy your dinner. In a few days? Break things off. Pick one of those better schools. Chester, or Lockland. Transfer. The tuition won't be a problem."

"Boys!" called Mrs. Shelton from the kitchen. "Turkey's ready."

Mr. Shelton clapped Eli on the shoulder. "Come on," he said cheerfully. "I'm starving."

"Dad," warned Charlotte when they met her in the dining room. "Did you put him through the wringer?"

"Just a little." Mr. Shelton kissed his daughter on the cheek. "It's my duty to put the fear of God into whoever you bring home."

She turned her warm brown gaze on Eli. "I hope he wasn't being too rough on you."

Eli laughed softly and shook his head. "Not at all."

They took their seats, the table falling to easy conversation—so much spoken, so little said—as they passed platters and bowls.

And as Eli and Charlotte walked back to their car that night, she slipped her arm through his. "Everything okay?"

Eli glanced back at the front door, where Mr. Shelton stood watching. "Yes," he said, kissing her temple. "Everything's perfect."

XIX

TWO YEARS AGO

ELI ran his fingers along the shelf where he kept the old case files. His own black folder sat like a stain at the edge of the row, a punctuation mark shifted to fit the growing sentence. Nineteen EOs tracked, hunted, captured, over a period of less than two years. Not bad, considering his limitations.

Eli had insisted on keeping the old folders, telling Stell that past work would inform future cases.

It was a partial truth—there were indeed patterns between EOs, shared traits, the same shadow cast over different faces. But the larger truth was simple: Eli found the markers satisfying. Not as satisfying as wrapping his hands around an EO's throat, feeling a pulse falter and still beneath his fingers. But an echo of that old calm still accompanied each closed case, the pleasant sense of things askew being set right.

There was another facet to the collection, a grim truth laid bare in the sheer number of folders.

"What have we done?" Eli muttered to himself.

But it was Victor who answered.

"What makes you think *we* did anything?"

He looked up and saw the thin blond ghost leaning back against the fiberglass wall.

"The number of EOs," said Eli, gesturing to the shelf, "it's sky-rocketed over the last decade. What if we did something? What if we tore something in the fabric of the world? What if we set something in motion?"

Victor rolled his eyes. "We are not gods, Eli."

"But we *played* God."

"What if *God* played God?" Victor pushed off the wall. "What if EOs were part of His plan? What if these people, the ones you've spent your life slaughtering, were *supposed* to come back the way they did? What if you've been attempting to undo the very work of that higher power you worship?"

"Don't you ever wonder if it's our fault?"

Victor tipped his head. "Tell me, is it blasphemy, or simply arrogance, taking credit for God's work?"

Eli shook his head. "You've never understood."

Footsteps sounded nearby.

The wall went clear.

"Who are you talking to?" asked Stell.

"Myself," muttered Eli, waving Victor's ghost away like a wisp of smoke. "I've been thinking more about that electrokinetic teen . . ." He looked up. Stell was dressed for fieldwork, his broad frame cinched into a reinforced black suit.

"How did the extraction go?" asked Eli, managing to keep most of the disdain out of his voice. He'd spent two weeks researching the EO—Helen Andreas, forty-one, with the ability to disassemble and rebuild structures with a single touch. Eli had given EON's agents as much insight as he could, considering the confines of his situation.

"Not well," said Stell darkly. "Andreas was dead when we got there."

Eli frowned. EOs, despite their destructive tendencies, rarely veered toward suicide. Their sense of self-preservation was too strong. "Was it an accident?"

"Not likely," said Stell, holding a photo up to the fiberglass. In it, Andreas lay on the ground, blood pooling beneath her and a small dark circle burrowed into her forehead.

"Interesting," said Eli. "Any leads?"

"No . . ." Stell hesitated. There was something he wasn't saying. Eli waited him out. After a long moment, the man finally went on. "This wasn't an isolated incident. Two months ago, another suspected EO was found in the same way, in the basement of a club." Stell slid both pages through the slot. "Will Connelly. We were still monitoring him, since we didn't have enough data to construe the exact nature of his ability and assess his priority level, but we had suspected it was regenerative. Obviously not a power as efficient as your own, but something like it. At the time we assumed his death was a one-off, a run-in with the wrong people, someone to whom he owed a debt. Now . . ."

"Once is chance, twice, coincidence," said Eli. "Collect a third, and you have a pattern." He looked up from the paper. "The weapon?"

"Unregistered."

"Keep the ballistics on file anyway. If he—or she—is actively hunting EOs, it's only a matter of time before they strike again. In fact," continued Eli, "pull every killing that matches this style of execution over the last . . ."—Eli considered—"three years."

"Three? That's an oddly specific number."

And it was. Three years—that was how long Eli had been at EON. That was how long he'd been out of work. If there had been another hunter during his tenure, he would have known.

Which meant someone new had taken his place.

XX

SIXTEEN YEARS AGO

LOCKLAND UNIVERSITY

ELI arrived at Lockland nearly a week before the start of the spring semester.

He hadn't picked just *any* school—if Charlotte's father was picking up the tab, Eli intended to stretch the bill. Lockland was one of the best-ranked programs in the country. Now, he crossed the intimate campus, savoring the quiet stretches of lawn. It was a solid week before classes were due to start, and the place was luxuriously empty.

But his heart sank when he reached the dorms. He'd been hoping for a solo suite. Instead, he found a different setup: two desks, two beds, one window halfway between them. One of the beds was empty. On the other, a lean figure had stretched out, one arm behind his head, the other holding up a book.

At the sound of Eli's approach, the book fell away, revealing a slim face, wolfish blue eyes, and lank blond hair.

"You must be Eliot."

"Eli," he corrected, setting his backpack on the floor.

The other boy swung his legs off the bed and stood. He was an inch or two taller than Eli, but all angles, edges.

"Victor," he said, slipping his hands into his pockets. "Vale."

Eli cracked a smile. "Name like that, you should be a superhero."

Victor gestured down at himself. He was dressed in black jeans and a black polo. "Can you really see me in spandex?" The blue eyes flicked toward Eli's single suitcase, the box balanced on top. "You travel light."

Eli nodded at Victor's own side of the room. "You came early."

Victor shrugged. "Family is best in small doses."

Eli wasn't sure how to answer that, so he said nothing. The silence stretched between them, and then Victor cocked his head in a lupine way and said, "Are you hungry?"

VICTOR speared another piece of broccoli.

"So, what are you studying?"

They were sitting in a large dining hall on campus, the restaurant stations along the wall each a capsule of a food culture.

"Pre-med," answered Eli.

"You too?" Victor stabbed a strip of beef. "And what brings you to the discipline?" His eyes flicked up and Eli felt . . . exposed. It was unsettling, the way that pale gaze bored into him. Not curious so much as cutting.

Eli looked down at his own food. "Same as most," he said. "I guess I felt a calling. You?"

"It seemed like an obvious fit," said Victor. "I've always been good at math and science, anything that can be distilled down into equations, cause and effect, absolutes."

Eli twirled pasta on his fork. "But medicine doesn't adhere to absolutes. Life isn't an equation. A person is more than the sum of their parts."

"Are they?" asked Victor. His expression was steady, his voice flat.

It was maddening—Eli was so used to disarming people, coaxing them into feeding him emotional cues, giving him something to play against.

But Victor showed no interest in playing.

"Of course," pressed Eli. "The parts themselves—muscle, organ, bone, blood—make a *body,* not a person. Without a divine spark, without a soul, they are only so much meat."

Victor clicked his tongue in disapproval. "You're religious, then."

"I believe in God," said Eli steadily.

"Well," said Victor, nudging away his plate. "You can live in the heavens. I'll take the earthly sphere."

A girl appeared, dropping into the seat beside Victor. "What have we here?" She mussed his fair hair with an ease clearly born of habit. Interesting. Victor didn't strike Eli as the type to welcome casual contact, but he didn't pull away, only favored her with a bored smile.

"Angie," said Victor, "meet Eli."

She flashed him a smile, and Eli felt like a mirror turned toward the sun, relieved to have a source of light he could reflect.

"We were just discussing God's place in medicine," said Victor. "Care to weigh in?"

"I'll pass." She plucked a piece of broccoli from his plate.

"It's rude to steal food."

"You never finish anything. Didn't your parents teach you to eat your vegetables?"

"No," said Victor blandly, "they told me to tap into my inner psyche and realize the truths of my potential. Vegetables never really came up."

Angie shot Eli a conspiratorial glance. "Victor's parents are self-help gurus."

"Victor's parents," said Victor, "are hacks."

Angie laughed, a small, affectionate sound. "You're such a weirdo sometimes."

"Only sometimes?" asked Victor. "I'll have to try harder." Those blue eyes flicked to Eli. "Normal is overrated."

Eli tensed—a small, inward clenching that didn't reach his face. *Normal is overrated.* Spoken like someone who didn't have to work so hard at it. Who hadn't needed *normal* to survive.

Victor cleared his throat. "Angie here is the brightest light in our engineering department."

She rolled her eyes. "Victor's too proud to fish for praise, but he's top of the pre-med class."

"But you haven't heard," said Victor soberly. "Eli here is going to give me a run for my money."

Angie eyed him with newfound interest. "Is that so?"

Eli smiled. "I'll do my best."

XXI

TWO YEARS AGO

EON

"**YOU** were right," said Stell.

Eli rose from his cot. "Don't sound so disappointed."

"We pulled the execution-style killings, then ran those deaths through our system to see if any of them had EO markers." Stell fed a piece of paper through the slot in the wall. "Meet Justin Gladwell."

Eli took it, staring down at the sparsely detailed profile, the mug shot of a man in his thirties with a two-day-old shadow. "Gunned down nearly a year ago. Abilities unknown. He wasn't even on our radar."

"They're outpacing you," said Eli, spreading the three profiles on his table. Justin Gladwell. Will Connelly. Helen Andreas. "Congratulations. You appear to have a new hunter."

"And you," said Stell, "appear to have a copycat."

Eli bristled a little. He didn't care for the idea of a surrogate. "No," he said, considering the series of corpses. "I would have tailored their deaths to suit. Would have made it look . . . organic. This person . . ."—he rapped his fingers on the table—"is preoccupied by something else."

"What do you mean?"

"I mean," said Eli, "that the killer clearly sees the executions as necessary, but I doubt it's their sole objective."

"We need to find this person as soon as possible," said Stell.

"You want me to hunt a hunter."

Stell raised a brow. "Is that going to be a problem?"

"On the contrary," said Eli. "I've been waiting for a challenge." He crossed his arms, studying the pictures. "One thing's almost certain."

"What's that?"

"Your hunter is an EO."

Stell stiffened. "How do you know?"

"Well, I don't *know*," said Eli. "I can only hypothesize. But what are the odds of an ordinary human successfully executing three distinct EOs without the slightest signs of resistance?" Eli held Gladwell's photograph up to the fiberglass. "A single, consistently positioned, point-blank headshot, in all three cases. A level of accuracy that means one of two things—either the shooter is an expert marksman, or the victims didn't put up a fight. Blood spray suggests they were conscious and upright when they were shot. Which means they simply stood there. Do you know many *ordinary* people who could convince or compel a person to go so willingly to their death?"

Eli didn't wait for an answer. He shook his head, studying the pictures, his thoughts turning. One week. Two months. Nine months.

"These killings are far apart," he mused. "Which suggests that either your hunter isn't very good at finding EOs, *or* they're not looking for *all* EOs."

"You think they're targeting specific people?"

"Or specific abilities," said Eli.

"Any ideas?"

Eli steepled his fingers.

Determining an EO's abilities postmortem was an impossible task. Abilities were hyperspecific, informed not only by the way in which the EO died, but also by their reason for wanting to live. He could speculate—but Eli hated speculating. It was dangerous, and inefficient. Educated guesswork was still guesswork, not a substitute for firsthand experience. Paper clues could only tell you so much—look at Sydney and Serena Clarke. The same near-death experience—a deep plunge in a frozen lake—resulting in two wildly disparate abilities. People were individual. Their psychology was specific. The trick, then, was to aim for vague shapes. Focus only on the outlines, the broadest conditions, and collect enough of those that he could find the pattern, the picture.

"Give me everything you can on these three," he said, sweeping his hand over the photos. "They may be dead, but that doesn't mean they don't still have secrets to tell."

Eli pointed at a box by Stell's feet. "What are those?"

Stell nudged it with his shoe. "These," he said, "are all the execution-style killings that fit the hunter's MO, but *not* the EO profile."

Humans. Of course. He hadn't considered that the hunter's scope might go beyond EOs. But that was because his own hadn't. What a careless assumption. "Can I see them?"

The box was too big for the fiberglass cubby, so Stell had to feed the papers through, a handful at a time. "What are you thinking?" Stell asked as Eli set the ream of paper on the table.

The dots floated in his mind, shifting as he tried to find the lines between them. "There's a pattern here," said Eli. "I haven't found it yet, but I will."

XXII

"TO see a world in a grain of sand . . ."

Thunder rumbled in the distance, the clouds flushing blue. It was the start of senior year, and after unpacking, they'd gone up on the roof to watch the storm roll in.

". . . and Heaven in a wildflower," continued Eli.

He lifted his palm until it seemed to rest just beneath the lightning.

"Hold infinity in the palm of your hand . . ."

"Honestly, Eli," said Victor, perching on one of the folding chairs that scattered the makeshift patio, "spare me the scripture."

Eli's hand fell away. "It's not the Bible," he said testily. "It's Blake. Get some culture." He swept the bottle of scotch away from Victor. "And the point holds. There is no harm in seeing a creator behind the creation."

"There is when you purport to study *science*."

Eli shook his head. Victor didn't understand—would never understand—that it wasn't a matter of faith *or* science. The two were inextricable.

Eli took a cautious sip from the stolen bottle and sank into a second chair as the storm crept closer. It was their first night back, the first night in their new shared apartment. Victor had spent his summer avoiding his parents on some remote family vacation while getting a head start on organic chemistry. Eli had spent his at Lockland, interning under Professor Lyne. He cut a sideways glance at his friend, who was sitting forward, elbows on his knees, his attention seemingly transfixed on the distant lightning.

Initially, Victor had presented a dilemma. Eli Cardale's persona, so carefully constructed over the last decade, found little audience with his sober new roommate. There was no need for a steady smile, affability, the practiced ease. There was no point to them, not when Victor seemed so utterly disinterested. No, *disinterested* was the wrong word—Victor's attention was constant, acute—but the more charming Eli tried to be, the less Victor responded to it. In fact, he seemed *annoyed* by the effort. As if Victor knew it was just that. An effort. A show. Eli found himself culling the unnecessary trappings, trimming his persona down to the essentials.

And when he did that, Victor warmed.

Turned toward Eli like a face toward a mirror. Like to like. It frightened and thrilled Eli, to be seen, and to see himself reflected. Not *all* of himself—they were still so different—but there was something vital, a core of the same precious metal glinting through the rock.

Lightning flashed arterial lines of blue over the rooftop, and seconds later, the world around them shook with a concussive force. Eli felt the tremor through his bones. He loved storms—they made him feel small, a single stitch in a vast pattern, a drop of water in a downpour.

Moments later, the rain began to fall.

In seconds, the first drops became a downpour.

"Shit," muttered Victor, springing up from his seat.

He jogged toward the roof door.

Eli rose, but didn't follow. Within seconds he was soaked through.

"You coming?" shouted Victor over the rain.

"You go ahead," said Eli, the downpour erasing his voice. He tipped his head back and let himself be swallowed by the storm.

An hour later, Eli padded barefoot across the apartment, dripping rainwater in his wake.

Victor's door was closed, the lights out.

After reaching his room, Eli peeled off his soaked clothes and sank into his chair as the storm faded beyond the windows.

Two in the morning, classes starting the next day, but sleep still eluded him.

His cell phone sat on the desk, a handful of texts from Angie, but Eli wasn't in the mood for that, and anyhow, she was probably asleep by now. He ran a hand through his damp hair, slicking it back, and tapped his computer awake.

Something stuck with him, from the roof. The image of the lightning in his palm. Eli had spent the better part of the summer studying electromagnetism in the human body. The literal and metaphorical spark of life. Now, drifting in that exhausted early-hours space, the darkened room and the artificial light of the laptop keeping him conscious if not fully awake, his fingers slid over the keyboard, and he began to search.

For what, he wasn't exactly sure.

One screen, one page, one site, gave way to another, Eli's attention wandering between articles and essays and forums like a mind lost in a dream. But Eli wasn't lost. He was just trying to find the thread. He'd encountered a theory, some weeks before, on another insomniac night. Over the last month, it had grown roots, fed on his focus.

Eli still didn't know what made him click that first link. Victor would have blamed idle curiosity, or fatigue, but in Eli's trancelike state it felt eerily familiar. A hand resting over his own. A blessing. A push.

The theory Eli had discovered was this: that sudden, extreme trauma could lead to a cataclysmic, even permanent shift in physical nature and ability. That through life-or-death trauma, people could be rewired, remade.

It was pseudoscience at best.

But pseudoscience wasn't *automatically* wrong. It was simply a theory that hadn't been adequately proven. What if it could be? After all, people in duress did extraordinary things. Claimed feats of strength, moments of heightened ability. Was the leap so extreme? Could something happen in that life-or-death moment, that tunnel between darkness and light? Was it madness, to believe? Or arrogance, to not?

The page loaded, and Eli's heart quickened as he stared at the word across the top of the screen.

ExtraOrdinary.

XXIII

ONE AND A HALF YEARS AGO

ELI knelt on the cell floor, a dozen pages spread before him. He'd narrowed the massive stack of killings to thirty. And then twenty. And now, at last, to six.

Malcolm Jones. Theodore Goslin. Ian Hausbender. Amy Tao. Alice Clayton. Ethan Barrymore.

Three drug dealers, two doctors, and a pharmacist.

He slipped the first three pages through the slot. "Run the ballistics in these against your executed EOs."

Stell turned through the papers. "There are a hundred gang and cartel killings in this pile. Why these three?"

"A magician doesn't reveal his secrets," said Eli blandly.

"And you're not a magician—you're a murderer."

Eli sighed. "How could I forget?" He nodded at the massive stack from which he'd culled the six names. "There are a hundred and seven gang and cartel killings in there, to be exact. Eighty-three of which we can rule out because they don't fit the clean point-blank execution model I requested. Of the remaining twenty-four, fourteen had records for specializing in illegal weapons, ten in pharmaceuticals. Given the fact that your target has used the same gun for each and every execution, I decided to assume this wasn't about acquiring weapons. We can narrow the list down even further because Jones's, Goslin's, and Hausbender's executions all involved other victims, which, in addition to furthering my theory that the man you're looking for is using a supernatural method of compulsion on his victims, negates the need for multiple samples from each scene, rendering three out of the original ten."

"You're sure it's a man?"

"I'm not *sure* of anything," said Eli, "but the odds favor a male killer. Female killers are rarer, and they tend to prefer more hands-on methods."

"And you think he's after drug dealers?" asked Stell.

Eli shook his head. "I think he's after *drugs*." He retrieved the other three profiles from the floor. "My theory is that your killer is either an addict, or very sick. Which brings me to these. Amy Tao, Alice Clayton, and Ethan Barrymore. The first two are doctors, the third is a pharmacist."

Stell paced beyond the fiberglass wall. "And the dead EOs? How do they factor in?"

"I stand by my theory that our hunter was—and probably still is—targeting specific abilities. Andreas's was destructive, but also re-storative. Connelly's regenerative."

"Which supports your theory that he's sick."

There was, thought Eli, a grudging respect in Stell's voice.

"It's still only a theory," he demurred. "Let's start by confirming the ballistics."

THE results came back two days later.

Alice Clayton and Malcolm Jones.

A doctor and a drug dealer, added to the tally of three dead EOs.

Eli's picture was growing. But it was still missing something.

He kept coming back to the gun.

Their hunter was methodical, precise—he had to know that vary-ing the style of execution would have helped cover the trail. And yet he'd chosen to maintain a single technique. There were reasons people adhered to such a pattern—sometimes it was a signature, other times a matter of comfort, or precision, but in this case Eli had a feeling that the killer didn't want to get their hands dirty. Shooting was cold, efficient, and distant. But it was also clean. Sterile. It could be done at a distance, with no risk of biological data at the scene. The killer's choice of weapon, despite the drawbacks of pattern, suggested they cared more about maintaining their own anonymity than hiding the trail of bodies. Which in turn suggested that the killer's DNA was already in the system.

An EO who was known to authorities.

Eli's pulse quickened as pieces clicked together in the back of his mind.

It was madness. Irrational. Impulsive. But Eli felt again that gentle pressure at his back, guiding him forward as he booted the computer and started searching for strange or sudden deaths in the practicing medical field.

Eli spent the next forty-eight sleepless hours skimming every database and obit and news story. He knew he was making leaps instead of strides, but the ground was smooth and sloped beneath his feet. So instead of catching himself, Eli let gravity do the work.

And then, finally, he found an obituary for Dr. Adam Porter. A leading neurologist, discovered dead after hours at a private practice. It had been a heart attack, according to the coroner's report, but not at his desk, or on the way to his car, or safely at home. No, the body had been found on the hospital linoleum floor, next to a smoking MRI, its power blown.

A freak accident.

A massive current.

The patient records from that night were missing, a neat hole carved out in a busy schedule, but Eli could read the outline by the edges it left behind.

He knew the shape.

He'd seen it before.

Angie's body, twisted on the floor of the lab at Lockland, her back arched, mouth open, the last seconds of her life immortalized by pain.

A heart attack, they'd said.

A freak accident.

A massive current.

And at the center of both, an EO with the skill to hunt, the ability to manipulate his victim's bodies. Someone already in the system—because they were supposed to be dead.

"I killed you," muttered Eli.

Victor appeared again, as if summoned. Cold blue eyes and a cunning smirk. "You did."

"Then how?"

"Do you really need to ask?"

Eli clenched his teeth.

Sydney Clarke.

Serena had insisted on dispatching her little sister herself. Obviously her resolve had wavered. Sydney was still alive.

The girl who had a nasty habit of bringing people *back*. And of bringing EOs back wrong, too. Eli had seen it for himself when Sydney resurrected one of his prior kills, sent him back like a toy on the fritz, a note from Victor in hand.

I made a friend.

Now Eli got to his feet and looked up into the nearest camera. "Stell?" he asked, first quietly, and then louder.

A cool voice responded via the intercom. "The director is unavailable."

"When will he be back?" he demanded, but the voice didn't answer.

Eli bristled. He needed to see Stell, needed to look him in the eyes, ask him how he could be so stupid, ask him why he didn't burn the body.

He looked around for something to use, some way to get the director's attention.

But everything was bolted down. Except, of course, for him. He slammed his fist into the fiberglass wall.

There was a low tone as the walls began to charge.

"Inmate," ordered the disembodied voice. "Stand down."

Eli did not. He hit the fiberglass a second time. An alarm went off, and an instant later, a burst of electricity shot up Eli's arm and sent him staggering backward, his pulse losing rhythm for a single measure before it settled. He started toward the wall a third time, but before his fist connected, the lights cut out, and Eli was plunged into absolute black.

The sensory deprivation was so sudden, the darkness was so absolute, Eli felt like he was falling. He reached out to brace himself and stumbled, searched several seconds for the metal chair before sinking into it to wait.

Why didn't you burn the body?

Why didn't you . . .

But as Eli sat in the dark, playing the question over and over in his mind, he felt that invisible hand, the one that had been a guide for so long, now pulling him back. If Eli gave Victor over to Stell, over to EON, they would take him *alive*. Put him in a cell. No. Eli would not—could not—allow those half measures. Victor was too dangerous, he had to be put down, and Stell had already failed once.

Eli wouldn't entrust the task to him a second time.

The lights came up, the far wall went clear, and the director stormed into sight, dressed in a tailored black suit, his tie loose at the throat.

"What the hell?" demanded Stell. "You better have something groundbreaking after that stunt."

Eli faltered for only a second, then straightened, committed to his course.

"Actually," he said coldly. "I hit a *dead end.*"

It wasn't a lie.

Suspicion flickered across Stell's face. "That's surprising, given how you've spent the last week. You seemed to be making strides."

Eli swore inwardly. He'd been so stunned by the discovery, so eager for the confrontation, and so startled by his own recanting, he hadn't considered the ramifications of changing his mind. The whiplash. A break in the pattern.

"Where did it fall apart?" pressed Stell.

"It hasn't," said Eli. "I just don't have any more leads."

"Then why the *fuck* did you call for me?" demanded the director.

Eli had made a mistake. He wasn't prone to making mistakes, except where Victor Vale was concerned. Victor had always possessed the unnerving ability to get under Eli's skin, interrupt his focus. And now Eli needed to disrupt Stell's own, find a way to redirect his attention, twist suspicion into . . . something easier. Anger—that was such a loud emotion.

"I guess," said Eli, infusing his voice with as much derision as he could muster, "I wanted to see what you would do. Now I know."

Stell looked at him, mouth open in surprise. And then, predictably, it crumpled into fury. "Do you *want* me to send you back to the lab?"

"That threat is beginning to feel stale."

Stell drew back, as if struck. "Is it?" he said darkly. "Allow me to refresh your memory."

Eli tensed as Stell raised his wristwatch to his mouth and spoke into a hidden comm, the words too low for him to hear.

"Wait," started Eli, his voice cut off by a metallic scrape overhead. Four small sprinklers emerged from the ceiling at the front of the cell. Icy water rained down, soaking Eli through in seconds.

He started to back up, but Stell's voice made him stop.

"Don't you dare retreat."

Eli held his ground. "Fine." He looked down at his hands, then up at Stell. "I won't melt."

"I know," said the director grimly.

Eli barely heard the hum over the sound of the water. He realized too late what was happening, managed just a step toward the fiberglass before the current hit him.

It was everywhere. Tearing up his legs, arcing through his chest, lighting every nerve. Eli buckled to his hands and knees as the electricity tore through him, conducted through the water. Enough volts to level a small beast, but Eli's own regeneration kept him conscious, caught in a suspended state of electrocution.

His jaw locked, a low, animal sound tearing between his teeth.

Stell turned and stormed away, his hand lifting in an almost dismissive motion. The wall went solid, white, and several terrible lurching seconds later, the current finally died. Eli collapsed to his side on the slick floor as the sprinklers slowed, and stopped.

He rolled onto his back, chest heaving.

And then, slowly, Eli got up, and crossed to the desk, sinking into the chair before the computer. Since the system was twinned with Stell's, the director would be able to pull up everything, be able to read the lines, if not the space between them.

Eli began to query other deaths, other causes, other leads. He couldn't bury the search that led him to Adam Porter, that missing link, but he could keep Stell from following the clean pattern of Eli's own thoughts. With every subsequent search, Eli frayed the thread, ventured down a course he'd earlier abandoned. Hopefully it would read as frustration with his own failure, a furious need to find the truth.

But as his fingers flew over the keyboard, creating a tangled web of false leads and dead ends, his own thoughts coalesced into a single, smooth train.

Eli would save Victor for himself.

XXIV

ELI had spent the better part of an hour listening to Stell talk about his new target. Marcella Renee Riggins, mob wife turned murderess. He flipped through the pages in the file as the director spoke, setting aside the newspaper clipping and the EON-issued backstory, focusing instead on the crime scene stills from the hospital—the bed with its rusted bar, its ruined sheets, and the much more striking hole in the hospital room wall.

"... nearly died in a fire, seems to be burning everything—and everyone—she can get her hands on—"

"She's not burning them," said Eli, skimming the photos.

"The piles of ash beg to differ."

Eli traced a finger along the hole in the wall, then flipped to the crime scene close-up of the debris on the kitchen floor.

He rose and pressed the photo against the fiberglass. "Do you see that? The edges of the diamond?"

Stell squinted. "It looks dirty. Which would make sense, considering it's sitting in a pile of human remains."

"It's not dirty," said Eli. "It's graphite."

"I don't follow."

Obviously. "Marcella isn't burning things. She's *eroding* them. If she'd been using heat, you might have been able to combat it with extreme cold. But with a corrosive ability like this, you're better off killing her."

Stell crossed his arms. "Is that the only advice you have to offer?"

"In this case, it's certainly the *best,*" said Eli. He had seen power like Marcella's before. Raw, destructive, boundless. There was no place for power like that in this world. She would carve a swathe of chaos, until she was put down. "Do you know the half-life of carbon?"

"Off the top of my head?" asked Stell.

"It's nearly six thousand years. How long do you think it took her to kill the person wearing that diamond? How long do you think it will take her to penetrate whatever armor your men are wearing?"

"It won't be the first time our agents have gone up against someone with a touch-based ability."

"And assuming you capture her, do you even have a cell capable of containing someone with these powers?"

"Every power has its limits."

"Just listen—"

"I don't need to," cut in Stell. "Your philosophy is hardly a mystery at this point, Eli. If it were up to you, EON would never salvage anyone."

"It's in part *because* of me that you have salvaged the last twenty-two EOs. So listen when I tell you that someone this powerful belongs in the ground."

"You know the policy."

"I know you want to believe that all EOs are worth saving, but we aren't."

"We don't decide who lives and who dies," said Stell tersely. "We don't condemn EOs without confrontation."

"Now who's letting their ideals cloud their judgment?"

"Marcella will be offered the same opportunity as every other EO we engage—to come willingly. If she refuses, and the on-site team is unable to safely—"

"*Safely?*" snarled Eli. "This woman can reduce people to ash with a single touch. She can decay metal and stone. Do you value an EO's life above a human's? Because you are sending your agents on a suicide mission to sate your pride—"

"Stand down," said Stell.

Eli exhaled through clenched teeth. "If you don't kill her now, you'll wish you had."

Stell turned to go. "If you have no other suggestions—"

"Send me."

Stell glanced back, raising a thick brow. "What was that?"

"You want other options? Ones that won't get innocent humans killed?" Eli spread his arms. "Our abilities are complementary. She ruins. I regenerate. There's a cosmic elegance to it, don't you think?"

"And what if her power is faster?" asked Stell.

Eli's arms fell back to his sides. "Then I die," he said simply.

Once upon a time he had believed he survived because God willed it. That Eli was unbreakable because He had a purpose for him. These days, Eli didn't know what he believed, but he still hoped, fervently, desperately, that there was a reason for it.

Stell smiled grimly. "I appreciate the offer, Mr. Cardale. But I'm not letting you go that easily."

The wall went solid, swallowing the director from sight. Eli sighed, and crossed to his bed. He sank down onto his cot, elbows on his knees, fingers laced, head bowed. As if in prayer.

Eli hadn't expected Stell to say yes, of course.

But he had planted the seed. Had seen it take root behind Stell's eyes.

Now he simply had to wait for it to grow.

XXV

FOUR YEARS AGO

EON——LABORATORY WING

THOMAS Haverty was a man of vision.

So he wasn't at all surprised when Stell stripped him of his post at EON. Wasn't surprised when security escorted him from the lab, took his access card, his files, his crisp white coat. So many men of genius were stymied by short-sighted fools. Scientists condemned before they were lauded. Gods crucified before they were worshipped.

"This way, Mr. Haverty," said a soldier in a black suit.

"*Doctor,*" he corrected as he stepped through the scanner, spread his arms, and let them search his clothes, his skin, his skeleton, all to make sure he hadn't stolen anything from the lab. As if Haverty would do something so obvious, so stupid.

They escorted him all the way to the parking lot, and proceeded to search his car, too, before returning his keys and signaling the security post to let him out. The gates slid closed behind him with grim finality.

Haverty drove the twenty-four miles back to the outer edge of Merit, to a small apartment on the southern side of the city. He let himself in, set the keys in their designated tray, peeled off his coat and shoes, and rolled up his sleeves.

A few stray flecks of Mr. Cardale's blood still stained the inside of his wrist, beyond the protection of his latex gloves. Haverty considered the dots for a moment, the strange pattern like a smattering of stars, a constellation waiting to be discovered.

He held his wrist out and went to his office. A windowless room, sterile and white and lined with refrigerated shelves of samples, vials of blood, small glass jars containing a dozen different drugs, folder after folder of hand-copied notes.

No, Haverty hadn't been foolish enough to steal from EON on his way out. Instead, he'd done it every day. Stolen his research one piece at a time. A single sample. A slide. An ampule. Each token small enough to be claimed an accident, if he'd been caught. A slip of the mind. Patience really was the highest virtue. And progress was a thing achieved one halting step at a time.

Every night—or morning—when he'd returned home, Haverty had taken up a notepad and reprinted word for word the notes he'd made in the sanctum of the EON compound.

Men ahead of their time were always, by definition, outside of it.

Haverty was no different. Stell couldn't see—EON couldn't see—but *he* knew that the ends would justify the means. He would show them. He would crack the ExtraOrdinary code, and change the face of science, and they would welcome him back. They would worship him.

He crossed the lab and drew a small glass slide from a top drawer, along with a scalpel, delicately scraping flecks of Eliot Cardale's brown-red blood onto the surface.

He had so much work to do.

XXVI

FOUR WEEKS AGO

SOUTHERN MERIT

NICK Folsetti sank onto the bench beside the block of lockers and began unwinding the tape from his hands. He ran his tongue along his inside cheek—he could still taste the tang of blood where his opponent had landed a punch.

The last of the tape came free, and Nick flexed, watching the skin on his knuckles tighten, harden to something like stone. It *wasn't* stone, of course, or anything else. It was more like all the softness went out of him. All the weakness erased. He flexed again, his fingers gaining a sudden flush of color as they softened back into flesh and bone.

Nick could only harden himself in pieces—hands, ribs, shins, jaw—and even then, it was a conscious thing.

But it was a hell of a thing.

He'd heard the whispers, of the soldiers who came looking for people like him. Had gone down the online rabbit hole, dug up everything he could on ExtraOrdinaries in those first few days before he realized that was probably a giant red flag and switched to incognito searches on public computers.

EON—that's what they were called. He kept picturing them like the people on TV shows, the ones who believed in ghosts or monsters or aliens. Nick had never been gullible, he didn't *really* think they existed, these hunters.

But then again, up until six months ago, when Nick, fresh out of the hospital, put his hand through a wall, and the *wall* was the only thing that broke, he hadn't believed in people like him either.

The bookie, Tavish, whistled from the doorway, a fresh toothpick between his teeth.

"For a guy your size, you sure can throw a punch." His chin bobbed toward the hall, the room, the ring. "Bigger stages than this, you know."

"You want me gone?" asked Nick.

"I didn't say that," said Tavish, shifting the toothpick in his mouth. "Just saying, you ever looking to go big, I could help you . . . for a cut."

"I'm not looking for more attention," said Nick. "Just cash."

"Suit yourself." The envelope arced through the air, landing on the bench beside him. It wasn't all that thick, but it was untraceable, and more than enough to get by until the next fight. Which was all Nick needed.

"See you in three nights," said Tavish, disappearing down the hall.

Nick thumbed through the cash, then tucked it in his coat and headed out.

The alley light above the door was on the fritz again, the alley a tangle of shadows, the kind that played tricks on your eyes this late at night.

Nick lit a cigarette, the red tip dancing before him in the dark.

There was a rager going on in one of the nearby warehouses, the heavy pulse of the club's bass blanketing the streets. Nick couldn't hear his own heart over the beat, let alone the footsteps coming up behind him.

Didn't know someone was there until the sudden flash of pain pierced his side. It caught him off guard, and for a second Nick thought he'd been shot, but when he looked down he saw, jutting between his ribs, a short metal dart. An empty vial.

He rounded, dizzy, expecting to see a cop, or a thug, or even an EON soldier, but there was only a single man, short and balding, wearing round glasses and a white lab coat.

That was the last thing Nick saw before his vision blurred, and his legs buckled, and everything went dark.

NICK came to in a steel room—a shipping crate, or maybe a storage locker, he couldn't tell. His vision slid in and out of focus, his head pounding. Memory flickered back. The dart. The vial.

He tried to move, and felt the pull of restraints around his wrists and ankles, the rustle of plastic sheeting beneath his head.

Nick flexed, hardening his wrists, but it was no use. Solidity wasn't the same as strength. The bonds had just enough give. They didn't snap. He fought, then, thrashing against the table, until someone clicked their tongue.

"How quickly we devolve," said a voice behind his head. "People become animals the moment they are caged."

Nick twisted, craning until he caught the edge of a white coat.

"I apologize for the state of my lab," said the voice. "It's not ideal, I know, but science doesn't bow to aesthetics."

"Who the fuck *are* you?" demanded Nick, twisting desperately against the restraints.

The white coat approached the table, and became a man. Thin. Balding. With round glasses and deep-set eyes the color of slate.

"My name," said the man, adjusting latex gloves, "is Dr. Haverty."

Something glinted in his hand, thin and silver and sharp. A scalpel. "I promise, what's about to happen is in the interest of progress."

The man leaned in, bringing his blade to rest above Nick's left eye. The point came into perfect focus, close enough to brush his lashes, while the doctor slid into a blur of white beyond.

Nick gritted his teeth, and tried to retreat, out of the scalpel's path, but there was nowhere to go, so instead he forced all his focus into hardening his left eye. The scalpel came to rest against it with the plink of metal on ice.

The blur of the doctor's face parted into a smile. "Fascinating."

The scalpel vanished, and the doctor retreated from view. Nick heard the scrape and shuffle of tools, and then Haverty reappeared, holding a syringe, its contents a vivid, viscous blue.

"What do you want?" pleaded Nick as the needle disappeared from sight.

Seconds later, a pain pierced the base of his skull. Cold began to flood his limbs.

"What do I want?" echoed Haverty, as Nick shivered, shuddered, spasmed. "What all men of science want. To learn."

3

ASCENSION

I

THREE WEEKS AGO

EON

"**WHAT** about you, Rush?"

Dominic blinked. He was sitting at a table on the upper level of the canteen, Holtz on one side and Bara on the other. After getting Dom the job, Holtz had stayed close, helped him fit in at EON. A cheerful blond kid—Dom couldn't help but think of him that way, even though Holtz was a year older—with a mischievous smile and a perpetually good mood, they'd served together, two tours, before Dom stepped on an IED and found himself retired. It was nice to have a shared shift break, Bara's presence notwithstanding.

Rios sat alone one table over, the way she always did, a book open beside her food. Every time a soldier passed too close, she shot them a look, and they retreated.

"What *about* me?" asked Dom.

"If you were an EO," said Bara around a mouthful of sandwich, "what would your power be?"

It was an innocuous question—inevitable, even, given the environment. But Dom's mouth still went dry. "I—don't know."

"Oh, come on," pressed Bara. "You can't tell me you haven't thought of it."

"I'd want X-ray vision," said Holtz. "Or the ability to fly. Or the ability to transform my car into other cars whenever I get bored."

Rios looked up from her own table. "Your mind," she said, "truly is a marvel."

Holtz beamed, as if it were a compliment.

"But," she continued, "if you bothered to read the eval files, you'd know that an EO's power is tethered to the method of their NDE and the state of their mind at the time of incident. So tell me," she said, turning in her chair, "what kind of accident gets you the power to change the model of your car?"

Holtz made a comical frown, as if genuinely trying to puzzle it out, but Bara was clearly bored.

"What about you, Rios?" he shot back. "What would *your* power be?"

She returned to her book. "I'd settle for the ability to create quiet."

Holtz let out a nervous laugh.

Dominic let his eyes slide over the group.

He hadn't expected it to get easier—hadn't *wanted* it to get easier—but it had. That was the thing, it was amazing what you could get used to, how quickly the strange became mundane, the extraordinary normal. After leaving the army, he'd missed the camaraderie, the common ground. Hell, he'd missed the uniforms, the orders, the sense of routine.

What Dominic could never get used to were EON's *cells*. Or rather, the people kept inside them.

The complex's crisp white walls had become familiar—the obscure maze reduced to clean lines of rote muscle memory—but there would never be anything comfortable about the purpose of this place. If Dom ever found himself forgetting the building's true design, all he had to do was look at the surveillance footage, click through the images of three dozen holding cells.

Now and then, when Dom drew rounds, he had walk those cells, deliver meals, listen to the EOs beyond the fiberglass beg for him to let them out. Sometimes, when he drew eval, he had to sit across from them—the prisoners in their cells and Dominic in his camouflage as human—and ask them about their lives, their deaths, their memories, their minds. He had to pretend he didn't understand what they meant when they talked about those final moments, the desperate thoughts that followed them down into the dark, the ones that pulled them back out.

Across the table, Holtz and Bara were still tossing around hypothetical powers, and Rios had gone back to her book, but Dominic stared down at his food, his appetite suddenly gone.

II

TWO YEARS AGO

DOMINIC'S APARTMENT

HE turned the business card over in his hands, waiting for Victor to call him back.

The black ink caught the light, illuminating the three letters.

EON.

Ten minutes later, the phone finally rang.

"Take the job."

Dominic froze. "You're not serious." But he could tell by the ensuing silence that Victor was. "These are the guys that hunt us. Capture us. Kill us. And you want me to *work for them?*"

"You have the background, the qualifications—"

"And if they peg me as an EO?"

A short, impatient sigh. "You have the ability to step outside of time, Dominic. If *you* can't avoid capture—"

"I can step out of time," said Dominic, "but I can't walk through walls. I can't open locks." Dom ran a hand through his hair. "With all due respect—"

"That saying usually precedes a no," said Victor coolly.

"What you're asking me to do—"

"I'm not asking."

Victor was a hundred miles away, but still Dominic flinched at the threat. He owed Victor everything, and they both knew it.

"All right."

Victor hung up, and Dom stared at the phone for a long time before he turned the card over, and dialed.

A black van came for him at dawn.

Dominic had been waiting on the curb, watched as a man in street clothes climbed out and opened the back doors. Dom forced himself forward. His steps were slow, a body operating against drag.

He didn't want to do this. Every self-preserving nerve in his body was saying no. He didn't know what Victor was thinking, or how many steps ahead he was thinking it. In Dom's head, Victor went around acting like the world was one big game of chess. Tapping people and saying, "You're a pawn, you're a knight, you're a rook."

Dom chafed a little at the thought, but then, he'd learned not to ask questions in the army. To trust the orders as they came down, knowing that he couldn't see the whole scope. War needed both kinds of people—those who played the long game and those who played the short one.

Victor was the former.

Dominic was the latter.

That didn't make him a pawn.

It made him a good soldier.

He willed his body toward the van. But before he could climb in, the man held out a ziplock bag. "Phone, watch, anything that transmits data and isn't hardwired to your body."

Dominic had been careful—there were only a handful of numbers in his phone, and none of them named; Victor was *boss man,* Mitch was *big man,* Syd was *tiny terror*—but he still felt a nervous prickle as the bag disappeared and he was ushered into the van.

It wasn't empty.

Four other people—three men and one woman—were already sitting inside, their backs against the windowless metal walls. Dom took a seat as the doors slammed and the van pulled away. No one spoke, but he could tell the others were military—or ex-military—by the set of their shoulders, their close-cropped or tightly wound hair, the steady blankness in their faces. One had a prosthetic arm—an elaborate piece of biotech from the elbow down—and Dom watched the man's mechanical fingers tap absently on his leg.

There was one more pickup—a young black woman—and then the ground changed under the tires, the world outside drowned out by the engine as the van gained speed.

Dom had spent half his career in convoys like this, being transported from one base to another.

One of the men went to check his watch before remembering it had been confiscated. Dominic didn't mind—he could wait.

TIME moved strangely for Dom.

Or at least, he moved strangely in time.

On paper he was only thirty-three, but he felt like he'd been alive for longer—and he guessed that, in a way, he had. Dom could step out of the flow of time, into the shadows, where the whole world became a painting in shades of gray, a dark between, a nowhere, where he was the only thing that moved.

Dom had never done the math, but he figured that he'd probably spent weeks—if not months—on the other side, the *out*side, his own timeline stretching out, losing shape.

Once, as an experiment, he had stepped into the shadows and stayed there, curious to know how long he could last out of time. It was like holding your breath, and at the same time it wasn't—there was oxygen in the space between, but there was also weight, pressure—a pressure that had nearly broken him before, when every step was pain. A pressure that now registered as drag, challenging, but by no means impermeable.

Since then, every morning and every night, Dominic spent time out of time. Sometimes he only moved around his apartment, and sometimes he went further afield, measuring the ground he could cover, instead of the seconds that passed.

AS the transport van slowed, Dom's attention was pulled back to the metal bench, the darkened hull, the other waiting bodies.

A few minutes later, it finally came to a stop. The doors opened, and they were ushered out onto smooth asphalt. Dominic squinted, disoriented by the sudden morning light. They were standing in front of a building that had to be EON.

From the outside, it looked . . . innocuous. Bland, even. There was a perimeter wall, but no barbed wire, no obvious gunner posts.

The group reached the front doors, which parted with the hiss of an airlock. The lobby—if you could call it a lobby—was sleek and open, but between the front doors and that space was a security port. One by one, the six were called forward by name and instructed to empty their pockets and step into the scanner.

Klinberg. Matthews. Linfield.

Dominic's pulse quickened.

Bara. Plinetti.

Victor had said they couldn't hold him, but he didn't *know* that, not for sure. These people, their entire job was capturing people like him. Surely their technology had been adapted to that task. What if they'd found a way to measure the difference between a human and EOs? What if they could detect people like him?

"Rusher," said an officer, ushering Dominic forward. He let out a low breath and stepped into the scan.

An error sound—a ringing alarm—echoed through the lobby.

Dom staggered backward out of the scan, braced for the walls to open and black-clad soldiers to come pouring in. He was ready to step out of the world and into the shadows, ready to forfeit his identity, his anonymity, the whole fucking thing, and face Victor's wrath—but the officer only rolled his eyes. "You got parts?"

"What?" asked Dominic, dazed.

"Metal. In your body. You got to specify that kind of thing before you go in."

The soldier briskly typed in a new set of commands. "Okay. Now go."

Dom forced himself to step back in, praying the scan couldn't pick up his panic.

"Hold still."

He felt like he was being Xeroxed. A bright band of white light tracked up and then back down his body.

"Step out."

Dominic did, fighting to stop the tremor from showing in his limbs.

One of the other guys—Bara—clamped a hand on his shoulder. "Jeez, man, how tight are you wound?"

Dom managed a nervous chuckle. "Not much for loud noises," he said. "Blame an IED."

"Bad luck, man." The grip loosened. "But they put you back together well."

Dom nodded. "Well enough."

They were led to a room with no chairs, nowhere to sit, no signs of comfort at all. Just bare walls, empty floor. The door swung shut behind them. And locked.

"You think it's a test?" asked one of the women—Plinetti—after thirty minutes.

"If so, it's a shit one," said Matthews, stretching out on the floor. "It'll take more than a white box to fuck with me."

Dom rocked on his heels, shoulders tipping back against the wall.

"Could use some coffee," said Bara with a yawn.

The last guy—Klinberg—spoke up. "Hey," he said in a mock whisper. "You ever seen one?"

"One what?" asked the other woman. Linfield.

"You know. What they keep here."

What, he'd said. Not *who*. Dom resisted the urge to correct him as the door swung open and a female soldier walked in. She was tall and lean, with warm brown skin and short black hair. Most of the recruits sprang to their feet—attention was a hard habit to break— but the guy on the ground rose slowly, almost lazily.

"I'm Agent Rios," said the soldier, "and I'll be leading you through today's orientation." She strode the length of the room. "Some of you are wondering what we do here. EON is separated into Containment, Observation, and Neutralization. Containment teams are dedicated to the location, pursuit, and capture of EOs. Observation of those EOs is stationed here at the base."

Klinberg raised his hand. "Which team gets to kill them?"

Dominic's chest tightened, but Rios's expression didn't falter. "Neutralization is a last resort, and its teams are built from those who've proven themselves in other departments. Safe to say, Klinberg, *you* won't be killing EOs any time soon. If that's a deterrent for you, let me know so I can address the remaining five candidates without your distraction."

Klinberg had the sense to shut up.

"Before we begin," continued Rios, "you're about to sign a nondisclosure agreement. If you break it, you will not be arrested. You will not be sued." She smiled grimly. "You will simply *disappear*."

A tablet was passed around, and one by one they pressed their thumbs against the screen. Once it was back in Rios's hands, the soldier continued speaking. "Most of you have heard the term *EO*. And most of you are probably skeptical. But the fastest way to disabuse you of doubt is through a demonstration."

The doors opened at her back.

"Follow me."

"KEEP your hands inside the ride," whispered Klinberg as they filed into the hall.

Remember this place, thought Dominic as he fell in line.

Remember everything. But it was a maze of white, sterile and uniform and disorienting. They passed through several sets of doors, each sealed, requiring a swipe from Agent Rios's key card.

"Hey," whispered Bara. "I heard they have that killer here. The one that offed, like, a hundred other EOs. You think it's true?"

Dom didn't answer. Was Eli really somewhere in this building?

Agent Rios tapped a comm on her shoulder. "Cell Eight, status?"

"*Irritable,*" answered the person on the other end.

A grim smile crossed her lips. "Perfect."

She swiped them through a final door, and Dominic felt his heart lurch. They were in a hangar, empty except for a freestanding cell in the center of the room. It was a cube made of fiberglass, and trapped inside, like a firefly in a jar, was a woman.

She knelt in the middle of the floor, wearing a kind of jumpsuit, its fabric glossy, as if coated.

"Tabitha," said Agent Rios, her voice even.

"Let me out."

The recruits moved around the cube, as if she were a piece of art, or a specimen, something to be considered from every side.

Matthews even rapped his knuckles on the glass, as if he were at a zoo. "Don't feed the animals," he muttered under his breath.

Dominic felt sick.

The prisoner rose to her feet. "Let me *out.*"

"Ask nicely," said Rios.

The prisoner was beginning to glow, the light coming from beneath her skin, a deep red-orange like heated metal. "*Let me out!*" she screamed, her voice crackling.

And then, she *ignited.*

Flame licked up her skin, engulfing her from head to toe, her hair standing up in a plume of blue-white light, like the tip of a match.

Several of the recruits recoiled. One covered his mouth. Others stared in fascination. Surprise. Fear.

Dominic feigned shock, but the fear was real. It crept through his limbs, a warning, that old gut feeling that said *wrong wrong*

wrong—just like it had the second before Dom's foot hit the IED, the instant before his world changed forever. A fear that had less to do with the woman on fire, and more to do with the cell holding her, the heat that didn't even penetrate the foot-thick fiberglass.

Rios hit a switch on the wall, and sprinklers went off inside the cell, followed by the sizzle of a doused fire. The cube filled with steam, and when the water cut off and the white smoke cleared, the prisoner sat in a heap on the floor of the cell, soaking wet and heaving for breath.

"All right," said Rios, "show-and-tell's over." She turned toward the recruits. "Any questions?"

THE black van was waiting at the end of the day.

All the way back to the city, the other recruits chatted, making small talk, but Dom closed his eyes and focused on his breathing.

The "demonstration" had been followed by an interview, an explanation of training protocol, a psych eval, each procedure executed in a way so grounded, so ordinary, that they'd been clearly designed to make candidates forget the strangeness of EON's purpose.

But Dominic *couldn't* forget. He was still shaken from the sight of the woman on fire, and certain that he'd never get out with his secret intact, so he was surprised—and suspicious—when, at the end of it all, Rios told him to report back the next day for further training.

Dom closed his eyes as the van sped on. One by one it stopped and the others were deposited outside their homes. One by one, until he was the only one left, and as the van doors slammed shut on him, and him alone, Dom was gripped anew by panic. He was sure that he could feel freeway moving beneath the tires, sure that they were taking him back to EON, to his own fiberglass cube.

"Rusher."

Dominic looked up and realized that the van was idling, the back doors open, his apartment building visible beyond in the dusky light. The soldier handed Dom the ziplock bag containing his phone, and Dom got out, but as he climbed the steps and went inside, he couldn't shake the feeling he was being watched.

There, on the street, an unfamiliar car. He switched the TV on, returned to the window—it was still there, idling. Dom changed into workout clothes, took a deep breath, and slipped out of time.

The world went silent, and heavy, and gray, all the sound and movement leached out of the room. Dom made his way to the front door, fighting against the drag of frozen time.

Back when every step was pain, Dom couldn't bear to spend more than a few moments in this heavy, dark place. But after months of training, his limbs and lungs moved steadily—if not easily— against the resistance.

He descended the stairs, his steps soundless when earlier they had echoed. Through the front doors and onto the curb. Dom paused beside the unfamiliar car and bent to examine the figure in the driver's seat, a cell half raised to their ear. The man had the look of ex-mil, and the file on the seat beside him was printed with Dominic's name.

He looked back and up at his apartment, the glow of the TV a splash of light against the curtains. Then he turned and walked two blocks to the nearest subway. Halfway down the stairs, he stepped back out of the shadows and into the world, into light and color and time, and vanished into the evening commute.

"THEY'RE watching my place," he said when Victor answered the phone.

He was jogging through a small park, his breath coming in short, even beats.

"I'd expect as much," said Victor, unfazed.

Dom slowed to a walk. "Why am I doing this?"

"Because ignorance is only bliss if you want to get caught."

With that, Victor hung up.

Dominic returned to EON the next day, via the black van, to find the initial group of six reduced to five. No Klinberg. By the third day, Matthews was gone too. Rios led them through exercises, drills, tests, and Dom did exactly as he was told. Tried to keep his head down and his expression blank. And still he expected to be cut.

Wanted to be cut.

He was heading back to the van on the third day when he was stopped by Rios.

"Director Stell would like a word."

Dominic stiffened. He'd never met the man, but he knew Stell's reputation. Knew he was the detective who sent Victor to prison back in college. The man who tracked Eli to Merit. And, of course, the man who'd started EON.

Run, said a voice in Dom's head.

He looked from Rios to the compound's entrance, the sliding doors hissing closed.

Run before they shut.

But if he did, that would be the end of it. His identity would be known, his cover blown. And then Dom would have to keep running. Always.

He forced himself to fall in line.

Rios led him to an office at the end of a long white hall. She knocked once, and opened the door.

Director Stell sat in a high-backed chair on the opposite side of a broad steel desk. He had black hair just starting to silver, his face reduced to angles as he stared down at a tablet.

"Mr. Rusher. Please sit down."

"Sir." Dominic sat.

The door closed behind him with a click.

"Something has been bothering me," said Stell without looking up. "You ever forget something, and you can't remember what it is? It's a vicious little mind game. Distracting, too. Like an itch you can't scratch." Stell set the tablet down, and Dominic saw his own face staring up from the screen. Not the photo taken in the security scan, or one pulled from hall surveillance. No, the photo was a few years old, from his time in the service. "It was your name," continued Stell. "I knew I'd heard it before, but I couldn't remember where." Stell turned the tablet and nudged it across the steel table. "Do you know what that is?"

Dominic scanned the screen. Beside his photo was a kind of profile, basic details—age, birthday, parents—along with facts about his life—address, schooling, etc.—but there was an error.

Dominic's middle name was listed here as Eliston.

His real middle name was Alexander.

"Have you heard of Eli Ever?" asked Stell.

Dom stilled, searching for the right answer, the right amount of knowledge. It had been public news—but how much of it, and which pieces? He'd only met Eli once, and only for an instant, the breath it took to step into the Falcon Price and pull Sydney—and her dog—out.

"The serial killer?" ventured Dom.

Stell nodded. "Eliot Cardale—known as Eli Ever in the press—was one of the most dangerous ExtraOrdinaries in existence. He killed nearly forty people, and briefly used the Merit police databases—and the police force, for that matter—to create a list of targets, profiles of those he suspected to be EOs. This," said Stell slowly, "is one of those profiles."

Once, when Dominic was overseas, he'd walked into a room and found a live bomb. Not like the IED he'd stepped on. No, he'd never had time to see that explosion coming. But the bomb in this room had been as big as a steel drum, and the whole place was booby-trapped around it. He remembered looking down, seeing the trigger wire, barely an inch in front of his left boot.

Dom had wanted nothing more than to run away, as far as possible, but he hadn't known where the other wires were, or even how he'd made it that far without triggering them. He'd had to pick his way out, one agonizing step at a time.

And here he was again, his footing precarious—one wrong move, and everything would blow.

"You're asking if I'm an EO."

Stell's gaze was steady, unflinching. "We have no way of knowing if every person Eli targeted was actually—"

Dominic slammed the tablet down on the table. "I gave my flesh and blood and bones to this country. I gave everything I had to this country. I *almost* died for this country. And I didn't get any special powers out of it. I wish I had—instead, I got a body full of scrap parts, and a lot of pain, but I'm still here, still doing what I can, because I want to keep people safe. Now, if you don't want to hire me, that's your choice. But have the balls to make up a better reason than this . . . *sir.*"

Dominic sat back, breathless, hoping the outburst had been enough to convince the other man.

The silence stretched out. And then, at last, Stell nodded and said, "We'll be in touch."

Dismissed, Dom rose from his chair and left. He went into the men's room across the hall, and into the safety of a stall, before vomiting up everything in his stomach.

III

THREE WEEKS AGO

EON

BARA smacked his palm on the table and got up.

"Hate to eat and run," he said, "but I've got a mission."

"No way," said Holtz, "they cleared *you* for fieldwork?" He turned on Rios. "What gives? I've been petitioning for weeks to get on Containment."

Bara smoothed his uniform. "It's because I'm such an asset."

Rios snorted. "It's because you're totally useless here."

Bara put a hand to his heart, as if wounded, then shot back, "What about you?"

"What about me?"

"You don't do fieldwork."

She met his gaze, her gray eyes flat. "Someone has to make sure the monsters don't get out."

Dom was surprised. He'd been there for two years, and witnessed a handful of attempts—an EO managed to put a hole in one of the fiberglass walls, another tore free from restraints during a routine med check—but he'd never heard of an actual escape.

"Has an EO ever gotten out?"

Rios's mouth twitched at the corner. "People don't get out of EON, Rusher. Not once we put them here."

People. Rios was one of the only soldiers who referred to the EOs that way.

"Who're you hunting?" asked Holtz, who'd clearly resigned him-self to living vicariously.

"Some crazy housewife," said Bara. "Burns holes in shit. Found her husband's secret apartment, at the Heights."

Holtz—who had had many girlfriends—shook his head. "Never underestimate an angry woman."

"Never underestimate a *woman*," amended Rios.

Bara shrugged. "Yeah, yeah. Place your bets. Poke your fun. But when she's rotting in a cell, you're all buying me drinks."

MEANWHILE, IN MERIT...

June closed her eyes and listened to the rain beat against her black umbrella.

She wished she were in a field somewhere, arms spread wide to catch the thunder, instead of standing on the curb outside the sleek urban high-rise.

She'd been waiting for nigh on ten minutes before someone fi-nally came through the revolving doors, and just her luck, he was all paunch in an ill-fitting suit, complete with five-o'clock shadow and a comb-over.

June sighed. Beggars couldn't be choosers, she supposed. She started toward the building, brushing past the man at the corner. The barest touch—the kind that goes unnoticed amid the jostle and drip of a rainy day—and she had all she needed. He was on his way and she was on hers. She didn't bother changing, not until she reached the Heights' front doors.

An older man sat behind a concierge desk in the lobby. "Forget something, Mr. Gosterly?"

June made a short, gruff sound and muttered, "Always."

The elevator doors opened, and by the time they closed behind her, the reflection in the polished metal was hers again. Well, not *hers*. But the one she'd started with that morning. Peasant skirt and a leather jacket rolled to the elbows, a sly smile and hair that fell in loose brown curls. She'd picked it off the subway like a girl shopping the racks. It was one of her favorites.

As the elevator rose, she pulled out her cell and texted Syd.

For a long moment, nothing. And then three dots appeared beside the girl's name, to show that she was typing.

June watched, restless for an answer.

When it came to Sydney, she'd never been good at waiting.

IV

THREE YEARS AGO

CAPITAL CITY

IT had taken an entire year for June to find them again, and when she did, it was entirely by accident. Almost as if it were fate.

The trouble was, June didn't believe in fate. At least, she didn't *want* to believe in it, because fate meant everything happened for a reason, and there were too many things she wished never had. Besides, it was hard to believe in a higher power or a grand design when you killed people for a living.

But then fate—or luck, or whatever it was—went and handed her Sydney.

A year of looking for the man in black, with no luck, and then, fifteen hundred miles from Dresden, where they'd first crossed paths, June cut through a park on the way to a job and saw the blond girl again.

A year—but it was impossibly, undeniably her. She had been—and seemed to still be—at that age where changes happened overnight. Bodies grew inches, curves—but the girl looked the same. *Exactly* the same. Same blond bob and ice blue eyes, same narrow build, same giant black dog waiting like a shadow at her side.

June scanned the park—there was no sign of the man in black, but she glimpsed the other one sitting in the grass, tattoos wrapped around his forearms and a book open on his knee. She saw a flash of pink nearby, a forgotten Frisbee. She picked it up, spun it between her fingers, and then lobbed the plastic disc at the man's head.

It connected with a light crack, and June jogged up to him, a bouncy young brunette, all apologies and sunshine.

"It's all right," he said, rubbing the back of his head. "Takes more than a Frisbee to knock me over."

He offered it back, and when her fingers brushed his, his life flickered through her like a film reel. He was so open, so human. Mitch Turner. Forty-three. Foster homes and skinned knees and bloody knuckles in a street brawl. Computer screens and car tires screeching. Handcuffs and a prison cell and a cafeteria, a man with a makeshift knife, a muffled threat, and then—June saw a face she recognized.

And thanks to Mitch, she now had a name to go with it.

Victor Vale.

In Mitch's mind, the man was lean but not yet gaunt, washed out in prison grays instead of fitted blacks. A flick of his wrist, and another man who threatened collapsed with a scream.

That meeting, like a hinge in Mitch's mind—beyond that moment, his memories were all marked by Victor's blue eyes, his pale hair. Until they found *her.* Sydney, bloody and rain-soaked in a too-big coat. Sydney, who wasn't human. Sydney, who Mitch didn't know what to do with, how to handle. Sydney, and now a different kind of fear.

Loss.

And tucked into all of that, like a slip of paper in a book, a last memory. Another blond girl. A body buried by fire. A choice smothered by regret.

"Sorry," June heard herself say again, even as the man's memories flashed through her head. "My aim is just awful."

"Don't worry about it," said Mitch, radiating kindness, warmth.

He sat back in the grass with his book and smiled. June smiled back and said good-bye, her focus already turning to the girl under the tree.

Unknown Number: I forgot to tell you.
Unknown Number: My name is Sydney.

June cradled the cell phone in her palm. She already knew the girl's name, of course, but it was better, coming from her. June wanted things to happen naturally, even if they hadn't started that way.

Nice to meet you, Sydney, she wrote back. *I'm June.*

Good, she thought with a smile.

Now they could be proper friends.

V

THREE WEEKS AGO

THE HEIGHTS

THE elevator chimed as it reached the fourteenth floor. June stepped out into the hall and approached the cream-colored door. She half expected to find a spare key on the doorframe or under the mat, but there was nothing. No matter. Two thin bits of metal and a half minute later, she was in.

Marcella Riggins's apartment was pretty much what she expected: leather sofa, plush white rug, copper sconces, all money, no soul.

Still, there were a few surprising touches. The chunk of wood missing from the bedroom door, the rotted line like burned paper showing the path of destruction. The tiny, glittering pieces of glass on the counter and strewn across the floor. But the thing June inspected first was the record player. It was the kind rich people bought for decoration instead of function. But a small stack of albums leaned beside it, even if they too were just for show, and June flipped through until she found something upbeat, savoring the scratch of the needle.

Music poured into the apartment.

June closed her eyes and swayed a little.

The song reminded her of summer. Of laughter and champagne, the cold splash of pool water, of veranda curtains and strong hands and the scrape of the slate walk against her cheek and—

The song scratched to a stop as June removed the needle.

The past was the past.

Dead and buried.

She wandered through the bedroom, drew an absent hand across the clothes in the closet—half of which appeared to have fallen victim to Marcella's wrath. Her cell buzzed.

> **Syd**: I'm so bored.
> **Syd**: I wish I was there.

June wrote back.

> **June**: You could be.
> **Syd**: I can't.

The words were routine, at this point, even if they both knew the outcome wasn't really possible.

After all, June could be anyone, while Sydney, it seemed, could only be herself. Conspicuous in its constancy, Sydney's presence would negate June's own advantage. And, of course, there was the matter of the *others*—of Mitch, and more importantly, of Victor. June hadn't, at first, understood the nature of that relationship, or the degree of Sydney's attachment, until Sydney finally broke down and told her everything.

It was last fall, and they were on one of their late-night calls, each of them perched on a rooftop, cities apart but under the same sky. Syd was tired—tired of living out of a backpack, tired of never settling down, tired of not getting to live a normal life.

June had wondered, of course, why they moved around so much— had spent a good long while assuming they were on the run. But there was more, she knew it, and she'd been waiting for Syd to confide in her.

That night, she was tired enough to tell the truth. "Victor's looking for someone who can help him."

"Help him how?"

"He's sick." A long pause. "I made him sick."

"How could *you* make him sick?"

"I thought I could save him. I tried. But it didn't work. Not the way it should have."

June hesitated then. She'd seen Sydney *save* small animals, knew what her intervention meant. "You *resurrected* Victor?"

The answer was barely a whisper. "Yes. I've brought people back before . . ." And then, still so softly, "But it's harder, when they're like us. You have to reach so much farther into the dark. I thought I grabbed hold of all the thread, but it was frayed, pieces everywhere, and I must have missed one, and now . . . his power isn't working right."

That last bit, like an opening in armor, a chance to ask the question that had plagued June since the day she brushed arms with the man in black. The mystery of his power—she'd glimpsed *something*, in Mitch's mind, the vague shape of it anyhow, had gleaned more from the big guy's fear, and from the careful way Sydney spoke, that Victor could do more than start cars or solve puzzles with his eyes closed.

"What *is* Victor's power?" she asked now, heard the girl swallow audibly.

"He hurts people."

A small shiver. "Sydney," June said slowly. "Has he ever hurt you?"

"No." And then, "Not on purpose."

Anger cut through June like a knife. Anger, and the grim determination to pry Sydney free from Victor's vise.

So far, she hadn't succeeded.

It didn't stop her from trying.

"If you ever want to leave . . ."

But June always knew the answer before it came.

June sighed. Sydney still blamed herself for Victor's situation, and until June could find a way to separate the girl from her shadow, Syd would say those same two words.

June put the phone away, turning her attention back to the task at hand, and the issue of Marcella Riggins. She plucked a framed photo from the dresser. No question, the woman was a stunner. Black hair, pale skin, long limbs. Pretty in the way that made nothing else about you matter. June had been that kind of pretty, once.

It was overrated.

June tossed the photo onto the bed and went to the window, intending to keep watch for Marcella.

Instead, she spotted a black van idling at the mouth of an alley.

That wouldn't do.

She donned the Mr. Gosterly costume a second time and went back downstairs. As she stepped through the revolving doors, she shed the aspect in favor of something even less form-fitting—a middle-aged man, haggard from too many nights spent sleeping rough. The homeless fellow staggered, as if drunk, and caught himself against the hood of the idling van. Then, without looking up, began to unbuckle his worn belt and relieve himself against the vehicle.

A door swung open, slammed closed.

"Hey!" shouted a voice, grabbing her borrowed body from behind.

June turned and stumbled forward into the soldier, as if losing his balance, and as she did, a switchblade slid out from her fingers with a neat little *snick*. She drove the blade up into the soldier's throat, then eased his body down against the alley wall.

One down.

How many more to go?

MEANWHILE, ACROSS TOWN . . .

Marcella sat on the patio of Le Soleil, sipping her latte as rain dripped from the awning and a hundred strangers passed beneath black umbrellas.

She couldn't shake the feeling she was being watched. She was, of course, used to being *noticed,* but this felt different. Intrusive. And yet there was no obvious source.

Despite her concern, Marcella wasn't in disguise—lying low had never been her style. But she'd conceded to a more subtle aesthetic, with her black hair in a simple high ponytail, her trademark stiletto pumps exchanged for more functional heeled black boots. Her nails, freshly painted gold, rapped against the side of her cup as she studied the subway station across the street. Marcella mapped out the station in her mind, envisioning the escalators that led down one level, and then two, terminating at the bank of storage lockers that ran along a white tile wall.

The locker in question was one of five they had, scattered across Merit. It had been Marcella's idea, to skim off the funds, in case a situation arose. Admittedly, she'd never envisioned a situation quite like *this.*

A siren wailed, and Marcella's fingers tensed on her coffee cup as the patrol car whipped around a nearby corner. But it surged past without stopping, and Marcella exhaled and brought the latte to her lips.

It was strange—in the days since her confrontation with Marcus, she'd been on edge, waiting for the cops to show up at any moment. She wasn't a fool. She knew they were the ones who'd kept her survival a secret. Knew her departure from the hospital was anything but subtle. And yet no one showed up, either to kill or to collect her.

She wondered what she would do when they did.

"Anything else?" asked the waiter.

Marcella smiled up at him from behind her sunglasses. "Just the check."

She paid and stood, flinching a little as she did—the burns were healing, but her skin was still tender and tight, aching with every motion. A useful reminder of Marcus's crime, and a shortcut to summoning this new power, if and when she needed it.

Marcella crossed the street and into the station.

She made her way to the lockers, found the number—the day they met—and spun the code Marcus had habitually used into the combination lock.

It didn't open.

She tried a second time, then sighed.

Her husband continued to disappoint her.

Marcella wrapped her fingers around the lock, and watched it rust away, the metal crumbling in her palm. The door swung open, and she pulled a stylish black-and-gold purse from the cubby. She drew the zipper back and examined the stacks of cash totaling fifty thousand.

It wasn't enough, of course, but it was a start.

For what? she asked herself.

The truth was, Marcella wasn't sure what to do next. Where to go. Who to become. Marcus had gone from being a foothold to a shackle, a hindrance.

Marcella took the purse and made her way back up to the street, and hailed a cab.

"Where to?" asked the driver as she slid into the backseat.

Marcella sat back and crossed her legs.

"The Heights."

The city slid past, innocuous enough, but when Marcella climbed out of the cab ten minutes later, she felt it again, that prickle like eyes against the back of her neck.

"Mrs. Riggins," said Ainsley, the Heights's concierge. His voice was steady, but his gaze lingered on her as she crossed the lobby, a careful tension in his face. He was standing too stiff, too still, working too hard at seeming calm.

Shit, thought Marcella, stepping smoothly into the elevator. As it rose, she unzipped the black-and-gold bag and reached past the money, fingers closing around the familiar grip of a handgun.

Marcella drew the weapon out, admiring the sleek chrome finish as she ejected the clip, checked the rounds, slid the safety off, each gesture performed with studied ease.

It was like wearing heels, she thought, racking the slide.

Just a matter of practice.

VI

TWO YEARS AGO

MERIT ARMORY

IT was her birthday, and they had the whole place to themselves.

Marcella could have picked a restaurant, a museum, a movie theater—any place she wanted—and Marcus would have found a way to make it hers for the night. He'd been surprised when she'd chosen the gun range.

She'd always wanted to learn how to shoot.

Her heels clicked across the linoleum, the bright fluorescents glaring down on case after case of weapons.

Marcus laid a dozen handguns on the counter, and Marcella ran her hands over the different models. They reminded her of tarot cards. When she was young Marcella had gone to a carnival, snuck into a little tent to learn her fortune. An old woman—the perfect image of a mythological or mythic crone—had spread the cards, and told her not to think, just to reach for the one that reached for her.

She had drawn the Queen of Pentacles.

The fortune teller told her it symbolized ambition.

"Power," said the woman, "belongs to those who *take* it."

Marcella's fingers closed around a sleek chrome Beretta.

"This one," she said with a smile.

Marcus took up a box of bullets and led her through into the shooting gallery.

He lifted a target—a full silhouette, head to toe, and marked by rings—and clipped it to the line. He hit a button, and the target skated away, five, ten, then fifteen meters before it stopped and hung suspended, waiting.

Marcus showed her how to load the magazine—it would take her months to manage without chipping a nail—and offered her the gun. It felt heavy in her hand. Lethal.

"What you're holding," he said, "is a weapon. It only has one purpose, and that's to kill."

Marcus turned Marcella to face the target, and wrapped himself around her like a coat, tracing the lines of her body with his own. His chest to her shoulders. His arms along her arms, hands shaping hers around the gun. She could feel his excitement pressing against her, but the gun range wasn't just a kinky setting for a birthday fuck. There would be time for that, later, but first, she wanted to learn.

She leaned her head back against her husband's shoulder. "Darling," she breathed. "A little space."

He retreated, and Marcella focused on the target, aimed, and fired.

The shot rang out across the concrete range. Her heart raced from the thrill. Her hands thrummed from the kickback.

On the paper target, a neat hole had been torn in the right shoulder.

"Not bad," said Marcus, "if you're shooting an amateur."

He took the gun from her hand. "The problem," he said, casually ejecting the magazine, "is that most professionals wear vests." He checked the rounds. "You shoot them in the chest, and you're dead." He slid the ammo back in with a swift, violent motion. His hands moved over the gun with the same short, efficient strokes he so often used on her. A confidence born out of practice.

Marcus swung the gun up, sighted for an instant, and then fired two quick shots. His hand barely moved, but the distance between the bullets could be measured in feet, not inches. The first struck the target in the leg. The second burrowed a neat hole between the cutout's eyes.

"Why bother with the first shot," she asked, "if you know you can make the second?"

Her husband smiled. "Because in my line of work, darling, the targets don't stand still. And most of the time, they're armed. Accuracy is much harder in the moment. The first shot throws the target off guard. The second is the kill."

Marcella pursed her lips. "Sounds messy."

"Death is messy."

She took back the gun, squared herself toward the target, and fired again. It tore the paper several inches to the right of the head.

"You missed," said Marcus, as if that wasn't obvious.

Marcella rolled her neck, exhaled, and then emptied the rest of the clip into the paper target. Some of the shots went wide, but a few punctured the paper head and chest, stomach, and groin.

"There," she said, setting the gun down. "I think he's dead."

A moment later, Marcus's mouth was on hers, their shuffling feet scattering the spent cartridges as he took her up against the back wall. The sex was brief, and rough, her nails leaving lines beneath his shirt, but Marcella's attention kept sliding past her husband to the ruined target, hanging like a shadow at his back.

Marcella didn't shoot any more that night. But she went back to the range alone, week after week, until her aim was perfect.

VII

THE elevator doors opened, and Marcella stepped out, one hand resting on the gun inside her bag. Out of the corner of her eye, she glimpsed a man walking casually toward her. He looked innocuous enough, dressed in a pullover and slacks, but black combat boots showed beneath the hems.

"Marcella Riggins?" he asked, continuing his slow advance.

She turned toward him. "Do I know you?"

"No, ma'am," he said with a smile. "But I was hoping we could talk."

"About what?" she asked.

His smile stiffened, set. "About what happened the other night."

"What happened . . ." she echoed, as if wracking her memory. "Do you mean when my husband tried to burn our house down around me? Or when I melted his face off with my bare hands?"

The man's expression stayed steady, even. His steps slowed, but didn't stop, each stride closing the gap between them.

"I think you should stay there . . ." Marcella drew the gun from her bag, not all the way, just enough to let him see the chrome polish along the back of the barrel.

"Come on, now," he said, lifting his hands as if she were a wild animal, something to be corralled. "You don't want to make a scene."

Marcella tipped her head. "What makes you think that?"

She swung the gun up and fired.

Her first shot took the man in the knee.

He gasped, buckled, and before he could even reach for the weapon holstered at his ankle, she fired a second shot into his head.

He collapsed, blood staining the runner.

She heard the steps behind her too late, and turned in time to see a dark figure, a soldier, armored head to toe in black tactical gear. Turned in time to see the arc of electricity leap from the end of a baton with a static hiss. Marcella's hand shot up and caught the weapon just as it skimmed her shoulder. Pain tore through her, sudden and bright, but Marcella tightened her grip, fingers flaring red. The strange light wrapped up over her wrist, a perfect mirror of the rot spreading through the instrument, then the hand holding it.

The attacker let go and staggered back with a yelp, clutching their arm, and Marcella slammed her heel into their chest, sending them to the floor. She knelt on top of them, fingers closing around the front of the soldier's helmet.

"Come on, darling," she said, "let me see your face."

The helmet warped, weakened, until she could tear the faceplate away.

A woman stared up at her, pain contorting the lines of her face.

Marcella tsked. "Not a good look," she said, wrapping her hand around the woman's exposed throat to stifle her scream as her body withered.

Then, the harsh metal sound of someone racking a round. Marcella looked up and saw a third soldier, his gun already leveled at her head. Her own weapon sat discarded several feet away—she'd dropped it when she went to catch the baton.

"Stand up," ordered the soldier.

Marcella considered him.

He was so focused on her, he didn't register the shape moving behind him, not until it reached out and wrapped an arm around his throat.

The shape—a man built like a heavyweight boxer—wrenched

the soldier back, and the gun went off, a steel dart grazing Marcella's cheek before burying itself in the wall behind her head.

The soldier didn't get a chance to fire again. The other man gripped the soldier's mask and wrenched it sideways, breaking his neck with an audible crack. When he let go, the soldier's body crumpled to the floor.

Marcella hadn't wasted any time. She was up again, the gun back in her hand and trained on the man who, for his part, seemed unfazed.

"Careful, now," he said, in a broad, musical voice. "Shoot me and you'll just kill a twenty-three-year-old from the suburbs who loves his ma."

"Who are you?" she demanded.

"Well, now, that's a little complicated."

And then, in front of Marcella's eyes, the man *changed*. Rippled, and was gone, replaced by a young woman with loose brown curls. "You can call me June." Marcella's eyes narrowed, and the woman smiled at her surprise. "Didn't think you were *that* special, did you?" She looked down at the three corpses, arms crossed. "You shouldn't leave these here for anyone to find." She knelt, and just like that, she was the boxer again, getting his hands under a pair of shoulders.

Marcella stared down in genuine surprise.

June looked up, impatient. "A little help?"

MARCELLA pressed a hand towel to her cheek, her gun balanced on the edge of the sink. The thin line was still weeping blood. She checked her reflection in the bathroom mirror and hissed in annoyance.

The cut would heal, but they'd ruined a perfectly nice shirt.

"Who are you?" Marcella called over her shoulder to the living room, where the shapeshifter was patting down the soldiers' bodies.

"I told you," June called back in a lilting voice.

"No," said Marcella, "you really didn't."

She tossed the cloth aside and took up her gun, returning to the living room. The bodies lay side by side on the floor, the last—the one missing half its skull—staining her polished wood.

Death is messy.

"Don't be precious," said June, reading her face. "I doubt you'll want to hang about now anyway."

"Fucking cops," muttered Marcella.

"These aren't cops," said June. "They're trouble." She tore a small black patch from the shoulder of one uniform and held it up for Marcella to see. "Or more accurately, they're EON."

Marcella raised a brow. The patch itself was unmarked, save for a simple black *X* ghosted on the cloth. "Is that supposed to mean something to me?"

June rose to her feet. "It should," she said, stretching. "It stands for ExtraOrdinary Observation and Neutralization. ExtraOrdinary—EO—that's us. Which makes *them* the neutralizers." She nudged a body with the tip of her shoe. "Sharks that come swimming when you make a splash. You're lucky I found you, Ms. Riggins."

Marcella took up the half-ruined helmet. She upended it, shaking out the ash. "How *did* you find me?"

"Ah. Bethany."

Marcella scowled at the memory of her ex-friend. Her late husband's late mistress. *"Bethany."*

"Perky young thing, tits up to here."

"I know who she is."

"She liked to talk. A lot. About Marcus, and the place he'd put aside for her."

Marcella didn't realize she was gripping the helmet until it fell apart in her glowing hands. "And you?" she asked, dusting her palms. "Are you looking for my husband?"

"Oh, he's well dead. You made sure of that." June whistled. "That's quite a talent you have there."

"You don't know the half of it."

"I know you walked into a room with five men sitting round a table playing cards, and when you left, two were ash, one had a bullet in his head, and the other two are saying all kinds of strange things." June smiled conspiratorially. "Next time, you should probably just kill them all. No good having survivors running their mouths. See, Marcella," she added, stepping closer, "the problem is, one of those men, the ones you killed that night—he was mine."

"My condolences," said Marcella dryly.

June waved her hand. "Mine to *kill*. And in my line of work, it's poor form to take a bounty off another."

Marcella raised a brow. "You're a hit man?"

"Hey now, no need to be sexist. We come in all shapes. But yeah, sure. And the way I see it, you owe me a death."

Marcella crossed her arms. "Is that so."

"It is."

"Anyone in particular?"

"Matter of fact, I think you know him. Antony Hutch."

Marcella bristled at the name. A memory of the rooftop party, Hutch's wet, wandering gaze, his patronizing smile.

June was still talking. "He and I, we've got some unfinished business, of a personal nature. He's a hard man to catch on his ass. But see, I hear that he's looking for *you*."

Marcella wasn't surprised. After all, she had cut down his numbers. "You want me to kill Antony Hutch?"

June's expression darkened. "No. I just want you to get me close enough to say hello. And then, as far as I'm concerned, we're square. What do you say?"

"I could do that," said Marcella, tapping the gun against her leg. "Or I could just kill you."

"You could," countered June with a wry smile, "but it wouldn't be me you were killing."

Marcella's brow furrowed. "How's that?"

"Hard to explain," said June. "Easier to show you. This little dress-up game of mine, it's nothing. But you get me in a room with Tony Hutch, and you'll see what I can *really* do."

Marcella was intrigued. "Deal."

"Lovely," said June with a sudden, dazzling smile. She crossed to the window. "In the meantime, we should probably get out of here. Only a matter of time before they send more."

"I suppose you're right . . ." Marcella considered the bodies on her floor. "But it would be rude to go without leaving a note."

"FUCKING hell," muttered Stell.

He'd already passed a scene in the lobby, where the concierge—an older man named Richard Ainsley—lay slumped forward in his chair, his throat slit.

The scene on the fourteenth floor told its own story.

Ash streaked across the hall runner, and a fine mist of blood spattered the floor and wall. Stell freed a dart from a neighbor's door. All the signs of a fight, but no bodies.

"Sir," called Holtz. "You should see this."

Stell stepped around the dark stains and through the open door into Marcella's apartment.

Two techs were securing the scene, bagging and recording everything they could, but as they stepped out of the way, Stell saw why Holtz had called him in.

If you don't kill her now, you'll wish you had.

Marcella Riggins hadn't tried to hide her work. On the contrary, she'd put it on display. The three agents' bodies—what was left of them—lay on the floor, their limbs arranged in a disturbing tableau.

A macabre version of *see no evil, hear no evil, speak no evil.*

The first soldier, missing a part of his skull, had his hands against his ears. The second, with a broken neck, had his own armored gloves over his eyes. And the third, little more than brittle bones inside a tactical suit, had no head at all.

Sitting like a centerpiece on the glass coffee table was a single ruined helmet.

How long do you think it will take her to penetrate whatever armor your men are wearing?

Stell examined the helmet and found a folded piece of paper tucked beneath.

Inside, in elegant, curving letters, there was a single line.

Stay out of my way.

Stell pinched the bridge of his nose. "Where were the rest of the agents?"

He'd assigned six to the mission. Six operatives for a single EO. It should have been enough. More than enough.

"We found one by the transport vehicle," said Holtz. "Two more in an alley." He didn't need to say that they were dead. The ensuing silence said enough.

"Cause of death?" asked Stell quietly.

"None of them were melted, if that's what you're asking. One broken neck. Two blades, to the throat and gut. Is it possible," ventured the young agent, "that Marcella wasn't acting alone?"

"Anything's possible," said Stell. But it did make sense. So far Marcella Riggins seemed to favor her bare hands or a gun, but four of the soldiers he'd sent had been killed in other, more varied ways.

Stell looked around. "Tell me this building has security."

"Closed circuit, in the public spaces," offered one of the techs. "Someone deleted the files, but they were clearly in a hurry. We should be able to pull footage from the lobby and hall."

"Good," said Stell. "Send it over as soon as you have it."

"What now?" asked Holtz.

Stell ground his teeth, and walked out.

VIII

ELI turned through Marcella's file. Across the cell, Victor leaned, hands in his pockets, against the wall.

For so long, he'd thought Victor was haunting him—now that Eli knew that the man was *alive,* he knew the phantom was nothing but a figment of his own imagination. A touch of madness. He did his best to ignore it.

Footsteps sounded beyond the wall. Eli knew by the tread that it was Stell. And he knew, too, that the director of EON was angry.

The wall went clear, but Eli kept his head bowed over his work.

"I take it," he said dryly, "that the extraction was a resounding success."

"You know it wasn't."

"How many died?"

There was a long, weighted silence. "All of them."

"What a waste," muttered Eli, shutting the file in front of him. "All in the name of policy."

"No doubt you're feeling smug."

Eli rose from his chair. "Believe it or not, Director, I take no pleasure in the loss of innocent life." He plucked the latest photos from the cubby where Stell had set them. "I only hope you're ready to do the right thing."

Eli turned through the shots from the Heights. "She's not exactly subtle, is she?"

Stell only grunted.

Eli studied the rest of the photos and notes, reconstructing the fight in his mind.

He noticed two things fairly quickly. One—Marcella had a flair for the dramatic.

Two—she wasn't acting alone.

There was the obvious issue of timing, and the method of the killings, of course—but for Eli, the most damning evidence was subtler—a matter of gesture, aesthetic. The scene up on the fourteenth floor was grand, gruesome, theatrical; the killings near the transport van were simple, brutal, and efficient.

One was an exhibitionist.

The other was a trained killer.

Marcella was clearly the first, but then, who was the second? An ally? A colleague? Or simply someone with a vested interest?

"She's not alone," he mused aloud.

"You think so too," said Stell.

It was only a hypothesis, of course, but one soon confirmed by the arrival of security footage from the Heights. Eli had pulled the files up on his computer, while Stell did the same on his tablet, and together they watched in silence as Marcella executed the first two agents. Eli saw, with grim satisfaction, the appearance of the second figure, a large man who snapped the third agent's neck.

And then, as Eli watched, the man became a woman.

It happened between frames, the change so sudden it seemed like a glitch. But it wasn't a glitch at all. It was an *EO*.

A shapeshifter, by the looks of it. An insidious ability, one of the hardest kinds of EO to find.

"Son of a bitch," muttered Stell.

"I hope you're not going to insist on sparing this new one for the sake of policy."

"No," Stell answered grimly. "I think we've established that *neither* of them intends to cooperate. We'll have to plan accordingly."

"One or two, it makes no difference," said Eli. "They may not be human, but they're still mortal. Find them. Kill them. And be done with it."

"You make it sound simple."

Eli shrugged. It was, in theory. The task itself would be more challenging. It took all his restraint, but Eli did not suggest his own involvement a second time. That seed was too freshly planted, its roots too fragile. Besides, he knew what Stell's next course of action would be—he'd suggested it himself. A sniper at a safe distance, a clean-cut execution. If it went well, no more innocents would die. Of course, if it went well, there would be no need to let *him* out.

Eli tensed. That hand on his, the subtle pressure pushing him forward, pulling him back—for so long, he'd assumed it was God, but doubt was a slow, insidious force, wearing away at solid things. Eli still wanted, more than anything, to believe, knew that to demand proof, to ask for a sign, was not the same . . . but he needed something.

And so he told himself, if God willed it . . . if the mission failed . . . if it was meant to be—

And if it wasn't? If Eli was truly on his own?

No—he had seen his opportunity, and he had taken it. And now he had to wait.

Had to have faith.

"You know what you have to do," said Eli.

Stell nodded. "We have to find them again first."

"That shouldn't be hard," said Eli. "Marcella doesn't strike me as the type to run from a fight."

IX

MARCELLA'S steel heels clicked across the lobby of the National building.

June followed a step behind, her steps muffled in her gladiator flats. She had taken on a new aspect—that's what she called them—this time, as a lanky girl with shoulder-length black hair and wide, dark eyes, spindly legs jutting from a pair of white shorts. She was barely sixteen by the looks of it, and when Marcella had asked, June had simply said, "I heard he likes them young."

"Can I help you?" asked the man behind the desk.

Marcella settled the sunglasses in her hair, blue eyes and long lashes on full display. "I certainly hope so," she said in a breathy voice.

She had long ago learned how to turn men into puppets.

It was simple, no special powers needed.

She smiled, and so did the man behind the desk.

She leaned in, and he leaned in to meet her.

"We're here to see Tony."

Marcella didn't have an appointment, but June was right: Hutch *had* been looking for her—he'd left a dozen voicemails on her cell since the card game. Half a minute later, they were on their way upstairs.

June slumped back against the elevator wall. She had gone suspiciously quiet, her mouth now pressed into a grim line. Her earlier humor had vanished, her gaze flicking nervously between the number pad on the wall, and her own reflection, and the gold trim on the ceiling.

The elevator chimed, and the doors slid open onto an elegantly appointed foyer, bookended by a pair of men in dark suits, their holsters visible beneath their tailored jackets. Beyond them, frosted glass doors led into the penthouse.

"Gentlemen," said Marcella, stepping forward.

Her outfit left little room for concealed weapons, but one of the suits still insisted on patting her down, his hands lingering on her hips and under her breasts. When the other guy reached to search June, she just sneered, and Marcella cleared her throat. "I'm pretty sure there are laws against that."

The suit huffed but stood down, clearly deciding it wasn't worth the fight. He tapped a code into a wall panel, and the frosted doors slid open. The space beyond looked more like a living room than an office. Broad white sofas and low glass coffee tables, decanters arranged along a sideboard.

Tony Hutch sat behind a glossy black desk, reading a paper, the city gleaming in the floor-to-ceiling windows at his back. Beyond the glass, a slate patio gave way to a shimmering blue pool, steam rising where the heated surface met the cool spring air.

Tony looked up from his paper and smiled.

They say people grow on you, and maybe that was true, because every time Marcella saw Tony, she felt the need to scrub him off her skin.

He rose and circled the desk, arms wide.

"Marcella, if beauty were a crime . . ." he said, reaching for her hand.

"Then I'd be running this city instead of you," she said dryly.

Tony laughed, even as his attention flicked sideways. "And who's this?"

"My niece, J—"

"Jessica," cut in June, holding out her hand, her accent smothered to a soft edge.

Tony took it, his eyes wandering over her. "Good looks clearly run in the family," he said, brushing his lips against her knuckles. With his head bent, he didn't see June's eyes narrow to slits. Marcella wondered, again, what June had meant by *personal business*.

The two suits were hovering by the glass doors, hands resting on their holsters, but Tony waved them away. "Stand down, boys." A wink. "I think I can handle things here."

Amazing, thought Marcella. Hutch had obviously seen her handiwork at the poker game, and still he treated her like a prop, a pretty but powerless bauble.

How many men would she have to turn to dust before one took her seriously?

The security retreated, and Tony turned toward the sideboard.

"Sit, sit," he said, gesturing at the two chairs in front of the desk. "Can I get you girls a drink?"

He didn't wait for an answer, just started scooping ice into crystal tumblers.

Marcella sank into a chair, but June wandered the suite, restless, examining the art. Marcella turned her attention to Tony. "Did you know about Bethany?"

Tony tutted. "Oh, that," he said, waving it away. "Look, I told Marc to get rid of her, but you know how men are. If dicks and hearts were in the same place—I mean, how many times have I tried to lure you away from your husband—but then, that's not why you're here."

"Why *am* I here, Tony?"

He returned to his chair. "You're here because you've got the sense to come when you're called. You're here to help me understand what the fuck is going on, because I've been hearing a lot of crazy shit, Marce, and all I know is three of my best guys are dead, and the other two seem to have the addled notion that it was *you* who killed them."

"Because it was."

Tony laughed, but there was no humor in it. "I'm not in the mood for games, Marce. I know you and Marcus had a spat—"

"A spat?" cut in Marcella. "He slammed my head against a table. He pinned my body beneath fifty pounds of iron, and set our house on fire with me inside it."

"And yet here you are, alive and well, while my top enforcer is a pile of dust on Sam McGuire's floor. So, you're gonna help me understand what really happened." He didn't bother to say *or else,* only sat back. "Look, I'm not an unreasonable man. You help me, and I'll help you."

Her mouth twitched. "How will you help me?"

"You were always too good for Marcus. I could give you the kind of life you deserve. The kind you're worth . . ."—that slimy smile—"if you ask nice."

Ask nice.

Play nice.

Marcella was so *fucking tired* of nice.

Across the room June let out a short, derisive laugh.

The smile slipped from Tony's face. "Something funny, kid?"

June turned toward them. "I asked you nice once, Tony," she said flatly. "It didn't make a bit of difference."

Tony's eyes narrowed. "Have we met before?"

June leaned her elbows on the back of the empty chair, and pouted. "Oh, Tony." This time, when she spoke, her accent was on full display, strong and sweet. "Don't you recognize me?"

The color drained from his face. "No . . ." Marcella didn't know if it was shock or a denial, but one hand went for the top drawer of his desk.

"Really?" June straightened, and as she did, the teen girl disappeared, replaced by a perfect replica of Tony Hutch himself. "What about now?"

Marcella watched as the Tony Hutch *behind* the desk drew a gun from the top drawer and fired three quick rounds into June's chest.

June looked down as the blood blossomed, sudden and bright across her shirt, but she didn't cry out, didn't fall, just smiled. Behind the desk, the *real* Hutch gasped and clutched his chest as three perfect holes appeared, blood spilling down his front.

"What was it you said to me?" asked June, leaning on the desk. "Ah, yes . . . Don't fight it, baby. You know you like it rough."

His lungs hitched once, twice, body shuddering to a stop.

As the man died, June seemingly lost hold of her powers.

The reflection of Tony fell away like clothes that no longer fit, and for an instant Marcella glimpsed someone *else*—a girl with auburn curls and hazel eyes and freckles like a band of stars across her nose—but it was only for an instant, and then June was back again, as the skinny dark-haired teen she'd worn into the office.

Marcella watched it all in amazement as the true potential of June's power settled over her.

The girl wasn't just a mirror, or a mimic.

She was a *living voodoo doll.*

Marcella broke into a grin just as the frosted doors were flung open and the two guards barreled in, weapons drawn.

June whipped around, no longer the teen girl, but a perfect mimic of the man who'd tried to frisk her. He raised his gun but faltered at the sight of himself, and in that instant of hesitation, June swept a letter opener from the desk and drove it down into her hand. Which was *his* hand.

The man gasped and dropped his gun as blood poured between his fingers. The second guard wavered—the shock of seeing Hutch dead, of seeing his partner suddenly in two places—and Marcella took the opportunity to grab Tony's gun from the desk and shoot the man in the head.

He dropped like a ball of lead. The other scrambled for his fallen weapon, but Marcella was there first, pinning his wounded hand to the floor with the heel of her shoe.

"You crazy bitch," he bleated as she bent down and wrapped her hand around his mouth.

"That's no way to talk to a lady," she said, digging her nails into his skin. It withered in her grip, flesh peeling back to reveal bone that thinned and cracked until the slightest pressure made it shatter.

Marcella straightened, dusting her palms. She swore softly. There was a crack in her manicure.

June whistled a low, appreciative sound. "Well, that was fun." She was perched on the sofa, legs swinging girlishly. She hopped down and started toward the glass doors, their surface now flecked with blood.

"Come on," she said, passing Tony's sideboard. "I need a *real* drink."

X

THREE WEEKS AGO

EAST MERIT

MARCELLA had been to her fair share of bars, but these days, most of them had glowing stained glass, leather booths—at the very least, a *menu*.

The Palisades had cracked windows, wooden stools, and a grimy chalkboard.

It wasn't that Marcella didn't know this world—the world of astringent well drinks and tabs paid in petty cash—but she'd left it behind on purpose. June, on the other hand, seemed right at home, elbows leaning on the sticky counter. She was herself again—not the girl Marcella had glimpsed so briefly in Hutch's office, or the one June had worn on their way in, but the one she had met at the Heights, with those loose brown waves, that long peasant skirt.

June ordered a double whiskey for herself and a martini for Marcella, which turned out to be straight vodka, ungarnished. Which, at the moment, she really didn't mind. She stood at the bar, sipping the drink.

"Fuck's sake, sit down," said June, swinging around in her seat. "And stop wrinkling your nose." The girl lifted her drink. "To a good day's work."

Marcella reluctantly perched on the stool, studying June over her glass.

She was brimming with questions. Two weeks ago, Marcella had been a beautiful, ambitious, but slightly bored housewife, with no idea that people like June, like *her*, existed. Now, she was a widow, one with the ability to ruin anything she touched, and she wasn't even the only one with powers.

"Can you be anyone?" she asked June.

"Anyone I touch," said the girl. "If they're alive. And if they're *human*."

"How does it work?"

"Dunno," said June. "How do you burn people alive?"

"I don't," said Marcella. "Burn them, that is. It's more like . . ."— she considered the drink in her hand—"ruining. Wood rots. Steel rusts. Glass returns to sand. People fall apart."

"What does it *feel* like?"

Like fire, thought Marcella, but that wasn't quite right. She remembered how it felt when Marcus crumbled in her arms. The simple, almost elegant way he came apart. There was something *raw* about her power. Something limitless. She said as much.

"Everything's got a limit," said June. "You should find yours."

The girl's gaze darkened, and Marcella remembered the space between bodies, the brief glimpse of that other shape. "Did you feel it?" she asked. "When he shot you?"

June raised a brow. "I don't feel anything."

"Must be nice."

June hummed thoughtfully, and then asked a very different kind of question. "Do you remember your last thoughts?"

And the strange thing was, Marcella did.

Marcella—who never remembered her own dreams, who rarely remembered a phone number or a catchphrase, who'd said a thousand angry things in the heat of passion and never recalled a single one of them—couldn't seem to forget. The words echoed inside her skull.

"*I will ruin you,*" she recited, softly. Almost reverently.

Now, somehow, she could.

It was as if she'd forged the power through her own formidable will, tempered it with pain and anger and the vicious desire to see her husband pay.

And so she had to wonder: what kind of life—what kind of *death*—made a power like June's? When Marcella asked, the girl went quiet, and in that quiet, Marcella felt the girl gaze into her own internal flame.

"My last thought?" June said at last. "That I would survive. And no one would *ever* be able to hurt me again."

Marcella raised her glass. "And now no one can. And on top of it, you can be anyone you want."

"Except myself." There was no self-pity in June's voice, only a wry humor. "Irony's a bitch."

"So is karma." Marcella twirled her glass. "You know my story," she said. "What's yours?"

"Private," said June shortly.

"Come on," she prompted.

June raised a brow. "Oh, sorry, if you thought this was a girls'-night-out kind of thing, where we get drunk and bond, I'll have to pass."

Marcella looked around. "Then what are we doing here?"

"Celebrating," said June, tossing back her drink and signaling for another before pulling a slip of rolled paper from her pocket. At first, Marcella thought it was a cigarette, but then, as June unfurled it, Marcella realized it was a *list*.

Four names in tight scrawl.

Three of them had already been crossed out.

And there, at the bottom—Antony Hutch.

As Marcella watched, June plucked a pen from the edge of the bar and struck the name out. "Well, that's done," she said, half to herself. And just like that, June was back, a manic light in her eyes as she spun in her seat, folded her arms on the bar. "What do *you* plan to do next?"

Marcella looked into her empty glass. "I think," she said slowly, "I'll take over the mob."

June snorted into her drink. "Brilliant."

But Marcella wasn't joking.

She had only settled for a place at her husband's side because no one would give her a seat at the table.

But she was done settling.

According to Marcus, power belonged to the man with the biggest gun. Marcella thought of the remains of Tony Hutch's body, staining his white carpet.

"How many of us do you think there are?"

"EOs?" June hesitated. "Who knows? More than you'd think. We don't exactly go around advertising."

"But you can find them."

The glass was halfway to June's mouth. Now it stopped. "What?"

"Your power," said Marcella. "You said when you touch someone, you can take their appearance, but only if they're human. Doesn't that mean you can tell when they're *not?*"

June's smile flickered, and returned twice as bright. "You're awfully sharp."

"So I've been told."

June stretched on her stool. "Sure, I can tell. Why? You looking to find more of us?"

"Maybe."

"Why?" June shot her a sideways glance. "Trying to eliminate the competition?"

"Hardly." She finished her drink and set the empty glass down, running a gold nail around the rim. "Men look at anyone with power and see only a threat, an obstacle in their path. They never have the sense to see power for what it really is."

"And what's that?" asked June.

"*Potential.*" Marcella tightened her fingers on the stem of her glass. "This ability of mine," she said as her hand glowed red, "is a weapon." As she spoke, the glass dissolved to sand, slipping through her fingers. "But why settle for one weapon when you can have an arsenal?"

"Because an arsenal stands out," said June.

Marcella's lips twitched. "Maybe it should. People with powers like ours, why should we hide? The life I had is gone. There's no getting it back. I'd rather make a new one. A better one. One where I don't have to pretend to be *weak* to survive."

June chewed her lip thoughtfully. And then, having answered what private question she'd been pondering, June sprang to her feet.

"Come on."

Marcella didn't know if it was the girl's sudden, infectious energy, or if she simply had nowhere else to go, but she stepped down from her stool.

"Where are we going?" asked Marcella.

June glanced back, a wicked light in her eyes.

"I'm in the mood for music."

IF the Palisades had been a dump, the Marina was worse. An underground bunker, half bar and half seedy jazz club, and every surface sticky. Small round tables, trimmed by rickety chairs, half of them empty. A low stage along the back wall, bare but for a few instruments and a standing mic.

June slung herself into a vacant seat and gestured to the chair across from her.

"What are we doing here?" asked Marcella, eyeing the whole situation with suspicion.

"Darling," said June, with dramatic flair. "You must learn to blend in." As she said the words, she changed, shedding the bohemian brunette for an older black man in a faded button-down, sleeves rolled to the elbows.

Marcella stiffened. The lights were low, but not *that* low. She glanced around. "Not exactly subtle."

June chuckled, her voice smoky in the old man's throat. "I thought you were done with hiding." She flicked her hand dismissively at the half-empty club. "People can see an awful lot, and believe none of it." The old man rocked backward in his seat, the front legs coming off the floor as his face vanished into the club's deep shadow. When the chair tipped forward again, June was back to one of her usual selves, loose brown waves tumbling into her face. "Won't you sit?"

Marcella lowered herself into the wooden chair as June went on. "Truth be told, I didn't bring you for the music. Not directly. But if you're interested in other EOs, I might have a treasure for you."

She drew a phone from her pocket and scrolled through her texts, before turning the cell toward Marcella.

A single name stood out on the screen: *Jonathan Richard Royce.*

"Who is he?" she asked.

"A sax player," said June, "a decent one at that. Or he was, until he went and got addicted to heroin. Finds himself in debt to Jack Caprese."

Caprese, thought Marcella. That was a name she knew. Merit was carved up among four men: Hutch, Kolhoff, Mellis, and Caprese.

Hutch had the biggest portion, but Caprese had big eyes, and bigger teeth these days. And a bottomless appetite.

"He couldn't break the habit," continued June. "But he couldn't afford it, either. So Caprese's men go over to sort out the balance. Break a few fingers. Only Jonathan's wife is home too. She pulls a gun, and it all goes sideways. Wife dies. According to medical records, so does Royce. For a few minutes, anyway. But in the end, he pulls through. So Caprese sends more guys around, and those end up dead too. Now no one wants to take credit for a botched kill, and no one wants it getting out that they failed, but for all that they still need Royce in the ground. So they outsource."

"They called you."

June smiled. "Yeah, they called me. But I couldn't kill him."

Marcella raised a brow. "What, you had a change of heart?"

"Hardly," said June. "I mean I really *tried* to kill him. And I *couldn't.*"

XI

THREE WEEKS AGO

JONATHAN Royce owned one good suit, and it didn't even fit.

It had, once upon a time—when he was thirty pounds heavier—but now, it slumped and sagged, always on the verge of slipping off. Just like his wedding ring, staying on only because of a twice-broken knuckle. Jonathan had never been a large man, but these days he was all harsh angles, underslept and undernourished. It was ironic, really—Jonathan looked like an addict, even though he'd been clean since Claire's death.

Everyone he knew had dabbled—drugs and music went hand in hand, and the jazz scene was no exception.

But heroin was a hell of a high.

Not the roller coaster peaks of cocaine, or the mellow *que sera sera* of good weed, but a dreamy wave, a blissful way out of your own life, and your own head, a summer midnight swim in the ocean bare-assed kind of freedom—at first. Jonathan had seen the addiction coming, watched it roll in like a tide, but he was already wet, and he couldn't drag himself back to shore.

And just like a high tide, an undertow, it came and washed everything away.

Money. Joy. Safety. Sanity.

Every day, the tide a little higher. Every day, the water a little deeper. Every day, a little farther from shore. Easy to get swept away. All you gotta do is stop swimming.

Jonathan looped the tie around his neck, fumbling with the knot, his fingers aching.

It had been nearly a year, and the joints still hurt every day.

He wasn't even surprised, the night Caprese's men came to visit. He was already high. Claire was out with friends and Jonathan didn't have their money and he knew it and they knew it and there was the hammer and his hands—but then there she was walking in, there was Claire, screaming, there was Claire, pulling out a gun— where had she gotten that gun?—and then there was noise and pain and darkness.

Jonathan should have left Merit, after that.

Should have bailed the moment he came to in that hospital room with two broken hands and three bullet holes in his stomach and chest. But Claire's blood was still mingled with his on their kitchen floor, and he just couldn't bring himself to *go*. It just didn't make sense, that she was dead, that he was not—Claire didn't deserve it, didn't deserve this, to become a past tense, a footnote in someone else's story—and Jonathan had the strange but unshakable idea that he hadn't made it either. That he was a ghost, anchored to the place where it all happened, bound there until some grim business was done. So he stayed, and wore that one good suit he had to her funeral, dripped ash on it chain-smoking cigarettes in a cheap hotel room afterward, waiting for Caprese's men to find him and finish the job.

Funny thing, but until that night when Caprese's men showed up, Jonathan had never killed anyone before.

He thought it would be harder.

It *should* have been harder, should have been impossible, considering the number of men, the number of shots fired, but so much about that day was impossible. The blue-white shine, like a shield, knocking their bullets away. The cacophony of sound and violence, and when it was over, Jonathan, standing alone among the corpses.

Unscathed.

Untouched.

In his rare metaphysical moments, Jonathan thought it was Claire, looking out for him. But in his masochistic moments, of which there were far more, he knew it was punishment, the universe mocking him for what he'd failed to do.

The clock chimed seven, and Jonathan knotted his worn-out tie. He slid on the jacket, picked up his saxophone case, and headed to work.

His breath fogged before him as he walked, this part of Merit already dark, like it couldn't be bothered with streetlights. It was a half mile to the Marina, a patch of Merit they'd labeled Green Walk on the map, another bit of irony considering there was nothing but stone and asphalt in every direction.

The Ghost of Green Walk.

That was him. The man who couldn't die.

He was already—

"Hey," snarled a voice. "Give me your money."

Jonathan hadn't heard him coming, hadn't really been listening. But he felt the barrel jab into his back, a single nervous thrust, and he turned to find a kid, maybe sixteen, gripping the gun in both hands like it was a bat.

"Go home."

"You deaf or stupid?" growled the kid. "Don't you see this gun? I said, give me your fucking money."

"Or what?"

"Or I'll fucking shoot you."

Jonathan tipped his head back, looked at the sky. "So shoot."

Half the time, they didn't have the balls to fire. This one did. Not that it made any difference. The gun went off and the air glinted around Jonathan, like flint striking stone; that shine, like Claire's arms around him, telling him it wasn't his time, wasn't his turn. The bullet ricocheted, flung into the dark.

"The fuck?" said the kid.

"Quit while you're ahead," warned Jonathan, right before the kid emptied the magazine at Jonathan's head. Seven shots, and six of them rebounded uselessly into the dark, sparkling off bricks, asphalt, shattering a window. But the last bullet snapped back and hit the kid in the knee, and he went down screaming.

Jonathan sighed, and stepped over the writhing form, checking his watch.

He was late for work.

THE Marina was half-empty.

It was always half-empty. Jonathan recognized most of the people who *did* show up, but something was different. He knew the moment he stepped in, like the air was full of snow. It was the two women near the back, the one like something out of a catalogue, red lips and glossy black hair, the other younger, with a mane of brown curls and a dangerous smile.

They watched him the whole set.

Maybe once upon a time, he'd drawn that kind of attention. But that was back when his hands could do better, back when he fit into the suit, back when his smile came easy, mostly because he was already high.

Jonathan was checked out—he made it through his set, hit the notes by habit instead of passion, and then went to the bar, carried on a wave of weak applause and a strong tide of self-loathing.

"Club soda," he said, sliding onto a stool. He could still feel eyes on him. Every now and then, Caprese sent someone around to try again, but it never took. Those two women didn't look like Caprese's usual killers, but maybe that was the point. He heard the neat click of the heels a second before the knockout appeared at his shoulder.

"Mr. Royce." Her voice was warm and sleek and laced with smoke.

The brunette hopped up on a stool. "Johnny boy," she said, and there was something about her accent, familiar, as if they'd met before, but he was sure he'd never seen her face.

"If Caprese sent you . . ." he muttered.

"Caprese," said the dark-haired woman, turning the name over in her mouth. "He's the one that killed your wife, right?"

Jonathan said nothing.

"And yet," she continued, "Jack Caprese is still alive. Flourishing, I've heard. While you're here in this shithole of a club, wasting away."

"Oy," chirped the other woman. "I like this place."

"Who are you?" asked Jonathan.

"June," said the brunette.

"Marcella," said the black-haired beauty. "But when it comes to people like us, the real question isn't who, is it? It's *what*."

The woman pressed a single gold nail against the bar and, as Jonathan watched, her finger glowed red, and the wood beneath began to warp and rot, wearing a hole straight through. The brunette—June—slid a coaster over the damage, only she wasn't the brunette anymore. She was Chris, the Palisades bartender, even though Chris was still on the other side of the counter, back turned while he polished a highball glass. By the time he turned back, so had she.

Jonathan's mouth went dry.

They had powers, like his shine. But the shine was a gift. The shine was a curse. The shine was *his*. There weren't supposed to be others with him, here in this hell.

"What do you want?" he asked, voice barely a whisper.

"That," said the beautiful woman, "is what I was just about to ask *you*."

Jonathan stared down into his club soda. He wanted his life back. But he had no life, not anymore. He wanted death, but he'd been deprived of that, too.

That night, after Caprese's men were all dead, and Jonathan wasn't, when the room was silent and dark and the world was empty, he had put the gun to his head and pulled the trigger, and that should have been the end of it, but it wasn't, because the shine was there again, like it or not, and that made him think of Claire, and how pissed she'd be, him throwing away a second shot. And thinking of Claire made him want to get high again, to float out to sea.

But the shine wouldn't let him.

Jonathan had told himself that he wouldn't try again.

He wouldn't let her down.

But it was like a whole new kind of drug, using that shine. A fearsome reminder that he was still alive.

June was frowning, as if she could read Jonathan's mind. But Marcella smiled.

"Why sit around sulking," she said, "when you could hurt the people who hurt you?"

But he *had* hurt them—he'd killed the men who killed Claire, and the ones who came for him, and everyone else Caprese sent. Every single one—except—

"Caprese," murmured Jonathan.

Was *that* why the shine wouldn't let him rest?

Why he couldn't get to Claire?

"I can help you get to him," said Marcella. She leaned in, close enough for him to smell her perfume. "I've heard a little about your talent, but I'd love to know more." She reached out and brought her fingers to rest against his arm. It was such a simple gesture, almost kind, right up until her palm flared red. The shine flashed along his skin, and she pulled back, considering her hand. "Hm," she said, as if she hadn't just tried to ruin him. "How do you do it?"

"I don't *do* anything," said Jonathan bitterly. "It just happens. Someone tries to hurt me—hell, I try to hurt myself—and it's there. Shielding me."

"Well, bully for you," said June, leaning back on the counter.

Marcella made a small, displeased hum. "I don't see how that helps me."

Jonathan stared into his glass. "I can share it."

Marcella's blue eyes narrowed. "What do you mean?"

Jonathan shook his head. This was how the shine mocked him. How he knew it wasn't a gift at all, but a curse, a shallow cut, not deep enough to kill, but more than enough to hurt. He'd just wanted to protect Claire, and he'd failed. Now, when he finally could, it was too late. She was already gone.

"Jonathan," pressed Marcella.

"I can shield someone else," he admitted, "so long as I can see them."

Marcella smiled. It was a dazzling smile, the kind that made you want to smile back, even when there was nothing to smile about.

"Well, in that case," she said, "let's talk about revenge."

XII

THREE WEEKS AGO

VICTOR'S steps rustled in underbrush.

It was almost dusk, the sky sinking into violent shades around him as he picked his way through the woods. Now and then the silence was punctuated by distant gunfire as, across the reserve, hunters picked off their prey before the last of the light failed.

Victor was hunting too. He trailed a broad man in an orange vest, the shock of color picking him out from the surrounding mottle of green and gray. The trees were sparse, surrounded by fields to every side. A few miles south, a small cabin, the full extent of the man's footprint.

Despite his current attire, Ian Campbell had been a hard man to find.

He'd gone off the grid after his accident, a disappearance almost as complete as death.

Almost.

But in this day and age, it was impossible not to leave a mark.

It had taken Mitch months to track this particular EO down. But he'd done it. Because he knew, just as Victor knew, that they were running out of options. The stack of paper had dwindled down to a few spare sheets, and as the leads shrank, the length of Victor's deaths grew, the seconds ticking upward until they threatened to brush that lethal edge, the medically established threshold of no return.

A soft bleating sound alerted Victor to the likely object of Campbell's attention.

An injured deer lay in the brush, its side opened by a scattering of buckshot. As Victor slowed to watch from the shadow of a nearby tree, Campbell crouched over the injured deer, making gentle noises as he laid a hand on the animal's side.

And then, as Victor watched, the buckshot rose back up through muscle and skin, and rolled down the animal's sides into the grass.

Victor's breath caught.

He had become so accustomed to disappointment—to tracking EO after EO down, only to learn that their powers were incompatible, or worse, irrelevant—so he was caught off guard by the sight of Campbell's power. The realization that he'd finally found someone who could help.

The deer rose on unsteady legs, and then bounded away through the trees, unhurt.

Campbell watched it go. Victor watched Campbell.

"Is it a kindness," asked Victor, his voice breaking the stillness, "to loose prey back into the world, simply to be shot again?"

Campbell, to his credit, didn't jump. He straightened, brushing his palms against his jeans. "Can't do much about the hunters," he said. "But never could pass up a creature in pain."

Victor laughed, a humorless, hollow sound. "Then you should have no qualms about helping me."

Campbell's expression narrowed. "Animals are innocent," he said. "*People* are another matter. Most, I've found, don't deserve the help."

Victor bristled—it sounded like something Eli would say. His fingers twitched, the air beginning to hum, but Campbell surprised him by stepping forward instead of away.

"How are you hurt?" he asked.

Victor hesitated, unsure how to answer such a simple question with such a complicated answer. In the end, he said, "Mortally."

Campbell gave him a long, measured look.

"All right," he said. "I'll do what I can."

Victor's heart stuttered, not from an episode, but from hope. A thing so rare he'd forgotten what it felt like. He had been prepared to use force.

"There are limits," continued Campbell. "I can't stop nature. Can't change its course. I can't rewind death, but I *can* undo a violence."

"Then," said Victor, whose deaths had been shaped by blood and pain, "you are well suited to this."

Campbell held out his hand, and Victor, who had never been comfortable with contact, forced himself to still as the EO's hand came to rest on his shoulder.

Campbell closed his eyes, and Victor waited. Waited for humming in his skull to disappear, waited for the crackle in his nerves to ease and the ticking clock to finally stop—

But nothing happened.

After a long, empty second, Campbell's hand fell away, and Victor knew that he'd found another dead end. But he'd seen Campbell's power. It should have worked. It had to work.

"I'm sorry," said the man, shaking his head. "I can't help you."

"Why not?" snarled Victor.

For the first time, Campbell backed away. "When I said I could—I meant—I can heal a violence done by *someone else*. But whatever's happened to you, however you're hurt, you've done it to yourself."

Victor's anger sliced through him like a knife, sudden and deep. His hand clenched into a fist, and Campbell staggered back into the brush, a pained sob wrenching from his throat.

"Get up," demanded Victor. But he raised his hand as he said it, forcing Campbell upright. *"Fix me."*

"I can't!" gasped Campbell. "I told you, I can only heal the *innocent*. You're not a victim."

"Who are you to judge me?" growled Victor.

"No one," said Campbell. "The power judges for itself. I'm *sorry*, I—"

Victor shoved Campbell away with a snarl. Behind his eyes, he saw his death—not the most recent, or the one at Eli's hands, but the very first, the one in the lab at Lockland, the way he'd climbed onto the table, pressed his bare back against the cold steel, summoned death to him like a demon, a slave, an order.

In the woods, Campbell had struggled back to his feet.

Victor half expected the EO to run, but he didn't.

Darkness had swept in around them, but even in the lightless woods, Victor saw the genuine sadness in the other EO's eyes.

Victor briefly considered letting the man go. But if he'd found Campbell, it was only a matter of time before EON did too. Their reach seemed farther by the day.

"I'm sorry," said Campbell again.

"Me too," said Victor, drawing his gun.

The shots echoed through the woods.

The body collapsed, and Victor sighed, and slumped back against the nearest tree, the humming louder than ever in his head. He closed his eyes, suddenly, immeasurably tired.

If you kill all the EOs you meet, how are you better than Eli?

Whatever's happened to you, however you're hurt, you've done it to yourself.

His cell broke the silence. Victor dragged his eyes open and answered the call, rising to his feet. "Dominic." He heard the telltale sounds of a bar in the background. "You have news?"

"There's a new EO," said Dom. "A bold one. Name's Marcella Riggins."

"Is she a viable lead?" asked Victor as he started back the way he'd come.

"No," said Dom. "Her power is definitely of a destructive nature."

Victor sighed. "Then what is she to me?"

"I just thought you'd want to know. She's just drawing a lot of attention."

"Good," said Victor shortly. "Then EON can waste their time hunting her instead of me."

He knew, of course, thanks to Dominic, that they were already chasing him. Or rather, chasing *someone*. And he had a good idea who was leading the charge.

Victor had been disgusted, but not surprised, when he'd learned about the way Stell was using Eli Ever. Putting him back to work. Eli always did have a knack for finding his way to the center of a stage, and Stell had fallen for his charms before. Victor wondered if *that* was why EON hadn't gotten closer. Not because their pet had failed to see Victor's hand in the killings, but because he *had*.

It would be so like Eli, that self-righteous, self-absorbed need to handle things himself.

And every day the noose failed to tighten, Victor's suspicions grew.

As for Marcella Riggins, let her have the spotlight, as long as she could hold it. When it came to EOs, there was a kind of natural selection. Most had the sense to stay in the shadows, but when the need for attention outweighed a sense of self-preservation, the scales tended to balance themselves.

And people like Marcella never lasted long.

XIII

THREE WEEKS AGO

JUST OUTSIDE MERIT

RAIN slipped through the warehouse roof, the steady drip of water masking the clip of Marcella's heels against the concrete floor. The old cannery sat on the outskirts of town, a skeleton of pillars and steel beams and a rotting roof, one of the designated parcels of neutral ground in the city.

Their voices drifted through the bones of the building.

". . . in his own office . . ."

". . . it can't stand . . ."

". . . who's going to handle . . ."

". . . just one woman . . ."

". . . no way she's working alone . . ."

"What is it with men and places like this?" mused Marcella, her voice loud enough to carry as three heads came into sight. "I swear, you always pick the most morose places to gather."

The men turned toward her. Joe Kolhoff. Bob Mellis. Jack Caprese. She'd half expected to find them sitting at another round table, these self-proclaimed knights of Merit, but instead she found them huddled in the center of the dreary, leaking space.

Unbelievable, thought Marcella. Her husband reduced to ash, Tony dead at his desk, and yet they *still* didn't even bother to draw their guns. Neutral ground rules dictated that bosses didn't carry, but surely no one actually went into a meeting like this without at least *one* piece of artillery.

"Is it the ambiance?" Marcella wondered as she made her way toward them. "Or does like simply call to like? Defunct. Outdated. Obsolete. So many old buildings in this city," she said, nails trailing across a concrete pillar. "It's insane the money they waste on repairs and refurbishments. Sometimes it's better to just raze the whole thing and start fresh, don't you think?"

"The once-late Marcella Riggins," sneered Kolhoff. "You've got some nerve—"

"Oh, I like to think I've got a great deal of nerve, Joe."

"If you had a damn bit of *sense*," said Mellis, "you would have run."

"In these shoes?" she teased, glancing down at her steel heels. "And miss this lovely meeting?"

"You weren't invited," said Kolhoff.

"What can I say? My ears were burning."

"How did you find us?" demanded Caprese.

Marcella wandered between the pillars, nails skating over concrete. "My husband used to have a saying. *Knowledge may be power, but money buys both.*" Her hand fell away. "Turns out some of Hutch's men were more than willing to change sides, in exchange for a promotion."

"Bullshit," hissed Caprese. "Family doesn't turn."

Marcella rolled her eyes. "The amazing thing about these *families* of yours," she said, dragging her hand along another pillar, "is that they're only family to the ones on top. Head far enough down the tree, and you find a whole lot of people who don't really care who's in charge, as long as they're getting paid." She let her eyes wander to the warehouse wall, the lot beyond, where half a dozen black sedans idled. "I wonder how many of *your* men will jump at the chance to work for me, the moment you're gone."

Kolhoff bristled. Mellis drew a knife from his back pocket, flicking it lazily open. Caprese, finally, produced a gun. "I always thought you were a brazen bitch," he said, training the barrel on her, "but you're obviously a stupid one, too, coming here alone."

Marcella continued her path between the pillars, unconcerned by the weapons. "Who said I came alone?"

Jonathan's dress shoes tapped out a rhythm on the concrete as he came into sight. He moved as if in a trance, his dark eyes trained on Caprese as he walked straight toward him. The mob boss squeezed off a shot, and the bullet struck the air in front of Jonathan with a burst of blue-white light before ricocheting off, sparking on the concrete floor.

"What the fuck . . ." snarled Caprese, firing again and again as Jonathan closed the distance between them, bullets skating off before one finally bounced back, hitting Caprese squarely in the knee. He gasped, and buckled, clutching his leg.

Jonathan didn't say anything. He simply drew his own gun, aimed at the kneeling man's forehead, and fired.

Kolhoff and Mellis froze, their eyes wide as Caprese's body slumped, lifeless, to the cold ground.

Marcella clicked her tongue, pressing her hand flat against the final pillar. "If you had a damn bit of sense," she said, red light seeping from her palm, "you would have run."

The concrete beneath her hand gave way, and as it did, the other pillars began to shudder and lurch, each already weakened by her passing touch. The building let out a heavy groan as the columns crumbled and the roof bowed, buckled.

Mellis and Kolhoff were running now, but there was no point. June had already locked the doors. A massive chunk of stone came crashing down, Marcella in its path.

She watched it fall, fascinated, limbs fizzing with excitement and fear.

"Jonathan," she said, but he was already looking, and the air around her shimmered with blue-white light just before the rubble struck. Rocks shattered against the forcefield and slid off, raining harmlessly down around her.

Marcella remembered the first time she witnessed a demolition. The thing that struck her most, after that initial boom, was the quiet grace, the way the whole behemoth had sagged sleepily, sinking less like a mass of bricks and steel than a failed soufflé. It was, admittedly, a little less peaceful from this angle, and not nearly as quiet.

But Marcella savored it all the same.

Savored the men's screams, the warping metal and the broken rock and the way the whole world shook as the building fell down around them, burying Kolhoff, and Mellis, and Caprese. Three more men who'd stood in her way.

The wreckage carved a circle of destruction around Marcella, around Jonathan, leaving them unharmed, though barricaded. Contained. But there was nothing that could hold her now. Marcella brought her fingers to the nearest block of concrete and pressed, her whole hand flaring crimson, a violent light spreading like fire up her arm.

The concrete weakened, cracked, shattered, the obstacles laid to waste, the path made clear.

Marcella had yet to test the limit of her power. Or rather, had yet to *find* it. The destruction came so easily.

She strode out of the ruined building, Jonathan trailing like a shadow.

June was waiting at the edge of the rubble, eyes wide. "That wasn't exactly subtle."

Marcella only smiled. "Sometimes subtlety is overrated."

June gestured to the suited men spilling out of the waiting black sedans. "And what do we tell the cavalry?"

Marcella considered the men.

"Let's tell them," she said, "that the Merit mob is under new management."

∞

MARCELLA collapsed onto the cream leather sofa, laughter bubbling across her lips. "You should have seen their faces, June . . ."

The city stretched beyond the floor-to-ceiling glass, glittering in the last shards of light.

Marcella had always wanted to live in the National.

Now that she was here, Hutch's penthouse felt like a temporary stop on the way to bigger, better things. But it was still a pretty one. Especially now that the blood had been scrubbed out. A few stubborn flecks remained, but Marcella didn't mind them. No, they were reminders of what she'd done. What she was capable of doing. Enemies reduced to stains under her feet.

As far as the standard personnel were concerned, Tony Hutch had gone on holiday, something he was prone to do.

He'd always been a man of many vices, used to his privacy.

Jonathan slipped like a ghost down the hall, but June lingered, perched on the edge of the sofa.

"You know," she said. "One body doesn't draw much notice. The trouble is when they start adding up. Mob boys don't exactly phone the feds every time someone bites it, but you're testing them. Do you not remember what I said, about EON?"

"All the more reason to stand out."

June crossed her arms. "How do you figure?"

Marcella curled a clump of black hair absently around one finger. "When people stay in the dark, it's easier to make them disappear." She sat up. "I just brought down an entire building. You can be anyone you want. And Jonathan can render us untouchable. We're not just impressive, we're invincible. We *should* stand out."

June shook her head. "If you want to survive—"

"But I don't want to *survive*," sneered Marcella. "I want to *thrive*. And I promise you, I'm just getting started."

The girl rolled her eyes. "What now? You're going to throw yourself a fucking party?"

A slow smile spread across Marcella's mouth. It wasn't such a bad idea.

"No," said June. "No, that was a joke—"

A gunshot went off from another room.

"Dammit," hissed Marcella, rising to her feet.

June followed, and together they found Jonathan standing in one of the bedrooms, the gun hanging limply from his fingers, a hole in the far wall where the bullet had ricocheted.

"What are you doing?" demanded Marcella.

"Didn't work," he murmured. "Thought it might. Now that Caprese's gone . . ."

"Sorry, Johnny," said June, "apparently you've still got work to do."

He sank onto the bed, head in his hands.

"Just wanted . . ." he said, gripping the gun in both hands, "to be with Claire . . ."

Marcella sighed, and pulled the weapon from his grip. His moroseness was killing her buzz.

"Come on," she said, turning on her heel, "we all clearly need a drink."

She didn't look back, but she heard Jonathan drag himself up from the bed and follow them into the main room.

June was in a restless mood, trading one aspect for another with every step. An old woman with a tattooed sleeve. A young black man in a tailored suit. A pretty twentysomething in a white minidress.

"You're making me dizzy," snapped Marcella.

June slumped onto the sofa, and took on a new aspect. She wasn't Marcella—couldn't be—but she was clearly meant to be close. Porcelain skin and black hair and legs for days. The face was too wide, the eyes green instead of blue. They followed Marcella to the sideboard lining the wall, with its collection of rare, expensive bourbons.

She set the gun on the crystal top and poured Jonathan a few fingers of something dark and strong. No ice.

"You missed quite a speech," said June. "Our girl's got big plans."

Marcella didn't rise to June's baiting. She handed the drink to

Jonathan. "That's right," she said. "And you're clearly meant to be a part of them." Marcella turned to June and offered her a glass. "What about you, June?"

She wasn't just asking about the drink, and they both knew it.

The other EO shook her head, but she was smiling, a playful, almost dangerous light in her eyes. "I've said my piece. Do as you please. After all, if EON comes calling, they won't catch *me*."

June took the drink, and Marcella held up her own. "A toast, to bigger, better—"

The window shattered behind them.

The bullet would have caught Marcella in the back, if Jonathan hadn't still been staring at her. Instead, it ricocheted in a burst of light, followed in quick succession by three more, shots whistling through the air.

One of them struck June. She stumbled, fell, her shape sloughing away as she did. For a second, barely a fraction of a second, Marcella saw the girl's true form again—the auburn hair, the band of freckles—and then that person was gone, replaced by a stranger, launching their body out of the line of fire.

"I told you—" started June.

"Not the time," snapped Marcella, as a decanter nearby exploded into glassy shards. "Keep your eyes on me," she ordered Jonathan. And then she turned, set down her glass of whiskey, and took up her gun.

The shots continued, a hail of fire that turned the air blue and white as Jonathan's forcefield reflected every shot. Marcella moved with a careful, calculated grace, forcing herself not to flinch amid the onslaught. It was exhilarating, knowing that her life wasn't, for the moment, in her own hands. Knowing that if Jonathan looked away, the shield would fall, and she'd be hit.

But sometimes, you had to have a little faith.

Marcella marched across the penthouse to the shattered floor-to-ceiling windows, the jagged rim of glass gaping open like a mouth. She touched the edge, and the remaining shards crumbled, crystals caught up and swept away by a gust of cold night air as Marcella stepped through the empty window, heels grinding on glass and sand and debris.

This, she thought, crossing the balcony, *is why you don't hide.*

This, she thought, lifting her own gun, *is why you let them see your strength.*

Marcella squinted through the flash and spark of Jonathan's shine, trying to find the flares of light that marked the sniper's rifle in the dark as she fired, again and again, emptying her clip into the night.

XIV

TWO WEEKS AGO

DOWNTOWN WHITTON

SYDNEY ran her fingers over the small bones.

Dol had found the bird in the gutter earlier that day, if it could be called a bird—it was a gnarled mess of sinew and feather, a single ruined wing. It was pitiful to start with, and worse still after Syd had pried it from the big dog's mouth, and now it lay sadly on a worn kitchen towel atop her borrowed bed. Dol watched, his chin resting on the comforter.

Somewhere beyond the doors, Mitch was making dinner, and humming an old song. They each had their own ways of coping with the stress, the fear, the hope. She turned her attention to the bird.

"What do you think?" she asked Dol.

The dog sighed, still sulking over the stolen prize. She scratched his ears—the closer he was, the stronger she could feel the threads that bound them, and the easier it was to remind her fingers what they were searching for.

Sydney took a deep breath, glanced at the red metal tin beside the bed, and then closed her eyes. She felt her way forward, let her hands come to rest on the sad remains, and reached.

It felt like a long fall.

It felt like emptiness and cold.

It felt like forever—and then Syd registered the faint blush of light, the twist and curl of a thread. No, not a thread. A dozen wisp-thin filaments, fragments scattered across the black stretch behind her eyes. They swam across her vision like fish, darting away from her touch, and Sydney's lungs began to ache, but she didn't give up. Slowly, painstakingly, she gathered the filaments, imagined fitting the fraying threads back together. Knotting them.

It took hours. Days. Years.

And only an instant.

As she tied the final knot, the thread glimmered, pulsed, became a flutter of feathers against her palm.

Sydney's eyes flew open as the bird moved beneath her fingers.

A sound escaped her throat, half laugh, half sob, a mixture of victory and shock, and then the sound was overtaken by the furious wing-beats and the squawk of a very surprised pigeon trying to escape the confines of her grip.

It pecked at her knuckles, and Sydney let go—a rookie mistake, as the bird took flight in the narrow room, searching for freedom, bouncing off the light fixture and the window, Dol bobbing his head as if trying to catch airborne apples.

Sydney lunged for the window and threw it open, and the bird escaped into the night in a flurry of gray feathers.

She stared after it, amazed.

She'd done it.

It was a bird, not a human, but Sydney had still taken only a few mangled bones and made the creature whole. Brought it back to life.

In seconds, she was across the room, prying the lid off the red metal tin. The last—the only—pieces of Serena Clarke lay nested inside, wrapped in a scrap of fabric. Sydney reached for them, heart racing—and stopped.

Her hand hovered over the remains.

What if it wasn't enough?

A bird wasn't a girl. If she tried, and failed, she'd never get another chance.

If she tried, and failed—but what else could she do? The rest of Serena was ash, scattered across a city hundreds of miles away.

Would it make a difference?

Sydney had never wondered if the *where* mattered as much as the *what*, but now, as she nestled the lid back on the tin, she thought, *Ghosts are tied to the place where they died.* She didn't believe in ghosts, but she had to believe in something—that thread of light, the closest thing she could find to a soul. If there was any of Serena left, beyond the bones in this box, it would be there.

Sydney would just have to wait.

XV

TWO WEEKS AGO

STELL'S plane had landed at dawn. He didn't know why a video conference wouldn't suffice, but the board had insisted on his presence, and short of outright defiance, Stell had had no choice but to go.

In his absence, he'd left Rios with strict instructions. No procedures were to be put into effect in his absence. No commands given or followed unless they came expressly from him.

The last thing Stell needed was a mutiny.

Now he stared across the nondescript conference table at five nondescript faces atop nondescript suits. Stell suspected that by the time he left the room, he wouldn't be able to pick any of them out of a lineup, let alone a crowd.

"First a failed EO capture," said the woman in black, "now a failed extermination."

"You've made quite a mess," added the man in gray.

"We've faced difficult EOs before," said Stell. "It's only a matter of time—"

"Only a matter of time," cut in the man in black, "before EON and its interests are both dragged into the spotlight."

"My team is doing everything we can," said Stell.

"That isn't strictly true," said the man in black. "We called you here because we believe your personal bias has prevented you from utilizing every asset at your disposal."

"Bias?" challenged Stell.

"We don't deny," added the woman in navy, "that you've been *integral* to the development of this organization—"

"*Development?* I *created* EON. I brought you the first intel, I explained the threat level—hell, I had to convince *several* of you of the very legitimacy of EOs."

The man in charcoal cleared his throat. "We are not questioning your contribution."

The man in gray leaned forward. "We know you have a strong personal attachment to the early ideals of this organization."

"Which is why," said in the woman in black, "you're not objectively qualified to judge its current needs."

"My subjectivity is an asset," said Stell. "You seem to think we're dealing with manufactured weaponry here. Only I seem to realize we're dealing with *people*."

"A case could be made," said the man in charcoal, "that they are *both*."

Stell shook his head. It always came back to this—to money, and power, and the board's desire for both. If the board had their way, they'd turn each and every captured EO into a weapon. Preferably single-use.

"Marcella Riggins makes a mockery of EON, and of you," said the woman in navy. "You claim you are doing everything you can, using every tool at your disposal, and yet you keep settling for low-range munitions when you have one perfectly suited to the task."

He understood then, with painful clarity.

Eli.

"At least *low-range* munitions have safety catches. Eli Cardale does not. I won't authorize him for use in the field."

The man in charcoal sat forward. "You yourself have advocated for this kind of utility."

"This is different," said Stell. "Eli isn't an ex-soldier. He's a mass murderer."

"One who has been cooperative for more than four years."

Stell shook his head. "You don't know him like I do."

"And so we return to the issue of objectivity," said the woman in navy.

"Insight isn't the same as bias," snapped Stell. "You think we have a mess on our hands right now. It's nothing compared to what would happen if we set him free."

"Who said anything about *free*?" asked the man in black. "There *are* countermeasures. According to our records, tracking devices were installed—"

"It's not just a matter of *losing* Eli," said Stell. "It's what he'll do before we find him again. He can't be controlled."

At this, the man in gray produced a briefcase. "With that in mind," he said, sliding it down the table, "a sturdier solution."

The clasps came open to reveal a smooth steel ring, nested on a bed of black. When Stell reached in, he discovered it was actually two rings, one pressed into the other. A seam ran along each circle, so that the fused collar could hinge open and closed.

"Haverty's methods were admittedly problematic," said the woman in black, "but in this case, they were also useful. His initial tests explored Cardale's general ability to heal. His second series explored the extent of that healing—and its limitations."

A small remote, flat as a credit card and half as wide, lay impressed in the fabric beneath the collar, a single button on the smooth dark surface.

"Haverty discovered a threshold. Anything smaller than, say, a pill, and Cardale's body could absorb it. Anything larger, and his body would physically reject the intrusion. However, if he was unable to reject the object, his body could not heal."

Stell thought of Eli, awake on the operating table, his chest pinned open as Haverty worked.

"We've had R and D on this project for months. Go ahead, try it."

Stell pressed the concave button, and the collar's inner ring collapsed, folding at the seam so that the band of metal transformed into a vicious spike.

"It's designed," explained the man in black, "to sever a human spinal column between the fourth and fifth vertebrae. In an ordinary person, such an injury would result in permanent paralysis. Due to Cardale's condition, the effects would obviously be temporary, but they should be just as effective."

"This is, of course, only an suggestion." The woman in navy shot him a thin smile.

"You are still EON's *director,* after all."

Stell returned the collar to the case, the board's logic warring with the lead weight in his stomach.

"But we would strongly advise you to handle this EO, and handle her swiftly. Using any and *every* means necessary."

BACK IN MERIT

Stell's house key always stuck in the lock.

He knew he should get it fixed, but he didn't spend much time at home. Slept in his own bed one night in three. Ate most of his meals in EON's canteen. He wasn't sure what made him drive from the airport into the city instead of back toward EON, didn't even realize what he was doing until he was halfway there. But his head was still cluttered from the meeting with the board, and the two whiskeys on the plane had done nothing to clear it, and Stell realized he didn't want to step through those doors until he knew exactly what he planned to do.

About Marcella.

About Eli.

Stell shrugged out of his coat. Lit a cigarette, even before he set the steel briefcase on the kitchen table. Slid the clasps.

The smooth metal collar sat nested in its velvet groove.

You are not using your assets.

Was the board right?

Send me.

Stell lowered himself into a chair.

You will never see the outside of this cell.

Was he letting his past color his judgment?

Or was he just listening to his gut?

He rubbed his eyes. Took a long drag of the cigarette, filling his lungs with smoke. The collar glinted in its case, EON's solution— but not Stell's. Not yet.

His cell rang. Stell answered without looking at the screen.

"Hello?"

He'd expected Rios, or a member of the board, but the voice on the line was smooth, sultry.

"Joseph," it said with all the warmth of an old friend.

He frowned, stubbing out the cigarette. "Who is this?"

"You really have to ask?"

"Do I know you?"

"I should hope so. After all, your men have spent a great deal of time shooting at me."

Stell's fingers tightened imperceptibly on the phone.

Marcella Riggins.

"If I didn't know any better, I'd think you had something against me."

"How did you get this number?"

He could hear the smile in her voice. "I'm getting tired of killing your agents. Are you getting tired of burying them?" She didn't wait for him to answer. "Perhaps," she continued, "we could find a more sophisticated solution . . ."

"Most EOs only get one chance," said Stell. "I'm giving you two. Surrender now, and—"

A soft laugh. "Now, Joseph," she chided. "Why would I do a thing like that?"

"So you just called to gloat."

"Not at all."

"Then why?"

"I thought," she said airily, "perhaps we could get a drink."

That, at last, caught Stell off guard. "To what end?" he demanded. "So you can try to kill me?"

"That would be pointless. If I wanted you dead, you would be. You think this number is the only thing I know? I have to say, your choice of decor is tragically bland."

Stell's head snapped up.

"Of course," she went on, "you're really not home much, are you?"

Stell said nothing, but shifted so his back was to the wall, his eyes on the windows.

"Only a few photos," she went on, "—two sisters, I presume, by the way they look at you—"

"You've made your point," he said through clenched teeth.

"Well, in that case, I'll be at Canica Bar around seven. Don't make me drink alone."

Before he could answer, she hung up.

Stell slumped back against the wall, head spinning. He couldn't go. He *shouldn't* go. Marcella was a target, an enemy, someone to be dispatched, not negotiated with.

But he had to do something.

He looked from the steel briefcase to the cell phone in his hand.

Stell swore under his breath, and grabbed his coat.

XVI

TWO WEEKS AGO

DOWNTOWN MERIT

SOME women spent years planning their wedding.

Marcella had spent the last decade planning a hostile takeover.

Of course, she'd always assumed Marcus would be the face of it, but this was far more satisfying.

With the four heads of the Merit mob so cleanly dispatched, and the factions thrown into chaos—a chaos bolstered by rumor and eyewitness testimony—the bulk were already scrambling for solid ground. So many, so willing to serve.

There would be scuffles, of course, and Marcella was prepared for those, ready to subdue the ones who would invariably vie for control, ready to pay off the officials who might get in her way.

There was still the matter of EON, but Marcella had a play for that, too.

She put her back to the window, surveying the room, Jonathan polishing his saxophone in a chair, June perched on the spine of the sofa, playing on her phone. With Hutch's suite at the National ruined, they'd taken up residence in an uptown penthouse at First and White. One with windows made of reflective glass.

Fool me once, thought Marcella, as someone knocked.

Jonathan answered the door, stepping aside to reveal a trim man in a silk suit.

"Oliver!" Marcella smiled at the sight of him—smiled wider at the rack of clothes filling the foyer. Between the house fire and the incident at the Heights, Marcella was in dire need of a new wardrobe.

"Shit, Marce," said Oliver, "you've got some heavy security downstairs. Felt me up, down, and in between."

"Sorry," she said. "It's been a busy week."

"Excuse me for being a bit wary at the moment," said June. "But who the fuck is this?"

"This is Oliver," said Marcella cheerfully. "My personal shopper."

June burst into raucous laughter. "People are trying to kill you—kill *us*—and you've got time for a fucking wardrobe change?"

Oliver smirked. "Spoken like someone who doesn't understand the power of appearance."

"That so?" June hopped down from the back of the sofa. She moved toward Oliver, taking on and shedding a different appearance with every step. "Maybe you should explain it to me?"

Oliver went very still.

"And that," said Marcella dryly, "would be June."

His gaze shifted unsteadily back to her. "I, uh, heard . . . about Marcus. Hell, I heard about *you*. Lots of strange talk."

"Whatever you've heard," said June, "it's probably true."

Marcella gestured at Jonathan, standing in his worn-out suit. "Ollie, did you bring what I asked for?"

In reply, Oliver pulled a garment bag from the rack and unzipped it far enough to reveal a sharp black suit. Marcella plucked it from Oliver's hand.

"A gift," she said, offering the bag to Jonathan.

"Nothing for me?" inquired June.

"You already have a full closet," said Marcella. She turned toward the bedroom. "Come on. Let's see what you've brought."

By the time he started unzipping dress bags, Oliver had regained his usual color. "Gotta say, I was a little surprised to get your call," he said, adding hurriedly, "and glad, of course. You always were my favorite mannequin."

She plucked a few blouses from the rack as Oliver began to lay out dresses on the bed. For a moment the image overlaid with another in her mind, the garments left waiting atop tousled sheets.

Marcella let go of the blouse in her hand before she ruined it.

"You have outdone yourself," she said, eyes traveling over the array. A lace halter, trimmed in black leather. A crimson blazer with sharp shoulders and tapered wrists. A black gown with a dipping collar and a silk obi tie. A line of perfect, steel-heeled shoes.

She lifted one. The polish was so high, Marcella could almost see herself in the shine. Red lips and black hair painted themselves on the metal finish, her reflection warping, as if she were on fire.

Oliver turned his back while Marcella stripped and donned a short red dress that drew a clean line across her shoulder blades. She considered herself in the bedroom's full-length mirror, let her eyes travel appraisingly over the burns that traced along her left collarbone, the inside of her right forearm, the top of one pale thigh.

They were healing, the skin slipping from pink to silver.

"That one's stunning on you," said Oliver at Marcella's back. Her eyes slid past her own reflection just in time to see him draw a slim switchblade from his bag. Marcella didn't flinch.

"Zip me up?" she said lightly.

"Of course." Oliver started toward her, and Marcella waited until he was almost an arm's length away before turning suddenly. He slashed, and she caught the knife in her hand, her palm already glowing red. Before the weapon could so much as scratch her skin, it had crumbled.

"What a pity," she said, wrapping her other hand around Oliver's throat. "You had such good taste."

He managed the beginnings of a scream before the skin and muscle gave way to bone, and then ash, and then nothing.

"Christ," said June, appearing in the doorway. She took in the scene. "Well, that's what you get for having a personal shopper." She nodded at Oliver's remains. "Is there anyone who *doesn't* want to kill you?"

"Occupational hazard, it seems," said Marcella.

"So it seems," said June. "And how long do you think before our friends at EON try their luck again?"

Marcella turned back to the mirror, flicking a stray bit of ash from the hem of her dress. She met her reflection, and smiled.

"Let me worry about them."

XVII

TWO WEEKS AGO

A long chandelier rippled across the ceiling, spilling soft light over crystal and marble and clean linen.

Stell adjusted his tie, grateful he was still dressed from the meeting at Capstone.

"You have a reservation, sir?" asked the maître d'.

"I'm meeting someone," said Stell, cautiously. "I'm early but—"

"You can wait at the bar," said the maître d', nodding to a curve of glass and oak.

Stell ordered a whiskey several shelves higher than his usual brand and scanned the guests—some of the most powerful and prominent people in Merit. The district attorney. The mayor's wife. Corporate heads, and politicians, and more than one star athlete.

He saw *her* as soon as she arrived.

It was impossible *not* to see her, even in Canica's low light.

She was dressed in red—not exactly subtle, but nothing about her would have ever merited that word. Her black hair curled in loose waves around her face. Her lips were the same shade as the dress, her eyes a striking blue.

Stell had seen photos, of course.

None of them did Marcella Riggins justice.

Stell could sense other heads turning as she made her way to a table in the center of the restaurant. He took up his glass from the bar and followed.

When she saw him, a smile broke the sharp line of her red lips.

"Joseph," she said, wielding his first name like a weapon. "So glad you decided to come."

Her voice was warm, tinged with smoke.

"Ms. Riggins," said Stell, sinking into the chair opposite.

"Morgan," she corrected as a glass of red wine was laid at her elbow. "Given all that's happened, I no longer feel inclined to use my husband's name. But please, call me Marcella."

She spoke with an airy confidence, one gold nail toying with the rim of her glass, and Stell realized that it wasn't Marcella's *beauty* that had failed to translate in any of the photos he'd seen. It was something else.

Something he'd seen before.

In Victor Vale. In Eli Ever.

A rare kind of strength. A dangerous will.

Someone this powerful belongs in the ground.

Suddenly he understood Eli's stance, the stubborn resolve behind his declaration. Stell's hand drifted toward his holstered gun.

If you don't kill her, you'll wish you had.

His fingers brushed the safety.

But Marcella only laughed. "Come on, Joseph," she said. "I'm sure you've noticed, weapons don't really work on me."

Stell had seen the footage, of course—Marcella on the shattered balcony, the sniper's shots skating off the air around her. He'd also seen the image of the thin man in the dark suit. The one, he realized, who was now sitting several tables over, wearing sunglasses, despite the restaurant's low light. The set of the man's shoulders, the angle of his face, suggested he was staring directly at them.

Another EO, Stell wagered.

"Don't mind Jonathan," said Marcella. "It's not that I don't trust you, Joseph," she added congenially. "But, well, we're still getting to know each other."

A fresh whiskey appeared at Stell's elbow. He didn't remember finishing his first, but the glass was empty. He lifted the new tumbler, took a sip, and stopped, recognizing the taste.

It was a brand Stell kept in his apartment. One that he only poured when he had something in particular to celebrate.

Marcella smiled, knowingly. Her long legs uncrossed and recrossed, high heels glinting like knives at the edge of his sight.

"Tell me," she said, twirling the wineglass stem between her fingers. "Do you have the place surrounded?"

"No," said Stell. "Believe it or not, I'm not eager for anyone to know I'm sitting down with a terrorist."

Marcella pursed her lips. "It will take more than harsh words to wound me, Joseph."

The way she used his name, as if he were the wineglass between her fingers, something to be toyed with. "You wanted to meet," he said curtly. "Tell me why."

"EON," she said simply.

"What about it?"

"You seem to target us because of *what* we are, not *who*. That kind of indiscriminate attack is shortsighted, to say the least." Marcella leaned back in her seat. "Why make another enemy, when you could have an ally?"

"An ally," echoed Stell. "What could you possibly offer me?"

A slow, crimson smile. "What do you *want*? Less violence? Safer streets? Organized crime really has gotten out of hand lately."

Stell raised a brow. "You think you can change the course of the *mob*?"

Marcella's smile shone. "Haven't you heard? I *am* the mob now." She rapped her nails on the linen tablecloth. "No, you want to deal in kind, don't you? A more relevant currency? You want . . . EOs."

"You would hand over your own?"

"My own what?" Marcella scoffed. "Who are they to me?" Stell looked past her again to the man in the dark suit. Marcella read his expression. "I'm afraid June and Jonathan are not up for trade. They belong to me. But surely there are others, ones that have eluded your grasp?"

Stell hesitated. Of course, some EOs were harder to catch than others, but there was only one that had proved, so far, impossible.

"There is an EO," he said slowly, "one who seems to be targeting their own kind." He didn't elaborate, didn't share Eli's theory regarding their motivations. "So far they've killed seven other EOs."

Marcella's eyes widened in mock surprise. "Isn't that *your* job?"

"I don't approve of needless death," said Stell. "Regardless of whether the victim was human, or not."

"Ah, a man with morals."

"My *morals* are the only reason I agreed to this meeting. Because I'm tired of burying good soldiers—"

"And because you haven't figured out how to stop me," said Marcella. Stell swallowed, but she waved him away. "This is a last resort. Why else would you sit down with a terrorist?"

"Do you want a ceasefire, or not?" asked Stell tightly.

Marcella considered her wine. "This EO—am I to search in the dark, or will you give me a starting mark?"

Stell drew a notepad from his pocket and scribbled down a list. He tore the sheet off. "The last five cities where the killer struck," he explained, sliding the paper across the table.

Marcella slipped the sheet into her purse without reading it. "I'll see what I can do."

"You have two weeks," countered Stell.

It was long enough to produce results, but not long enough for Marcella to waste time. She was right—and she was wrong—this wasn't the last resort. Stell *did* have a way to stop her. But it wasn't the one he wanted. Two weeks would give him time to think, to plan, and if he couldn't find another option, then two weeks was how long he had to decide which was worse—letting Marcella walk free, or Eli.

"Two weeks," mused Marcella.

"That's how long this service buys you," said Stell. "If you succeed in producing the killer, then perhaps we can continue to find common ground. If you fail, then I'm afraid your value to EON will not merit your continued freedom."

"A man who knows what he wants," said Marcella with a feline smile.

"There is another term—you will stop drawing so much attention to yourself."

"*That's* going to be hard," she teased.

"Then stop drawing attention to your *power*," clarified Stell. "No more public demonstrations. No more grand displays. The last thing this city needs is a reason to fall apart."

"We certainly wouldn't want that," said Marcella coyly. "I'll find your target for you, Joseph. And in exchange, you will stay out of my business, and out of my way." She lifted her glass. "Do we have a deal?"

XVIII

ELI studied the footage again, and again.

The mission at the National should have been simple.

But nothing about Marcella Riggins was proving simple.

"You should be celebrating," said Victor's ghost. "Isn't this what you wanted?"

Eli didn't answer. He focused on the footage from the scene, advanced the surveillance one frame at a time, watching as the glass shattered, the bullet—which should have taken Marcella in the back of the head—ricocheted, sparking off an invisible shield.

Eli paused the footage there, rapping his fingers thoughtfully on the table.

The odds of a single EO possessing more than one power were slim to none. No, it was far more likely, he surmised, that this particular skill belonged to the third, as yet unidentified EO, the one lurking like a shadow at the very back of the room.

Three EOs, working together—that itself was unusual. The vast majority were loners, isolated by either necessity or choice. Few looked for others, let alone found them.

"We did," observed Victor.

It was true. Both Eli and Victor had arrived at the same conclusion—that there was strength in numbers, potential in the complementary pairing of powers.

Now, apparently, so had Marcella.

Eli rolled the footage forward and watched her step through the hail of bullets onto the balcony. Watched as every single shot ricocheted. Watched as she raised her own gun in the general direction of the sniper.

There was something so brazen about the gesture . . .

EOs ran.

EOs hid.

Under pressure, an EO might fight back.

But they didn't do *this*.

Didn't *perform*.

Didn't use their powers with such obvious relish.

EOs were broken by definition, made reckless by the absence, the emptiness, the knowledge that their lives were over. It drove them to steal, to ruin, to self-destruct.

Marcella wasn't self-destructing.

She was preening. Baiting them. Daring them to try again, try harder.

She had taken out her husband—and that made sense, an act of revenge. Of closure. But then, she'd taken out his *competition*. That wasn't the mark of someone with nothing to lose. No, that was the mark of someone with something to *gain*. That was *ambition*. And ambition plus power was a very dangerous combination.

What would she do, if left unchecked?

The phantom in his head was right—he'd asked for a sign that he was needed, that this was right.

Marcella couldn't be allowed to continue in this manner.

And soon Stell would realize, if he hadn't already, that Eli was the only one who could put her down.

Footsteps sounded from beyond the fiberglass, and he looked up from the computer as Stell appeared on the other side of the wall.

"There you are," said Eli, rising to his feet. "I've gone through all the footage from the failed execution, and we're obviously going to need a much more tailored approach, especially considering there are . . ." Eli trailed off as Stell set a new case file in the tray.

"What's that?"

"We got a hit on a suspected EO two hours south of Merit."

Eli frowned. "And Marcella?"

"She isn't the only target we're tracking."

"But she's the most dangerous," said Eli. "And in the last three days she's collected two more. What are we going to do about—"

"*We* aren't going to do anything," said Stell shortly. "Your job is to analyze the files I give you. Or have you forgotten that you exist at the mercy of EON?"

Eli clenched his teeth. "There are three EOs working *together* in Merit, and you're just going to ignore them?"

"I'm not ignoring *anything*," countered Stell. "But we can't afford another failed op. Marcella and her partners need to be handled cautiously. You have two weeks to devise that *more tailored approach* you spoke of."

Eli drew up short. "Why two weeks?"

Stell hesitated at that. "Because," he said slowly, "that is how long I've given her to prove her worth as an asset."

Eli reeled. "You made a *deal*? With an *EO*?"

"The world is not black and white," said Stell. "Sometimes there are other options."

"Where were *mine*?" snapped Eli. "The lab or the cell—those are the only ones *I* was given."

"You killed forty people."

"And how many has she killed already? How many more lives will she destroy by the time you see fit to put her down?" Stell didn't answer. "How could you be so stupid?"

"You will remember your place," warned Stell.

"Why?" demanded Eli. "Tell me why you would make a deal with her."

But Eli knew. Of course he knew. *This* was how far Stell was willing to go to keep him in this cage, contained, controlled.

"What did you mean," he said through gritted teeth, "when you said her worth as an asset?"

Stell cleared his throat. "I've given her a mission. A chance to succeed where you have failed."

Eli stilled. No. The open file. The unsolved case. Victor.

"The hunter is *mine,*" he growled.

"You've had two years," said Stell. "Perhaps it's time for fresh eyes."

Eli didn't realize he'd approached the fiberglass until he slammed his fist against it.

This time, the gesture wasn't calculated. It was pure rage, a moment of violent emotion turned to violent action. Pain flashed through him, and the wall hummed in warning, but Eli's hand was already falling away.

Stell's mouth twitched, a grim smile. "I'll leave you to your work."

Eli watched the director go until the wall went white, and then he turned and slumped back against it, sliding to the floor.

All of his patience, his subtle pressures. The ground beneath him shuddered, threatened to break. One misstep, and it would crumble, and he would lose Victor and Marcella both, and with them, justice, closure, and any hope of freedom. It might already be too late.

He studied the back of his hand, where a single smear of blood marred the knuckles.

"How many will die for the sake of his pride?" mused Victor.

Eli looked up and saw the phantom standing over him again.

He shook his head. "Stell would rather let the city burn than admit that we are on the same side."

Victor stared at the wall as if it were still a window. "He doesn't know how patient you are," he said. "Doesn't know you like I do."

Eli cleaned the blood from his hand.

"No," he said softly. "No one ever has."

XIX

TWO WEEKS AGO

FIRST AND WHITE

JUNE whistled softly as she rinsed the blood from her hands.

Marcella had swept out of the penthouse in her red dress, Jonathan trailing like a shadow at her heels. She didn't say where she was going, or when she'd be back, didn't ask June to come with, which was fine with her. Jonathan might be a lap dog, but June preferred to work alone.

Which, mind you, wasn't the same as *being* alone. Too much silence, too much space. But idle hands and all that—which is how June ended up wrists deep in someone else's blood.

She hadn't taken a new job in more than week. Hadn't needed to. Hutch had been the final name on her personal list, and Marcella had been working up a roster of *obstacles,* as she called them— men and women most likely to resist her rapid ascent—so whenever June got bored, she just went out and knocked a few off the list.

Marcella didn't seem to mind.

Some people were matches, a bit of light and no heat. And some were furnaces, all heat but little light. And then, once in a blue moon, there was a bonfire, something so hot and bright you couldn't stand too near without burning.

Marcella was a bonfire if ever June saw one.

Of course, even bonfires eventually went out, smothered by their own ashes. But in the meantime, June had to admire the other woman's ambition, and had to admit she was actually enjoying herself.

The only thing missing was Sydney's soft laugh, her bright smile . . .

June snapped the water off, dried her hands, met her gaze in the reflection.

No. Not hers. Not her hazel eyes. Not her red hair. Not her freckles.

But she'd found herself taking this aspect—brown waves, green eyes, sharp chin—more and more often. It felt strange, holding on to one face long enough for other people to remember it.

Was it worth it? Syd had asked her that night, when she confessed to giving up her face, her life, herself. And it was, it *was,* but that didn't stop June from craving the light of recognition in someone's eyes. The comfort of being seen, being known.

She could be anyone, these days, a million outfits at her disposal, but she tried not to get too attached to any one of them. After all, people died, and when they did, their shape vanished from her closet. (Sometimes she didn't even know they were gone until she went looking.)

Only one shape was guaranteed to be there, and it was the one she wouldn't wear.

June heard the door swing open, the signature click of Marcella's heels on the marble floor. June went to find her, and passed Jonathan on his way to the balcony, a cigarette between his teeth. Marcella shrugged out of a white trench coat.

"What have you been up to?" asked June, leaning against the wall.

"Making connections," said Marcella. She drew a folded piece of paper from her purse. "Since you have a knack for finding people—"

"I have a knack for *killing* people," corrected June. "Finding them is simply a prerequisite."

"Well, I have a job for you." Marcella held out the slip. "Did you know that there's someone out there killing EOs?"

"Yeah," said June, taking the folded slip. "It's called EON."

Marcella persisted. "I'm talking about an *EO*. Someone like us, *killing* people like us. Which I find rather vexing."

June unfolded the paper, her gaze flitting over the list.

Fulton.
Dresden.
South Broughton.
Brenthaven.
Halloway.

She stilled, recognition flitting like a pulse inside her chest. "What is this?"

"The locations," said Marcella, "of the EO's last five kills."

June didn't look at her phone, but she knew that if she did, if she opened her texts from Sydney, she'd see these same places listed, each in response to the question June always asked.

Where are you these days?

June wanted to know, because the world was big, wanted to know because Sydney was hers to protect. She read the list again.

So this was what Victor had been doing. Why the three of them were always on the move. But June doubted that he was purely an executioner. Doubted it was that simple.

We're looking for someone who can help.

Maybe that was true. Maybe Victor was being *thorough*. Covering his tracks afterward. It made sense, considering he was supposed to be dead.

"Let me get this straight," said June, pocketing the list, "there's an EO out there killing other EOs. And you want to find him."

"*EON* wants to find him," said Marcella. "And they want my help."

June let out a short, humorless laugh. "That's what you meant by *making connections*?"

"Indeed," said Marcella. "I told you I would handle them. But I had to give the boys something, and it was either you and Jonathan, or this." Marcella leaned on the marble counter. "They've given me two weeks to find this EO killer."

"And what happens then?"

"Oh," mused Marcella, tracing the veins in the stone, "I imagine that Director Stell will decide I'm more trouble than I'm worth."

"You don't seem worried," said June.

Marcella straightened. "He's underestimated what I can do with two weeks. In the meantime, I suppose we should find that EO."

June's mind was turning, but she kept her voice airy, light. "What are you going to do with him?"

"You know," said Marcella, "I haven't decided yet."

XX

JUNE had texted Sydney on her way to the car, sat idling there until she saw the three small dots that signaled an incoming reply.

Syd: Whitton.

June put the location into her GPS, and shifted into gear as the map came up on the screen.

From there it was easy to find them.

How's the view? she'd asked. *Tell me what you see.*

Such a simple question, made routine by years of checking in, asking such small, seemingly innocuous questions as a way to condense the distance between them. June soon learned that Sydney and Victor and Mitch were staying in a nondescript apartment building, a ten-story stack of tan stone blocks on a street filled with the same, the only relief a small park on the corner, the bright flags on the hotel across the street.

June checked in to that same hotel the next day, and waited. Waited for proof that Victor was the EO killer, that he was the person Stell was looking for, the one Marcella promised to find.

She had been waiting for three days.

Victor came and went, a constant, restless force, carving slow circles through the small city, and June would follow at a distance, snapping photos with her phone. But so far, he'd yet to make a move. June was getting restless.

Still, it hadn't *all* been a waste of time. She'd gotten to see Syd—hadn't let the girl see her, of course, there would be time for that later—but once, she'd trailed Mitch and Sydney to a movie, sat right behind them, and let herself pretend they were there together, like a family.

It had been nice.

But mostly, June waited.

She hated waiting.

Right now, she was pacing on the curb outside the hotel, dressed as an old man, a cigarette hanging from her fingers.

She looked up, now and then, waiting for the balcony door five floors up and two over to slide open, waiting for Syd to emerge into the afternoon sun.

A few minutes later, she did.

That familiar blond bob caught the light as she stepped out onto the patio. June smiled—despite Sydney's complaints, she *was* growing up. The changes were subtle, sure, but June knew people well enough to read those subtleties, even if they had less to do with height and weight and more to do with posture, poise.

Syd had explained the problem of her aging, sometime around her sixteenth birthday. It was the cold—or, at least, that was Victor's theory—that the hypothermia she'd suffered had slowed *everything* about her. Syd had complained that, at the rate things seemed to be going, her teens would take forever. But then June had pointed out that so would her twenties, and in her own experience, those were the best years, anyway. Syd had gotten quiet then, silence stretching across cities.

"And by the time I'm thirty," she'd said, "everyone I know will be dead. Except for Eli."

Eli. The way Sydney said that name, as if she was afraid that speaking it too loud would somehow summon him.

"What about you?" she'd asked June with sudden curiosity. "Do you age?"

June had hesitated. She'd glimpsed the shape that hung in the back of her wardrobe, the one she never took out. It hung so perfectly still, beneath its film of disuse, but there was no denying.

"I do."

Now, June watched as Sydney sank into a patio chair, head bowed over her phone even as she put her feet up on that giant black dog, who didn't seem to mind at all.

A few seconds later, June's cell gave a soft ping.

Syd: Are you still in Merit?

She tipped her head up to savor the warm blue sky, and then lied.

June: Yeah. It's raining. I hope the weather's nicer there.

The front door across the street swung open, and a wraith of a man stepped out, shielding his eyes from the sun. It had been three years since June had seen Victor Vale. He didn't look well. His face was a rock worn with deep hollows. And the way he moved—as if he were a length of cord, strung so tight that any force might snap it.

He hurts people, Sydney had said.

But June had been watching for days, and aside from the way strangers bent out of his path, she hadn't seen him use his power once. He didn't look that strong.

He's sick. It's my fault.

Victor started down the block. June stubbed out her cigarette and followed, merging with a small group of pedestrians as it passed. With each intersection, strangers peeled away, but others joined, and all the while June kept Victor in her sights. He moved like a ghost through the city, slipping out of its bright heart and into seedier parts, before arriving in a district known as the Brickworks.

Four warehouses, squat brick buildings like pillars, or compass points, framed the blocks that made up the Brickworks, and between them, a network of bars, betting shops, strip clubs, and darker fare.

You didn't need a line or a fence to find the place where good neighborhoods gave way to bad ones. June had lived in enough of both to know by feel. The shift from new steel to old stone. Double-glazed windows to spidering glass. The polish worn off, and never repainted. Curbs glittering with the remains of the last broken bottle.

The Brickworks didn't even pretend to be respectable.

Few places could exude that much trouble in the middle of the day, and given the sheer number of illicit businesses, June guessed the local police were getting a cut to look the other way. By the time she stepped across the proverbial tracks, she'd shifted into an old biker, all gristle and bone and tattooed sleeves.

It wasn't the first time Victor's wanderings had led him—and by extension June—to this corner of the city. He was obviously look-ing for someone. But the tangle of buildings and the broad daylight made it hard to follow too closely. June fell back, and when Victor's pale head vanished through a door at the back of a bar, she changed tactics, returned to the street and circled until she found a half-rusted ladder hanging from a structurally unstable fire escape.

June hauled herself up onto the nearest warehouse roof, boots skimming the tar as, somewhere nearby, a door crashed open. She crossed the roof in time to see a man go crashing backward into a stack of empty crates, muttering curses.

Victor came into view a few seconds later. The man on the ground got up and started toward Victor, only to buckle, as if he'd been struck.

Victor's cool voice wafted up like smoke.

"I will ask you one more time . . ."

The man said something, the words low and unintelligible from June's position on the roof. But Victor clearly heard him. With a single, upward flick of his hand, the man was forced up to his feet, and Victor shot him in the head.

The silencer muffled the violence of the gun's retort, but not its impact. Blood sprayed across the bricks, and the man fell lifeless to the ground. A second later, something seemed to fall in Victor, too. His poise, so tightly held, began to fray, and he swayed a little on his feet before slumping back against the opposite wall. He ran a hand through his light hair, and let his head tip back against the brick as he looked up.

June lunged backward, breath held, waiting for some sign that he'd seen her. But Victor's gaze had been miles away. She heard his footsteps, slow and even, and by the time she chanced another look over the rooftop edge, he had disappeared around the corner.

JUNE found him again, at the edge of the Brickworks, followed half a block behind as she dialed Marcella's number.

She hesitated before she hit Call, not because she had any lingering doubts, but simply because the words would carry weight, consequence, and not just for Victor. Putting him in EON's path meant endangering Sydney, too.

But June would be there. She'd keep her girl safe.

The phone rang once, and then Marcella answered. "Well?"

June studied the man in black. "His name is Victor Vale."

"That was fast," said Marcella. "And you're sure he's the one they're looking for?"

"Positive," said June.

"And his power?"

"Pain," said June.

She could hear Marcella's smile. "*Interesting.* Is he alone?"

"Yes," said June. "As far as I can tell."

The words came out effortlessly. Lying was a skill made easy by habit.

Besides, Sydney was *hers,* and June didn't know if she wanted to share. If she could get the girl to Merit, maybe. If Marcella succeeded, if the time came when EOs didn't have to hide, or run. June knew Sydney was tired of running. In the meantime, there was no need for Marcella to know about the girl. Not yet.

"I'll stay here," continued June. "Keep an eye on things. Wouldn't want Victor to slip away." She frankly didn't care if EON got their hands on Victor, but she wasn't about to let Sydney fall into the same trap. "Unless you need me," she added.

"No," said Marcella. "We'll survive a little longer without your sparkling wit."

"You know you miss me," said June. "Has Merit built a statue in your honor yet?"

Marcella only laughed. "Not yet," she said, "but they will."

And June honestly couldn't tell if she was joking.

AS June followed Victor home, she toyed with the idea of killing him then and there.

She knew she *shouldn't,* but the idea was tempting. It would certainly make things simpler. And she was pretty sure she could manage the kill—the pain wasn't an issue, but that physical control of his would likely make things difficult. Still, June did love a challenge. She turned the idea over like a butterfly knife as she walked. After all, Marcella planned to hand Victor over to EON. Wouldn't it be a mercy, to cut him down instead? It was a boon, of course, that in killing Victor, Sydney would be free—free of her guilt and her attachment.

June was still mulling it over when, halfway down the block, Victor stumbled.

His step changed, lost its smooth stride. She saw him lurch to a stop, and then start again, his steps faster, more urgent.

June quickened her pace, but as Victor reached the intersection, the light changed, and there was a jostle of bodies, a taxi pulled too far forward, honking horns and hurrying shapes, and in that second, June lost him.

She swore, doubling back.

She hadn't been that far behind.

Where could he have gone?

He wasn't on the main road, which meant he'd slipped down a side street. June checked one, and then another, and she was at the mouth of the third when she caught sight of him, his back to her, doubled over and clutching at the wall. She started toward him, shifting into a middle-aged woman with mousy brown hair, innocuous, forgettable, and was just about to call out, ask if he was all right, when Victor collapsed.

As he did, the air around him rippled, and a second later, something slammed into June with all the force of a truck. If a truck were made of current instead of steel.

June was thrown backward, her latest shape sloughing away by the time she hit the pavement. Had she been anyone else, the force would have killed her.

As it was, she *felt* it. Not the blast itself, but the back of her head where it hit the ground. Pain cut a shallow line across her scalp, and June sat up, rubbing her head. Her fingers came away dotted with red, and her breath caught, not at the sight of the blood, but the arm, familiar pale skin dotted with freckles.

She was herself. Vulnerable. Exposed.

"Fuck." June staggered to her feet, swapping out the body—*her* body—for another, shuddering with relief as the pain was erased along with every other trace of her true form.

And then she remembered Victor.

He was slumped, motionless, against the alley wall. His head lolled against his chest.

He's sick, Sydney had said. *I made him sick.*

But the body on the ground wasn't just sick. It was *dead*. No pulse, no color, no signs of life.

Amazing—after all the time June had spent persuading herself *not* to kill him, he'd gone and died anyway.

At least, she *thought* he was dead. He certainly *looked* dead.

Cautiously, June moved toward the body.

She crouched, and touched his shoulder, and as she did, something leapt through her fingers, flickered through her mind. Memories. Not all of them, not even a handful, only one. A lab. A redhead. A current. A scream. It moved through her like static shock, a single glimpse, brief, and impossible, bright, and then gone.

June recoiled, shaking out her hand, and then she drew her gun and brought the barrel to rest against the man's forehead. Whether or not he was really dead, she could make it stick. He'd made it so easy. Maybe fate was shining on June after all.

She thumbed off the safety, let her finger come to rest against the trigger.

And then stopped.

June could think of a dozen reasons to make sure Victor was dead, and only one to stay her hand.

Sydney.

This was the one thing Sydney would never forgive, if she found out. Besides, June didn't want to steal the girl this way. Wanted to win her, fair and square. She'd told Sydney once that people should choose their family, and she'd meant it.

June wanted Sydney to *choose* her.

So she lowered the gun. Was just sliding the weapon back into her coat when suddenly, impossibly, Victor *moved*.

June nearly jumped out of her skin.

Few things caught her by surprise these days, but the sight of Victor Vale, shuddering back to life, was enough to give her a fright. His fingers twitched, a small current running visibly over his skin, and then his chest inflated as he drew a deep breath, and opened his eyes, and looked up.

"Oh, Christ," said June, one hand to her racing heart. "I thought you were dead!"

For a moment, Victor stared at her with the blank gaze of the very drunk, or the hopelessly lost. And then, quick as a spark, the light went on behind his eyes.

If he was surprised to find himself sitting on the ground, it didn't show.

He started to say something, and then stopped, and drew a small black object from between his teeth. A mouth guard. June realized that whatever had happened just now, it wasn't the first time.

Victor was looking at June now, his gaze cold and clear.

"Do I know you?" he asked, and there was no thickness in his voice, no disorientation, only study.

"Don't think so," said June, talking as fast as she could think, relieved she'd shifted into another disarming body, the black-haired girl she'd used in Hutch's office. "I was just walking past and saw you lying on the ground. Should I call an ambulance?"

"No," said Victor quietly, rising to his feet.

"No offense, sir, but you didn't look too well a moment ago."

"I have a condition."

Bullshit, thought June. Seizures were a condition. What she'd seen just now was death.

"I'm fine now," he insisted.

That bit seemed true. Whatever had come over Victor, it was already gone. The man who stood before her now was the picture of control. He turned, heading back toward the street.

June had a clear shot at the back of his head, but she also had the strange certainty that if she went for her gun now, she'd never get the shot off.

The air was humming with power, and none of it was hers. So June's hand stayed at her side as she watched Victor go, swearing inwardly.

She should have killed him when she had the chance.

XXI

ONE WEEK AGO

SYDNEY Clarke was getting stronger.

She'd resurrected three more birds since the first, each feat performed using fewer and fewer pieces.

She was just setting her latest victory free when she heard the front door close.

Victor was home.

She hadn't told him yet, about the successes—she knew he'd be proud, wanted to see that pride turned toward her—but she didn't want to jinx them, didn't want him to look at her and glimpse the motive behind her progress, the reason for her intensity.

Victor was too good at seeing through things.

Sydney shut the window and started toward the bedroom door, but halfway there, she felt her steps slow, something catch in her throat.

The two voices beyond were muffled, but distinct.

Victor's, low and steady. "He was incompatible."

Mitch's halting reply. "That was the last one."

Something pitched inside Sydney's chest.

The last one.

She pressed a hand against her sternum, as if trying to stop its fall. She realized what it was as it slipped between her fingers. Hope.

"I see." That was all Victor said.

As if it were a mild setback and not a death knell.

Sydney's head came to rest against the bedroom door, her most recent victory forgotten. She waited until the space beyond was quiet. And then she stepped out into the hall.

The door to Victor's room was closed, and Mitch was a dark shape out on the patio, his head bowed, his elbows resting on the rail.

In the kitchen, a piece of paper sat crumpled on top of the trash. Sydney drew it out, smoothed it on the counter.

It was Victor's last EO profile.

His last lead.

The page had been reduced to a wall of black lines, interrupted only by five letters, scattered across the page.

FIXME.

Sydney held her breath. Behind her eyes, the surface of a lake cracked under Victor's feet.

XXII

ONE WEEK AGO

DOWNTOWN MERIT

BY the end of the first week, Stell knew he'd made a terrible mistake.

He knew it when he saw the sinkhole on Broadway. Knew it when he was called to the collapsed building on Ninth. And he certainly knew it when he stepped into the ballroom at the Continental.

He moved through the vast space, a hazard mask cinched over his nose and mouth. The ballroom was high-ceilinged and ornate, a popular place for business execs and powerful families alike to throw parties. Stell assumed that was what had been happening the night before. After all, the tables were still laid out, the gossamer and ribbons still drew ghostly lines through the air.

Only the *people* were missing.

No, not missing. A fine patina of ash covered every surface. It was all that was left of the forty-one guests in the Continental's evening register.

Needless to say, the scene had tripped the Merit PD's *strange shit* alarm.

Stell had seen enough—he retreated into the hall, pulling the mask from his face as he dialed.

Two rings later, Marcella's smooth voice answered. "Hello, Joseph."

"Do you want to tell me," hissed Stell, "what I'm looking at right now?"

"I couldn't say."

"Then I'll tell *you*," he snapped. "I'm standing outside a ballroom at the Continental. It looks like a fucking snowstorm in there."

"How peculiar."

"What part of lying low did you *not* understand?"

"Well," she said coyly, "I didn't sign my name in the ashes."

He pinched the bridge of his nose. "You are making it very hard to look the other way."

"Crime *has* gone down, as promised."

"No," said Stell, "it's simply been *consolidated*." He lowered his voice as he paced the hall. "Tell me you have something to show me, besides this gross display. Preferably something related to the subject of our mutual interest."

Marcella sighed. "You really do take the fun out of things. I thought we could have lunch to celebrate, but since you're obviously busy, I'll go ahead and tell you now. I found your EO killer."

Stell stiffened. "Is he with you now?"

"No," said Marcella. "But don't worry. A deal's a deal. And I still have a week."

"Marcella—"

"I'm sending you a photo. To whet your appetite."

XXIII

SHE really was clever, thought Eli.

He lay, stretched out on the cot, staring up at his reflection in the mirror ceiling as he turned the problem like a coin between his fingers.

Through some combination of strategy and luck, Marcella had managed to flank herself with two compatible powers. He lined them up in his mind.

The ruiner. The shapeshifter. The forcefield.

Up close. Long distance. And everything between. Together, their powers were nearly impregnable. But find a way to separate them, and Marcella would die just like anyone else.

Footsteps sounded beyond the glass, and a second later, the far wall went clear, revealing a very red-faced Stell. "Did you know?"

Eli blinked and sat up. "I'm not omniscient, Director. You'll have to be more specific."

Stell slammed a piece of paper against the barrier. A printout. A photograph. Eli swung his legs off the cot and approached the glass. Stilled when he saw the face in the photo. There he was, the narrow face, hawkish in profile, chin grazing the collar of his trench coat. Not a good photo, not a *clear* photo, but Eli would recognize him anywhere.

Victor Vale.

"Two years," said Stell. "That's how long you've had to track him down, and Marcella delivers this in less than two weeks. You buried it. You *knew*."

But Eli realized, staring at the photo, that he hadn't known, not really. He'd wanted to be right, wanted to be sure, but there had always been that fissure, a line of doubt. Now, it sealed, smoothed, solid enough to bear the weight of the truth.

"I guess you didn't burn the body."

"God *dammit*, Eli," snarled Stell. He shook his head. "How is this possible?"

"Victor's always been terrible at staying dead."

"*How?*" demanded Stell.

"Serena's little sister had the inconvenient ability to resurrect the dead."

"Sydney Clarke? You listed her among your kills."

"Technically," said Eli, "Serena was supposed to take care of her. Obviously she got cold feet."

One more thing he'd have to handle himself.

Eli dragged his gaze away from the photo. "What are you going to do about him?"

"I'm going to find him. You two can each have a cell to rot in."

"Oh, great," said Eli dryly. "We can be neighbors."

"This isn't a fucking joke," snapped Stell. "All your talk of cooperation, I knew it was a ruse. I *knew* you couldn't be trusted."

"In the name of *God*," scoffed Eli. "How many excuses will you find to vindicate your own stubbornness?"

"He's been out there, killing humans and EOs, and you *knew*."

"I *suspected*—"

"And you didn't say anything."

"You didn't burn the body!" roared Eli. "I put him down, and *you* let him get back up. Victor Vale's continued existence, and the deaths he's since accrued—those are *your* failures, not mine. Yes, I kept my suspicions from you, because I hoped I was *wrong*, hoped that you hadn't been so foolish, hadn't failed so catastrophically. And if you had, well, then I knew my warnings would fall on deaf ears. You want Victor? Fine. I'll help you take him *again*."

He went to the low shelf, drew the hunter's folder from the row of case files.

"Unless you'd rather let Marcella lead you through her hoops instead."

He dropped the folder in the open tray.

"I'm sure once she figures out Victor's value, she'll make you pay every cent."

Stell said nothing, his face a poor imitation of a stone wall as he slowly reached for the file. But Eli, of course, could still see every crack.

"My advisement," he said, "is on the last page."

Stell skimmed the instructions in silence, and then looked up. "You think this will work?"

"It's how *I'd* catch him," said Eli, truthfully.

Stell turned to go, but Eli called him back.

"Look me in the eye," said Eli, "and tell me that when you find Victor, you will kill him once and for all."

Stell met his gaze. "I'll do as I see fit."

Eli flashed a feral grin. "Of course you will," he said.

And so will I.

XXIV

SYDNEY was back on the ice.

It stretched in every direction. She couldn't see the banks, couldn't see anything but the frozen stretch of lake ahead, behind, the plume of her own breath.

"Hello?" she called.

Her voice echoed across the lake.

The ice crackled just behind her and she spun around, expecting to see Eli.

But there was no one there.

And then, from somewhere in the distance, a sound.

Not the cracking of the lake. A short, sharp tone.

Sydney sat up.

She didn't remember falling asleep, but she was curled on the sofa, Dol at her feet and thin morning light seeping in the windows.

The sharp tone sounded again, and Syd looked around for her phone before she realized that the sound was coming from Mitch's computer. The laptop sat open on the table a few feet away, pinging like a beacon.

Sydney tapped the computer awake.

Mitch's black lock screen came up, and she typed in the password—*benedición*. The screen gave way to a matrix of code, way beyond the basics he'd been teaching her. But Syd's attention went to the corner of the screen, where a small icon bounced up and down.

Results (1).

Sydney clicked the icon, and a new window popped up.

Her breath caught. She recognized the page's format from the paper she'd found crumpled in the trash. It was a profile. A distinguished man, dark-skinned with a trim white beard, staring out at her from a professional photo.

Ellis Dumont. Fifty-seven. A surgeon who'd been in an accident the year before. He hadn't abandoned his old life; maybe that was why he hadn't shown up in the system. Not enough markers. But this—this was the important part. Ever since he'd returned to work, his patients' recovery rate had skyrocketed. There were links to news articles, pieces praising this man with a near prescient ability to discover what was wrong.

She scrolled down the page until she found Dumont's current location.

Merit Central Hospital.

Sydney surged to her feet and hurried down the hall. The soft hush of the shower spilled from Mitch's room. Victor's door was ajar, the space beyond dark. She could just make out the lines of his body on the bed, his back to her.

The first and only time she'd ever woken him, it had been from a nightmare, and he'd lit her up like a Christmas tree. The pain had echoed in her nerves for hours.

She knew it probably wouldn't happen again, but it was still hard to force herself forward. In the end, it was a wasted fear.

"I'm not asleep," said Victor softly.

He sat up and turned to face Sydney, his eyes narrowing.

"What is it?"

Sydney's heart was racing. "There's something you should see."

She sat, perched on the edge of the sofa, as Victor read the profile, his expression carefully blank. She wished she could read his mind. Hell, she wished she could read his face.

Mitch appeared in the doorway, large towel draped over his bare shoulders. "What's going on?"

"Get your things," said Victor, rising to his feet.

"We're going to Merit."

XXV

FIRST AND WHITE

MARCELLA leaned back in her chair and admired the view.

The city spilled away beyond her floor-to-ceiling windows, rolled out like a carpet beneath her feet.

Once upon a time she'd stood on the rooftop of a college frat and thought she could see all of Merit. But it had only been a few small blocks, the rest swallowed up by higher buildings. *This* was a real view. *This* was her city.

She turned back toward the desk, where the cards sat waiting.

They'd arrived in a lovely silk box—one hundred crisp white invitations, the front of each embossed with an elegant gold *M*.

She drew one from the box and flicked it open.

The words were printed in curling black, the edges embossed with gold.

Marcella Morgan and her associates
request your presence at the exclusive reveal
of Merit's most extraordinary venture.
The future of the city starts now.

The Old Courthouse.
This Friday, the 23rd. 6 p.m.
Invitation admits 2.

Marcella smiled, turning the card between her fingers.

What now? June had asked. *You're going to throw yourself a fucking party?*

Marcella knew the girl had meant it as a joke, but Stell had tipped his hand, the night they met, and let a face card show.

No more grand displays. The last thing this city needs . . .

But, of course, Stell hadn't really been talking about the city. He meant *EON*. Yes, a little publicity would be bad for their business.

And so, that was exactly what Marcella planned to give them.

She was done playing by other people's rules. Done hiding. If you lived in the dark, you died in the dark. But stand in the light, and it was that much harder to make you disappear.

And Marcella Renee Morgan wasn't going anywhere.

XXVI

TWO DAYS AGO

ON THE ROAD

MITCHELL Turner had a bad feeling.

He got them, now and then, the way other people got migraines or déjà vu.

Sometimes it was dull, abstract, a sense of wrongness that crept in like night, slow but inevitable. Other times it was sudden and sharp, like a pain in his side. Mitch didn't know where the feelings came from, but he knew to listen when they did.

Bad feelings were warnings, when you had bad luck.

And all Mitch's life, he'd had bad luck.

Bad luck made sure he was the one who got caught.

Bad luck landed him in jail.

Bad luck crossed his path with Victor's—though he didn't see it at the time.

It was like a rubber band. Mitch could only get so far away before the invisible hand slipped and he went crashing back into trouble. Other people were always surprised when bad things happened. When good things stopped. Not him. When Mitch had one of those feelings, he listened.

Watched his step.

Kept one eye on the breakable things in his life.

He glanced in the rearview mirror and saw Sydney, curled up in her red bomber jacket, booted feet draped over Dol. She was wearing a pink wig, the synthetic strands falling over her eyes. Mitch shot a surreptitious glance at the passenger's seat and saw Victor staring out the window, his face unreadable as ever.

Merit rose in the distance ahead of them.

"Everything that goes around, comes around," said Victor. His cool blue gaze cut sideways. "You should keep driving."

Mitch frowned in confusion.

"If this doesn't work," added Victor softly. "Even if it does. Take Syd and—"

"We're not leaving," said Sydney, bolt upright in the backseat.

Victor sighed. "I should have," he murmured.

The bad feeling nipped like a shadow at Mitch's heels. How long had it been following him? Days? Weeks? Months? Had it been there since the night at Falcon Price, when he set fire to Serena's body? Or was it simply the fact that when it came to Mitch's luck, it was only a matter of time before it ran out?

"How far?" asked Sydney in the backseat.

Mitch's throat felt dry when he answered.

"We're almost there."

FUCK.

June had overslept, woken with the sun full up and in her eyes. This is why she preferred killing to stalking—you could do it on your own schedule.

She lurched out of bed, stumbled to the window, studied the apartments across the street. There was no sign of Syd on the balcony. No glimpse of Victor or Mitch in the rooms beyond. For days, they'd passed like shadows through the apartment, lounged on furniture, taken the dog for walks.

Now, the curtains were pulled back, and the place looked barren.

June swore, and got dressed.

She crossed the road, caught the door just as someone was coming out. They didn't even look twice—and why should they? She was just a kid, thirteen, gangly, innocent. June loped up the stairs, shifting again before she reached the fifth-floor landing, ready to pass herself off as a college kid, canvassing for politicians.

She knocked on their door, but no one answered.

June pressed her ear to the wood, swore again at the wall of silence, then produced a few narrow picks and let herself in.

The door swung open.

The apartment was empty.

A horrible déjà vu—of another city, another abandoned place, a full year of useless searching—but June steadied herself. Sydney was no longer a stranger. They knew each other. Trusted each other. June returned to her hotel room and fetched her phone from the bedside table, sighing with relief.

Sydney had already texted.

Syd: You'll never guess where we're going.

June knew the answer before she even read Sydney's next message. *Merit.*

Five minutes later, June was on the road, driving a solid twenty over the speed limit as she barreled toward Merit in their wake. She called Marcella on the way.

"He's on the move," she said, catching herself before she said *they.* "And headed to Merit."

"Well," said Marcella, "I wonder what gave him that idea."

"It wasn't you?"

"No," she said, sounding a little put out. "But this is better. See that he gets here safely. We'll welcome him with open arms."

June frowned as she wove around a semi. "I thought you were trading him to EON."

"I never said that," replied Marcella pointedly. "I told you I hadn't decided yet. And I haven't. You know I like to know my options, and I have to admit that Stell's reaction to the news of Victor Vale has piqued my interest. I've done a little homework, and this Vale is quite an interesting case. He could turn out to be an asset. Or perhaps not. But I certainly don't plan on handing him over to EON until I've had a chance to meet him."

Never one to waste a weapon, thought June.

"Who knows," mused Marcella. "Maybe he'll prove pliable."

Victor struck June as many things—*pliable* wasn't one of them. If anything, he seemed to be rather intransigent, cold smoke to Marcella's fire. But opposites attracted for a reason. Would it be such a bad thing? June had always assumed she'd have to pry Sydney from Victor's grasp, but maybe she wouldn't have to. Maybe he would join them, three EOs becoming five. That was a nice number, wasn't it? Five. Almost a family.

Marcella was still talking.

"I want you to make contact," she was saying. "Arrange a meeting with our new friend. I'll send you the details. Oh, and June?"

"Yeah?"

"Somebody convinced Victor to come to Merit, and it wasn't me."

"My money's on EON."

"That would probably be a good bet. Obviously, we can't let them get to Victor first. So do try not to lose him."

June swore again, and gunned the engine.

4

JUDGMENT DAY

I

THE DAY BEFORE

MERIT

THE Kingsley was a blade of a building, thrust up through the city's skyline.

But Victor hadn't chosen the place for the modern aesthetics. No, the selling point had been its underground parking, which mitigated the problems of exposure—a tattooed man with a shaved head, a giant black dog, and a short blond child would always stand out, even in a city like Merit—and the closed-circuit security, which Mitch would have hacked by the time they unpacked, and—much to Sydney's apparent delight—a rooftop garden.

Mitch set their bags down inside the door.

"Don't get comfortable," said Victor. "We're not staying long."

Mitch and Sydney shouldn't have come at all, but Victor had long given up trying to dissuade them. Attachment was a vexing thing, as pernicious as weeds.

He should have left, before it ever took root.

"I'll be back," he said, turning toward the door.

Sydney caught his arm. "Be careful," she said.

What a nuisance, Victor told himself, even as he rested his hand on her head.

"Careful is a calculated risk," he said. "And I'm very good at making those."

Victor pulled away, forcing Syd to let go, and left without looking back.

He took the elevator to the street and stepped out, alone, into the
afternoon sun, checking his watch. It was just after three. According
to Mitch, the doctor's shift at Merit Central ended at five. Victor
would be there to meet him.

Ellis Dumont.

A more spiritual person might have seen the EO's sudden appearance as a sign of divine intervention, but Victor had never put much
stock in fate, and even less in faith. Dumont's presence in the matrix was convenient to the point of suspicion, his location in Merit
its own red flag.

No, Dumont was either a gift or a trap.

Victor was inclined to think the latter.

But he couldn't afford to stake his life on it.

His latest episode had crossed the four-minute threshold. He'd
come back, but Victor knew he was playing a dangerous game. The
odds were terrible, the stakes monumental.

It was Russian roulette, except that a bullet would be a cleaner end.

He had considered that, a quick, clean death. Not a suicide, of
course—a reset. But that would introduce another factor, another
risk. If he died again—truly died—would Sydney be able to bring
him back? And if she did, how much of his power would be left?
How much of *him*?

Four blocks later, Victor turned the corner and stepped through
the sliding glass doors into a gym. He would have preferred to meet
in a bar, but Dominic Rusher was five years sober, and in a moment
of distraction Victor had agreed to meet him here instead.

He'd always hated gyms.

He'd avoided sports in school, avoided the weight yard in prison,
preferring to hone his strength in other ways. He *had* enjoyed swimming, once. The soothing repetition, the measured breath, the way
physical mass had no bearing on skill.

Now, as he strode past the hulking, sweating masses lifting

weights, he had a vivid memory of watching football players trying to swim, attacking the pool as if they could muscle it out of the way. The current worked against them. They sank like stones. Spluttered for air. Bested by something as simple and natural as water.

Dominic was waiting for him in the locker room.

At first glance, Victor hardly recognized the ex-soldier. If the last five years had whittled Victor down, they'd had the opposite effect on Dom. The change was startling—apparently, as startling as Victor's own transformation.

Dominic's eyes widened. "Victor. You look . . ."

"Yeah, like shit, I know." He tipped his shoulder against the steel lockers. "How's the job?"

Dom scratched his head. "Well enough, all things considered. But remember that EO I told you about? The one making a scene?"

"Marcella." Victor hadn't meant to hold on to that name, but something about it, about her, had stuck in his mind. "How long did she last?"

Dom shook his head. "They haven't caught her yet."

"Really?" Victor had to admit, he was impressed.

"But the thing is," said Dom, "they don't seem to be *trying*. And she's not exactly keeping the lowest profile. She killed six of our agents, clipped a sniper—hell, every day she does something new. But orders are to hold." He lowered his voice. "There's something going on. I just don't know what. Above my pay grade, obviously."

"And Eli?" prompted Victor.

"Still in his vault." Dom shot him a nervous look. "For now."

Victor's eyes narrowed. "What do you mean?"

"It's just a rumor," said Dom, "but apparently some of the higher-ups think he should be playing a more *active* role."

"They wouldn't do something that stupid."

But then, people did stupid things all the time. And Eli could charm almost anyone.

"Anything else?" he asked.

Dominic hesitated, rubbing at his neck. "It's getting worse."

"I've noticed," said Victor dryly.

"Yesterday Holtz found me heaving my guts out in a closet. And last week I broke into a cold sweat in the middle of a training seminar. I've claimed hangover, PTSD, anything I can think of, but I'm running out of lies."

And I'm running out of lives, thought Victor, pushing off the lockers.

"Good luck," called Dom as he left.

But Victor didn't need luck.

He needed a doctor.

SYDNEY stepped out into the sun on the rooftop garden of the Kingsley building.

It was a blue sky day, but the air was still cold. It made her think of the lake, her thirteenth birthday, the skin of ice over the melted water. Her fingers tightened on her cell. The text had come in while she was unpacking, three short words that made her nervous.

> **June**: Call me. Now.

Sydney called.

It rang, and rang, and when June finally answered, all Syd heard was music, too loud and fraying at the edges. June's lilting voice broke through, telling her to hold on, and a second later the music dropped away, replaced by the low hum of an engine.

"Sydney," said June, her voice high and clear. "Just the girl I need."

"Hey," said Syd. "We just got to Merit. What's going on? Are you here?"

"On my way back," said June. "Had a bit of work outside the city. Look," she went on, "I need you to do something for me."

There was a tension in June's voice, an urgency Syd had never heard before.

"What is it?" she asked.

A short exhale, like static on the line. "I need you to tell me where Victor is."

The words fell like a rock in Sydney's stomach. "What?"

"Listen to me," pressed the other girl. "He's in trouble. There are some really dangerous people in Merit, and they know he's here, and they're looking for him. I want to keep him safe, I do—and I *can*—but I need your help."

Safe. Syd's mind tripped over the word. If Victor was in trouble—but *why* was he in trouble, and how did June know? Who was looking for him? EON?

She started to ask, but June cut her off.

June, who'd never even raised her voice.

"Do you trust me or not?"

She did. She wanted to. But—

"Where is he, Sydney?"

She swallowed. "Merit Central Hospital."

II

THE DAY BEFORE

MERIT CENTRAL HOSPITAL

IT was seventeen minutes past five.

Victor leaned back against Dumont's gray sedan in the hospital parking garage and scrolled through Dom's texts as he waited for the doctor. The buzzing in his skull seemed to ratchet up as he skimmed the most recent times.

3 minutes, 49 seconds.

3 minutes, 52 seconds.

3 minutes, 56 seconds.

4 minutes, 04 seconds.

The stairwell door clattered open across the garage.

Victor glanced up and saw Dumont, dark skin, gray hair, head bowed over his tablet as he headed toward his car. Toward Victor.

Victor didn't move, simply waited for the doctor to come to him.

"Dr. Dumont?"

The man looked up, brows furrowing. Victor thought he saw something cross the doctor's face. Not surprise, exactly, but fear. "Can I help you?"

Victor studied him, fingers flexing. "I certainly hope so."

Dumont looked around the parking garage. "I'm off work," he said, "but you can make an appointment—"

Victor didn't have time for this—he took hold of the doctor's nerves, and twisted. Dumont buckled with a shocked cry. He clutched his chest, sweat breaking out along his brow.

Having made his point, Victor let go.

Dumont sagged back against his car. "You're—an EO."

"Just like you," said Victor.

"I don't—hurt people," said Dumont.

"No? Then how does *your* power work?"

Dumont let out a shaky breath. "I can see—how people are broken. I can—see how—to put them back together."

Relief swept through Victor. Finally, a promising lead.

"Good," he said, stepping toward the doctor. "Show me."

Dumont shook his head. Victor was about take hold of the doctor's nerves again when the stairwell door swung open and a small huddle of nurses stepped out, talking animatedly. A car beeped nearby. Victor shifted to block their view.

"Not here," muttered Dumont.

"Then where?" asked Victor.

The doctor nodded at the hospital. "My office is on the seventh—"

"No," said Victor. Too many eyes. Too many doors.

Dumont rubbed his forehead. "The fifth floor is under renovation. It should be empty. That's the best I can do."

Victor hesitated, but the humming in his head was spreading to his limbs. He was running out of time.

"Fine," he said, "lead the way."

MEANWHILE, ACROSS TOWN . . .

Sydney tried to call Victor, but it went straight to voicemail every time.

What did June mean when she said he was in trouble?

They'd been careful. They were always careful.

Do you trust me or not?

In that moment, Sydney had. She hoped she hadn't made a mistake.

Footsteps sounded behind her. Sydney's hand went automatically to the gun she now kept tucked in her coat, thumb already resting against the safety.

But then she recognized the heavy tread, and turned to see Mitch striding toward her across the rooftop garden.

"There you are," he said cheerfully.

She let go of the gun. "Hey," she said. "Just admiring the view." She tried to keep her voice light, but her head was still spinning, and she was afraid it would show on her face, so she turned her back on Mitch. "It's weird, isn't it? How cities change. Buildings go up, and come down, and it looks the same—and different."

"Like you," said Mitch, ruffling her pink wig. The gesture was light, easy, but there was a strain in his voice, and the silence, when it fell, was heavy. Syd's mind was on Victor, but she knew Mitch's was on her sister.

They'd never talked about what really happened to Serena. It had been too soon, and then too late. The wound had healed, as best as it could.

But now that they were back in Merit, the finished Falcon Price building glinting in the distance, the air was thick with everything they'd never said.

"Hey, Syd," started Mitch, but she cut him off.

"Do you ever wish you were an EO?"

Mitch's brow crinkled, caught off guard by the question. He didn't answer right away. He'd always been careful like that, sorting out his words before he said them.

"I remember when I first met Victor," he said at last. "These guys inside were giving me a hard time, and he just . . ." Mitch slid his hand through the air. "He made it look so easy. I guess to him it probably was. But watching it made me feel . . . small."

Syd laughed. "You're the biggest guy I know."

He flashed her a smile, but it was sad at the edges. "Sometimes it feels like I'm in a fight, and all I've got are my hands, and the other guy has a knife. But that guy with the knife, eventually he's going to face someone with a gun. And the one with the gun is going to go up against someone with a bomb. The truth is, Syd, there will always be somebody stronger than you. That's just the way the world works." He looked up at the shining skyscraper. "It doesn't matter if you're a human versus a human or a human versus an EO or an EO versus an EO. You do what you can. You fight, and you win, until you don't."

Sydney swallowed, and turned her attention back to the skyline.

"Any word from Victor?" she asked, trying to keep her voice light.

Mitch shook his head. "Not yet. But don't worry." His hand came to rest on her shoulder. "He can take care of himself."

MERIT CENTRAL HOSPITAL

Their steps echoed on the stairs.

"What exactly happens at the apex of these episodes?" asked Dumont.

"Nerve impairment. Muscular seizure." Victor ticked off the symptoms. "Atrial fibrillation. Cardiac arrest. Death."

Dumont glanced back. *"Death?"*

Victor nodded.

"Do you know how many times you've died? Are we talking about three to four recurrences or a dozen—"

"One hundred and thirty-two."

The doctor's face went slack. "That's . . . not possible."

Victor considered him dryly. "I assure you, I've kept track."

"But the sheer strain on your body." Dumont shook his head. "You shouldn't be alive."

"That is both the cause and the crux of our problem, isn't it?"

"Have you experienced cognitive impairment?"

Victor hesitated. "There's a brief period of disorientation immediately after. And it's getting longer."

"It's a miracle you're still forming sentences."

Miracle. Victor had always hated that word.

They reached the fifth floor, and Dumont pushed open a set of doors. He hit a switch and the lights came on, one shuddering wave at a time, illuminating a broad floor that was indeed in the process of being torn apart and put back together. Plastic sheeting hung in makeshift curtains, equipment covered in white tarps, and for an instant Victor imagined himself back in the half-built Falcon Price building, voices bouncing off concrete.

"There are some exam rooms this way," said Dumont, but Victor refused to move.

"This is far enough."

They were standing in the middle of the tangled space. Victor would have preferred a clean line of sight to the exits, but the tarping made that impossible.

Dumont set his things down and shrugged out of his coat.

"How long have you been an EO?" asked Victor.

"Two years," said the doctor.

Two years. And he'd only just shown up in their search matrix.

"Go ahead and sit down," said Dumont, gesturing to a chair. Victor continued to stand.

"Tell me something, Doctor. When you were dying, what were your final thoughts?"

"My final thoughts?" echoed Dumont, considering. "I thought about my family . . . how much I'd miss them . . . how I didn't want to leave . . ." He stumbled over the answer, as if he couldn't remember. Perhaps he was simply nervous, but as he stammered, Victor was reminded of an actor forgetting their lines.

"And you said your power is to diagnose a person's ailments?"

It didn't fit.

An EO's near-death experience was colored so strongly by their last moments, their will to survive, but also their dire, most desperate wishes. Dumont's final moments, final thoughts, should have shaped his power, and yet—

The doctor managed a nervous smile. "I thought I was meant to be diagnosing *you*."

Victor parroted the smile. "Yes, of course. Go ahead."

But Dumont hesitated, patting his shirt pocket.

"Is something wrong?" asked Victor, fingers drifting toward his holstered gun.

"I don't have my glasses." Dumont turned away. "I must have left them downstairs. I'll just go and—"

But Victor was already behind him.

He couldn't afford to use his power—pain generated noise, and noise drew attention—so Victor settled for pressing the gun against the base of the doctor's spine and wrapping his free hand over the doctor's mouth. "The trouble with conventional weapons," he said in the doctor's ear, "is that the damage they do is so permanent. If you make a sound, you will never walk again. Do you understand?"

Dumont nodded once.

"You're not an EO, are you?"

A short sideways flick. *No.*

"Are they waiting for your signal?"

The doctor shook his head and tried to speak, his words muffled against Victor's palm. Victor drew his hand away, and the doctor repeated himself.

"They're already here."

As if on cue, Victor heard doors swing open, the shuffle of steps.

"I'm sorry," continued Dumont. "They have people at my house. Watching my family. They said if I—"

Victor cut him off. "Your motives are irrelevant. The only thing I need to know is how to get out." He slid the gun's safety off. "Exits. Tell me."

"There's a service elevator—the others won't stop here—and two internal stairs."

And of course, there was the way they'd come in, the most direct route—and the one with the least amount of cover.

Boots shuffled across the linoleum nearby, the harsh overhead lights casting shadows on the plastic sheeting. Victor needed to be able to see his targets. But he didn't need to be able to see them *clearly*.

He reached for the nearest shadow and it buckled with a cry as the pretense of surprise shattered, and shots rang out, and the fifth floor plunged into chaos.

VICTOR'S hand twitched, and two more soldiers went down screaming, before they cut the lights. A second later he heard the telltale sound of a metal clasp, the hiss of air, and then the canisters came rolling across the ground, filling the air with smoke.

"Hold your breath," he ordered, dragging Dumont back against the wall as scopes traced red lines through the billowing white. The smoke burned Victor's eyes, clawing at his senses, and through it all the crackle of energy was spreading through his limbs—warning.

Not yet, he thought. *Not yet.*

The service elevator groaned open, and Victor had time to see the barrel of a gun, the first traces of black armor, combat boots. He twisted sideways, releasing his hostage as he ducked out of the soldiers' line of fire.

Dumont threw up his hands as Victor reached the stairwell.

"Don't shoot!" called the doctor, coughing as the smoke hit his lungs.

The soldiers pushed past him as Victor surged into the stairwell and started down.

More footsteps rose up from below, but Victor had the high ground now. By the time the first soldier saw him, Victor already had their nerves in his grasp. He twisted the dial all the way up, and they fell, like puppets without strings.

Victor rounded their bodies and continued down. He was nearly to the third-floor landing when the first spasm hit.

For a second, he thought he'd been shot.

Then he realized, with horror, that he was out of time. The current arced through him, lighting his nerves, and he bowed his head, steadying himself against the rail before forcing his body onward.

He made it to the first floor, and opened the door just in time to see a soldier heading straight for him, weapon raised. Before Victor could summon the strength or the focus to bring the soldier down, someone else had done it for him.

A silencer swung into view, followed by three muted thumps as the gun fired point-blank into the side of the soldier's head. It wasn't enough to pierce the helmet, but it caught him off guard, and half a second later the shooter—a female doctor—stepped into sight. She stepped right into the soldier's arms, and then—almost elegantly—drove a blade up under his helmet.

The soldier dropped like a stone, and the female doctor turned on Victor.

"Don't just stand there," she hissed, her voice strangely familiar. Footsteps sounded overhead and below. *"Find another way out."*

Victor had questions, but there was no time to ask.

He turned and continued down the stairs toward the hospital sublevels. Burst through a set of doors into an empty hall, the sign at the end marked MORGUE in small, mocking letters. But beyond that—an exit sign. Halfway there, the next spasm hit, and Victor stumbled, one shoulder slamming hard into the concrete wall. His knee buckled, and he went down.

He tried to force himself back up as the doors swung open behind him.

"Stay down!" ordered a soldier as Victor collapsed to the floor.

"We've got him," said one voice.

"He's down," said another.

He couldn't get up, couldn't get away. But Victor still had one weapon. The current climbed higher, the dial turned up, and he held on as long as possible, clutching to life one fractured, agonizing second at a time until the boots came into sight.

And then, Victor let go.

Let the pain crash over him in a final wave, washing everything away.

VICTOR came to in the dark.

His vision slid in and out for a second before finally coming into focus. He was lying on a gurney, the ceiling much lower than it should be. Victor tested his limbs, expecting to find them restrained, but there was nothing on his wrists or ankles. He tried to sit up, and pain closed tightly around his chest. Two of his ribs felt broken, but he could still breathe.

"I started CPR," said a voice. "But I was worried it would do more damage than good."

Victor turned his head and saw the figure in the dark.

Dumont.

The doctor was sitting on a bench a couple feet away, half hidden by shadow.

Victor looked around, and realized he was lying in the back of an ambulance.

The seconds before his episode came back in fragments, broken frames, but they didn't explain how he'd gotten from the basement floor to here.

"I found you," explained the doctor, unprompted, "outside the morgue. Well, I found the soldiers first."

"You didn't turn me over to EON," observed Victor. "Why?"

Dumont examined his hands. "You could have killed me up on the fifth floor. You didn't."

It hadn't been an act of mercy. There had simply been no point.

"And the soldiers?" asked Victor.

"They were already dead."

"So was I."

Dumont nodded. "Medicine is full of calculated risks and split-second decisions. I made one."

"You could have walked away."

"I may not be ExtraOrdinary," said Dumont, "but I *am* a doctor. And I took an oath."

A siren tore through the air nearby, and Victor tensed, but it was only another ambulance, pulling out of the bay. The bay . . .

"We're still at the hospital?" asked Victor.

"Obviously," said Dumont. "I said I'd help you live, not help you *escape*. Frankly, I was beginning to doubt your odds of doing either."

Victor frowned, feeling his pockets for his phone. "How long was I gone?"

"Nearly four and a half minutes."

Victor swore under his breath. No wonder the doctor hadn't driven away.

"I should run some tests," continued Dumont, producing a pen-light, "make sure your cognitive function hasn't been—"

"That won't be necessary," said Victor. There was nothing Dumont could do for him now—nothing that would make a difference. And while four and a half minutes was far too long to be dead, it wasn't long enough for EON's enforcement team to clear out. They would still be on-site. How long until more joined them?

Victor nodded at the front of the ambulance. "I assume you can drive?"

Dumont hesitated. "I can, but . . ."

"Get behind the wheel."

Dumont didn't move.

Victor wasn't in the mood to torture him, so he resorted to logic instead. "You said they had eyes on your family. If you go back in there now, they'll know you helped me escape."

Dumont frowned. "And how does driving you away make me less complicit?"

"You're not an accomplice," said Victor, producing a pair of cable-ties from a toolbox. "You're a hostage. I can tie you to the steering wheel now, or later. It's up to you."

The doctor silently climbed behind the wheel. Victor took the passenger's seat. He flipped the sirens on.

"Where am I going?" asked Dumont.

Victor turned the question over. "There's a bus station on the southern edge of the city. Drive."

Dumont hit the gas, and the ambulance peeled out of the bay. After a few blocks, Victor killed the sirens and the lights. He sat back in the seat, flexing his fingers. He could feel the doctor cutting glances at him.

"Eyes on the road," said Victor.

Ten minutes later, the bus depot came into sight, and Victor pointed to an empty stretch of sidewalk.

"There," he said.

As Dumont started guiding the ambulance off the road, Victor reached over, took the wheel, and jerked it, forcing the vehicle up onto the curb.

"Don't forget," he said, "you're in distress." Before Dumont could protest, Victor zip-tied his hands to the wheel. "Do you have a phone on you?" Dumont nodded at his pocket.

Victor drew the cell from the doctor's coat and threw it out the window.

"There," he said, climbing out of the ambulance.

Now he had a head start.

III

THE DAY BEFORE

EON

STELL stood before the bay of screens, arms crossed, watching it all fall apart. Radio chatter crackled from the speaker on the desk.

"No sign of target."

"Soldiers down."

"Seal the perimeter."

What a goddamned catastrophe, thought Stell, sinking down into his chair.

Eli's trap had succeeded, but his own agents had failed. Three of them were dead—two bleeding from their ears and noses on a sublevel, one knifed in the throat on the first floor—the rest had been fucking useless.

Whether Victor had seen past the bait to the hook, or simply wriggled free, one thing was clear—he hadn't done it alone.

Several of Stell's agents had been shot at by a male orderly, a receptionist, and a female doctor—but Stell had a feeling they were all the same person. One of his men had shot back, caught the doctor in the shoulder. At that same moment, halfway across the hospital, a doctor matching her *exact* description had collapsed, bleeding, in the middle of scrubbing in for surgery.

The shapeshifter—*Marcella's* shapeshifter—had been there.

And she'd helped Victor escape.

Stell took up his phone and dialed.

"Joseph," said that smooth voice.

"Where is Victor Vale?" demanded Stell through gritted teeth.

"You were cheating."

"This isn't a game. You agreed to deliver him. Instead, you are the reason he's still free. When do you intend to uphold your end of the deal?"

Marcella sighed. "Men are always so impatient. Perhaps it comes from a lifetime of being given what you want, when you want it. Sometimes, Joseph, you just have to wait."

"When?"

"Tomorrow," said Marcella. "Before the party."

Stell's chest tightened. "What party?"

"Didn't you get my invitation?" A stack of mail sat forgotten on the edge of Stell's desk. He began rifling through it. "I considered holding on to him until after . . ."

Stell found the card, crisp and white, with a gold *M* embossed on the front. It was unstamped. Someone had delivered it by hand. Stell broke the seal.

"It would certainly keep you out of my way," Marcella was saying, "but then again, I wouldn't want you to miss the show . . ."

Marcella Morgan and her associates . . .

Stell read the invitation once, and then again—he couldn't believe what he was looking at. He didn't *want* to believe it.

. . . Merit's most extraordinary venture.

"This is the opposite of lying low," he growled.

"What can I say? I've never been understated."

"We had a deal."

"We did," said Marcella. "For two weeks. Beyond that, we both knew it wouldn't last. But I have appreciated the ceasefire. It gave me time to print my invitations."

"Marcella—"

But she'd already hung up.

Stell swept a mug from his table. It shattered, dark drops of coffee painting the floor.

In seconds, Rios was there.

"Sir?" she asked, surveying the broken cup, the papers displaced in his search for the card, the crisp white invitation crumpled in his hand.

Stell slumped back in his chair, Eli's voice playing in his head.

You made a deal?

Someone this powerful belongs in the ground.

Send me.

Stell's gaze went to the slim silver briefcase the board had given him, the collar nested inside.

Agent Rios was still standing there, silent, waiting.

Stell rose to his feet. "Prepare a transport team for tomorrow."

Rios raised a brow. "For which prisoner?"

"Cardale."

STELL found Eli sitting on the edge of his cot, fingers laced and head bowed, as if he were praying.

Or simply waiting.

At the sound of Stell's approach, his head drifted up. "Director. Has my trap yielded any results?"

Stell hesitated. "Not yet," he lied. There was no reason for Eli to know about Vale's escape, and a dozen reasons to keep him in the dark. Especially considering what he was about to do. "Have you been considering the problem of Marcella?"

Eli rose. "My assessment hasn't changed."

"I'm not asking for your sentence," said Stell, "I'm asking for your method. How would you dispatch her?"

"How would *I*?"

"You *do* still believe you are the best equipped for the task."

A ghost of a smile. "I do."

"Let me be very clear," said Stell. "I don't trust you."

"You don't have to," said Eli.

Stell shook his head. What was he thinking? "We still don't know if you can even defeat Marcella."

Eli smiled grimly. "Haverty spent a year trying to find the limits of my regeneration. He never succeeded."

"Her power isn't the only problem," said Stell. "After all, Marcella is not acting alone."

"Neither am I," pressed Eli, gesturing at the cell, at EON. "The hard part isn't killing three EOs, Director. It's collecting them in one place, and then separating them so they can't work together. Do that, and your agents can take care of the other two EOs while I see to Marcella. I assure you, under the right conditions, defeating them is more than possible."

Conditions.

Stell slid Marcella's invitation through the fiberglass slot. "Will this work?"

Eli took the card, his eyes dancing across the words.

"Yes," he said, "I think it will."

IV

THE NIGHT BEFORE

MERIT

VICTOR needed a drink.

He spotted a bleak stretch of low buildings, bland, forgettable, a bar sandwiched between them, and started across the street, digging his cell from his pocket.

Mitch answered on the second ring.

"We were getting worried. What happened with Dumont?"

"It was a trap," said Victor flatly. "He was only human."

Mitch swore. "EON?"

"Indeed," said Victor. "I got away, but I won't risk leading them back to the Kingsley."

"Is that him?" called Syd in the background. "What happened?"

"Should we leave?" asked Mitch.

Yes, thought Victor. But they couldn't. Not now. The movement would only draw EON's further attention. They'd set their trap at the hospital, lain in wait. They'd gotten Victor to come to them, which meant they hadn't been able to find him. But that didn't mean they *wouldn't*. Did they already know about Sydney? What would happen if they found her instead?

"Stay in the apartment," he said. "Don't answer the door. Don't let anyone in. Call me if you notice anything or anyone outside."

"What about you?" asked Mitch.

But Victor didn't have an answer to that question yet, so instead he hung up and stepped into the bar. It was a dive, poorly lit and more than half-empty. He ordered a whiskey and settled into a booth along the back wall where he could keep an eye on the bar's only door and the handful of patrons while he waited.

Victor had pocketed a battered paperback from the center console of the ambulance—now he dug it out, along with a black felt pen, and let the broken spine fall open under his hand.

Old habits. The pen cut a steady path, blacking out the first line, and then the second. He felt his pulse slow with each erasure, each measure of text reduced to a solid black streak. The first word was always the hardest to find. Now and then, he searched for a specific one, and then erased the text around it, but most of the time, though Victor was loath to admit it, even to himself, the practice felt less like a physical act than a metaphysical one.

He let the pen skate across the page, waiting for a word to stop its path. He cut through *pride, fall, change,* before finally coming to a stop at the word *find.* His pen skipped over a solo *a* two lines later, then continued down the page until it found *way.*

Victor was running out of time, and out of leads, but he wasn't giving up.

Sydney, Mitch, Dominic—they all behaved as though surrender were a risk, an option. But it wasn't. Some fractional part of Victor wished he could stop trying, stop fighting, but it simply wasn't in him. That same stubborn will to survive, the very trait that first made him into an EO, now prevented him from acquiescing. From admitting defeat.

Whatever's happened to you, however you're hurt, you've done it to yourself.

That's what Campbell had said. And the EO was right. Victor had always been the master of his fate. He had climbed onto that steel table. He had coerced Angie into flipping the switch. He had goaded Eli into killing him five years before, knowing Sydney would bring him back.

Every action had been his own design, every step his own making.

If there was a way out of this, he would find it.

If there wasn't, he would make one himself.

The bar's only door swung open, and a few moments later Victor heard a voice, the words lost in the crowd, but the accent unmistakable.

He looked up.

There was a small, brunette woman with fox-sharp features leaning across the bar. He'd never seen the person before, but Victor knew it was her—the woman from the strip club. The concerned Samaritan from the alley, too. And of course, most recently, the doctor who'd helped him escape EON. It wasn't just the accent that Victor recognized. It was the look in the woman's eyes—*behind* her eyes, really—as she glanced toward him, the mischievous smile that lit her face. If it *was* her face.

They were an EO—that much was obvious.

He watched as the shapeshifter took up their drink and headed toward him.

"Is this seat taken?" Again, that lilting voice.

"That depends," said Victor. "The Glass Tower—was that the first time we met?"

A wry smile cut across the vulpine face. "It was."

"But not the last."

"No," said the EO, sinking into the chair across from him. "Not the last."

Victor curled his fingers around his glass. "Who are you?"

"Think of me as a kind of guardian angel. You can call me June."

"Is that your real name?"

"Ah," said June wistfully, "*real* is a murky thing, for someone like me."

The woman sat forward, and as she did, she changed. There was no hinge, no transition—the brunette girl dissolved, replaced by strawberry curls and dark blue eyes in a heart-shaped face.

"Do you like it?" asked June, as if she were asking his opinion of a new dress, not a distorted reflection of the only girl Victor had ever loved. "It's the best I can do, considering the real one is dead."

"Change," said Victor tersely.

"Aw," June sulked. "But I picked her just for you."

"*Change*," he ordered.

The blue-eyed gaze leveled on him, a challenge, a dare. Victor rose to meet it. His fingers twitched as he took hold of her nerves, turned the dial in her chest—but if the woman felt any pain, it didn't register on her face. Her power—somehow it was shielding her.

"Sorry," said June with a wan smile. "You can't hurt *me*."

A faint emphasis on the last word.

Victor leaned forward. "I don't need to."

He splayed his hand across the worn wood table, pinning her body to the chair.

A faint crease formed between June's eyes, the only hint of struggle as she fought his hold.

"There are so many nerves in a human body," said Victor. "Pain is only one of the possible signals. A single instrument in a symphony."

A smirk fought its way onto the girl's mouth. "But how long do you think you can hold me? An hour? A day? Until your next death? I wonder, which one of us will give up first?"

They were at an impasse.

Victor let go.

June exhaled, rolling her neck. As she did, the girl with the strawberry curls fell away, replaced by the brunette she'd been wearing before. "There. All better?"

"Why have you been following me?" asked Victor.

"I have a vested interest," said June. "And I'm not the only one. There's an EO in this city who would very much like to meet you. Perhaps you've heard of her."

Marcella Riggins.

The EO currently treating Merit like her own personal playground. The one who, against all odds, had yet to burn out.

"I see," said Victor slowly. "So you're just the messenger."

A flicker of annoyance crossed June's face. "Hardly."

"And why," he asked, "would I want to meet with Marcella?"

June shrugged. "Curiosity? The fact you've got nothing to lose? Or maybe—you'll do it for Sydney's sake."

Victor's expression darkened. "Is that supposed to be a threat?"

"No," said June, and for once there was no mischief, no malice, in her voice. Her expression was open, honest. She hadn't changed faces, but the difference was just as striking. "I do care what happens to that girl."

"You don't even know her."

"Everyone's got secrets, Victor. Even our darling Syd. How do you think I found you today at Merit Central? She looks out for you, and you should be doing the same for her. I know you're sick. I've seen you die. And we both know Sydney's got a long life ahead. What happens when you're not around to protect her?" The earnestness dissolved, replaced once more by that wry twist of the lips, that sly glint of light behind the eyes. "She's a powerful girl, our Syd. She'll need allies when you're gone, and we both know you already killed her first choice."

Victor looked down into his drink. "Is that what Marcella is, then? An ally?"

"Marcella," said June pointedly, "is *powerful.*"

"What exactly *is* her power?"

"Come see for yourself."

June swiped the battered paperback and pen.

"Tomorrow," she said, scribbling the details on the inside cover. "And just so you know," she added, rising. "When Marcella makes an offer, she only does it once." She nudged the book back toward him.

"Don't waste it."

V

THE NIGHT BEFORE

FIRST AND WHITE

JUNE hummed softly as the elevator rose.

When she reached the top floor, she found two men in dark suits standing outside the penthouse door. They were new, and one had the poor sense to try to stop her as she passed.

"Where do you think you're going?"

June looked down at the hand on her shoulder. When she looked back up at the man, she was *him,* down to the last hairy knuckle and acne scar.

"I go where I please," she said, her accent coming through in his deep voice.

The security pulled back as if burned.

"I'm . . . I'm sorry," he said, genuine fear flashing across his face. That—that was a pleasant change. She'd gotten surprise, shock, even awe once or twice, but never such a simple thing as *fear.* They hadn't known *who* she was, but they knew *what.* An EO. And it clearly scared the shit out of them.

Maybe Marcella was right. Maybe EOs shouldn't be the ones hiding.

"Not to worry," said June, cheerfully, shifting back into the brunette. "Honest mistake."

They scrambled to open the door, and she stepped into the penthouse, marveling a little at the strange comfort of *returning.*

We really need a dog, she thought. *Something to greet you when you get home.*

She reached the open living room, where Jonathan sat slumped on a leather sofa, palms pressed against his eyes.

"Johnny boy, why so glum?" Her steps slowed at the sight of a large red-brown stain on the floor. "Well, that's new."

"Yeah," said Jonathan, looking up, "she's been busy."

"I can see that. And where is our fearless leader tonight?" Jonathan didn't answer, didn't need to. Marcella's voice streamed from her office.

"Why would I want flowers?"

"They're lilies," said a man's voice. "I thought they'd make an elegant centerpiece."

"*I'm* the elegant centerpiece."

"Without something to soften the space, I'm afraid it will look awfully *austere.*"

"This is the beginning of a new age," snapped Marcella, "not a fucking sweet sixteen. Get rid of them."

The man hesitated. ". . . If you're sure . . ."

June heard the telltale click of heels on marble. "Well, perhaps you do know best . . ." There was a shuffle, a gasp, and June stepped through the door just in time to see the man crumble in Marcella's grip.

"Oh, I've missed this," said June pleasantly as what was left of the man fell to the floor. She considered the ruined heap, adorned only by a few tattered bits of silk and a silver cufflink. Marcella was burning hotter, faster, and—as far as June could tell—she still had yet to find her limit.

Marcella leaned back against her desk and took up a cloth, wiping her hands. "I've always hated having to repeat myself." She glanced up. "Shouldn't you be watching over our new arrival?"

"I've had enough babysitting for one day," said June. "I delivered your message."

"*And?*"

"He's a tough one to predict, but I think he'll come."

"I certainly hope so," said Marcella. "I *am* glad you made it back in time."

"For what?" asked June.

Marcella handed her a card.

June took it up, turned it over, eyes flitting over the paper. She shook her head, baffled and amused. "Jesus, Marcella, anyone ever told you that you're batshit crazy?"

Marcella pursed her lips. "Several times," she said. "It's an insult men love to aim at ambitious women. But aren't you forgetting, June—this was *your* idea."

"It was a joke and you know it." June flicked the card away. "How many people did you send that to?"

Marcella ticked them off on her fingers. "The mayor, the chief of police, the district attorney, the director of EON." She waved her hand. "And a few hundred of the most powerful—well, *formerly* most powerful—people in this fine city."

June shook her head in disbelief. "Drawing this kind of attention is a *very bad idea*. You're putting a target on our backs."

"There's already one there. Haven't you noticed? They're going to come for us, one way or another, June, and if we stay hidden, no one will ever know we were there. So let them see us. Let them see what we can do." Marcella smiled, that radiant, seductive smile. "Admit it, June. There's a part of you that wants to stand in that light. No more running. No more hiding."

Marcella didn't understand that June would *always* be hiding. But the woman was right about one thing.

People had tried to bend June. Tried to break her. Tried to make her feel small.

Perhaps it was time for them to understand how small *they* were. June could never be herself, not the self she was before, but she could be someone. She could be seen.

And when EON came calling, well, they wouldn't catch *her*.

Which left only one question, really.

Who was she going to wear?

VI

THE LAST MORNING

MERIT

SYDNEY crashed to her hands and knees on the ice.

She tried to get away, but Eli grabbed the collar of her coat, dragging her backward.

"Come now, Sydney," he said. "Let's finish what we started."

She sat up, gasping for air.

Syd didn't remember falling asleep. She'd spent most of the night tossing and turning, restless. It wasn't the Kingsley—she'd spent five years getting used to strange new places. It was Victor—or rather, his absence.

The apartment felt wrong, too empty without him.

He had a way of taking up space, and even when he started to move like a ghost, coming and going, he never *stayed* gone. There was always that thread connecting him to Sydney, and whenever he was out late, she'd lie in bed and feel it spool away beneath her hand, and then draw tight when he returned.

But Victor hadn't come back last night.

Dumont had been a trap, and Victor had almost been caught in it. He'd gotten away, and wouldn't come back until it was safe. He'd gotten away—and Sydney knew he'd had help. She checked her phone again, saw the notes from last night.

Syd: thank you

June: of course ;)

Syd got up and wandered out of her room, found Mitch at the table twisting a pair of wires and fitting them into a small black box. Sydney was always amazed that such big hands could do such precise work.

"What's that?" she asked.

Mitch smiled. "Just a precaution," he said, holding up the device. She realized she'd seen it before, or something like it, spotted them in the corners of doorways wherever she and Mitch and Victor played house.

"Have you heard from him?"

Mitch nodded. "This morning," he said. "And as soon as he gets back, we're leaving."

Sydney's chest tightened. She couldn't leave Merit. Not yet. Not before she tried—

She ducked back into her room and got dressed, pulled on the boots and the bomber jacket, and then went to the dresser, where she'd hidden the small red tin. She tucked the box deep in her pocket and started out into the apartment and toward the front door.

"Come on, Dol," she called.

The dog drew up his lazy head.

"Syd," said Mitch. "We need to stay inside."

"And he needs a walk," protested Sydney.

Dol, for his part, didn't seem excited.

"I took him out earlier on the rooftop," said Mitch. "The building's gardener won't be happy, but it'll have to do. I'm sorry, kiddo. I don't like being cooped up either, but it isn't safe—"

Sydney shook her head. "If EON knew where we were, they would have already come for us."

Mitch sighed. "Maybe. But I'm not willing to take the chance."

There was a steadiness to his words, a stern resolve. Sydney chewed her lip, considering. Mitch had never *prevented* her from leaving before, not physically. She wondered if he would.

She didn't want to make him do that. She sighed, shrugging out of her coat.

"Fine."

Mitch relaxed, visibly relieved. "All right. I'll start lunch. You hungry?"

Syd smiled. "Always," she said. "I'm going to take a shower first."

Mitch was already in the kitchen, turning on the stove, as she slipped down the hall, tugging the coat back on. She went straight past the bathroom and into Mitch's bedroom, sliding the window open as Dol padded into the room behind her.

"Stay," she whispered.

The dog opened his mouth, as if to bark, but his tongue simply lolled.

"Good boy," she said, swinging her leg over the sill. "Keep Mitch safe."

Syd was about to climb down the fire escape, but then she hesitated, digging out the playing card she always kept with her—the one Victor had plucked from the fallen deck so long ago, and then slipped like a secret into her palm.

The king of spades.

It was battered now, edges worn from five years of back pockets, a rough crease along the middle.

In their game, a face card meant freedom.

Syd told herself she wasn't breaking the rules—and if she was, well, she wasn't the only one.

She dropped the card on the floor, and tugged the window shut behind her.

VII

THE LAST MORNING

VICTOR stood on the street, the stolen paperback open in his hand.

He'd lingered in the bar until just after midnight before checking into a nearby motel, the kind that clearly wasn't eager to draw police attention. After a few restless hours on creaking springs, he'd gotten up again, and walked the thirty-four blocks through the waking heart of Merit to the address June had scribbled inside the battered front cover.

119 Alexander Place. 12 p.m.

It was, of all things, an art gallery. Large glass windows looked out onto the curb, revealing glimpses of the paintings inside. It was almost noon, and Victor hadn't decided yet if he was going in.

He weighed the options in his mind, along with June's words.

It could simply be another kind of trap. Or it could be an opportunity. But in the end, it was sheer curiosity that propelled him forward. For the EO who had managed to evade EON's net. For the woman who had held her ground instead of running.

Victor crossed the street, climbed the three short steps, and stepped into the White Hall Gallery.

It was larger than it looked from the street—a series of broad, blank rooms, linked together by archways. Abstract paintings dotted the walls, blotches of color against the white. In his black attire, Victor felt like an ink spill. Ideal for slipping through crowds on the street, but far more conspicuous in such a stark environment. So he didn't bother trying to blend in, didn't pretend to admire the art, simply set off to find Marcella.

A handful of men and women stood scattered through the rooms, but none of them were real patrons. Victor glimpsed holsters beneath fitted suits, fingers resting on the open mouths of handbags. Hired guns, he thought, wondering if June was hidden among them. He didn't spot anyone with her tells.

But he did find Marcella.

She was in the largest gallery, facing away from him, her black hair pulled up, a silk blouse dipping low between her shoulder blades. Still, he knew it was her. Not because he'd seen a photograph, but because of the way she stood, with all the casual grace of a predator. Victor was used to being the strongest person in the room, and it was both familiar and unsettling to see that confidence on someone else.

They weren't alone in the room.

A thin man in a black suit leaned against the wall between two paintings. His dark hair was slicked back, his eyes hidden behind a pair of sunglasses. The white walls made the gallery unnaturally bright, but not bright enough to merit shades—meaning they served an alternate purpose.

"I've never understood art," mused Marcella, loud enough for Victor to know she was addressing him. "I've been to a hundred galleries, stared at a thousand paintings, waiting to feel inspired or awestruck or enamored—but the only thing I ever really felt was *bored*."

As Victor watched, she reached out and pressed one gold nail to the surface of the painting. Under Marcella's touch, the canvas rotted, and crumbled, pieces drifting to the floor.

"Don't worry," she said, turning on one metal heel. "I own the building, and everything in it." She raised a brow. "Except for you, of course." She gave him a cursory look. "Do you like art, Mr. Vale? My husband did. He always had a fondness for beautiful things." Marcella lifted her chin. "Do you think I'm beautiful?"

Victor considered her—the willowy limbs, the red lips, the blue eyes framed by thick black lashes. He glanced from her, to the ruins of the painting on the gallery floor, and back. "I think you're powerful."

Marcella smiled, clearly pleased with the answer.

Victor sensed a ghost of movement at his back, and glanced over his shoulder to see another man enter the room, one with a goatee and a mischievous smile.

"I believe you've already met June," said Marcella. "In one form or another."

The man winked, that telltale light in his eyes.

"And this is Jonathan," said Marcella, flicking her fingers in the direction of the thin man against the wall.

Jonathan didn't answer, beyond the slight nod of his head.

"So," said Victor, "instead of art, you're collecting EOs."

Marcella's red lips split into a smile. "Do you know what I wanted to be when I grew up?"

"President?"

Her smile widened. "Powerful." Her steel heels clicked against the marble as she came toward him. "When you think about it, it's really all anyone ever wants. Once upon a time, power was determined by lineage—the age of blood. Then it was determined by money—the age of gold. But I think it's time for a new age, Victor. The age of power itself."

"Let me guess," said Victor. "I'm either with you or against you."

Marcella tsked. "Such black-and-white thinking. I swear, men are so busy looking for enemies, they rarely remember to make friends." She shook her head. "Why can't we work together?"

"I work alone."

Marcella raised a knowing brow. "Now, we both know that's not true."

Victor's eyes narrowed, but he said nothing. Marcella seemed more than happy to hold the stage.

"Money in the right hands can get all kinds of things. Knowledge. Insight. Eli Ever's files from his time with the Merit PD, perhaps. He and Serena Clarke made quite a pair, but I think you got the better deal with her little sister, Sydney."

Victor kept his poise, but across the room June stiffened, the color draining from her face. "Marcella—"

But the woman held up a hand, gold nails catching the light.

"I've heard about your own talents," she continued. "I'd like to see them for myself."

"You want me to audition?"

Her lips twitched. "Call it what you like. I've shown you mine. And Jonathan's. And June's, for that matter. I think it's only fair . . ."

Victor needed no further prompting. He flexed his hand toward the thin man in the suit, expecting him to buckle immediately— and was surprised when instead, the air in front of him flashed blue and white with an almost electric crackle. And beyond that, nothing happened. Strange. Victor could *feel* the other man's nerves, just as present as before he'd tried to impact them. But in that exact instant, it had been like a short-circuit, almost like lightning trying to strike something grounded.

A forcefield.

Marcella smiled. "Oh, sorry. I should have said, Jonathan's off-limits." She looked around. "A little help?"

She hardly raised her voice, but the room began to fill. The six men and women Victor had passed earlier came spilling in.

Marcella smiled.

"I have a reward," she said, "for whoever brings this man to his knees."

For a moment, no one moved.

And then, everyone did.

A brick of a man lunged toward him, and Victor took hold of nerves, and twisted violently. The man buckled, screaming, as Victor leveled the two approaching in his wake, then turned toward a woman as she drew a blade.

A conductor's flick of Victor's fingers, and she collapsed too.

The fifth went down on his side, curling in against the pain, while the sixth tried to reach for his gun—Victor forced his hand flat to the marble and continued turning the dials up until all six writhed and spasmed on the floor.

He held Marcella's gaze, waiting for her to say *enough,* order him to stop. Waiting for any sign of her discomfort. But Marcella only watched the scene unfold, her blue eyes bright, unflinching.

Up until then, she had reminded Victor of Serena, expecting the world to bend to her will. But in that moment, she reminded him of *Eli.* That zealous light in her eyes, the coiled energy, the conviction.

Victor had seen enough.

He turned his power on Marcella. Not a subtle impression, either, but a sudden, blunt-force blow, strong enough to fry nerves and level a body. She should have collapsed on the spot, buckled like dead weight to the cold marble. Instead, Marcella took a single surprised breath and then Jonathan's head flicked imperceptibly toward her. As soon as it did, the air crackled, the space around Marcella filling with the same blue-white flare that had shielded Jonathan moments before.

Victor realized his error. Marcella was more like Eli than he'd guessed. Her uncanny self-assurance was an arrogance born from invincibility. Albeit a borrowed one.

Victor dropped his hold on the rest of the room, and left them gasping on the floor.

Marcella pursed her lips as the shield flickered out. "That wasn't very sporting."

"Forgive me," answered Victor dryly. "I guess I got carried away." He looked down at the men and women on the floor. "I take it I failed your test."

"Oh, I wouldn't say that. Your performance was . . . illuminating."

Marcella produced a crisp white envelope.

June took the card and delivered it to Victor.

"What's this?" he asked.

"An invitation."

They stood there for a second, neither willing to put their back to the other.

At last Marcella broke into a smile. "You can see yourself out," she said. "But I do hope we meet again."

Victor wanted nothing less, but he had a feeling they would.

"**WELL**," said Marcella, watching Victor go. "That was enlightening."

June hadn't said a word since Marcella mentioned Sydney, hadn't trusted herself to speak. Now she cleared her throat.

"Do you still think he might be useful?"

"Undoubtedly," said Marcella, taking out her phone.

"Should I follow him?"

"No need." Marcella punched in a number. "I've seen enough." Someone answered, and Marcella said, "He's staying at the Kingsley, on Fifteenth. But right now, he's moving west on Alexander. Happy hunting, Joseph."

June's stomach dropped.

How did Marcella already know where they were staying? Where *Sydney* was staying?

She gave June a bland look. "You didn't think you were the only one keeping an eye on things, did you?"

June swallowed. "Do what you want with Victor, but Sydney isn't part of this."

"Maybe she wouldn't have been," said Marcella, pointedly, "if you'd told me the truth about the girl's power instead of keeping her to yourself." She flicked her fingers dismissively toward the door. "But go ahead. See if you can get to her before they do."

VIII

THE LAST MORNING

"**SYDNEY!**" called Mitch, flipping the grilled cheese in the pan.

She didn't answer.

That bad feeling, the one he'd had on the way to Merit, began to crystalize from a general dread into something specific. Like the vague first signs of an illness that suddenly sharpened into the flu.

"Sydney!" he called again, shifting the pan off the stove so lunch wouldn't burn. He started toward the bathroom, slowing when he noticed the door was open. As was the door to Syd's room.

And the one to his own.

Mitch glimpsed a black tail swishing absently just inside the door, and found Dol sprawled on his bedroom floor, facing the window and chewing on a scrap of paper.

Mitch knelt down and pried the paper from the dog's lolling mouth, stilling at the sight of the crown, the sideways profile. It was a face card.

The king of spades.

Mitch was on his feet, already dialing Sydney's cell. It rang, and rang, and rang, but no one answered. He swore, and was just about to chuck the phone onto the bed when it went off in his hand.

Mitch answered, praying it was Syd.

"Pack up," ordered Victor. "We're leaving."

Mitch made an uneasy sound.

"What is it?" demanded Victor.

"Sydney," said Mitch. "She's not here."

A short exhale. "Where?"

"I don't know. I was making lunch and—"

Victor cut him off. "Just find her."

SYDNEY stood on the curb, looking up.

Five years ago, the Falcon Price had been a construction project, rebar and concrete surrounded by a plywood fence. Now, it rose high above her, a gleaming tower of glass and steel. All the evidence of the crimes committed that night hidden beneath fresh cement, drywall, plaster.

She didn't know what she'd expected to find. What she'd expected to *feel*. A ghost? A remnant of her sister? But now that Sydney was here, she could only see Serena rolling her eyes at that idea.

Syd knelt, reaching into her bag for the secret she'd carried so long. She eased the lid off the red metal tin, folded back the strip of cloth. For the first time in five years, Sydney let her fingers skim the soot-covered shards of bone. The finger joint. The piece of rib. The knot of a hipbone. All that was left of Serena Clarke. All that was left—besides whatever was left here.

Sydney laid the bones out on top of their cloth wrapping, arranged them just so, leaving a fraction of space for the missing, drawing imaginary lines where the other bones should be.

She took a deep, shuddering breath, and was about to bring her hands to the remains when her phone rang, the high sound cutting through the quiet. How stupid. She should have shut it off. If she had already gotten started, if her hands and her mind had been reaching past the bones when that noise happened, Sydney could have lost the thread, could have fumbled her only chance. Ruined everything.

She dug the phone from her pocket and saw Mitch's name flash across the screen. Sydney switched the cell off, and turned her attention back to her sister's bones.

IX

THE LAST AFTERNOON

"**WHAT** do you mean, *transport protocol*?"

Dominic had been in the locker room, buttoning up his uniform shirt, when Holtz burst in, face bright. He'd finally been tapped for field duty. Or rather, for transport.

"They're letting Stell's hunting dog out," he said.

Dom's chest tightened. "What?"

"Eli Cardale. They're letting him out of his cage—to go after that crazy mob wife, the one who killed Bara."

Dom was on his feet. "They can't."

"Well, they are," said Holtz.

"When?"

"Right now. Orders came in from the director. He was gonna handle it himself, but there's some big op going down in the city— another EO—and Stell just blew through like a storm. Before he left, he told us to initiate the extraction . . ."

But Dom was still stuck on the words before. "Another EO?"

"Yeah," said Holtz, pulling a suit of matte black armor from the wall. "That mystery guy, the one who's been killing off other EOs."

Dom's mouth had gone dry.

"What are the odds?" mused Holtz. "So much excitement in one day."

Holtz finished strapping in and turned to go, but Dominic caught his arm. "Wait."

The other soldier frowned down at the place where Dom's fingers dug into his sleeve. But what could Dom say? What could he do? He couldn't stop the missions—all he could do was warn Victor.

Dom forced himself to let go.

"Just be careful," he said. "Don't go ending up like Bara."

Holtz flashed that cheerful, dogged smile, and was gone.

Dominic counted to ten, then twenty, waiting until Holtz's steps had receded, until he was left with only the thud of his heart. Then he walked out of the locker room, turned right, and headed for Stell's office—and the only phone inside the building.

He kept his gait even, his steps casual—but with every forward stride, Dom knew he was going further down a one-way road. He stopped outside the director's door. Last chance to turn around.

Dom pushed open the door, and stepped inside.

VICTOR knew he was being followed.

He sensed the weight of their steps, felt their attention like a drag. At first he assumed it was June, or one of Marcella's human guards, but as their steps quickened, and the sound of one person became two, Victor began to suspect another source. He'd been heading directly back to the Kingsley. Now, he veered left, cutting through a crowded stretch of downtown Merit's restaurants and cafés.

His phone buzzed in his pocket.

He didn't recognize the number, but answered without slowing his step.

"They're on to you," said Dominic, his voice low, urgent.

"Yeah," said Victor, "thanks for the heads-up."

"It gets worse," said Dom. "They're letting Eli out."

The words were a knife, driven so precisely between Victor's ribs.

"To catch me?"

"No," said Dom. "I think it's actually meant to catch *Marcella*."

Victor swore under his breath. "You can't let that happen."

"How am I supposed to stop it?"

"Figure it out," said Victor, hanging up.

He could feel them lapping at his heels. Hear the sound of car doors swinging closed.

Victor crossed the street and stepped into a nearby park, a sprawling network of running paths, vendor carts, open lawns, packed tight with people in the midday sun. He didn't look back. He hadn't been able to pick his pursuers out of the crowd, not yet. Population was working in their favor, but it could also work in his.

Victor picked up his pace, allowing a hint of urgency to creep into his stride.

Catch up, he thought.

He heard a set of steps quickening, clearly expecting him to break into a run. Instead, Victor turned on his heel.

He doubled back on the crowded path, and started walking again in the opposite direction, forcing his pursuer to either stop and retreat, or maintain the illusion by continuing toward him.

Nobody stopped.

No one retreated.

Usually people bent away from Victor, their attention veering like water around a stone. But now, in the tangle of joggers and walkers and ambling groups, one man was still looking straight at him.

The man was young and dressed in civilian clothes, but he had the gait of a soldier, and the moment their eyes met, a ripple of tension crossed the younger man's face. He drew a gun, but as he swung the weapon up, Victor flicked his own fingers, a single, vicious pull of an invisible thread, and the man fell to his knees on the path, the gun skidding out of his hand. Victor kept walking as the crowd turned, half in worry at the man's scream and half in horror at the sight of the weapon on the park's pavement.

Chaos erupted, and in that chaos Victor cut left, onto a different path, aiming for the street side of the park. Halfway there, a second figure rushed toward him, a woman with cropped dark hair.

She didn't draw a weapon, but she had one hand to her ear and her lips were moving.

A group of cyclists whipped around the corner and Victor cut across the path just before they passed, a sudden, whooshing barricade that bought him just enough time to step between two carts and out of the park.

Victor moved swiftly, cutting across traffic and down a side street, seconds before an unmarked van skidded around the corner at the other end. It drove straight at him. He reached for the man behind the wheel, turning the dial up until the driver lost control and the van veered, slamming into a hydrant. Victor heard more footsteps, the hiss of radio static. He ducked into the nearest subway stop, swept past the turnstile and down the stairs, taking them two at a time toward the train pulling into the station below.

He made his way to the very end of the platform, but instead of boarding the train, he slipped past the pedestrian barricade and into the mouth of the tunnel, pressing his body against the wall as the bells chimed and the subway doors hissed shut.

A man reached the platform just in time to watch the train slide by.

Victor lingered in the tunnel, watching the man scan the cars, hands on his hips, his black hair edging to gray.

Stell.

Even after five years, Victor recognized him immediately. He watched as the former detective turned around, finally, and stormed back up the stairs.

Victor knew he should try again to get to the Kingsley—but first, he needed to have a word with the director of EON.

The next train pulled in, and Victor slipped into the press of bodies following in Stell's wake.

X

THE LAST AFTERNOON

EON

DOM stared at Stell's bank of computer screens.

Figure it out.

His mind spun like tires in mud, searching for purchase, his attention flicking from the desk to the door to the grid of camera footage on the far wall. There, upper right, three soldiers in full gear moved down a white hall. In another window, the familiar shape of Eli Cardale sat waiting.

Fuck.

Dom turned toward the trio of screens on Stell's desk. He didn't know the first thing about hacking into computers.

But he knew someone who did.

Mitch answered on the second ring. "Who is this?"

"Mitch, it's Dominic."

A shuffle of movement. "This isn't a good time."

Footsteps sounded in the hall beyond Stell's office. Dom pressed the cell to his chest and held his breath. When they were gone, he raised the phone, talking quickly. "Sorry, but I'm working on Victor's orders."

"Aren't we all."

"I need to hack a computer."

The metal sound of a zipper sliding. "What kind?"

"The kind at EON."

The line went quiet, and Dom assumed Mitch was thinking, but then he heard a laptop click open, a booting sound. "What kind of encryption?"

"No idea." He tapped the computer away. "It's just a password screen."

Mitch made a sound like a muffled laugh. "Governments. Okay. Do exactly what I tell you . . ."

He started speaking a foreign language—that's what it sounded like, anyway—but Dom did as he was told, and three agonizing minutes later, a green ACCESS GRANTED appeared on the screen, and he was in.

Dom hung up, brought up the grid of folders, each one marked by a cell number. Every other computer in EON had a folder like this one. And every other folder started with *Cell 1*.

But Stell's computer had another option—*Cell 0*.

Dom opened the drive and Eli Ever—Eliot Cardale—appeared onscreen, sitting at a table in the center of his cell, turning through a black folder. As Dom keyed in the codes, his vision sharpened, his focus narrowing the way it had when he was in the field. Time seemed to slow. Everything fell away except the screen, the commands, and the blur of his fingers across the keyboard.

A second window appeared with the cell block controls, scanning past lighting and temperature to security, emergency, lockdown.

Dominic couldn't prevent EON from letting Eli out. But he could slow them down. He was just about to key in the codes Mitch had given him, send the whole cell into lockdown, when someone cleared their throat behind him.

Dom spun around, and saw Agent Rios standing there, looking unimpressed. He didn't have time to wonder where she'd come from, didn't even have time to step *out* of time—into the safety of the shadows—before Rios slammed a cattle prod into his chest and Dom's world went white.

ELI was getting restless.

He scanned the images in the black folder one last time as he waited for Stell.

The director had made the plan very clear—Eli would be escorted from the facility under guard and, upon completion of the mission, returned to his cell. If he disobeyed in any way, at any point, he would be returned to the lab instead, where he would spend the rest of his existence being dissected.

That was *Stell's* plan.

Eli had his own.

Steps sounded beyond the wall, and he set his file aside and rose, expecting as usual to see Stell. Instead, when the wall went clear, he saw a fleet of EON soldiers dressed in black, their faces hidden behind sleek, close-fitting masks. Even with the visors up, only their eyes were visible. One pair green, one blue, one brown.

"All this fuss," muttered Green Eyes, sizing him up. "Doesn't look all that dangerous to me."

"Oh," said Eli, crossing the cell, "there are EOs out there *far* more dangerous than I am."

"But how many people have *they* killed?" asked Blue Eyes. "I'm guessing it's less than you."

Eli shrugged. "That depends."

"On what?" asked Brown Eyes—a woman, judging by her voice.

"Whether you consider EOs people," said Eli.

"Enough," said Blue Eyes, stepping toward the barrier. "Let's get going."

Eli held his ground. "Where is Director Stell?"

"Busy."

Eli doubted Stell would hand over such a delicate task—unless it was truly urgent.

Or personal.

Could Stell have already found Victor?

Ships in the night, thought Eli grimly. But he couldn't afford to worry about Victor Vale right now.

"Inmate," ordered Blue Eyes. "Approach the divide and put your hands through the slot."

Eli did, felt the heavy metal cuffs close around his wrists.

"Now turn around, place your back to the slot, and kneel."

Eli hesitated. That wasn't protocol. Cautiously, he did as he was told, expecting a dark hood to come down over his head. Instead, cold metal slid around his throat. Eli tensed, resisted the urge to pull away as the steel closed around his throat.

"The hunting dog gets a collar," said Blue Eyes.

Eli stood, running his fingers along the band of metal. "What is this?"

Brown Eyes held up a slim remote. "Didn't think we'd let you out without a leash . . ."

She pressed a button, and a single high note, like a warning tone, sounded in Eli's ears before pain pierced the back of his neck. Eli's vision went white, his body folding beneath him.

"And down he goes," said Blue Eyes as he hit the cell floor.

Eli couldn't move, couldn't feel anything below the shard of metal driven between his vertebrae.

"Come on, Samson," said Green Eyes, "we're on a schedule."

The tone sounded again, and the steel spike withdrew. Eli gasped, chest lurching as his spine healed and sensation flooded back into his limbs. He pushed himself to his hands and knees, and then up to his feet. A small pool of blood on the cell floor was the only sign of what they'd done.

Brown Eyes waved the remote. "You try to escape, you try to attack us—hell, you piss us off—I'll put you down."

Eli studied the slim remote in the soldier's hand, and wondered if it was the only one.

"Why would I do that?" he said. "We're on the same side."

"Yeah, sure," said Green Eyes, thrusting a hood through the slot. "Put it on."

Eli was led, blind and bound, through doorways and down halls, a soldier gripping each arm. He felt the ground shift beneath him from concrete to linoleum, and then to asphalt. The air changed, a breeze grazing his skin, and he wished the hood were off, wished he could see the sky, breathe in fresh air. But there would be time for that. A few feet more, and then their progress halted. Eli was turned around, maneuvered until his back came up against the metal side of a van.

Doors swung open, and he was half dragged into the back of the van, forced a little too roughly onto a steel bench against one wall. A strap went around his legs, another around his chest. His hand-cuffs were locked to the bench seat between his knees. The soldiers climbed in, and the doors were thrown shut, and the van's engine revved as it pulled away from EON.

Eli smiled beneath the hood.

He was cuffed and collared—but he was one step closer to free.

XI

THE LAST AFTERNOON

A couple years ago, Mitch had taught Sydney about magnets.

They'd spent a whole day testing their effects, the attraction and repulsion. Syd had always thought of magnetic force as a pull, but she'd been shocked to discover the strength of their push. Even a small flat disc could exert so much force against another.

She felt that same repulsion now, as her fingers hovered over her sister's bones.

Sydney tried to will her hands down as something inside her heart pushed back.

Why couldn't she do it?

Sydney had to bring Serena back.

She was her *sister*.

Family isn't always blood.

June had said that—June, who'd never betrayed Sydney. June, who'd protected Victor. But she wasn't *Serena*.

And if EON was chasing them now, Serena could help. Serena could do anything. Could make *other people* do anything.

It was a terrifying power to start with—but how bad would it be if Serena came back *wrong*? What would that power look like when it was fractured, broken?

For so long, Sydney had assumed she was afraid of failing. Afraid that she'd slip, lose the threads, and with that, her only chance at reviving Serena.

But the longer she stared at her sister's bones, the more Sydney realized—she was just as scared of succeeding.

Why had she waited so long? Was it really because she thought it had to happen *here*? That the connection would be strongest back where it had first been broken?

Or—was it because it gave her an excuse to wait?

Because Sydney was afraid to see her sister again.

Because Sydney wasn't ready to face Serena.

Because Sydney wasn't sure she *should* bring her sister back, even if she could.

Tears blurred her vision.

She realized, suddenly, that in all her nightmares, Serena had never once saved her. She was there, on the banks of the frozen river, waiting, watching as Eli stalked Syd across the ice. As he wrestled her to the frozen ground. As he wrapped his hands around Syd's throat.

Serena hadn't pulled the trigger on Sydney that night.

But she hadn't stopped Eli from shooting her either.

Sydney missed her sister.

But she missed the version of Serena who had loved and protected Sydney, made her younger sister feel safe, and seen. And that Serena had died in ice, not fire.

Sydney's fingers finally came to rest against Serena's bones. But she didn't reach beyond them, didn't search for the lingering thread. She simply folded them up inside the strip of cloth, and put them back in the red metal tin.

Her legs were shaking as she pushed herself up to her feet.

Syd shoved the container deep into her pocket, heard the scrape of metal on metal as the tin came to rest against the gun. In her other pocket, her fingers found her cell phone. She dug it out as she left the Falcon Price lot and headed back toward the Kingsley, watched it restart in her palm. Her boots dragged to a stop.

There were so many missed calls.

A handful from Victor.

Then a dozen from Mitch.

And text after text after text from June.

Sydney took off running.

SHE tried to call Mitch, but it went straight to voicemail.

Tried to call Victor, but no one answered.

At last, June picked up. "Sydney."

"What's going on?" she asked.

"Where are you?" demanded June, sounding breathless.

"I had all these missed calls," said Syd, slowing to a walk, "and I can't get ahold of anyone, and I—"

"Where *are* you?" repeated June.

"On my way to the Kingsley."

"No," said June. "You can't go back there."

"I have to."

"It's too late."

Too late. What did she mean?

"Just stay where you are and I'll come to you. Sydney, listen to me—"

"I'm sorry," said Syd, right before she hung up. It had taken her twenty-five minutes to walk to the Falcon Price. She made it home in ten. The Kingsley finally came into sight, down the block and across the street. Syd slammed to a stop as she noticed the two black vans idling on the corner, one near the entrance, the other at the mouth of the parking garage. They were unmarked, but there was something ominous about the tinted glass, the windowless sides.

Arms wrapped around her shoulders.

A hand closed over her mouth.

Sydney twisted, tried to scream, but a familiar voice sounded in her ear.

"Don't fight, it's me."

The arms let go, and Syd turned to see June, or at least a version of her, one with loose brown curls and sharp green eyes. Sydney sagged in relief, but June's attention twitched, drawn to something over Syd's shoulder.

"Come on," said June, gripping her hand.

Syd resisted. "I can't just leave them."

"You can't save them like this. What are you going to do? Storm in there? Think. If you go in there now, you'll just get yourself caught by EON, and what good will you be to anyone then?"

June was right, and Syd hated that she was. Hated that her power wasn't enough to protect them.

"We need a plan," said June. "So we'll think of one. I promise." She squeezed Sydney's hand. "Come on."

This time, Syd let herself be pulled away.

IT was beginning to rain as Victor followed Stell through the streets of downtown Merit.

He plucked a black umbrella from a corner stand without paying, and vanished beneath it, one bloom of darkness among dozens. Half a block ahead, the detective stopped beside a black van and a sedan, and convened with a cluster of soldiers in sodden street clothes, their manner and posture nullifying any meaningful disguise.

Victor lingered nearby, folding himself into the huddle at the bus stop. He watched Stell rake a hand through his salt-and-pepper hair, the picture of frustration. Watched him gesture at the soldiers, who got back into their vehicles, while Stell himself set off on foot.

Victor fell in step behind him.

Stell walked for ten, fifteen minutes more before swiping into a residential building. Victor caught the front door just as the elevator closed. He watched it ascend one floor, then two, before stopping. Victor took the stairs instead and arrived just as Stell was unlocking the front door, watched the man stiffen as he registered the other man's presence, realized that he wasn't alone.

Stell turned, drawing his service weapon before he saw Victor, and froze.

Victor smiled. "Hello, Detective."

Stell's hand was steady on the gun. "It's been a while."

"I'm surprised it took you so long."

"In my defense," said Stell, "I assumed you were dead."

"You know what they say about assuming," said Victor dryly. "We EOs are hard to keep down." He nodded at the weapon. "Speaking of down."

Stell shook his head, grip tightening on the gun. "I can't do that."

Victor flexed his hand. "Are you sure?" He splayed his fingers, and shock crossed Stell's face like lightning as his own hand opened, let the gun fall to the floor.

"You're not the only one who's traded up," said Victor, moving toward the detective. The air caught audibly in Stell's throat as he tried to back away, and couldn't.

"Pain is specific, but relatively simple," continued Victor. "Now, animating a body, articulating it—that requires precision, the firing of certain nerves, the pulling of specific strings. Like a marionette."

"What do you want?" hissed Stell.

I want to stop dying, thought Victor.

But Stell couldn't help with that.

"I want you to keep Eli in his goddamn cage."

Surprise crossed the detective's face. "That isn't your call."

"How could you be so stupid?" growled Victor.

"I do what I have to," said Stell, "and I certainly don't answer to—"

Victor's hand clenched into a fist, and Stell doubled over in pain. He caught himself against the wall, gave a sharp whistle through gritted teeth, and a second later every other door in the hall swung open, soldiers streaming in, weapons raised.

"I want him alive," ordered Stell.

Careless, Victor chided himself. The cop had baited his own trap, and he had stepped inside.

"You've always preferred being predator to prey," observed Stell.

Victor's teeth clicked together. "Did Eli teach you that?"

"Give me a little credit," said Stell. "You guys aren't the only ones who can spot a pattern."

"What happens now?" asked Victor, trying to sense the number of bodies surrounding him. How much power would he have to use to level the ones he couldn't *see*?

"Now," said Stell, "you come with us. This doesn't have to get violent," he continued. "Get on your knees and—"

Victor didn't wait for him to finish. He reached out with everything he had. Two bodies hit the floor behind him, another buckling at the edge of his sight.

Then Stell shot Victor in the chest.

He staggered, his hand going to his ribs. But there was no blood, only a red dart, buried deep. A vial, already empty. Whatever it held, it was strong—Victor wrenched the dart out, but his limbs were already going numb.

He cranked the dial up on his own nerves, clung to the pain to regain focus.

Victor brought two more soldiers to their knees before another shot pierced his side. A third took him in the leg, and he felt himself slip. He tried to brace himself against the wall, but his legs were already folding, his vision flickered, then dimmed. He saw the soldiers swarming in; and then—

Nothing.

XII

THE LAST AFTERNOON

ACROSS TOWN

THREE blocks from the Kingsley, June was making instant cocoa while Sydney perched on the edge of the nondescript hotel bed. Outside, it had started to rain. Syd tried Victor's phone again, but it was off now, just like Mitch's. She'd even tried Dominic's number, but there was no answer there, either.

June had told her everything—EON's task force, their mission to catch Victor and Sydney, the simple fact that June had to choose quickly, knowing she only had time to reach one. She'd been so worried—and by the time she got to the Kingsley, the EON soldiers were already there.

Which meant that Mitch—

June seemed to read Syd's mind.

"The big guy can take care of himself," she said, carrying over two mugs, "and if he can't, what difference would *you* have made? No offense, Syd, but your power wouldn't protect him—it would only get you caught, and Mitch wouldn't have wanted that." She paused. "Drink up, you're shivering."

Sydney wrapped her fingers around the hot mug. June sank into a nearby chair. It was so weird, seeing her again. Syd had had the other girl's voice in her ear for more than three years, the words on her phone, but she'd only seen June's face once before, and of course, it wasn't really hers. It wasn't even the one she was wearing now.

Sydney took a long, scalding sip, cringing not at the heat but the sugar—June had made it way too sweet.

"What do you really look like?" she asked, blowing on the steam.

June winked. "Sorry, kiddo, a girl's gotta have some secrets."

Syd looked down at the cocoa and shook her head. "What am I going to do now?"

"*We*," said June, "are going to think of something. We'll get through this, you and me. We just have to lie low until it's over, and then—"

"Until *what* is over?" demanded Syd. "I can't just stay here when Victor and Mitch are in trouble."

June leaned forward, resting a hand on Syd's boot. "They're not the only ones who can protect you."

"It's not about protection," said Syd, pulling away. "They're my *family*."

June stiffened, but Sydney was already on her feet, abandoning the half-empty mug beside the bed.

June could have grabbed her, but she didn't. She simply watched her go.

Sydney was almost to the door, reaching for the handle, when it seemed to drift out of reach. The floor had tilted, too. And suddenly, it was all Syd could do to keep from falling over.

She squeezed her eyes shut, but that only made things worse.

When Sydney opened them again, June was there, reaching out to steady her. "It's okay," she said, her accent soft, melodic. "It's okay."

But it wasn't.

Syd tried to ask what was going on, but her tongue felt leaden, and when she tried to pull away, she stumbled, head spinning.

"You'll understand," June was saying. "When this is all over, you will . . ."

Sydney's vision blurred, and June's arms closed around her as she fell.

THE road jostled under Eli's feet as the transport made its way toward Merit.

Five minutes into the drive, the hood had come off, trading the dark, woven interior of the fabric for the dark, windowless interior of the van itself. Not a vast improvement, but certainly a step.

The brown-eyed soldier sat on the bench to Eli's right. The other two sat across from him. They rode in silence, Eli attempting to track the distance with one part of his mind, while the rest traced over the details of the plan he'd been given, pondered the problem of Marcella and her chosen compatriots.

He felt Brown Eyes staring at him.

"Something on your mind?" asked Eli.

"I'm trying to figure out how a guy like you kills thirty-nine people."

Eli raised a brow. "You can't kill what's already dead. You can only dispose of it."

"Does that apply to you, too?"

Eli considered. For so long, Eli had thought himself the exception, not the rule. Now he knew better. And yet Eli had been given this specific power. A memory flashed through his mind—kneeling on the floor, slicing open his wrists over and over and over to see how many times it would take before God let him die.

"I would bury myself if I could."

"Must be nice," said Green Eyes. "To be unkillable."

A second memory—of lying on that lab table, his heart in Haverty's hands.

Eli said nothing.

A few minutes later, the van came to a stop on a busy street—Eli could hear the noise even before the back door swung open and Stell himself climbed in. "Briggs," he said, nodding at the woman. "Samson. Holtz. Any trouble here?"

"No sir," they said in unison.

"Where have you been?" demanded Eli.

"Believe it or not," said Stell, "you weren't the highest priority."

He'd meant it as a jab, but Eli saw only its truth, written in the lines of the director's face.

Victor.

The van drove on for a few more blocks before pulling into an alley, where the three soldiers climbed out—but not Stell. He turned his attention to Eli. "They are going ahead to secure the room. In a minute, you and I are going to leave this van and go inside. You make a scene, and that collar will be only the *first* of your problems."

Eli held out his cuffed wrists. "If you want to keep a low profile, these should probably come off."

Stell leaned forward, but simply tossed a coat over Eli's outstretched hands, hiding them from view. Eli sighed, and followed the director out of the van. He looked up at the stretch of blue sky, and breathed in fresh air for the first time in five years.

Stell brought a hand to Eli's shoulder, kept it there as they wove through the cars in front of the hotel.

"Remember your instructions," warned Stell as they stepped through the doors and crossed the lobby to the bank of elevators.

The soldiers were waiting on the fifth floor.

Two in the hall, one still clearing the room.

They'd taken off their helmets in an effort to blend in, revealing three young, good-looking soldiers. A woman in her early thirties, compact and strong and stoic. A young man, handsome and blond, thirty at most, who looked like he would have won Most Likable while in school. A second man, wide-jawed and smug, who reminded Eli of the frat boys he'd hated in college, the kind who would crush a beer can on their heads as if the feat were something to be proud of.

Once inside, Stell finally removed Eli's handcuffs.

He rubbed his wrists—they weren't stiff, or sore, but it was a hard habit to shake, that urge, and the small gestures that made people ordinary. Human. Eli surveyed the room. It was an elegant hotel suite, with a large bed and two tall windows. A garment bag hung on the back of the bathroom door, another had been cast onto the bed. A chair sat beneath one of the large windows, a low desk beneath the other, its surface adorned with a pad of paper and a pen.

Eli started toward it.

"Stay away from the windows, inmate."

Eli ignored him, resting his hand on the desk. "We're here *because* of this window." His fingers closed around the pen. "This view."

He leaned across the desk and looked out at the Old Courthouse across the street.

What a perfect choice, thought Eli. After all, a courthouse was a place of judgment. Justice.

He straightened, slipping the pen up his sleeve, and started for the bathroom.

"Where do you think you're going?" demanded Green Eyes.

"To take a shower," said Eli. "I need to be presentable."

The soldiers looked to Stell, who stared at Eli for a long moment before nodding. "Sweep it," he ordered.

Eli waited while the soldiers secured the bathroom, making sure there was no way out, removing anything that might be even vaguely construed as a weapon. As if Eli himself weren't the weapon of choice today.

When the soldiers were satisfied, he unhooked the garment bag from the bathroom door and stepped inside. He was pulling it shut when one of the soldiers caught the door. "Leave it open."

"Suit yourself," said Eli.

He left a foot of clearance, for modesty. Hung up the borrowed suit, and turned on the shower.

With his back to the open door, Eli freed the stolen pen from the cuff of his EON-issued jacket and held it between his teeth as he stripped off the clothes, let them pool around his feet.

He stepped into the shower, the frosted glass door falling shut behind him. He ran his fingers over the surface of the steel collar, searching for a weakness, a groove or clasp. But he found none. Eli hissed in annoyance.

The collar, then, would have to wait.

He removed the stolen pen from his mouth, and under the static of the water's spray, snapped it in two.

It was hardly ideal, but it was the closest thing to a knife he was likely to get.

Eli closed his eyes, and summoned the pages from the black folder. He'd studied them thoroughly, memorized the photos and scans that had accompanied each of Haverty's experiments.

The record had been gruesome but revealing.

The first time Eli had noticed the shadow on an image of his forearm, he'd taken it for a swatch, just one of those markers used to signal direction on an X-ray. But then it showed up again on an MRI. A small metal rectangle, the faint impression of a grid.

And he knew exactly what it was.

Eli found the same mark on a scan of his lower spine. At his left hip. The base of his skull. Between his ribs. Disgust had welled like blood as Eli realized—every time Haverty had cut or pried or pinned him open, the doctor had left a tracking device behind. Each one small enough so that Eli's body, instead of rejecting the objects, simply healed around them.

It was time they came out.

Eli brought his makeshift scalpel to his forearm and pressed down. The skin split, blood rising instantly along the jagged edge, and an old voice in his head noted that the heat and moisture would act as anticoagulants, before he reminded that voice that his healing power rendered the fact irrelevant.

He clenched his teeth as he drove the plastic deeper.

Haverty had never bothered with shallow wounds. When he opened Eli up, he did it down to bone. The static of the spray would have provided a buffer, but Eli didn't make a sound.

Still, as his fingers slipped and slid, and blood ran down the drain, Eli felt a tremor of residual panic pass through him. The only kind of mark left by Haverty's work. Invisible, but insidious.

At last, the tracker came free, a sliver of dark metal clutched between stained fingers. Eli set it in the soap dish with a shaky breath.

One down.

Four to go.

THE KINGSLEY

Mitch rolled over, and spit a mouthful of blood onto the hardwood floor.

One eye was swelling shut, and he couldn't breathe through his broken nose, but he was alive. He could move. He could think.

For now, that would have to be enough.

The apartment was empty. The soldiers were gone.

They'd left Mitch behind.

Human.

That one word—a judgment, a sentence—had saved his life. The EON soldiers lacked either the time or the energy to deal with someone so tangential to their pursuit.

Mitch forced himself to his hands and knees with a groan. He had a muddled memory of movement, grasping at consciousness as the soldiers spoke.

We've got him.

It took a long time for the words to sink into Mitch's bruised skull.

Victor.

He got, haltingly, to his feet and looked around, taking in the trashed apartment, the bloodstained floor, the dog lying on the floor nearby.

"Sorry, boy," he murmured, wishing he could do more for Dol. But only Sydney could have helped him now, and Mitch had no idea where she was. He stood there, amid the carnage, torn between the need to wait for her and the need to go find Victor, and for a second the two forces seemed to pull him physically, painfully apart.

But Mitch couldn't do both, and he knew it, so he asked himself, what would Victor do? What would Syd? And when the answers were the same, he knew.

Mitch had to leave.

The question was where to *go*.

The soldiers had taken his laptop, and he had crushed his primary cell, but Mitch crouched—which turned out to hurt just as much as standing up—and felt under the lip of the sofa, dislodging the small black box and the burner smartphone that it was feeding into.

His *butler*.

In the old black-and-white movies he'd always loved, a good butler was neither seen nor heard, not until they were needed. And yet they were always there, tucked innocently into the background, and always seemed to know the comings and goings of the house.

The concept behind Mitch's device was the same.

He booted the phone and watched as the data from the soldiers' electronic tracking streamed in. Calls. Texts. Locations.

Three phones. And they were all in one place.

Got you.

All his life, people had underestimated Mitch. They took one look at his size, his bulk, his tattooed arms and shaved head, and made a snap judgment: slow, stupid, useless.

EON had underestimated him too.

Mitch looked around, found the playing card Sydney had left behind. He scribbled a quick instruction on the back, and rested the playing card on the dog's motionless side.

"Sorry, boy," he said again.

And then Mitch grabbed his coat, and his keys, and went to save Victor.

XIII

THE LAST AFTERNOON

VICTOR opened his eyes, and saw only himself staring back.

His lean limbs, sallow skin, black clothes, reflected in the polished ceiling. He was lying on a narrow cot against the wall of a square space, quickly discernible as some type of cell.

Panic slid like a needle beneath Victor's skin. Four years he'd spent in a place like this—no, not quite like this, not as clever, not as advanced—but just as empty. He had been buried alive in that solitary confinement cell, and every day Victor had sworn that once he got out he would *never* let himself be trapped again.

He brought a hand to his chest and felt the bruise between his ribs where the first dart had gone in, scraping bone. He sat up, paused for a moment to let the lingering nausea pass, then stood. There was no clock in here, no way to tell how long he'd been unconscious, aside from the constant hum of his power, its strength and volume growing with each passing minute.

Victor looked around, and resisted the urge to call out, unnerved by the idea that no one would answer, that the only response he'd be greeted by was his own echo. Instead, he studied the surroundings. The walls, which he'd originally taken for rock, were actually plastic, or maybe fiberglass. He could feel a subtle charge coursing through it—a deterrent, no doubt, against escape.

He looked up, scanning the ceiling for cameras, and was interrupted by a familiar voice filling the cell.

"Mr. Vale," said Stell. "We've come a long way, only to find ourselves back where we started. The difference, of course, is that this time, you won't be getting out."

"I wouldn't be so sure of that," said Victor, forcing his voice to hold its edge. "But I have to admit, this isn't exactly sporting."

"That's because this isn't a game. You're a murderer, and an escaped convict, and this is a prison."

"What happened to my trial?"

"You forfeited it."

"And Eli?"

"He serves another purpose."

"He's playing you," sneered Victor. "And by the time you figure out how, it will be too late."

Stell didn't rise to the bait, leaving Victor in silence. He was running out of patience, and out of time. He looked up at the cameras. He may be in a cage, but Victor *had* prepared for the possibility. He had left himself a key.

The question was—where was Dominic Rusher?

DOM tugged at the steel standard-issue handcuffs, but they were bolted to the table.

Three years, and his only fear had been waking up in an EON cell. Instead, he'd woken up in an interrogation room.

He was sitting in a metal chair, cuffed to a steel table, and he was alone, the only door clearly locked, the control panel on the wall marked by a solid red line.

Panic flickered through him, and Dom had to remind himself that they didn't *know* he was an EO.

Not yet.

And he needed to keep it that way as long as possible.

Dom was truly trapped—he could slip out of time, but it wouldn't do a damn bit of good, because even without time, he would still be *chained to a fucking table*. And he'd be even more screwed because the moment he crossed *back* into reality, the slip would show, the gap between where he'd been and where he was. Maybe it would just look like a stutter, a shutter, a glitch. But there were no glitches in a place like EON, and everyone watching him on camera would know what it meant. What he was.

So Dom waited, counting time in his head, wondering where Eli was now, hoping Victor, at least, had gotten away.

Finally, the keypad turned from red to green.

The door unsealed, and two soldiers came in.

Dom had been hoping for a friendly face, but instead he got Rios again, joined by a hard-edged, brutish soldier named Hancock. Dom's attention hung on the sliver of shrinking freedom as the door behind Rios swung shut, and the codes went red again.

Shit.

Rios crossed to the table and set down a file. Dom's file. He scanned the tops of the pages, searching for paperclips, staples, anything he might be able to use.

"Agent Rusher," said Rios. "You want to tell us what you were doing in the director's office?"

Dom had put his short time awake to good use. He was ready for this line of questioning. "I was trying to stop a murderer from escaping."

Rios raised a brow. "How do you figure that?"

Dom sat forward. "Do you know about Eli Ever? Or Eliot Cardale, or whatever name he wants to go by? Do you know what he did?"

"I've read his file," she said. "And I've read yours."

"Then you know I was one of his targets. I still don't know why—but I should be dead. Would have been, too, if Eli had gotten to me. So when I heard that Stell planned to have him transported off-site,

I couldn't let that happen, couldn't have that maniac loose in Merit again."

"That wasn't your call, soldier."

"So fire me," said Dom.

"That's not *my* call," said Rios. "You'll be held here until the director returns to make a decision."

Rios was shuffling the file as she spoke, and Dom caught sight of a metal staple just before Hancock's comm went off. The low static muffled the words, but one of them leapt out.

Vale.

Dom tried to hide the recognition on his face as Hancock lifted the comm to his ear.

Vale . . . awake . . .

"In the meantime," continued Rios. "I suggest—"

"How did you get into Stell's office?" asked Dom, changing directions. She looked up, a shadow crossing her face. Dom pressed on. "There's only one door, and I was facing it. But you showed up *behind* me."

Rios's eyes narrowed. "Hancock," she said. "Go call Stell. Ask him what he wants us to do next."

Dominic really did want to hear Rios's explanation, but not as much as he needed to get out. He waited as Hancock swiped his keycard, waited as the line turned green and the door clicked open.

"Now, Agent Rusher," she continued, "let's disc—"

He didn't give her a chance to finish. Dominic took a deep breath, like a swimmer before a dive, and jerked backward, the world parting around him as he slipped out of time, and into the shadows.

The room hung in perfect stillness, a painting in shades of gray—Rios, frozen, her face unreadable. Hancock, halfway through the door. Dominic, still handcuffed to the table.

He rose, pulling the stapled pages toward him, and got to work prying the bit of metal loose. He worked the sliver free, then straightened it out, and began fitting the slim bar between the teeth of the handcuff and the locking mechanism. It took several tries, the weight of the shadows like wet wool draped across his limbs, and a red welt rising on Dominic's wrist from the constant applied pressure, but finally the lock came loose. He pried the handcuff open, repeated the same grueling process with the other side, and was free.

Dom fastened the cuffs back around Rios's wrists, then ducked under Hancock's frozen arm into the hall. The air dragged around him like an ocean tide as he approached the nearest control room. There was only one other soldier there, a female agent named Linfield, sitting in front of a console, and frozen mid-stretch. Dominic freed the cattle prod from her holster and brought it to the base of her neck before stepping back into the flow of time.

A flash of blue-white light, the crackle of current, and Linfield slumped forward. Dom pushed her chair aside and started searching, hands flying across the keyboard.

He didn't have long. Every second Dom stood in the real world was a second exposed, a second he could be caught, captured, a second alarms were going up, and soldiers were invariably crashing toward him. And yet, despite it all, the world narrowed as he typed, his heart racing, but the pulse strong, steady. He'd always been good under pressure.

Dom didn't have time to figure out which cell Victor was being kept in, so he chose the fastest option.

He opened them all.

ONE minute Victor had been pacing the confines of his silent, empty cell, and the next the world was plunged into motion and sound. An alarm, high and bright, wailed as the farthest wall of the cell dropped away, the solid pane of fiberglass retracting into the floor.

Lights flashed white overhead, but instead of going into lockdown, the facility seemed to be *opening*. Coming apart. To every side, Victor heard the metal crank of seals breaking, doors unlocking.

About time.

He stepped out of the cell, only to find himself in a second, larger chamber, this one cast in concrete instead of plastic. It was roughly the size of a small airplane hangar—he circled until he found a door. It swung open under Victor's touch and gave way onto a white hall.

He made it three steps before whatever Dominic had managed to cause was suddenly reversed.

Doors slammed, locks sealed, alarms cut off and then started again, the lights no longer white but a deep arterial red, like a twisted game of Simon Says.

But Victor didn't stop moving.

Not when a hail of distant gunfire echoed in a nearby hall, not when boots sounded on slick linoleum, not when plumes of white gas began to pour through the overhead vents.

A barrier slammed across the hall in front of him and so Victor doubled back, holding his breath as he swung around a corner, found himself face to face with two EON soldiers, helmeted and armed.

He lunged for their nerves as their weapons flew up, but Victor was too late—their fingers reached the triggers an instant before his power could reach *them*.

The shots rang out, a burst of gunfire, and Victor lunged sideways, but the hall was narrow, and there was no escape.

A bullet—not a tranquilizer this time, but slim, piercing steel—grazed his side right before his power knocked the hands on the guns off course. But Victor's own hold faltered too, and in that stolen second the guns adjusted, retrained on his head, his heart.

The soldiers fired, the hall filling with the sharp retorts, and Victor braced for the impact.

It never came.

Instead, an arm wrapped around his shoulders, Dominic's body twisting in front of Victor like a shield as he pulled them both back into the dark.

The world went suddenly, perfectly, still.

They were standing in the same place, in the same hallway, but all the violence and urgency had been sucked out of the space, replaced by silence and calm. The advancing soldiers hovered, frozen in time, the bullets carving lines of motion as they hung suspended in the air.

Victor dragged in a few steadying breaths, but when he tried to speak, nothing came out. The shadows were a void, swallowing not only color and light, but also sound.

Dominic's face was a grim mask a foot from Victor's own as the soldier's hand tightened on his sleeve, and he tipped his head in a wordless command.

Follow me.

XIV

THE LAST EVENING

FIRST AND WHITE

ONCE again, Marcella had chosen to wear gold.

She'd come a long way since that pivotal night on the National's roof, shedding not only her husband but the scalloped decadence of that first dress, trading it for the polished sheen of white-gold silk. It molded to her body like liquid metal, rising up around her throat and plunging down between her shoulder blades, pooling in the small of her back.

To my beautiful wife.

In a certain light, the milky fabric seemed a second skin, the soft shimmer brushed onto bare flesh, turning her to gold.

What's the point of having beautiful things if you don't put them on display?

Marcella tucked a coil of black hair behind one ear, admiring the liquid way the gold earring fell from the lobe. A bracelet circled one wrist. Her nails, painted to match.

If beauty were a crime.

A net of white-gold beads, like a band of stars, over her hair.

Does she come with a warning label?

Her heels, thin as blades and just as sharp.

My wife, the business major.

The only drops of color the steady blue of her eyes and the vivid, vicious red of her lips.

You don't want to make a scene.

Her hand drifted to the mirror.

I always thought you were a brazen bitch.

The glass silvered under Marcella's touch, burning black in spots as if it were film, erosion spreading until it swallowed the gold dress and the blue eyes and the red lips set in a perfect smile.

Jonathan was leaning against the wall, fidgeting with his gun, ejecting and reinserting the magazine the way Marcus used to punch the end of his pen when he was restless.

Click, click. Click, click. Click, click.

"Stop that," she ordered, turning toward him. "How do I look?"

Jonathan gave her a long, considering stare. "Dangerous."

Marcella smiled. "Come zip me up."

He slid the gun back into its holster. "Your dress has no zipper."

She gestured at the heels. He came forward, and knelt, and she lifted one foot onto his waiting knee.

"No matter what happens tonight," she said, tipping up his chin. "Keep your eyes on me."

SYDNEY woke up in an empty bathtub.

She was curled on her side, wrapped in a large comforter in the deep white basin, and for a second she had no idea where she was. And then, haltingly, she remembered.

The Kingsley. June. The hotel, and the cup of too-sweet chocolate.

Sydney got to her feet, head pounding from whatever June had put in the drink—and grateful she hadn't drunk more of it. She stumbled out of the tub and tried the bathroom door, but the handle only turned a couple inches.

Syd knocked, and then pounded. Threw her shoulder into the door and felt the resistance, not of a lock, but an object forced against the other side. Syd turned, surveying the small, windowless room, and saw the note sitting on the sink.

I'll explain everything when this is over.
Just trust me.
-J

She felt herself tremble, not with fear, but anger. *Trust?* June had *drugged* her. Locked her in a hotel bathroom. She'd thought that June was different, that she saw Sydney as a friend, a sister, an equal. But for all that talk of trust, of independence, of letting Sydney make her own choices, June had still done *this*.

Syd had to get out of here.

Had to find Victor, and save Mitch.

She felt for her phone, only to remember she'd left it on the coffee table. But as she dug her hands into her bomber jacket, she felt the small metal tin with Serena's bones in one pocket, and the cool steel of the gun in the other. June obviously hadn't thought to frisk her. After everything, she'd treated Sydney like a naive child.

Syd drew out the gun, fingers flexing on the grip as she aimed at the doorknob, then reconsidered, shifted the barrel toward the hinges on the other side.

The shot echoed, deafening, against the tile and marble, hard surfaces reflecting it back at an earsplitting level.

Sydney fired twice more, then threw her weight into the door again, felt the hinges break, the wood swing free.

And she was out.

XV

THE LAST EVENING

EON

THE white halls stretched in a strange tableau.

Soldiers kneeling at corners, and frozen mid-stride in halls. A woman on fire, the flames licking at the soldiers trying to approach. A man on his knees on the ground, arms being wrenched behind him. Clouds of gas lit by the red strobe of the emergency lights.

And weaving through the scenes, Victor and Dom, making their way out of EON. It was slow, agonizingly slow, the air dragging like water at their arms and legs, and Victor holding Dom's sleeve like a blind man—and in some ways, he was blind, blind to the path through the maze.

And then Dominic dropped.

There was no warning. Not even a stumble.

He simply sank to the floor.

Victor knelt too—it was that or let go—but as Dom's back came to rest against the wall, Victor saw the front of his uniform, black on black, but shining wet.

The bullets had torn tidy, coin-sized holes.

The shootout in the hall. In that brief instant, when Dom had surged out of the shadows and before he'd pulled them back—

"You fool," muttered Victor, soundlessly.

He pressed his hand against the wound, felt the shirt soaked through with blood. How Dominic had stayed on his feet so long, Victor didn't know.

Dom shuddered, as if cold, so Victor severed his nerves, and said, "Get up."

But Dominic couldn't hear him.

"Get up," he mouthed again.

This time Dominic tried, rose a couple of inches, only to slip back to the floor. His mouth moved, the words lost, but Victor understood.

Sorry.

"Sorry," said the ex-soldier—and Victor realized that he could hear Dominic's voice this time. The shadows were crumbling around them, color and life sweeping in through the cracks. Victor tensed, tightened his hold on Dominic's arm. But it wasn't *his* grip that was slipping.

It was Dom's.

"Hold on," ordered Victor, but Dom's head lolled to the side, and the colorless, soundless space between time collapsed back into chaos and noise, gas and gunfire.

Blood slicked Victor's palms, streaked the floor, stretched behind them in a vivid breadcrumb trail, shockingly red against the sterile white surfaces.

Victor started to draw Dominic to his feet, but the ex-soldier was dead weight now, his skin gray, waxy, his eyes open, but unseeing. Victor let go, easing the body back against the wall as soldiers barreled around the corner.

This time Victor moved first.

No hesitation, no calculation, just blunt and brutal force.

He dropped them like stones in deep water.

Victor stepped over their limp bodies.

The facility's front doors came into sight, one long, empty hall standing between him and freedom.

And then a soldier stepped through the wall in front of him.

There was no sliding door, no hidden hall. She came straight out of the wall, as if it were an open door. She stood before him, unmasked, dark eyes sharp and a cattle prod hanging from one hand.

An *EO,* working for EON.

Victor didn't have time to be surprised.

The soldier lunged for him, blue light crackling across the top of the baton. Victor leapt backward, reaching for her nerves, but before he could get a grip on them, she cut sideways, vanished again through the wall.

An instant later, she was behind him.

Victor spun, catching her wrist just before the electric baton found bare skin.

"You're troublesome," he said, the words swallowed up by the wailing alarms.

He wrenched her nerves, and the soldier gasped in pain, but didn't crumple.

Instead, she slammed her boot into Victor's wounded side.

He went down hard on the white floor, and she was on top of him—or would have been, if his hand hadn't shot out at the last second, dragging her body to a stop.

The soldier fought his hold, even as he forced her hand to turn the cattle prod back on herself. Her eyes narrowed in concentration as her will warred with his, but Eli was loose, and Sydney was lost, and those two things made Victor immovable.

He flexed one hand, drove it toward his chest, and in a mirror motion, the soldier drove the cattle prod into her own.

Blue light, the crackle of energy, and the EO collapsed, unconscious.

Victor rose, swept around her body to the wide glass doors. But they didn't open.

There was no escape.

MITCH didn't know what to do.

His car idled a hundred feet beyond the high metal gates of the EON complex as the rain turned from a drizzle to a downpour.

He sat behind the wheel, now jury-rigging the butler's small black box to hack the gate's frequency instead of tracking signals. That would get him closer to the building, but it still didn't answer the problem of how he was going to get in, or rather, how he was going to get Victor *out*. Or even where to start looking for him.

There was a guard in a security booth inside the gate, and who knew how many officers inside the building, and it would take a hell of a lot more than a smartphone and a hacking fob to crack the security around a place like EON. Which meant, if Mitch was getting in, he'd have to use force.

He was still wracking his brain for the best of several bad plans when the rain eased a little, enough for Mitch to make out the building's front doors—and the distinctive figure standing just beyond them.

Victor.

Mitch hit the button on the black box, and the gates to EON began to slide open. He gunned the engine and shifted into drive, tires skidding in the rain before lurching forward through the gate, and straight toward EON.

Victor leapt out of the way just before Mitch crashed his car through the front doors. The glass, reinforced as it was, didn't shatter, but it did buckle, bow, and as Mitch reversed the car, Victor was able to pry the doors open and slip through.

He threw himself into the front seat.

Mitch's foot was already on the gas.

The guard from the security tower was running toward them, but Victor flicked his hand, as if the soldier were only a bug, a nuisance, and the other man collapsed.

Mitch's car, its front end a mess of crumpled metal, barreled through the open gate and drove away.

He checked the rearview mirror—nobody was behind them, not yet. He glanced sideways at Victor.

"That's a lot of blood."

"Most of it is Dominic's," replied Victor grimly.

Confusion washed over Mitch. He didn't want to ask. Didn't really need to. The only answer that mattered was in Victor's eyes as they avoided his.

"Where's Sydney?" he asked.

"I don't know."

"You drop me off," said Victor, "and you find her, and then you get the hell out of this city."

"Drop you off where?"

Victor pulled the invitation from his back pocket. It was crumpled, and bloodstained, but the gold lettering on the front was clear.

"The Old Courthouse."

XVI

THE LAST EVENING

THE rain was finally easing by the time Marcella stepped outside.

Three cars sat idling on the curb ahead, one elegant black town car flanked by two SUVs. The security detail swept around them, four men in crisp black suits, raised umbrellas masking them from sight.

Marcella wasn't taking any chances.

Stell would be getting desperate, and desperate men did reckless things.

They reached the sedan, and Jonathan held open her door. When he wasn't wallowing, he could be quite a gentleman.

Marcella slid into the backseat, and noticed she wasn't alone. A man sat across from her, tan and elegant in a pale gray suit. He was staring out the window, and sulking profoundly.

"Well?" asked Marcella. "Did you get to her in time?"

The man nodded, and spoke in that familiar lilt. "It was a near thing," said June, "but I did."

"Good," said Marcella briskly. "You'll bring her to me, of course, when this is done."

June's borrowed eyes flicked sideways, but when she spoke, her voice was steady. "Of course."

Jonathan climbed in on the other side. Marcella had no trouble seeing June behind her many faces—but Jonathan jumped a little at the sight of a stranger.

"Johnny boy," cooed June. "Rest easy, now, the prodigal EO has returned to the fold."

Marcella considered June. "Is that what you're wearing?"

The man's mouth tugged into a wry smile. "Am I too pretty?" And just like that, he vanished, smooth, high cheekbones replaced by a bag lady with a hooked nose. "Is this better?"

Marcella rolled her eyes, glad to see June restored to her usual humor.

"Surely," she said, "there's a happy medium."

June gave a dramatic sigh and dissolved into a middle-aged man with a groomed mustache and an attractive, if mildly forgettable face. "Better?"

"Much," said Marcella.

June gave her a sweeping look. "You look like Snow White killed the queen and stole the mirror."

Marcella flashed a cool smile. "I'll take that as a compliment."

June settled back in her seat. "You would."

ELI smoothed his hair back and buttoned his shirt.

He'd dumped the fragments of the broken pen into the toilet tank. The tracking devices he slipped into the pocket of his suit jacket.

It felt good to be back in real-world clothes, even if they were on the formal side. He'd donned a hundred different costumes in the service of his work. All he was missing was a weapon—a knife, a length of wire. But he could make do with his bare hands. He'd certainly done it before.

Eli was just knotting the borrowed tie when he heard the commotion beyond the bathroom door, the radio chatter mixing with Stell's gruff voice. Eli undid the knot and started again, working slowly as he listened.

"No . . . God dammit . . . who was it? No . . . we continue as planned . . ."

Eli waited until it was obvious there was nothing more to glean, then emerged, taking in the scene. Stell's cheeks were ruddy. He had never had much of a poker face. And only one man could cause so much consternation.

Victor.

"Everything okay?" asked Eli.

"Just focus on the task," ordered Stell, pulling on his own suit jacket and running a hand through salt-and-pepper hair. *More salt by the day,* thought Eli. Some people really *weren't* suited for this line of work.

He wasn't the only one who'd gotten dressed.

The woman now wore a silk black jumpsuit, the kind that belonged on a catwalk, not a field agent.

The young blond was still in his uniform, but the square-jawed soldier wore a black jacket over a crisp white shirt open at the throat.

Eli hummed thoughtfully. "The invitation only admits two."

In answer, Stell produced a second card.

"A replica?" wondered Eli aloud. If it was a copy, it was flawless.

"No," said Stell. "It's the one Marcella sent to the district attorney. Lucky for us, he's out of town." He handed the spare invitation to the female soldier. "Holtz," he said, nodding at the blond, "will stay outside."

"Always the short straw," muttered the soldier.

Stell checked his watch.

"It's time."

THE black van was gone when Sydney got back to the Kingsley.

She found the apartment door broken, ajar, and she drew her gun, clutching it in both hands as she stepped through.

The first thing Syd saw was blood. Fat drops of it, leading down the hall, then a small pool on the hardwood floor smeared by the edge of a handprint.

And the body.

Dol.

Syd scrambled to the dog's side, sinking to her knees beside his still form. She knocked the playing card from atop his chest, ran her fingers through his fur. Closed her eyes, and reached, felt the thread of the dog's life dancing away, dodging her grip. Every time, it was harder. Every time, she had to reach deeper. As Sydney worked, a terrible aching cold wound through her, and she felt her lungs seize, her breath trip, and then at last she caught the thread, dragged Dol back to life. Again.

The dog's chest heaved, and Syd sank back, gasping for air.

Her attention drifted to the king of spades, now overturned, a note in Mitch's tight script on the back.

Went to find Victor.

Syd got to her feet, and so did Dol, shaking off his death as if it were rain. He pressed himself against her side as if to ask, *What now?*

Syd looked around. She didn't have a phone.

Didn't have a clue where anyone had gone.

But she did have *something*—the invisible tether that ran between her and the things she brought back.

Sydney didn't know if it would be enough, but she had to try. She closed her eyes and reached for another thread. Felt it go taut against her fingers.

"Come on," she said to Dol, stepping around the blood.

When they reached the street, Syd paused, closing her eyes again. Felt her world tip ever so slightly to the left. As if to say, *This way.*

She started walking.

"DRIVE faster," said Victor, trying to ignore the buzzing in his skull, those first warnings of a building charge.

It would wait. It had to wait.

"Why?" demanded Mitch, even as he sped toward Merit. "Why are we going toward this mess instead of away?"

Victor found a roll of paper towels in the backseat and pressed them to the shallow wound along his ribs. "Eli will be there."

"All the more reason to go the other way. You two can circle each other forever, but there's only one way it ends, Victor, and it's not in your favor."

"Thanks for the confidence," said Victor, dryly.

Mitch shook his head. "You and your vengeance . . ."

But it wasn't vengeance.

Whatever's happened to you, however you're hurt, you've done it to yourself.

Campbell had been right.

Victor had to take responsibility. For himself. And for the monster he'd helped to create. Eli.

"You're going in like that?" Mitch was asking.

Victor turned the card over in his hand. "I have an invitation."

But he looked down at himself. Mitch had a point.

He'd lost his favorite trench coat, somewhere between the confrontation in Stell's hallway and waking up in the cell. A thin slice ran along his black T-shirt. He'd done his best to rinse the blood from his hands with a bottle of water, but it was still under his nails.

He had no weapons, and no plan.

Only the knowledge—the *certainty*—that Eli would run, the first chance he got.

And Victor would be there to stop him.

XVII

THE LAST NIGHT

THE OLD COURTHOUSE

ELI stepped through the doors into the grand foyer, wicking rain from his hair.

The venue was already brimming with people, men and women in evening attire. The toast of Merit, it seemed, all in one place. The two soldiers had already entered, several people ahead, and had immediately dissolved into the crowd.

Eli and Stell advanced, and were stopped by a pair of security guards with handheld metal detectors.

"Law enforcement," said Stell brusquely, displaying his sidearm.

"Sorry, sir," said the guard. "This is a weapons-free event."

The irony, thought Eli, spreading his arms as the baton drifted over him. Not so much as a beep. Stell reluctantly surrendered his gun. They passed a coat check station, and Eli shrugged out of his jacket and handed it to the clerk, watching the tracking devices drift away. That still left the problem of the collar, but between stepping out of the shower and into the suit, Eli had come up with a plan.

They stepped into the courthouse's grand atrium, a circular chamber surrounded by pillars and topped by a dome. Eli craned his head, admiring the building. It was a showpiece of classic architecture. High-ceilinged and hollow, equal parts elegant and austere.

Wrought-iron sconces bloomed like metal bouquets on each of the pillars. Broad silver dishes—an echo of the scales in Justice's hand—sat atop polished marble tables that seemed to rise straight out of the floor. A viewing balcony ran along the base of the dome, looking down on the atrium below, and in the atrium's center, on a marble stand, a bronze statue of Justice herself rose toward the ceiling, nearly two stories tall.

There was no sign of Marcella, not yet, but that didn't surprise Eli. She would make an entrance, that much he could predict. Jonathan, he guessed, wouldn't be far from her side, but June would be impossible to spot, at least until she made a move.

Eli spotted the two EON soldiers, carving their slow security sweeps through the thickening crowd.

The hall echoed with laughter, the light low, the air dancing with champagne flutes and jewelry and bodies clustering close. Bystanders. Moving pieces. Distractions.

Stell was at his shoulder.

"When the time comes," said Eli, "will you be able to get the bystanders out?"

"I'll do my best," said Stell. "Getting their attention might be difficult."

Eli scanned the space, thinking. The windows were high and narrow, useless, the crowd thick . . . but that could work in their favor. Panic was contagious. Like dominos, all you had to do was fell the first one.

"I'll be right back."

Stell caught his shoulder. "Where are you going?"

"To get you a gun." Eli nodded at Marcella's security, all dressed in trim black suits. "Haven't you noticed? The guests may not be allowed to carry, but her men certainly are."

Stell didn't let go.

"At some point," said Eli calmly, "you have to let out my leash."

The director stared at him for a long, hard moment, and then his hand finally fell away. Eli turned and slipped through the crowd, trailing one of the security guards as they split off down a hall toward the bathroom. Eli followed him in, watched the guard vanish into a stall, waited for another man at the sink to finish washing up and leave. Eli slid the bolt in the man's wake, and approached the stall door.

It swung open, and Eli slammed his shoe into the guard's chest, sent him reeling back into the wall. Eli caught him by the tie before he could fall, drew the guard's holstered gun, and pressed it tight to his chest to muffle the shots.

Eli eased the body back onto the seat.

It had been a long time since he killed a human. But forgiveness would have to wait.

He returned to Stell's side, and presented the director with the stolen gun, low and easy, as if it were a handshake among friends. Stell looked at him with bald surprise. They both knew that Eli was the one holding the weapon, Eli the one with his finger near the trigger. But he spun the weapon in his hand, offering Stell the grip instead of the barrel.

After a pause, Stell took the gun, and Eli turned and plucked a champagne flute from a passing tray. He might as well enjoy the party.

"LAST call for second thoughts," murmured June. "Or second call for last ones."

Rain drummed on the roof of the town car as it pulled up outside the Old Courthouse.

"Don't be somber," said Marcella. "It's a party."

"It's madness," countered June.

Marcella's lips twitched. "Good thing there's method in it."

It was a gamble, of course. A risk. An ambitious play.

But she used to tell Marcus, the world wasn't made for the faint of heart.

Nothing ventured, nothing gained.

And if Marcella's plan went up in flames, well, she'd take the whole damn city with her.

As she stepped out of the car, the broad umbrellas appeared again, ushering her to the waiting bronze doors of the Old Courthouse.

From inside, Marcella could hear the clink of ice and crystal glasses, the murmur and melody of an eager crowd. She brought her hand to the polished metal, splayed her fingers across the surface, gold nails gleaming, as June and Jonathan took their places behind her.

Marcella smiled.

"Showtime."

MITCH'S car screeched to a stop in front of the Old Courthouse.

Pain lanced through Victor's side as he got out, but he didn't dare turn it down, not with the episode building in his bones.

"Victor—" started Mitch.

He glanced back. "Remember what I said. Find Syd, and leave."

Victor climbed the short stone steps, pushed open the bronze doors, his free hand wrapped as casually as possible across his ribs. He handed his invitation to the suit at security, who hesitated at the blood flecking the cream paper.

He looked at Victor, who stared coldly back, leaning on the man's nerves as he did until the discomfort registered on his face.

The security waved him through.

Victor headed for the atrium, doubling back at the sight of the coat check. His eyes trailed over the jackets and shawls that had already been checked in, landing on a black wool trench on the left, with a high collar and black leather trim.

Victor flagged the clerk. "I lost my ticket," he said, "but I'm here to claim my coat." He nodded at the trench.

The kid—and he really was just a kid—wavered. "I . . . I'm sorry . . . I can't return a coat without a valid claim—"

Victor forced the kid's mouth shut, watched his eyes widen in surprise, confusion, horror as he pinned him still. "I can break your bones without lifting a finger," he said smoothly. "Would you like me to show you?"

The kid's nostrils flared in panic as he shook his head.

Victor released his hold, and the clerk stumbled back, gasping, fingers trembling as he pulled the trench from the rack.

He shrugged on the coat. He felt in the pockets and found a twenty. "Thanks," he said, tucking the cash into the short glass jar.

The atrium was crowded, full of bodies and noise. Victor made a slow circle of the chamber, hugging the outer edge as he wove between guests, scanning the crowd.

And then, across the hall, through the crowd, a familiar face.

One that hadn't changed in fifteen years.

Eli.

For a moment, the gala seemed to fade into the background, the details and sounds retreating until only the singular man stood in sharp detail.

Victor didn't realize his feet had begun to move until a hand pulled him back, dragged him sideways behind the nearest marble pillar. Victor was already reaching for the assailant's nerves when he saw the familiar tattoos spiraling up the man's broad arm.

"I told you to drive," said Victor, but then he noticed a sly gleam in Mitch's eyes, the strange set of his mouth, that familiar lilt present beneath Mitch's casual hello.

June.

"Get off me," ordered Victor.

June didn't let go. "You have to stop her."

"I'm not here for Marcella."

"You should be," said June. "She's got her sights on Sydney."

"Because of *you.*"

"No," protested June. "I never told her. But she knows, and now she wants her. And from what I've seen, Marcella—"

As if on cue, the crowd parted, and a golden figure ascended the stone dais in the center of the room.

Victor pulled free of June, looking to where Eli had been, but the man was gone. *Shit.* He scanned the crowd, searching the sea of dark suits until he caught movement. Most of the men and women were standing still, their attention transfixed on Marcella's ascent. Eli slid through them like a shark, his own focus just as clear.

Victor mirrored Eli's progress, the two of them cutting matching lines toward the dais, and the statue, and the woman in gold.

And then, at last, Eli noticed him.

Those cold, dark eyes slid past Marcella and landed on Victor. Surprise flickered across Eli's face, and then sank away, replaced by a grim smile as the barrel of a gun came up against the base of Victor's spine, and Stell's gruff voice sounded in his ear.

"That's far enough, Mr. Vale."

MARCELLA had spent her life on display.

But tonight, she finally felt *seen.*

Every pair of eyes was focused on her as she took the dais, every pair curious and bright and waiting for the reveal, because they knew there was more. More than beauty, more than charm. Whether they knew it or not, they'd come to see power.

When Marcella spoke, her voice carried, buoyed by the marble hall and the stillness of the crowd, their faces upturned, like flowers hungry for the light.

"I'm so glad," she said, "that you could join me tonight."

As she spoke, Marcella made a slow circle around the dais, savoring her hold on the gathered audience, the most powerful people in Merit—or so they *thought.*

"I know the invitation was a touch enigmatic, but I promise you, the best things are worth the wait, and what I have to offer you is better shown than told . . ."

JUNE took the stairs two at a time.

She'd shed Mitch's bulky frame for a slimmer one, and with the added quickness to her steps, she loped up to the balcony that overlooked the atrium with its sea of people. At their center, Marcella was making a slow circle around the base of the statue.

June found Jonathan tucked in a shadow, watching the show. He rested his elbows on the wrought-iron rail, all his focus on Marcella's luminous form.

"Some of you have money," Marcella's voice rang out, "and some of you have influence. Some of you were born with power, and others built it from nothing. But you are all here because you are impressive. You are lawyers, journalists, executives, law enforcement. You lead this city. You shape it. You protect it."

"Do you see that man?" said June, pointing to the pale blond head moving through the crowd.

"Victor Vale," said Jonathan blandly.

"Yeah."

If Victor wouldn't help her willingly, June would force his hand. He was a creature of self-preservation.

They all were.

"If he gets too close to Marcella," she said, "shoot him."

Jonathan drew his handgun from the holster under his suit jacket, his eyes never drifting from Marcella.

"Don't kill him," added June. "Not unless you have to. She doesn't want him dead."

Jonathan shrugged. His complacence had always annoyed her, but for once June was glad he didn't ask questions.

"Thanks, Johnny boy," she said, slipping back down the stairs.

"STELL." Victor gritted his teeth as, across the gallery, Eli continued his slow, methodical approach to the dais, where Marcella still held court.

"You understand the importance of power," she was saying. "What you don't yet understand is that *those* ideas of power are outdated."

Stell dug the gun into Victor's back. "I'm not letting you get in the way."

"Is that so?" Victor scanned the crowd.

"That is why I'm here," continued Marcella. "To open your eyes."

Eli was almost to the dais as her hand drifted up, coming to rest on the statue's bronze robes. "To show you what real power—"

Victor chose a man at random, and twisted his nerves.

A scream split the air, and for an instant Marcella's voice was washed out, the crowd's interest diverted. In that same instant, Victor rounded, slamming his elbow back into the side of Stell's head.

Stell's gun went off, but Victor was already out of the bullet's path, moving determinedly toward the platform, and Marcella, and Eli. At the sound of the firearm discharging, the tense crowd had shattered into panic. The guests surged away, a wave of bodies frantically pushing toward the exit. Only Victor and Eli still moved inward, toward the center of the room and the golden figure on her stand.

Victor was almost there when another gunshot went off, the ground sparking as the bullet struck the marble a foot away. He looked up and saw Jonathan up on the balcony, recognized the EO's intent just in time to see him line up a second shot.

The bullet tore through Victor's shoulder, the pain hot and white, blood welling instantly.

He swore, reaching for Jonathan's nerves before the man could fire a third time.

Victor caught them, turned the dial, as he had in the art gallery, and just like in the art gallery, the blue-white light of Jonathan's forcefield flared up, instantly shielding him. Victor felt his hold slipping, but this time he didn't let go.

Every object had a shatter point, a limitation to its tensile strength.

Apply enough force, and it *would* break.

XVIII

THE LAST NIGHT

THE OLD COURTHOUSE

FOR five years, Victor Vale had lived in Eli's head. First as a ghost, then as a phantom. But both, Eli realized now, had been critically flawed, a version of his rival that had been trapped in amber, unchanging—like him. The *real* Victor showed every one of the last five years, and then some, worn thin. He looked sick—just as Eli had suspected. No matter.

He would make things right.

But first—Marcella.

She was stepping down from the statue, her face contorted not with fear but with fury as she headed straight for Eli. "Are *you* behind this interruption?"

"Apologies," he said, "I was just so eager to meet you."

"You'll regret that," Marcella sneered, stepping within range.

Eli reached to grab her, but that blue-white light flashed up between them, forcing his hand away. Rebuffing him, but not *her*. Marcella stepped into the circle of his arms, and brought her fingers to his cheek.

"You really should have run with the rest of them," she said, hand flaring red.

Pain lashed across Eli's face, a wave of agony as his skin dissolved, exposing teeth, jaw. But even as the rot spread, he could feel it reversing, the muscle and skin healing. The amusement melted from Marcella's eyes and mouth, replaced by surprise, shock.

"Why would I run?" said Eli, his cheek knitting back together. "I'm here to kill you."

Marcella pulled back, suddenly uncertain.

He had missed that—the expression on their faces before they died. The way the scales trembled and shook before they fell into balance. As if the EO knew—that they were wrong, that their lives—what they took for lives—were stolen. That it was time to let go.

A gunshot went off nearby, and then another, and seconds later the air above flared blue and white, crackling with energy. Victor stood, head craned, and when Eli followed his gaze, he saw Jonathan at the heart of the storm. Victor spread his hands, and the air surged, the EO above swallowed from sight.

The surprise on Marcella's face cracked, showed fear.

Eli had a theory. He decided to test it.

With Jonathan preoccupied, Eli reached out and wrapped a hand around Marcella's throat.

There was no light around her this time, no forcefield shock, only soft white skin under his fingers.

Marcella's hands flew up, digging into Eli's arms, the sleeves of his suit quickly crumbling. The skin beneath peeled back, then healed, then peeled away again.

But Eli didn't let go.

Across the gallery, Stell and his soldiers were trying to clear the panicked crowd, while on the other side of the statue Victor continued to unleash his own power on Jonathan, as if the other EO were only a circuit, something to overload and interrupt.

To think that, in a way, the two of them were working together again. Like old times—or like they could have been, perhaps.

It was almost poetic, thought Eli, just before he saw an EON soldier appear behind Victor.

"No!" shouted Eli.

But either no one heard him, or they didn't care. The soldier reached Victor and wrapped an arm around his throat, hauling him backward and breaking his focus.

The blue-white light of Jonathan's forcefield vanished, and then reappeared an instant later, this time protectively thrown around Marcella.

There was a noise—like thunder—a violent crack—and then Eli was thrown backward. Pain tore through his back as he struck the nearest pillar, hitting several feet off the ground. But Eli didn't fall. He looked down and saw one of the sconce's metal limbs jutting from his chest.

Eli gritted his teeth as he struggled to push himself forward, pry his body off the iron bar.

Marcella started toward him, rubbing her throat.

"You must be Eli Ever," she said hoarsely. "The great EO executioner. I have to admit," she said, putting her hand against his stomach, "I'm underwhelmed."

Marcella pushed Eli back down the bar, iron scraping his insides as his back hit the pillar.

He let out a snarl.

"You don't seem to be healing," said Marcella, holding up a stained palm. "Still planning to kill me?"

"Yes," hissed Eli, blood leaking between his teeth.

Marcella clicked her tongue.

"Men."

She dug her nails into his injured stomach. Pain flared through Eli as layers of skin and muscle peeled away, and organs shriveled, and he began to die.

ELI'S strangled scream cut through the marble hall as Victor was forced to the floor.

"Can't hurt what you can't see," said the EON soldier at his back, which wasn't strictly true. Especially when they were foolish enough to have put their arm around his throat.

The soldier cried out, as if his arm had been broken. No doubt it felt that way. As soon as the limb slackened around Victor's throat, he swung up to his feet and turned on the soldier, felling the man with the short flick of a now-expert hand.

The soldier slumped, unconscious, to the marble, and Victor turned his attention back to Eli, pinned against a metal fixture, a few feet off the ground.

Shots echoed through the courthouse. Stell seemed to have figured out that Jonathan's particular ability required a line of sight, and was now emptying his own gun at the EO up on the balcony above. Blue-white light flared, but then Stell's gun clicked, the magazine already empty, and Jonathan retaliated, unleashing a hail of his own bullets, forcing both Victor and Stell to dive behind adjacent pillars.

Victor was genuinely torn.

If he took down Jonathan, Eli might be able to kill Marcella.

If he didn't, Marcella might actually kill Eli—a death Victor longed for.

And one he still wanted for himself.

In the end, Victor's decision was made for him, not by Eli, or Marcella, but by June.

June—who appeared before him, once again wearing Mitch, and put a gun to the big man's head. "I asked nicely, but you didn't listen."

June brought her finger to the trigger.

"Kill Marcella," she ordered, "or lose him."

Everything about June, from the steady hand, to the even gaze, told Victor that she would shoot Mitch, simply to make a point, let alone get what she wanted.

"When this is over," said Victor, "you and I are going to have words."

And with that, he rounded the pillar, already reaching for

Jonathan's nerves. The shield flared up anew, blue and white and defiant, and sweat beaded on Victor's skin. He'd never unloaded this much charge into one person, and his own nerves crackled and hummed from the sheer effort, threatening to short out once and for all.

But at last, the forcefield began to splinter.

ELI'S vision swam as Marcella's hand clawed deeper.

But he still saw the burst of light on the balcony behind her.

Eli's lips moved, as if in pleading, and when Marcella leaned closer, he slammed his head into hers as hard as he could. Without Jonathan's protection, the blow landed, and Marcella staggered back, holding her cheek. She spun, and saw Jonathan's own cracking shield. She started across the room toward Victor, leaving Eli pinned to the pillar.

The wrought-iron bar still jutted from his front, though Marcella had half ruined it—along with his stomach. Eli slammed his fist down into the rusted metal, and it crumbled away.

He got his foot up against the pillar behind him and pushed himself off the lower remains of the bar, dropping to the floor. Eli's stomach was a ruin of blood and gore, but without the wrought iron driven through it, the wound was already healing. Organs closing, tissue knitting back into clean, smooth flesh.

A deafening crack cut through the courthouse as Jonathan's force-field finally shattered. The EO toppled forward over the banister and fell, hitting the floor below with the dull thud of dead weight on stone.

Victor swayed and then sank to one knee, gasping from the effort. He didn't see Marcella moving toward him, her stride quickening as her hands began to glow.

Eli reached her first, wrapping his arms around her shoulders, pinning her back against him.

"Honestly," she snarled, "take a hint."

Her power flared, fast, and hot, and Eli's world went white with pain as she pitted her strength against his.

Back in the lab, Haverty had measured Eli's rate of recovery, the speed with which he healed, had marveled at the way it never slowed, like a battery that couldn't run down. But none of Haverty's tests had strained Eli's body the way that Marcella's power did now.

She tipped her head back against his shoulder. "Are you having fun yet?"

The air itself rippled with the strength of her will.

Marcella's power was no longer coming from her hands alone. It radiated around them both, warping the nearest table, sending hairline cracks across the thinning marble at their feet. It ate away his suit and her dress, melting, ruining, erasing everything, until they stood in a shallow pool of ash atop the weakening floor, Eli's arms—caught in a constant transformation from skin, to muscle, to bone, and back—pressed against Marcella's bare chest.

"If you're counting on my modesty," said Eli. "You should know, I have very little left."

Eli pressed himself against her, head bowed in a strange, almost loving embrace as at last the steel collar around his throat rusted, fell away.

Eli smiled through the agony, his final chains gone.

The ground beneath them was wearing visibly now. Eli tightened his grip, his body screaming in protest. "I've killed fifty EOs," he hissed, "and you're nowhere near the strongest."

Marcella's power wicked through the air. The bronze statue a dozen feet away began to rust, crumble. The pillars swayed, unsteady, and the whole building trembled, brittle, the marble beneath their feet wearing away, the same way Eli's body did, layer by layer.

The marble thinned like melting ice beneath them, first translucent, then transparent.

"It appears," said Marcella, "that we are evenly matched."

"No," said Eli as the floor splintered, cracked. "*You* can still die."

Eli slammed his foot down into the fragile marble, and it shattered beneath them.

VICTOR was halfway to his feet, one hand clutching his wounded
shoulder, when the floor gave way. He staggered backward, boots
searching for solid ground as the force of the crash rippled through
the building.

Only once he was beyond the wave of destruction did Victor see
the full scope of what had happened.

It was like a blast turned inward, an implosion.

One second Eli and Marcella were tangled together, engulfed in
light at the center of the atrium, and the next they were gone, plunging like meteors through the marble floor. The force of the collapse
set off a chain reaction. The walls shook. The pillars toppled. The
glass dome cracked and shattered.

The hole was vast, a drop of twenty, maybe thirty feet onto solid
stone floor.

There was no sign of June, but Victor saw Stell nearby, unconscious, one foot pinned beneath a broken pillar.

The building stopped shaking. Victor stepped to the edge of the
hole and looked down. Marcella lay stretched at the bottom of
the chasm, her limbs draped over broken stone, her black hair loose
and her head tilted at a wrong angle.

Rubble shifted, and Eli staggered to his feet beside her, naked and
bloody, his broken bones knitting themselves back together as he
rose. He looked down at Marcella's body, and crossed himself, and
then he craned his head and looked up through the broken floor.

His eyes met Victor's, and for a second neither man moved.

Run, thought Victor, and he could see the response in Eli's coiled
frame.

Chase me.

A rock came free near Eli's bare foot, skittering down the pile of rubble, and both surged into motion.

Eli spun, climbing over the wreckage, as Victor turned, searching for another way down. The nearest stairs had collapsed, the elevator was unresponsive. He finally found a stairwell, and took the steps two and three and four at a time, lunging down to the lower level, to the wreckage and the remains of Marcella Morgan.

But by the time Victor got there, Eli was already gone.

XIX

THE LAST NIGHT

THE building was a ruin, the tangle of stone still shifting and settling, as Eli climbed out of the wreckage. Dust and glass rained down around him as he pried open a door, found a back stairwell intact, and climbed. The door at the top opened onto a parking garage. Sirens wailed nearby as he strode, naked, across the concrete toward the side street.

It had been hard to walk away from Victor.

There would be time for him again. But first, Eli needed to put distance between himself and the courthouse—and EON's reach.

"Excuse me, sir," called a security guard, approaching, "you can't—"

Eli slammed his fist into the man's jaw.

The guard dropped like a stone, and Eli stripped him, tugging on the stolen uniform as he stepped around the arm of the parking barrier and out into the alley.

It had been five years since Eli's arrest, longer still since the last time he needed to disappear. Amazing how quickly the mind went down old paths. Eli felt calm, in control, his thoughts ticking off with soothing linearity.

Now, he just needed to—

Pain lanced his side.

Eli winced, and looked down to see a dart jutting between his ribs. He pulled the dart free and held it up to the light, squinting at the dregs of an electric blue liquid in the vial. A strange shiver ran through him. A tightness in his chest.

Footsteps sounded behind him, slow and steady, and Eli turned around, only to find a ghost.

A monster.

A devil in a white lab coat, deep-set eyes peering out from behind round glasses.

Dr. Haverty.

Eli's mouth went dry. He flashed back to steel tables slick with blood, felt hands inside his open chest, but despite the bile rising in his throat, Eli forced himself to hold his ground.

"All our time together," he said, tossing the dart away, "and you really thought something like that would work?"

Haverty cocked his head, glasses shining. "Let's find out."

The doctor swung the gun up, and fired a second dart into Eli's chest.

Eli looked down, expecting to see the neon liquid, but the contents of this vial were clear. He plucked out the dart.

"I don't sleep," he said, tossing it away, "but I still dream. And I've so often dreamed of killing you."

He started toward Haverty, but halfway there his front knee buckled. Folded, as if it had gone to sleep. The world rocked sideways, and Eli collapsed to his hands and knees in the street, limbs suddenly sluggish, head spinning.

This wasn't right.

None of this was right.

He was on his back now, Dr. Haverty kneeling beside him, measuring his pulse. Eli tried to pull free, but his body didn't listen.

And then, for the first time in thirteen years, Eli Ever passed out.

VICTOR surged out up the stairs and out into the parking garage, the steel door crashing behind him. His shoulder was still bleeding, leaving a veritable breadcrumb trail on the concrete. On top of that, the humming had spread to his limbs, the tone pitching to a whine inside his head. He was running out of time.

He scanned the garage—would Eli take a car, or set off on foot? There were no empty spaces, not here on the street level, and the odds of Eli wasting precious seconds on higher floors was slim.

On foot, then.

He started toward the exit, and saw the security guard slumped on the ground, his body propped up against the booth. He'd been stripped to shorts and socks. Victor stepped past him and out onto the side street.

There were too many alleys, too many ways for Eli to go, and every time Victor chose wrong, it would only increase Eli's lead.

Something shimmered on the ground nearby, and Victor knelt to retrieve it. A tranquilizer dart.

He looked up, and noted a pair of security cameras mounted high overhead.

He felt in the pockets of the stolen coat, and was relieved to find a cell phone. He dialed Mitch's number, hoping for once the man hadn't obeyed his orders.

It rang two times, three, and then Mitch picked up. "The courthouse is coming down! What the hell's going on?"

"Where are you?" asked Victor.

A moment's hesitation. "About two blocks away."

He was relieved to hear it.

"I still haven't gotten ahold of Syd."

"Well, since you're still here," said Victor, looking up at the security cameras, "I need you to hack something."

STELL ground his teeth as Holtz and Briggs helped pry his leg free from the wreckage.

He'd broken something, he knew, but he'd gotten lucky. Samson's body was buried somewhere at the bottom of the wreckage, swallowed up along with more than half of the courthouse floor. The rest of the building didn't look very stable.

"Another ambulance is on its way," said Briggs over the noise of the approaching sirens.

Holtz had kept the crowds at bay, done everything he could to minimize civilian exposure during the incident. But now emergency crews were rapidly arriving, and the crowd outside was too curious, too used to getting their way, demanding answers, explanations, casualty reports.

Stell's mind spun, but he only had a few minutes to contain the scene here.

Marcella Morgan's body lay draped atop the broken marble far below, a testament to her own destructive power.

Heaped at the farthest edge of the ruined floor was the second EO—Jonathan—one hand hanging like a rag doll over the chasm's edge.

There was no sign of June.

Or Victor.

Or Eli.

"Pull up the trackers."

"I already did," said Briggs, grimly.

She offered Stell Eli's coat in one hand. In the other, she held out five small tracking devices.

Stell's stomach dropped.

"It gets worse," said Holtz, producing the rusted remains of Eli's collar, broken, useless.

Stell swept the shards from Holtz's hand, and they rained down onto the ruined floor.

"Call in everyone we have," he ordered. "And find Cardale."

XX

THE LAST NIGHT

LOCATION UNCERTAIN

THE first thing Eli noticed was the smell.

The antiseptic odor of a lab, but beneath that, something sickly sweet. Like rot. Or chloroform. His other senses caught up, registered a too-bright light. Dull steel. His head was cotton, his thoughts syrup. Eli didn't remember what it felt like to be drunk—it had been so long since anything affected him—but he thought it must have been more pleasant. This—the dry-mouthed, head-pounding longing to retch—was not.

He tried to sit up.

Couldn't.

He was lying on a plastic sheet on top of a crate, his wrists zip-tied to the wood slats beneath. A strap ran across his mouth, holding his head down against the crate. Eli's fingers felt for something, anything, found only plastic.

"Not as fancy as my old lab, I know," said Haverty, swimming into focus. "But it will have to do. Needs must, and all." The doctor dipped out of Eli's sight, but never stopped talking. "I still have friends in EON, you know, and when they told me you were being released, well—I don't know if you believe in fate, Mr. Cardale"—he heard tools being shifted on a metal tray—"but surely you can see the poetry in our reunion. You are, after all, the reason for my breakthrough. It's only right that you're now going to be my first *true* test subject."

Haverty reappeared, holding a syringe in Eli's line of sight. That same electric blue liquid danced inside.

"This," he said, "is, as you might have guessed, a power suppressant."

Haverty brought the blade to Eli's chest and pressed down. The skin parted, blood welled, but as Haverty withdrew the knife, Eli *kept bleeding*. The pain continued too, a dull throb, until *slowly*, Eli felt the wound drag itself back together.

"Ah, I see," mused Haverty. "I erred on the side of a low dose, to start. I gave the last subject too much too fast and he just kind of . . . came apart. But, see, that's why you're the perfect candidate for this kind of trial." Haverty took up the syringe. "You always have been." He plunged the needle into Eli's neck.

It hurt, like cold water racing through his veins.

But the strangest thing wasn't the sensation of pain. It was the spark of memory—a bathtub filled with cracking ice. Pale fingers, trailing through the frigid water. Music on the radio.

Victor Vale, leaning against the sink.

You ready?

"Now," said Haverty, dragging Eli back to the present. "Let us try again."

XXI

THE LAST NIGHT

VICTOR paused outside the bland gray building. It was a storage facility. A two-story grid of climate-controlled, room-sized lockers where people abandoned furniture or art or boxes of old clothes. This was as far as Mitch's camera work had gotten Victor. But it was far enough.

There had been another man, according to Mitch. Glasses and a white coat. Eli, dragged behind him, unconscious.

Those words made no sense. The night of Eli's transformation, Victor had watched as Eli tried to drink himself into oblivion. But the liquor didn't even touch him.

After his death, nothing could.

Victor made his way through the ground-floor grid, scanning the roll-up doors for one without a lock. His shoulder had stopped bleeding, but it still ached—he didn't dampen the pain, needed every sense firing, especially with the charge building in his limbs, threatening to spill over.

Victor heard a male voice—one he didn't recognize—coming from a storage container on his left. He knelt, fingers curling around the base of the steel door as the voice carried on in a casual, conversational way. He inched the door up one foot, two, holding his breath as he braced for an inevitable rattle or clank. But the voice beyond didn't stop talking, didn't even seem to notice.

Victor ducked under the rolling door, and straightened.

Instantly he was hit by a stench, slightly noxious, and far too sweet. Chemical. But he soon forgot the smell as he registered the scene before him.

A tray of hospital-grade tools, a man in a white coat, his back to Victor and his gloves slick with blood as he leaned over a makeshift table. And there, strapped to the surface, Eli.

Blood spilled down his sides from a dozen shallow wounds.

He wasn't *healing*.

Victor cleared his throat.

The doctor didn't jump, didn't seem at all surprised by Victor's arrival.

He simply set the scalpel down and turned, revealing a thin face, deep-set eyes behind round glasses.

"You must be Mr. Vale."

"And who the hell are you?"

"My name," said the man, "is Dr. Haverty. Come in, take a—" Victor's hand closed into a fist. The doctor should have buckled, dropped to the floor screaming. He should have at least staggered, gasped in pain. But he didn't do any of those things. The doctor simply smiled. ". . . seat," he finished.

Victor didn't understand. Was the man another type of EO, someone whose own powers rendered him untouchable? But no—Victor had been able to feel June's nerves, even if he'd had no effect on them. This was different. When he reached for the doctor's body, Victor felt—nothing. He couldn't sense the man's nerves. And suddenly, Victor realized he couldn't sense his own, either.

Even the building episode, the terrible energy ready to spill over moments before, was now gone.

His body felt . . . like a body.

Dull weight. Clumsy muscle. Nothing more.

"That would be the gas," explained the doctor. "Remarkable, isn't it? It's not technically a gas, of course, just a compressed airborne version of the power-suppressant serum I'm currently testing on Mr. Cardale."

Victor registered motion over the doctor's shoulder, but he kept his focus on Haverty. Had the doctor himself turned around, he would have noticed Eli's fingers reaching out, feeling for the edge of the table—would have seen them find the scalpel Haverty had so foolishly set down. But Haverty's attention hung on Victor, and so he failed to notice Eli slipping free.

"I've read your file," the doctor continued. "Heard all about your fascinating power. I'd love to witness it myself, but as you can see, I'm in the middle of another—"

Haverty turned to gesture then, finally, at Eli on the table, but Eli was no longer there. He was on his feet now, scalpel flashing in the fluorescent light.

Eli struck, the knife parting the air—and the doctor's throat.

Haverty staggered back, clutching at his neck, but Eli had always had a deft hand. The scalpel bit swift and deep, severing jugular and windpipe, and the doctor sank to his knees, mouth opening and closing like a fish as blood pooled on the concrete beneath him.

"He never stopped talking," said Eli curtly.

Victor was very aware of the knife in Eli's hands, the absence of any weapon in his own. His eyes went to the tray of tools, more scalpels, a bone saw, a clamp.

Eli put a shoe up on Haverty's back and pushed the doctor's body over.

"That man can burn in hell." His dark eyes drifted up. "Victor." A pause. "You were supposed to stay dead."

"It didn't take."

A grim smile crossed Eli's face. "I have to say, you don't look well." His fingers tightened on the scalpel. "But don't worry, I'll put you out of your—"

Victor lunged for the tray of instruments, but Eli knocked it sideways.

Tools scattered across the floor, but before Victor could reach any of them Eli caught him around the middle, and they went down hard, Eli's scalpel driving down toward Victor's injured shoulder. He knocked Eli's arm off course at the last instant and the blade scraped against concrete, drawing sparks.

With Eli unable to heal and Victor unable to hurt—they were finally on equal ground.

Which wasn't *equal* at all.

Eli was still built like a twenty-two-year-old quarterback.

Victor was a gaunt thirty-five, and dying.

In the blink of an eye, Eli had forced his elbow up against Victor's throat, and Victor had to throw all his strength into keeping one arm from stabbing him and the other from crushing his windpipe.

"It always comes down to this, doesn't it?" said Eli. "To us. To what we did—"

Victor drove a knee up into Eli's wounded stomach, and Eli reeled, rolling sideways. Victor staggered to his feet, shoes slipping in Haverty's blood. He caught up one of the fallen instruments, a long thin knife, as Eli lunged at him again. Victor dodged back half a step, and kicked out Eli's knee. His scalpel-holding hand hit the ground for balance and Victor brought his boot down, pinning hand and blade both to the floor as he swung his own knife toward Eli's chest.

But Eli got his arm up just in time, and the knife sank into his wrist, blade driving deep, and through. Victor let out a guttural scream, but when he tried to pull free, Eli caught his hand in a vise grip, and twisted. Victor lost his balance and went down, Eli on top of him, the blade now in his grip. He brought it down, and Victor threw his hands up and caught Eli's wrists, the blood-slicked knife suspended between them.

Eli loomed over him, leaning his weight on the blade. Victor's arms trembled from the effort, but little by little, he lost ground until the tip of the knife parted the skin of his throat.

EVERY end may be a new beginning, but every beginning had to end.

Eli Ever understood that, leaning over his old friend.

Victor Vale, weary, bleeding, broken, *belonged* in the ground.

It was a mercy to put him there.

"My time will come," he said, as the knifepoint sliced Victor's skin. "But yours is now. And this time," he said, "I'll make sure you—"

A sound tore through the steel room, sudden and deafening.

Eli's grip faltered as pain, molten hot, tore through his back— through skin and muscle and something deeper.

Victor still lay beneath him, gasping, but alive, and Eli went to finish what he'd started, but the knife hung from his fingers. He couldn't feel it. Couldn't feel anything but the pain in his chest.

He looked down, and saw a broad red stain blossoming across his skin.

His breath hitched, copper filling his mouth, and then he was back on the floor of a darkened apartment at Lockland, sitting in a pool of blood, carving lines into his arms and asking God to tell him why, to take the power when he didn't need it anymore.

Now, as he looked up from the hole in his chest, he saw the girl, her white-blond hair and ice blue eyes, so familiar, beyond the barrel of the gun.

Serena?

But then Eli was falling—

He never hit the ground.

XXII

THE LAST NIGHT

SAFE

SYDNEY stood at the mouth of the storage locker, still gripping the gun.

Dol whined behind her, pacing nervously, but Sydney kept the weapon trained on Eli, waiting for him to get back up, to turn on her, to shake his head at her weapon, her futile attempt to stop him.

Eli didn't rise.

But Victor did. He struggled to his feet, one hand to the shallow wound at his throat as he said, "He's dead."

The words seemed wrong, impossible. Victor didn't seem to believe them, and neither could Sydney.

Eli was—*forever.* An immortal ghost, a monster who would follow Sydney through every nightmare, every year, plaguing her until there was no one left to hide behind, nowhere left to run.

Eli Ever wouldn't die.

Couldn't die.

But there he was on the ground—lifeless. She fired two more shots into his back, just to be sure. And then Victor was there, guiding the gun from her white-knuckled grip, repeating himself in a slow, steady voice.

"He's dead."

Sydney dragged her eyes away from Eli's body, and studied

Victor. The ribbon of blood running from his throat. The hole in his shoulder. The arm he'd wrapped around his ribs.

"You're hurt."

"I am," said Victor. "But I'm alive."

Car doors slammed nearby, and Victor tensed. "EON," he muttered, putting himself in front of Sydney as footsteps pounded down the hall. But Dol only watched, and waited, and when the door rose the rest of the way, it wasn't soldiers, but Mitch.

He paled as he took in the storage locker, the makeshift operating table, the bodies on the floor, Victor's injuries, and the gun in Sydney's hand. "EON's not far behind me," he said. "We have to go. Now."

Sydney started forward, but Victor didn't follow. She pulled on his arm, felt instantly guilty when she saw the pain cross his face, and realized how much of the blood in here must be his.

"Can you walk?" she pleaded.

"You go ahead," he said tightly.

"No," said Sydney. "We're not splitting up."

Victor turned and, cringing, knelt in front of her.

"There's something I have to do." Sydney was already shaking her head, but Victor reached out and put a hand on her cheek, the gesture so strange, so gentle, it stopped her cold.

"Syd," he said, "look at me."

She met his eyes. Those eyes that after everything still felt like family, like safety, like home.

"I have to do this. But I'll meet you as soon as I'm done."

"Where?"

"Where I first found you."

The location was burned into Syd's memory. The stretch of interstate outside the city.

The sign that read MERIT—23 MILES.

"I'll meet you at midnight."

"Do you promise?"

Victor held her gaze. "I promise."

Sydney knew he was lying.

She always knew when he was lying.

And she also knew she couldn't stop him. Wouldn't stop him. So she nodded, and followed Mitch out.

VICTOR didn't have much time.

He waited until Mitch and Syd were out of sight, and then returned to the storage unit. He fought to focus as he dragged his aching limbs across the room, stepping around Eli's body.

It was like a magnet, constantly drawing his eye, but Victor forced himself not to stop and look at it. Not to think about what it meant, that Eli Cardale was really, truly dead. The way the knowledge knocked Victor off-balance. A counterweight finally removed.

An opposite but equal force erased.

Instead, Victor turned his attention to Haverty's tools, and got to work.

EXODUS

I

AFTER

VICTOR ran his fingers over the surface of his phone.

11:45 p.m.

Fifteen minutes until midnight, and he was not on his way out of town.

Victor settled back into the worn armchair, tuning the dials of his own nerves, to test their strength. Haverty's serum had worn off a few hours before—it had been like a limb returning to feeling, nerves initially pins-and-needles sharp before finally settling back under control.

But as Victor's power returned, so had the humming in his head, the crackle of static. The beginnings of another episode. But only the beginnings. That was the strange thing—before stepping into the storage locker, his limbs had been buzzing, the current minutes from overtaking him. When Haverty's serum suppressed his power, it had suppressed the episode, too. Reset something, deep inside Victor's nervous system.

He drew a vial from his coat pocket—one of six that he'd collected from Haverty's storage locker. Its contents were an electric blue, even in the darkness of the empty apartment.

The liquid represented an extreme solution, but it also represented progress.

He'd have to be mindful—each time Victor used the serum, he

would be trading a death for a window of vulnerability, a period without powers—but he was already making notes—plans, really.

Perhaps, with the right dosage, he could find a balance. And *perhaps* was more than Victor had had to work with in a very long time.

His phone lit up—he had switched it to silent, but it still flashed brightly, a familiar number on the screen.

Sydney.

Victor didn't answer.

He watched the screen until it gave way again to darkness, then slipped the phone in his pocket as footsteps sounded beyond the door. A few seconds later, the rattle of a key in the lock, and Stell limped into view, one foot encased in a medical boot. He tossed his keys into a bowl, didn't bother turning on the lights, just hobbled to the kitchen and poured himself a drink.

The director of EON had the liquor halfway to his lips when he finally realized he wasn't alone.

He set the drink back down.

"Victor."

To his credit, Stell didn't hesitate, simply drew a gun and aimed it at Victor's head. Or at least, he meant to. But Victor stilled the man's hand.

Stell grimaced, fighting the invisible weight around his fingers. But it was a battle of wills, and Victor's would always be stronger.

Victor lifted his own hand, turning it, and like a puppet, so did Stell, until his gun was resting against his own head.

"It doesn't have to end like this," said Stell.

"Twice you locked me in a cage," said Victor. "I don't intend to let it happen a third time."

"And what will killing me do?" snapped Stell. "It won't stop the rise of EON. The initiative is bigger than me, and growing every day."

"I know," said Victor, guiding Stell's finger to the trigger.

"God dammit, *listen*. If you kill me, you will make yourself EON's number-one enemy, their primary target. They will never stop hunting you."

Victor smiled grimly.

"I know."

He closed his hand into a fist.

The gunshot split the room, and Victor's hand fell back to his side as Stell's body toppled to the floor.

Victor took a deep breath, steadying himself.

And then he pulled a slip of paper from his pocket. A page from the battered paperback, the lines blacked out except for five words.

Catch me if you can.

Victor left the door open behind him.

As he stepped out into the dark, he drew his phone from his pocket.

It was buzzing again, Sydney's name a streak of white against the black backdrop. Victor switched the phone off, and let it slip from his fingers into the nearest trash can.

And then he turned his collar up, and walked away.

II

AFTER

SYDNEY pressed the phone to her ear, listened as the ringing gave way to silence, the automated voicemail, the long beep.

It was fifteen minutes after midnight, and there was no sign of Victor. The car idled in the darkness just beyond the sign—MERIT—23 MILES—Mitch tense in the driver's seat, and Dol leaning out the back window.

Sydney paced the grassy shoulder and tried to call Victor one last time.

It went straight to voicemail.

Sydney hung up, and found herself about to text June—before she remembered that she no longer had her own phone. Which meant that Sydney didn't have June's number anymore. And even if she did . . .

Syd shoved the burner phone back in her pocket. She heard the car door open, Mitch's heavy steps in the grass as he approached.

"Hey, kid," he said. His voice was so gentle, as if afraid of telling her the truth. But Syd already knew—Victor was gone. She stared at the distant skyline of Merit, shoved her hands in her coat, felt her sister's bones in one pocket, the gun in the other.

"It's time to go," she said, returning to the car.

Mitch turned on the engine, pulled back onto the highway. The road stretched ahead, flat and even and endless, almost like the surface of a frozen lake at night.

Sydney resisted the urge to look back again.

Victor might be gone, but there was still that thread, tangling their lives. It had led Sydney to him once before, and it would lead her there again.

No matter how long or far she had to look.

Sooner or later, she would find him.

If Sydney had anything, it was time.

III

AFTER

EON

HOLTZ shivered, not at the sight of the corpse on the steel table, but from the cold.

The storage room was fucking freezing.

"Not so tough now," muttered Briggs, her breath a cloud of fog.

And it was true.

Lying there, under the cold white light, Eliot Cardale looked . . . young. All his age had been contained in those eyes, flat as a shark's. But now they were closed, and Cardale looked less like a serial-killing EO and more like Holtz's kid brother.

Holtz had always wondered at the gap between body and corpse, the place where a person stopped being a he or a she or a they, and instead became an *it*. Eliot Cardale still looked like a person, despite the shockingly pale skin, the still-glistening bullet wounds—small, dark circles with serrated edges.

Nobody knew how Haverty had been able to render Eli human—or at least mortal. Just like they didn't know who had shot the EO, or who had killed the ex-EON scientist—though everyone seemed to assume it was Victor Vale.

"Holtz," snapped Briggs. "I'm freezing my ass off, and you're making moony eyes at a corpse."

"Sorry," said Holtz, his breath pluming. "Just thinking."

"Well, stop *thinking*," she said, "and help me load this thing."

Together, they maneuvered Cardale's corpse into cold storage, which was basically just a permanent stretch of deep drawers in the basement of the EON complex, dedicated to indefinitely housing the remains of deceased EOs.

"One down," she said, scribbling notes on her clipboard, "one to go."

Holtz's eyes flicked to the other body that waited, patiently, on its own steel plank.

Rusher.

Holtz had avoided looking at his old friend as long as possible. Not just because of the gunshot wounds that stood out in livid marks against the old scars, but because he couldn't believe his eyes— Dominic had survived so much. They'd served together for four years, and worked here, side by side, for another three.

And all that time, Holtz had never known what Rusher was.

Rios was always telling them not to make assumptions, that EOs weren't ducks—they didn't have to walk like one and talk like one and smell like one to *be* one.

But still.

"It's crazy, isn't it?" he murmured. "Makes you wonder how many are out there. And *here*. If I was an EO, you better believe this is the last place I'd be."

Briggs wasn't listening.

He couldn't blame her.

EON was in a state of emergency. They'd gotten the place back under lockdown pretty quickly, but they'd still lost four EOs in the process, a third of the soldiers were in medical—five had died. The gala mission had been a total disaster, EON's first unkillable EO was dead, possibly from the efforts of their own ex-employee, and the director hadn't even bothered to come to work today.

Holtz needed a drink.

Briggs sealed the doors to cold storage and they climbed back to the main levels.

Holtz swiped through security and stepped outside, grateful that his shift was finally over.

His car sat waiting on the employee side of the lot. It was a sleek yellow speedster, the kind that took on an animal grace—it didn't just drive. It prowled and growled and rumbled and purred, and the other EON soldiers loved to give him shit for it, but Holtz hadn't craved many things since he'd gotten out of the army—just fast cars and pretty girls—and he was only willing to pay for one of them.

He climbed behind the wheel, engine revving pleasantly as he jacked up the heat, still trying to shake off the chill of cold storage, the lingering shock of the last twenty-four hours. As he pulled through the gate, Holtz cranked up the radio, trying to drown out the sound of the gravel drive. He shook his head—EON, he assumed, could surely afford to have paved their private road, but apparently they didn't want to encourage any traffic. So if you were a civilian, hitting gravel in this area was a sign you'd gone the wrong way.

Though some people didn't get the message—like this asshole, Holtz thought, looking down the road.

A car had parked on the shoulder, a low, black coupe, its taillights glaring and its hood raised.

Holtz slowed, wondering if he should call it in, but then he saw the girl. She'd had her head bent over the engine, but as he drew up beside her car, she straightened, scrubbing at her forehead.

Blond hair. Red lips. Tight-fitting jeans.

Holtz rolled down the window. "This is private property," he said. "I'm afraid you can't stop here."

"I didn't want to," she said, "the stupid thing just up and *died*."

Holtz caught the edge of an accent, a melodic lilt. God, he loved accents.

"And of course," the girl went on, kicking a tire, "I don't know shite about cars."

Holtz eyed the low black beast. "That's quite a car for someone who doesn't know shite."

She smiled at that, a dazzling, dimpled smile. "What can I

say?" she said in that musical voice. "I have a weakness for nice things." She pulled her hair up off her neck. "Think you can help?"

Holtz didn't know shite—*shit*—about cars either, but he wasn't about to admit it. He got out and rolled up his sleeves, approaching the engine. It reminded him of the fake bombs he'd had to defuse in basic training.

He toggled and poked and made low humming sounds as the girl stood at his shoulder, smelling of summer and sunshine. And then, miraculously, his fingers brushed over a hose and Holtz realized it had simply come free. He reconnected it.

"Try starting it now," he said, and a second later, the coupe's engine rumbled to life. The girl let out a joyful sound.

Holtz shut the hood, feeling triumphant.

"My hero," she said with mock sincerity but genuine affection. She dug through her wallet. "Here, let me pay you . . ."

"You don't have to do that," he said.

"You bailed me out," she said. "There has to be something I can do."

Holtz hesitated. She was out of his league, but—fuck it.

"You could let me buy you a drink."

He braced himself for the inevitable rejection, wasn't surprised when the girl shook her head. "No," she said, "that won't do. But I'll buy *you* one."

Holtz grinned like an idiot.

He would have gone with her right then, left the black coupe on the side of the private road and driven her anywhere she wanted, but she apologized—she was running crazy late, thanks to the breakdown—and asked if he would take a rain check.

Tomorrow night?

He agreed.

She held out her hand, palm up. "Got a phone?"

He offered up his cell, flushing slightly when her fingers lingered on his, their touch feather light, but electric. She added her name and number to his contacts and passed it back.

"Tomorrow, then?" she asked, turning toward her car.

"Tomorrow, then . . ." Holtz looked down at the entry in his phone. "April."

She glanced back at him through thick lashes, and winked, and Holtz climbed into his yellow speedster and drove away, still watching April, haloed in the rearview mirror. He kept waiting for her to disappear, but she didn't. Life was strange and wonderful sometimes.

And tomorrow, he had a date.

JUNE watched the yellow car shrink into the distance.

Idiot, she thought, starting up the road, this time on foot.

By the time she reached the gates of EON, she looked for all intents and purposes like Benjamin Holtz, Observation and Containment, age twenty-seven. Loved his little brother and hated his stepdad and still had nightmares about the things he'd seen overseas.

"What's this?" asked the security guard, rising from the booth.

"Stupid car broke down," she muttered, doing her best to imitate Holtz's northeastern accent.

"Ha!" said the security guard. "That's what you get for choosing style over substance."

"Yeah, yeah," said June.

"What you need is a good midlevel sedan—"

"Just let me in so I can grab a van and some cables and get my shit back on the road."

The gates parted, and June stepped through. Easy as pie. She crossed the lot on foot and whistled at the sight of the front doors. It looked like someone had driven a car into them. Inside, a soldier looked up from some kind of scanning station.

"Back so soon?" he asked, rising to his feet.

"Left my wallet somewhere."

"Won't get far without that."

"You're telling me."

Small talk was an art form, one of those things that made people's eyes gloss over. Go silent, and they might start wondering why. But keep them talking about nothing at all, and they wouldn't even blink.

"You know the drill," said the soldier.

June did not. This fell soundly in the realm of minutiae, something that rarely conveyed with a touch. Making a guess, she stepped into the scanner, and waited.

"Come on, Holtz," said the soldier. "Don't be a pain in my ass. Arms up."

She rolled her eyes, but spread her arms. It was like standing inside a copier, a beam of white light that moved from head to toe, followed by a short chime.

"All clear," said the soldier.

June saluted him, a casual flick of her fingers as she started down the hall. She needed to find a computer. It should have been easy, a building as fancy as this one, but every hallway looked alike. Identical, even. And every identical hallway was studded with even more identical doors, almost none of them marked, and the farther into the maze June went, the farther she'd have to walk out. So she settled instead for simplicity, pointing herself toward the nearest door. Halfway there, it swung open. A female soldier stepped out, took one look at Holtz, and rolled her eyes.

"Forget something?"

"Always," said June. She didn't pick up her pace, but her fingers caught the door just before it closed. June slipped inside, and found a small room with four computer consoles. Only one of them was occupied.

"Finally," the soldier said, "I've had to piss for an hour . . ."

He started to swivel toward June, but she was already there, one arm hooking around his throat. She pinned him against the chair, cutting off his ability to speak, to shout for help. His back arched as he fought her hold, throwing punches made clumsy by shock and the sudden lack of oxygen. But Benjamin Holtz was no weakling, and June had killed her fair share of men. The soldier did manage to get a pen and jam it back into June's thigh, but of course, it wasn't her thigh.

Sorry, Ben, she thought, tightening her hold.

Soon enough, the soldier stopped fighting. He went limp, and she let go, rolling his chair out of the way so she could get to his computer. June hummed as her fingers slid over the keyboard.

She had to hand it to EON. They had a very user-friendly system, and half a minute later she'd found the file she needed. It had been labeled ALIAS: JUNE. She skimmed through, curious to see what they'd found—which wasn't much. But still enough to merit the trip.

"Good-bye," she whispered, erasing the file—and herself—from the system.

June went out the way she'd come in.

Retraced her steps down the hall, past security and the gates, back to the waiting black coupe. June opened the car door, and by the time she climbed behind the wheel, she was herself again.

Not the leggy brunette, or the thin teen, or any of the dozen faces she'd recently worn, but a spritely girl, with strawberry curls and a splash of freckles across her high cheeks.

June let herself sit in that body for a moment, breathe with her own lungs, see with her own eyes. Just to remember what it felt like. And then she reached out and started the engine, sliding into something safer. The kind of person you wouldn't look twice at. The kind who gets lost in the crowd.

June glanced in the rearview mirror, checked her new face, and drove away.